Praise for
HAWKESMOOR

"Breathing new life into vampires isn't easy—after all, they're dead—but Anne Merino has managed it with aplomb. Like the vampire at its center, Robin Dashwood, Merino's HAWKESMOOR is both erudite and full of passion, witty and tragic, attuned to the classics yet utterly modern. If you're in the market for a new, fresh vampire saga or just a bloody good time, look no further."

— **Steve Hockensmith**, *New York Times* best-selling author of *Pride and Prejudice and Zombies: Dawn of the Dreadfuls*

"Delightfully well-crafted, intricate and enchantingly imaginative, I was drawn deep into this enjoyable read with its complex world and fascinating characters. It actually makes me feel excited for vampires again! Romance and adventure, with an odd charm all its own, and fully realized world-building. Highly recommended!"

— **Amanda McCabe**, award-winning author of *A Lady in Disguise*, *Nine Ladies Dancing* and *Miss Fortesque's Protector in Paris*

"Anne Merino's sweeping new novel HAWKESMOOR invites the reader upon a vampiric journey from Georgian England to the French Revolution to modern-day New York. HAWKESMOOR is beautifully written, crafted, and conceived; it is a vampire story unlike any other, offered by a writer unlike any other."

— **Sanjay Sighal**, author of *Tales of the Night Watchman*

"HAWKESMOOR is a delightful ride through vampires and time. Its mysteries draw in the reader irresistibly. And it's more fun than Anne Rice!"

—**Bryan Alexander**, Georgetown University, futurist, and author of the blog "Blogging Dracula since 2005"

"In HAWKESMOOR, Anne Merino has created a finely crafted tale which is both elegant and erotic. Its Gothic wit propels us grippingly through a vast historical panorama, steeped in vampiric lore, towards something almost cosmic and strangely timeless. Paradoxically, this thoroughly entertaining vampire chronicle casts a light on what it actually means to be human, which makes this a superbly rewarding read."

> —**Clifford Slapper**, author of *Bowie's Piano Man: The Life of Mike Garson*

"HAWKESMOOR is an irresistible yarn from the first paragraph onwards. It zips along, paced to hold the reader's attention, with liberal doses of shock, plus a twist that explains the title and sets the scene for the action that unfolds. I truly love this book—from me that's a meaningful statement because I hardly ever read fiction."

> —**Mary Finnigan**, journalist and author of *Psychedelic Suburbia: David Bowie and the Beckenham Arts Lab*

"By the time you're two pages into HAWKESMOOR, you know you're in the hands of a master storyteller. Already you've gently polished the surface of the vampire genre, and revealed some of its true nature, quite apart from the commonly held conceptions of our day. But you've yet to encounter the Welsh supernatural that storms in some centuries and pages later—a completely fresh and brilliant form of the Gothic imagination. And what of her characters? So well drawn, and with such attention to the fall of a phrase. Robin Dashwood—you may well fall for him, dashing as he is—or his centuries-long love. Oh, reader, read on!"

> —**Charles Cameron**, Oxford poet and contributor to *Children of Albion: Poetry of the Underground in Britain*

"Anne Merino has created a new vision of vampires, steeped in history and replete with ethical and moral challenges, yet modern and accessible, rich with the legends and histories that have fascinated readers for decades and the contemporary sensibility that compels readers of all ages today. This fast-paced novel is constantly unfolding unexpected twists and turns, making it impossible to put down. The reader will want to devour this book!"

—**June Guterman**, Academy Award®winning producer
and CEO of Looking Glass Films

"Just the magic readers need to believe again in heroes! Instantly, I took to the hero and heroine, unable to set HAWKESMOOR down until I reached the brilliantly executed ending. Like a gracious hostess, author Anne Merino invited us into a most exciting world to be part of a titled family lineage with secrets to keep. When I set the book down, I felt as if I had been a willing participant in this romantic thriller."

—**Sharon Day**, author of the SEEK Team Investigation
series and the blog "Ghost Hunting Theories"

"My life has been devoted to the study of the esoteric and paranormal so I sat down to read HAWKESMOOR with genuine interest, both instinctual and professional. This exquisitely written novel weaves an elegiac tale through time and alternate dimensions that is absolutely impossible to put down. A must read for lovers of the mysterious and beautiful."

—**Natalia O'Sullivan**, author of *Soul Rescuers: A 21st Century Guide to the Spirit World* and *The Ancestral Continuum*

Hawkesmoor

A NOVEL OF Vampire & Faerie

Anne Merino

RIVERCLIFF
BOOKS & MEDIA

RIVERCLIFF
BOOKS & MEDIA

Published by Rivercliff Books & Media
an imprint of Wetware Media, LLC
www.rivercliffbooks.com

Edited by Carol Stanley
Book cover by Gersi Rami
Editorial Assistant Janis Daddona

ISBN: 978-0-9971416-8-9

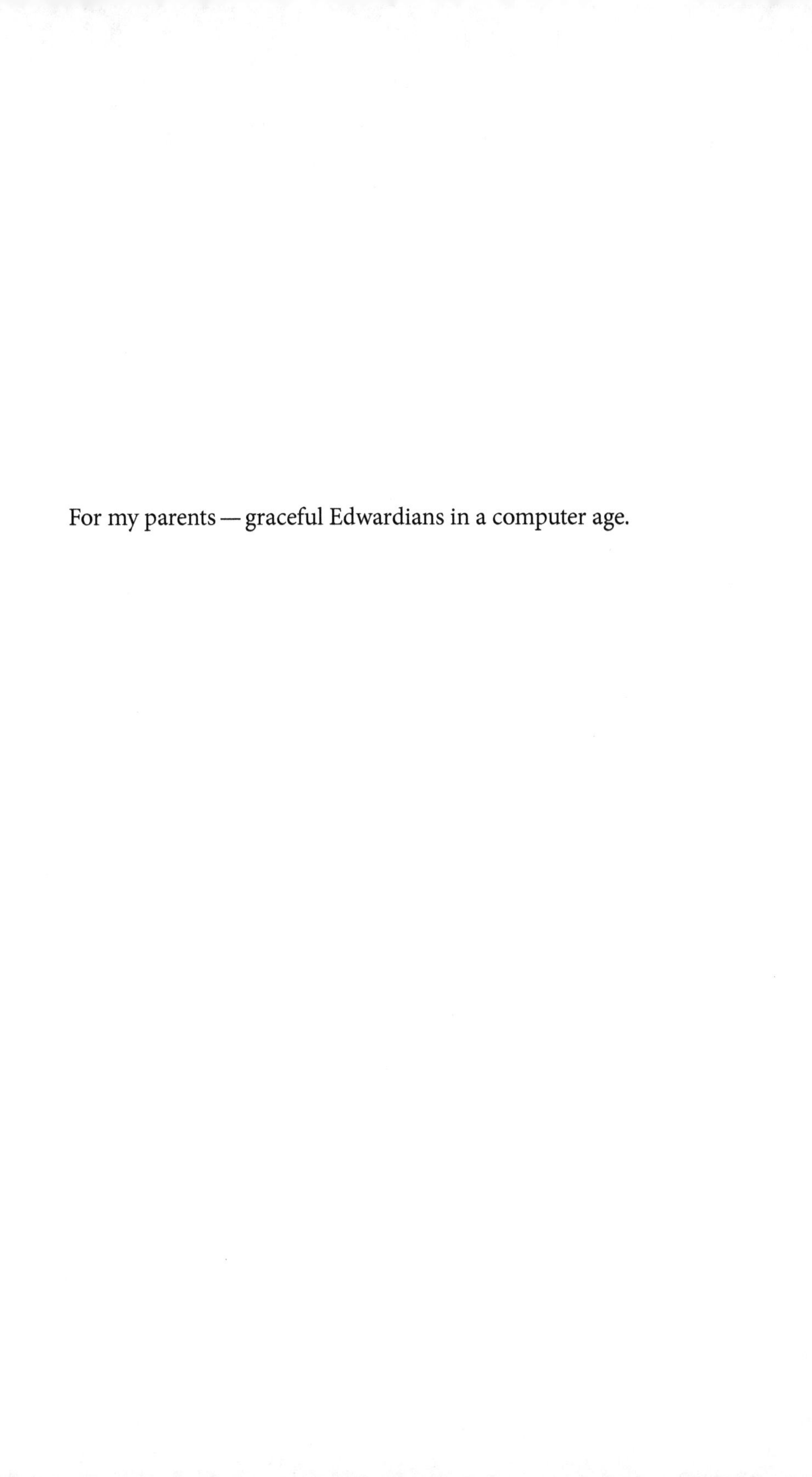

For my parents — graceful Edwardians in a computer age.

Acknowledgments

Although writing is often thought of as a solitary, lonely occupation, it takes quite a few people to shepherd a manuscript towards becoming a real book. Dr. Johnson had his Boswell. Even the Bronte sisters writing away in a remote parsonage in the middle of a Yorkshire moor had brother Branwell to poke the fire and bring them the occasional cup of tea. All writers have people to thank profusely for their kindness, support and invaluable assistance. Here are mine:

The lovely Lisa Duff at Rivercliff Books & Media (an imprint of Wetware Media) who took on *Hawkesmoor*. Thank you for believing in the novel and giving it a home.

My dear friend and editor, Carol Stanley, is smart, sophisticated and possesses a pithy sense of humor. This makes her a great deal of fun to work with on a book. Fortunately for me, she is also a gifted editor. Her astute and tactful suggestions for refining *Hawkesmoor* have made it a far better story.

Thank you, Patricia Potts, for your brilliant proofreading and copy-editing. You're another one I will never be able to thank enough.

High five to my wonderful friend, Loren Blowers, the phenomenal author of science fiction's epic Stingwisher series. We meet up and read each other's current projects. Often alcoholic beverages are involved. Loren's witty advice and encouragement has kept me clattering away at the laptop even when writing seems really difficult and unrewarding.

Thank you, Charles Cameron, for all around creative wizardry. You always have the good word and sage advice.

My sister, Mary Zoll-Montoya, always knows how to get a laugh. She is the only person I know who can announce — after a terrible plumbing crisis involving expensive, posh twin-ply toilet paper and an old septic system — that her household has "once again flown too near the Sun."

My two fascinating sons, Emlyn and David, who make life such fun and so worthwhile.

Beloved German Shepherd, Hector, who takes me for walks and away from the computer. Yes, writers should always thank their dogs.

And then there's my husband, Tom. A filmmaker and writer, Tom has great taste, strong opinions and the genuine gift of being honest about creative work. For more than twenty years, his opinion is the one I seek first, and the one that matters the most.

*Come away, O human child: To the waters and the wild
with a fairy, hand in hand, for the world's more full of
weeping than you can understand.*

— William Butler Yeats

1

Sunlight sparkled off a thousand different New York windows as Robin Dashwood sat out on his terrace, pretending to sip a morning cup of coffee.

There were just so many pointless misconceptions about vampires, he reflected, and the forever nocturnal bit had to be one of the silliest.

He'd been a vampire for more than three hundred years and he still found his morning coffee a high point in his waking hours.

Of course, the ritual of breathing in the rich fumes of the brew and remembering what it was like to enjoy actually drinking the stuff had changed dramatically over three centuries. It had been coffee in spectacular bone china served on heavy silver by doting valets once. Now he grabbed a cup in his own kitchen before heading off to teach his classes at nearby NYU.

Unlike other vampires who truly hated this new egalitarian era with its self-service mandate and constant industrial noise, Robin quite liked the 21st century. He could lose himself in all the self-absorbed hubbub. He seldom yearned for the grace and grandeur of earlier times anymore.

"Morning, professor," said the voice of his current girlfriend, Kate Ashby.

She was a young actress. Exceptionally pretty in a waifish sort of way and even moderately successful with a role on a television soap opera. They had a comfortable and flexible relationship that neither of them had ever expected to last as long as it already had. But then, he had a weakness for stalwart denizens of the theatre. What others might think of as shallow narcissism Robin saw as a valiant belief in themselves and their talent despite utter rejection. He found their dedication to their work and giddy belief in better futures completely disarming. The company of artists always gave him an all too brief sensation of being human. In keeping with the restless human spirit of actors, Robin had begun to sense Kate's growing boredom with her former history teacher and her growing interest in Los Angeles and its beguiling film community.

Robin glanced up from his newspaper and smiled slightly.

"Don't call me professor. It makes me feel so old." His voice was soft but rather hoarse around the edges, still imbued with the upper class English accent that betrayed the country of his human birth.

"You are so not old." She came across the little balcony to plunk her own mug of coffee on the wrought iron table.

"More than three hundred years old, actually." He smiled again as Kate dropped a kiss on his forehead.

She was a thin, gangly thing; he thought affectionately, all legs, elbows and long blond hair. It was an effect exaggerated by a plaid mini skirt and black leggings that disappeared into thick hobnail boots favored by the college-aged. He had a moment to remember how breathtaking women once were in their mysterious confections of velvet and silks, their dainty feet shod in whimsical satin slippers.

Robin breathed in one of the last drafts of rapidly cooling coffee. Women had seemed to float in clouds of quietly rustling layers of taffeta.

"Robin," Kate broke into his memories impatiently, "you *will* meet me there at eight o'clock? You heard what I said, right?"

He shook his head to clear the last vestiges of his memory. "I'm sorry, love. What about eight o'clock?"

Kate made a sour face. "You're such a space case! Opening night reception at the Glockner, remember? I promised my PR lady I'd go. Some boring historical thing. You'll probably love it. I left the invitation on the kitchen counter."

"A boring historical thing?" Robin frowned. "And why would a PR firm want its soap opera actresses at such a tedious event?"

"Important English people *with titles* will be there. Makes us actresses look respectable." Kate swallowed a long drink of her coffee. "I've got to run, Robin. I've got an audition for that new Taylor Mac thing before script run-throughs."

"Good luck then."

"Won't get it. I'm too mainstream pretty," she replied matter-of-fatly as she rose from her chair. "Put this message in your head: Glockner Gallery, eight o'clock tonight."

"I believe I have it now. Thank you." He returned his attention to the Eastern European situation in the paper.

"It's black tie, Robin, and I know you have a faculty meeting."

Robin let out a short breath to cool his rising temper. "I will be at the Glockner at eight o'clock tonight, gorgeously attired in my finest dinner suit and you, my love, can stop worrying about it."

"Okay. I trust you." Kate bent over and slid her arms down around his neck. She kissed his cheek. "It's just that you disappear sometimes and I can never find you."

"In my secret life," he said with a small yawn, "I kill people."

Kate giggled. "Yeah, right."

Robin put the boring historical thing out of his mind until he returned from rather a long day at the university.

"Martini time, young Professor Dashwood," announced his neighbor Arthur Silver, a spry 80-year-old who had once swallowed swords and fire in the Borscht Belt era.

"If only that were true," Robin said as he unlocked his mailbox in the foyer and retrieved its meager contents. "What's up, Arthur?"

Arthur put on his showman's barker voice. "Tonight, in the Bailey's main floor lounge, Daisy Meadows and the Fawcett Triplets will be performing torch song classics of the 30's." He lost the artificial tone. "You coming, Robin?"

Dashwood shook his head. "As much as I would prefer listening to Daisy and the Fawcett sisters, I have to squire Kate around a cocktail party."

"Well, if Daisy doesn't have her dentures refitted, they'll be doing a Sunday matinée."

"I wouldn't dream of missing that one."

He currently lived a dull life for a vampire Robin mused as he rode the old cage elevator up to the fifth floor. But its unremarkable qualities were what made it a private art piece.

It would have been easy to be like the handful of other vampires he had met over the last three hundred odd years; living out lives of world weary jet setters, flitting about in the guise of artists and rock singers. He too could be using his accumulated wealth to languish about trendy watering holes, drinking the chic dry and secretly pining for yesteryear when no one complained much when the odd serving wench or two went missing.

Instead he owned a colorful old five story building in Greenwich Village called The Bailey. The still elegant Bailey had always housed the theatre trade, from the days of Victorian music hall to vaudeville to Broadway. It remained a haven for retired stage personalities and young hopefuls. None of the Bailey's roster of theatre folk knew Robin Dashwood for their landlord and he never revealed, even to the oldest performer, how he'd caught most of their acts in their heydays.

He loved the theatre and its people. Surrounding himself with their peculiar brand of humor and survival instincts kept him in touch with his human past. Since buying the Bailey in 1908, he had found it a fascinating way of measuring the passage of time.

Robin shoved open the elevator cage door with his elbow as he struggled to hang onto his unwieldy stack of student essays.

He'd cried last week when Mabel Fierson had finally succumbed to the cancer in her lungs. She had been a beautiful creature in her time. Mabel the Ethereal was how they billed her in 1940s. He remembered her Isadora style of Greek dancing well. Of course, Isadora hadn't finished her performances by shedding her scarves one by one but then Isadora had never been the toast of the state fair circuit. Mabel the Ethereal had enchanted wide-eyed farm boys throughout the country and had undoubtedly broadened appreciation of the dance considerably during her long career.

Robin unlocked his flat and unceremoniously dumped his students' mid-term essays on the foyer table. He had little more than an hour to change clothes and dash over to the Art Institute.

Besides his history courses at NYU and his relationship with Kate, there wasn't much else. He still saw a little theatre and worked on his fourth scholarly book for his editor at Mercury Press. Of course, about once a week he had to feed.

Most vampires fed more often for the sheer hedonism of it but in true aesthetic spirit, Robin had learned to quell the powerful urge to steal human blood for nearly seven days. He was literally starving by then so he usually killed, rather than deploying the more refined small drink favored by really skillful vampires.

He hunted among drug addicts, vagrants, pan handlers, pimps and hard core criminals. A particular favorite being drug dealers who could be counted on to be fairly clean of narcotics themselves and well-nourished in comparison to their clientele. It was fortunate that he was starving when he found one of his victims. It was the only way he could stomach the sour effects of their badly depleted blood.

Robin bent to pick up a note that had fallen from one of the student papers. It was a love struck message from Maria, one of his eleven o'clock lecture attendees. She had developed a major attachment to him and had just started to send him little notes full of promises to do wonderful things for and to him. It was far from the first time a student had fallen into such a trap.

Vampires were magnetic creatures. It was helpful in gaining quick confidences that led inevitably to feeding. And like most vampires, Robin Dashwood was beyond beautiful. He tried to hide his tall, imperially slender frame in baggy suits and his luminous green eyes behind round bookish tortoiseshell spectacles with fake lenses. He wore his gleaming chestnut-colored hair quite long in a severe blunt cut that nearly brushed his thin shoulders and hoped it would conceal his features. It only enhanced the flawless planes of his angular face and the cool pale of his skin.

Robin hated to waste the evening at a society reception. He was in the mood to sit at his desk and work on the next segment of his biography of William Pitt. He loved the relative quiet of the flat when Kate wasn't home running over her deplorable dialogue for the next day's shoot or watching moronic comedies on the television or talking too loudly to her soap opera comrades on the phone.

It really was time to send her off to Hollywood and into the arms of some deserving young man out there. Kate wouldn't even mind very much. She was sufficiently armored with titanium self-regard that his vampire magnetism—a survival tool designed for making quick connections with prey—failed to make much of a dent once Kate had gotten used to him. In fact, it was what had held them together so long. Passionately in love with herself and her career, Kate remained oblivious to his occasionally odd schedule, never noticing with any genuine clarity that he never really ate or ever made any headway with a glass of wine. She provided him with plausible cover, enabling him to gracefully step around possible entanglements with other women and to exist with minimal complication.

A dark voice in his head reminded him he had another very tempting option for ridding himself of Kate Ashby.

He pushed the idea away with a shudder. It must be nearly time to go in search of a target. Tonight, after Kate was asleep, he'd find somebody.

Robin emerged from the Bailey impeccably turned out in his favorite dinner suit. Made for him in the 1930's, it possessed superb lines almost extinct in modern versions. It was a perfect spring evening — he even had little trouble flagging down a taxi. Perhaps going out wasn't such a bad idea after all.

"Where it be, mister?" asked the driver as he slid into the back seat.

"The Glockner Gallery, please."

The driver nodded jovially. "Yep, opening night party, right? I'm old school — remember when cabbies used to know what was happening anywhere in the city?"

"Would you happen to know what the opening is for? I honestly don't know myself." Robin reached into his breast pocket for the invitation as the cab pulled away from the curb. It would probably say something about the event. He hoped it wasn't another tiresome retrospective on the impact of fashion.

"Some English display of old furniture." The cabbie thought for a second. "From some castle. Hawk something Castle."

Robin froze. Surely he had heard the man incorrectly.

"Hawkesmoor Castle?" he asked in a low voice.

The driver beamed. "Yeah, that's it! Hawkesmoor Castle. Couldn't forget that name."

With trembling hands, Robin tore open the cream-colored envelope and read the engraved card inside. Lady Caroline DeBarry would be present to open an exhibit of fine English antiques from Hawkesmoor. All to benefit the current refurbishment project at the castle itself in Yorkshire, England.

He let out a small, strangled cry. The cabbie looked back in the rear view mirror in real concern.

"You okay back there, mister?"

Hawkesmoor Castle. The words swam in front of his face. Hawkesmoor Castle, his keep, his abandoned responsibility, his Earldom. The place where he should be buried next to the woman who should have been his Countess who would have had his sons. Elizabeth — her name still had the power to hurt him like a blow to the body.

"You want I should pull over?" The cabbie began slowing the yellow cab down a fraction. "Hey, mister!"

The hunger began to pound in his temples like a migraine. His joints ached with it. His horror at the sudden reemergence of Hawkesmoor Castle, the place of his birth and human death, had caused the blood hunger to accelerate.

This was a disaster. His head reeled at the possible ruination of the careful, predictable life he had so pointedly devised for himself. He had always been meticulous — hunting in the smallest hours of the night in black corners of New York where even angels dared not alight. But now, in the middle of bustling Soho, he was a vampire rising.

"Hey, mister," repeated the worried cab driver. "What should I do?"

Robin felt his eyes dilate — a targeting system booting up. His unique revenant chemistry was reconfiguring for attack. He inhaled desperately, trying to reroute the impulses to what was left of his humanity. The relentless migraine narrowed, focused and became a laser — a razor blade — ripping through his veins.

"Yes," Robin hissed, "pull over."

"I'll radio for an ambulance," the driver offered as he edged the vehicle off the main thoroughfare and double parked on a quiet side street. "Hang on, buddy!"

Robin was in a deadlock. Frantic attempts to defuse his vampire system were failing, lost in the hypersonic pulse in his veins that ignited every nerve ending. He felt his entire frame light up like a Roman candle — the pain was exhilarating. Robin Dashwood was off line. What remained was a devastating weapon.

"Please help me."

"Sure thing, mister." The cabbie jumped out and came around to the rear door. He held out a strong hand for Robin to grasp.

"I'm sorry," the vampire said hoarsely as he accepted the hand. It was the last flickering remnant of Robin Dashwood

"What the hell?" the cabbie began.

His superior vampire strength had the cabdriver in the back seat and neatly pinned with a crushed larynx before the man could finish his sentence.

2

Kate would be furious. He was over an hour late.

It had taken some time to repair the damage after he had dumped the unfortunate taxi driver in a convenient alleyway. The crisp white shirt had been drenched with blood so he had made a stop at Barney's to fetch a suitable substitute. A mind-boggling feat made considerably easier by one of his vampire traits.

Like humans, vampires possessed different attributes and individual talents. These could include mental telepathy, simple matter transformations, aerial abilities, tracking specific victims by molecule, short and long distance teleportation. Robin knew there were vampires of enormous personal powers throughout the world although he was not one of them. Those creatures not only came equipped with great natural abilities but also cultivated others with meticulous care. Robin had no desire to become a vampire king. He was content to quietly avoid human detection and survive.

After the kill, Robin had become a shade. It was the most important skill in his almost non-existent arsenal. He literally could will himself to evaporate and become one with the air. Humans could not see him although animals and some true psychics could sense him. In such a state, Robin could move swiftly and silently through human environments. This time, his shade had joined the shoppers in the busy aisles of Barney's, selected a clean shirt and made good his escape.

It had also taken him some time to summon enough courage to approach the guarded entrance to the Glockner Gallery. He was desperately afraid of what he would find there—a few of his former possessions, perhaps. The chance to touch one or two of them scanning for any trace lingering of his father or maybe even Elizabeth. Then there was the real possibility of learning what happened to all of them. A truth he had avoided learning for three hundred years. It hadn't been difficult to hide from the impact his disappearance had made to the people he loved. No historians particularly cared what happened so long ago in a remote Northern Earldom. Nobody cared any more what happened to his family and to his betrothed. He could pretend whatever he liked about them all—devise pleasant stories about how they went on about their lives without him.

But now, the reality might suddenly jump out at him from any corner of the exhibition.

Both anxious and exhilarated, he passed through the invitation-only checkpoint. The essence of the cabdriver had strengthened him. He was forced to admit that higher quality blood really did improve his physical state.

But a massive wave of homesickness swept over him as he stepped into the Glockner's exhibition hall. The temporary exhibit had been shrewdly fashioned with wonderfully painted flats, huge historical photographs and lavish flat screens with virtual tours of the actual castle. It was an eerie doppelganger of his Hawkesmoor. Frozen, and unable to take another step closer until he could absorb the shock, Robin saw a small collection of Hawkesmoor's more important furniture, paintings, tapestries and silver scattered about the surreal set. Even at a distance, he registered the regal presence of the six Venetian walnut parcel-gilt armchairs by Brustolon his mother had been so fond of. One of the Irish Waterford chandeliers from the state dining room. The Queen Anne state bed, along with its magnificent gilt wood suite of furniture. The Magadeline Feline silver Chapel Communion Service his father had commissioned to celebrate the birth of a son. And all the paintings of Hawkesmoor's noble residents.

"Mother," said Robin moving forward, almost breaking into a run.

He edged around the tightly knit groups of socialites milling about his possessions as they drank champagne and nattered about opera guilds or the horse show in the Hamptons. It was hanging over a plaster recreation of the green drawing room's Carrara marble fireplace. The really splendid Jonathan Richardson painting of his mother. Augusta, the sixth Countess of Hawkesmoor. She gazed down at him with a kind smile, more than a hint of her famous sense of merriment playing across her large green eyes.

"Mother," Robin repeated softly. His throat constricted painfully.

She was so peaceful, so content. She seemed to be saying to him, "We are all up here. All our pain and troubles long forgotten but where are you? Where are you?"

"The table with inlaid stones is just incredible," said a woman behind him in the Connecticut drawl favored by high society goddesses who lunched at the Four Seasons and Le Bernadin. "Sent to the castle from the Doge. We really must get back to Venice this year."

Robin turned his head slightly, taking quick note of a sleek Manhattan matron exquisitely turned out in Chanel couture and shimmering diamonds. He wiped away a tear that had suddenly spilled from his right eye. His mother might have liked her elegant 21st century counterpart.

"It's that girl in red that fascinates me," replied the woman's male companion, radiating vast wealth in a bespoke suit of merino wool, cashmere and silk. "Clearly a lady of sensitivity and breeding."

"Elizabeth, seventh Countess of Hawkesmoor," she sighed. "What a romantic name."

Robin felt the words enter his brain with an electric jolt that shook his entire frame. He spun around. Directly across the room was an immense full-length painting of Elizabeth — his Elizabeth.

It just wasn't possible. They had never married. He had disappeared the night of their betrothal ball. How could she be the seventh Countess?

Robin felt he had almost locked gazes with Elizabeth's painted eyes as he strode across the crowded hall. She was never so wan, he thought as he neared the massive portrait. Even her wonderful tawny hair seemed to have been stripped of its burnished gold. Elizabeth's naturally waving hair had been the bane of her lady's maid. It refused to be tamed by ribbons and pins, escaping all modish coifs to tumble haphazardly down her back. This Elizabeth, thin and serious, was drowning in an elaborate red velvet riding habit. She stood in quiet dignity, her oval face averted as if she were taken aback at all the strange modern people who stared up at her. The lush Acadian meadows behind Elizabeth's wasted frame was supposed to represent Hawkesmoor's prosperous farmlands.

Ha! thought Robin. *If they only knew how desolate and wild Hawkesmoor country really was.*

"Elizabeth, seventh Countess of Hawkesmoor," he read softly to himself from the glowing touchscreen that served as a much more modern version of the printed placard, "was a figure in one of Hawkesmoor Castle's more interesting historical tales. Formerly Lady Elizabeth Gwayr, she was, to all accounts, in a true love match with the future Earl: Richard Robin Francis, Lord Merritt. August 3, 1750, the eve of their betrothal ball, Lord Merritt vanished without a trace and despite a search that scoured England, was never seen again. Lady Elizabeth Gwayr was quickly married —some said with unseemly haste — to his cousin Ambrose Westmacott, who eventually inherited the Earldom."

Robin paused for a moment to take in a shallow breath before he could read the last sentence. Ambrose, that mutton-headed brute! He couldn't keep his thick paws off ale or the nearest chambermaid.

"Elizabeth died in 1764 after taking a terrible fall down the staircase in the Great Hall."

He took several shaky steps backwards and sat down on one of his mother's Brustolon chairs.

"Oh, for the love of all that's holy!" swore Lady Caroline's assistant, Beryl. "I knew it would happen! Some jerk is actually sitting on one of the Venetian chairs. I'll get security."

"No, don't." Lady Caroline followed the line of Beryl's pointing finger. "It could be a rich American who wants to write us a huge check to repair the roof."

"In exchange for a shiny gold plaque—lovingly restored by Goldstein's Mattress Kingdom," Beryl groaned, grabbing a glass of white wine from a passing waiter.

"We need money for Hawkesmoor," Caroline reminded her. "If we don't get a lot of it and soon… Well, you know. I'll go have a word with him."

"Right! I'll find that neurosurgeon and convince him to buy about a million pounds of upholstery restoration for Augusta's boudoir."

"And talk to Mr. Goldstein too." Caroline grinned. "I bet Augusta wouldn't say boo to a new mattress after all these years either."

Lady Caroline wove her way through the throngs of New Yorkers. She felt vaguely uncomfortable in the black velvet cocktail dress and wished fervently she were back home at Hawkesmoor. She'd be outside in a really soft pair of old pegged breeches and a sweater, enjoying the wild beauty of the moor country. If she wasn't forced to save Hawkesmoor Castle from ruin or sale to a theme park, she'd never stray from the moors for very long.

What a truly elegant man, Caroline thought suddenly as the Venetian chair trespasser came sharply into view. He sat back in the ornate chair with an easy grace, as if he were lord of the manor. He was staring fixedly at the Phillips painting of Countess Elizabeth. She liked the way his heavy curtain of hair fell about his slender shoulders.

He looked rather shell-shocked as if he'd just taken a shot of really bad news. She decided he hadn't meant to be thoughtless about the exhibit. He just needed a friendly face and a glass of cheap champagne.

"Hello," Caroline said, kneeling slightly by the carved armrest. "I'm Caroline DeBarry."

He slowly turned his handsome head and his green eyes widened in puzzlement at the sight of her.

"Corisande," he began hopefully and then closed his eyes. "No, you're not her." His voice was hollow.

"If you mean the Countess," Caroline supplied cheerfully, "some people imagine I resemble her because I live at the castle but I'm not related to Elizabeth at all. My ancestors took over the castle long after she died."

The beautiful green eyes opened again. "Forgive me, I've been very rude. You must wish to protect your lovely chair."

He clasped the armrests with his long hands, pushed up to his feet and stepped away from her.

"Don't disappear!" Caroline insisted, laying a hand on his forearm. "You're English, aren't you?"

"Yes." He studied her face intently for a moment and then averted his eyes to study a Chinese vase he didn't recall from his era. "I'm Robin Dashwood."

"It's nice to make your acquaintance, Mr. Dashwood." Caroline smiled at him. "Would you like me to show you about? There are quite a few really special pieces. We've got some awfully good ghost stories too. A Grey Lady and a ghost boy…"

"I'm afraid I have to be leaving," he interrupted, rubbing his right temple wearily. "But I'm glad to have met you, Lady Caroline."

"Thank you, Mr. Dashwood." She was surprised but not displeased when he lifted a hand to gently push an errant strand of strawberry blonde hair out of her eyes.

"You are so very like her," he said cryptically before moving away and leaving her to stare after him in fascination.

Robin was almost at a run. He headed for the exit, wiping at his wet eyes and roughly shaking off the clutches of a sharp-voiced blonde who called him *a total and complete jerk!*

He clattered down the wide modern steps of the Glockner Gallery and finally broke into a run when he reached street level. With a tortured cry only other vampires could hear, Robin melted into shadow and rose up with the cool night breeze.

3

Robin stared out the window by his desk, watching March rain strike the glass.

Elizabeth, he thought, tracing a raindrop with his finger as it slid down the windowpane, had lived out her short life married to his loathsome cousin, Ambrose. How unexpectedly cruel for both Elizabeth and himself.

He winced as furious crashing noises informed him that Kate was hurling her suitcases and cardboard boxes at a pair of highly entertained Mayflower moving men.

Lady Caroline sipped coffee from a chipped Glockner Gallery mug and plopped her feet up on a desk in the temporary private office. She studied the schematics for the exhibit with a disappointed sigh. Somehow the layout of the Queen Anne suite wasn't working. Six days into the run and the traffic pattern was still haphazard in that particular corner. She was afraid one of the pieces would get damaged over the exhibit's run.

It would have been nice to be able to afford the floor designer and a full time curator for the length of the showing but Hawkesmoor couldn't match the initial grant.

"I was not bred to be an administrator," Caroline muttered, tossing the papers into her file basket. "I'm good with horses and dogs."

It was a wet and dreary weekday. Attendance was spotty at best and the gallery essentially empty so she decided to creep out in her jeans and take a look at the Queen Anne suite herself. The really famous English treasure houses — the ones that had already sold their souls to the lucrative tourist trade — had professional people on staff that did these sorts of shows and did them very well. Poor old Hawkesmoor. It just had the last members of the DeBarry line to fight for it. One rumpled old Earl and his three children. Caroline took a final sip and put the mug aside. She wondered how her father was doing back home. It was lambing season and he had great hopes for his new crossbreeds. *They'll be a hardier moor sheep*, he had predicted with real excitement, *just see if they don't get more out of less acreage!*

The exhibit was tomblike as Caroline headed towards the spectacular crimson and gold Queen Anne State bed — due to its more obvious opulence — had become the main attraction.

She glanced up at Augusta, the sixth countess, on the way. Caroline had always loved the portrait. As a child she spent many rainy afternoons in Hawkesmoor's long Elizabethan gallery, studying all the past occupants of the castle. Caroline ticked off a few of her favorites in her head automatically: kind and smiling Augusta, stern George — the tenth Earl, plump, silly Adelaide, pious Henry — the ninth Earl, melancholy Elizabeth and of course, the mysterious Lord Merritt who had disappeared.

The story had always intrigued her. As a girl, she used to sit by the only portrait of him known to be in existence. A rather small work as portraits went and not signed by an artist. Richard Robin Francis stood by an open window overlooking the moors in the composition. He was tall, slender and romantically handsome with beautiful, angular features. She liked the clear-eyed intelligence of his gaze and the lovely spidery length of his pale hands that seemed to hint of an artistic nature. The artist had chosen to paint Lord Merritt in a severe black frock coat devoid of any of the elaborate embellishments so popular at the time. He looked as if he were in mourning although there was no record of a family death at that date. Caroline found it eerie — a kind of foreboding on the painter's part.

Lord Merritt had been thirty-two when he vanished. Quite late for a first marriage in those days but according to Augusta's diaries, the sixth Earl had wanted to wait for the young Lady Elizabeth to reach her eighteenth year. He keenly desired a union between ancient Saxon Gwayr family and the Norman line of the DuPlessis. It had become a DeBarry family parlor game, trying to figure out what had happened that summer night when Lord Merritt failed to appear at the betrothal ball.

Most people assumed he had been murdered by his cousin Ambrose who stood to inherit Hawkesmoor since the sixth Earl had no other issue. Caroline never understood the logic since Elizabeth had been hastily married to Ambrose Westmacott. Surely neither the Gwayr family nor the Earl would have wanted her married to Lord Merritt's murderer.

Still, she and her younger brother Peter had pretty much explored the length and depth of the castle searching for hidden rooms containing the rotting bones of Lord Merritt. To their immense disappointment, they never found him.

"It's Lady Caroline, isn't it?" came a quiet British voice at her shoulder.

She spun in her battered loafers to find the elegant Mr. Dashwood from the opening night party. He stood near her with his arms crossed and a thoughtful expression on his face.

Caroline had a moment to wish she had worn something chic — something Chanel or Stella McCartney. As usual, she had opted for jeans and a sweater, her long red-gold hair falling down her back in a thick, untidy jumble. She was a practical-minded country girl who kept up more with changes in equestrian gear and sheepdog trials than fashion.

But Dashwood, she noted immediately, was one of those rare creatures with innate style. The old-fashioned baggy brown suit and leather satchel over his shoulder were worn with easy grace and effortless elegance.

"Mr. Dashwood! It's nice to see you back again," Caroline said with what she hoped wasn't too much good cheer. Perhaps he would think her a perfect country bumpkin. Maybe he detested jolly people and preferred Bohemian coffee house types who understood the angst of a melancholy Russian poem when they heard one.

He pulled his tortoiseshell glasses off his face. "I had to come back."

Caroline widened her eyes in surprise. "Well, I'm glad you did. It's bloody boring around here today."

"You said something about showing me around the other night." Dashwood smiled at her as he slipped the glasses into his breast pocket. "Does the invitation still stand?"

"Oh, of course, yes." She found herself in danger of babbling. "I'd be happy to. There's a lot to take in. Are you fond of history, Mr. Dashwood?"

"Robin, please." He glanced away from her and up to the painting of Augusta. "I'm a professor of European history at NYU, actually. This exhibit is quite interesting to me."

"A historian! Gosh, that's brilliant. Come — help me figure out what to do about this Queen Anne bed." Caroline laughed out loud as Dashwood arched a quizzical eyebrow. "I mean; I really could use your advice. The visitors keep bumping into it."

"I am, of course, happy to look, but," he cocked his head to the side, "don't you have professionals to solve these sorts of problems?"

Caroline shrugged loosely and slid her hands into the pockets of her mother's 1970's era gray cashmere cardigan. She inhaled a long breath of the gallery's climate controlled air, trying to suppress a giggle. As a child and teenager, she had battled the unfortunate tendency to titter when highly anxious, frightened or intimidated. She was glad to have mostly conquered it as nervous giggles had made certain moments in her childhood extremely awkward. Caroline pushed away a searing memory of her A-level in biochemistry with an involuntary shudder. At least she thought she had mastered it. She cleared her throat.

"Hawkesmoor can't afford a full time art director and ours had to go back to England. We could only budget him in for opening week."

"Well then," Dashwood beamed at her, "let's go move your furniture."

An hour later, Caroline wiped sweat off her forehead with the back of her hand and flopped down on an edge of the enormous State Bed. A few motes of dust from the original velvet hangings rose up and floated in the air.

She watched as Robin Dashwood carefully made the final adjustment to a brass and oak traveling chest belonging to the Queen herself. He affectionately ran his hand over the brass-studded lid.

"AR," he said softly as his fingers found the monogram. "Anna Regina."

"You know I think it's going to work!" announced Caroline, indicating the new arrangement. "Thank you, Robin."

At her words, Robin's green-eyed gaze drifted from the chest to fix on something in the distance.

"That picture of the girl in red," he began slowly.

"Oh," Caroline yawned as she sat up to follow his direction, "you mean Elizabeth."

"Do you know much about her?" Robin clasped his long hands together uneasily.

"A fair amount, I suppose."

"I, uhm, read the interpretive screen by her portrait." Robin broke off his stare and crossed to the bed. He leaned against one of the massive pillars, looking down at Caroline. "Was she happy with Westmacott despite my … despite everything?"

"It's really hard to know as Augusta's private diaries from that period have never been found. We know they must have existed once because she was an exhaustive diarist — much of what we have gleaned of daily life in the 18th century Hawkesmoor comes from Augusta's diaries." Caroline wrinkled her brow in thought. "We do know, from Augusta's correspondence with her brother, the Marquess of Tantamount, that she absolutely detested Ambrose Westmacott. Augusta complained bitterly of his penchant for heavy drinking and generally coarse manners."

Caroline took in a short breath of surprise. Real sorrow pulled at Robin's handsome features. He crossed his arms almost protectively about his chest and turned slightly away from her, obscuring his face.

"In these letters, did she ever mention Elizabeth?"

"Well, Augusta was very fond of her. Remember she was supposed to have married Augusta's only child, Richard." Caroline glanced at her old tank wristwatch. The exhibit would be closing in another hour. "She must have regretted the marriage since Elizabeth was only Countess for a very short time."

"What do you mean, a very short time?" His voice was low and urgent.

"The old Earl finally died in 1764 and within forty-eight hours, Elizabeth was found dead at the bottom of the Great Hall staircase," she explained, wiping another bead of sweat away. "It's not hard to have misgivings about Ambrose. He promptly remarried, to his long-time mistress."

"I see," Robin said in an icy tone.

There was a long, awkward pause between them broken finally by Caroline who pushed herself reluctantly off Queen Anne's bed.

"I have to finish some paperwork before the exhibit closes," she said with real regret. "Thanks for all your help, Robin."

Robin seemed to shake himself out of a reverie. He half-smiled at her, his coppery hair falling rakishly across his face. The effect sent a shiver down her spine.

"I enjoyed this afternoon." He moved to pick up his brown leather satchel.

"If you are truly interested in the history of Hawkesmoor," Caroline started hesitantly.

It was not like her to go after handsome strangers she'd just met in foreign cities. She even had a regular boyfriend back home: Mark Halsey who ran the local riding school. He wanted to marry her and everything. She always imagined she would eventually. It seemed the expected, sensible course to take. Mark understood life at Hawkesmoor Castle. Unexciting but appropriate.

"Yes, Caroline?" Robin straightened to his full height.

But Robin Dashwood was so beautiful. His dark green eyes seemed to drink her in as if she was a glass of sacramental wine. It was unnerving and exciting. The mirror opposite of Mark Halsey.

"We could discuss it over dinner," she blurted out in a rush. "I mean, I'll stand treat. It's the least I can do."

"You are asking me out on a date?" Robin looked amused as he threw the satchel strap over his shoulder.

Caroline felt her throat run dry. Of course, he thought she was too dowdy and silly. He would like pale serious girls who wore Anna Sui dresses and wrote haiku about civil rights. She decided to fling herself into the unknown anyway.

"Gosh," she floundered awkwardly, "date is a strong word."

"I accept," Robin interjected with a dazzling smile.

But first he had to deal with his anger. Robin's mind roared with thoughts and memories. He clattered down the gallery's stairs to the wet street, ignoring the pounding rain.

It was just possible Ambrose could graduate to murder. He had always been a thickheaded bully and with an eager mistress to prod him into action, Robin could see him capable of murdering Elizabeth.

The very idea of Ambrose touching Elizabeth made his revenant blood run even colder than usual. If only he could go back for a few moments, he'd rip Ambrose's throat out.

There was an illegally sub-divided apartment building in Bedford-Stuyvesant that had become his newest killing field. Undocumented aliens, criminals with outstanding warrants and substance abusers paid cash to a conscienceless landlord to hide within its dismal walls. An excellent place to find his usual prey — remorseless bullies.

Robin cast aside Bed-Stuy as too far and too little. He wanted to hunt a different kind of bully, closer to home. It was a fine Manhattan evening. There would be corrupt Wall Street tax attorneys, real estate developers and sex-trafficking hedge-fund managers relaxing over martinis in posh watering holes all over the city. He'd find one and tear his or her throat out in Ambrose's stead.

4

Caroline thought she looked all right in the same black velvet dress she'd worn to the opening night reception. It was short, sleeveless and reminded her of a vintage *Breakfast at Tiffany's* kind of chic. At least it had in the dressing room of the Northern village shop near Hawkesmoor. Now she wished she had paid just a bit more attention to *Vogue* than *Horse and Hound*.

She waited in the hotel's magnificent lobby watching the gleaming marble entranceway for any sign of Robin Dashwood and listening to the heavy rain pound the pavement just outside.

An ever-vigilant hotel steward brought her a cup of tea and an iPad with a current news page up on its screen. The leading story was something about the sudden death of a prominent attorney. She shivered and put the tablet aside, returning to her own thoughts. The superlative service reminded her just what a stay in New York was doing to the balance on the family credit cards. There were a lot of built-in assumptions Americans had about British aristocrats and an especially popular one held that all upper class Brits were flush with pocket money despite any protestations to the contrary. It just didn't occur to them that the privilege of looking after a great estate like Hawkesmoor relentlessly drained the family exchequer every year. It didn't occur to them that an English Lady might find the cost of a top New York hotel intimidating. In order to be taken seriously by those who might help Hawkesmoor, she was obliged to spend far more than she and her father had originally planned for the trip. It was frustrating.

Budget things always made her irritable so Caroline forced her brain to switch subjects and found herself returning to Robin Dashwood. He was the definite high point of her trip to America. What a lovely mysterious man. It would be intriguing to find out more about him and why he chose to remain in such an alien place as New York.

Mark would not be best pleased with her little adventure, Caroline mused as she sipped her tea. He really considered himself to be the only one on the field — the official boyfriend. She had yet to accept any of his marriage proposals and perhaps she should. Why continue to delay the inevitable? After all, Mark should be the obvious choice. He was solid, and devoted to rural life. He would help her manage Hawkesmoor. He would be good for Hawkesmoor. He ought to be good enough for her.

"Caroline, forgive me," said a voice near her. "The rain held me up."

She jerked her head up, nearly spilling the contents of her teacup. How did he bloody move so quickly and silently?

Robin stood by her in a rain-drenched trench coat. The coppery hair was wet and clinging in heavy waves to the planes of his handsome head. He sneezed.

"Sorry." He pulled a white handkerchief out from his pocket. "I seem to have caught my death out there."

Caroline found herself beaming at him in relief. She realized just how much she had been looking forward to having dinner with Robin and fearing that he would fail to appear.

"You are soaked," she said sympathetically. "All because of me."

"All my own doing." He shook his head politely and promptly sneezed again. "I got off at the wrong subway stop. It's been a long day. Anyway, shall we go? There's a nice little French place around the corner."

"No," Caroline broke in, surprising herself with her decisiveness. "It makes much more sense to use room service."

Robin looked mildly surprised. "Here?" he asked cautiously.

"Why ever not? It's got a very pleasant sitting room I've never gotten to use." Caroline shrugged. "You could get warm and dry."

He tried to speak but sneezed instead.

"You have talked me into it," Robin said, once he could.

Really, he had to be more careful. Often addicts he preyed on had so polluted their blood supply that he had a reaction to it, rather like an allergy. Sometimes it was just the mild symptoms of a cold. Other times a raging flu-like reaction that put him to bed.

Still the annoying head cold had allowed him closer to Lady Caroline than he had dared hope.

Robin watched as she organized the room service cart with rather more seriousness than the job deserved. He was completely charmed by her natural warmth and already loved her infectious laugh that revealed both a keen sense of fun and occasional bouts with nerves. She was also artlessly beautiful with the face of a Norman princess — gorgeous creamy skin, high cheekbones and widely set eyes that flashed with humor and intelligence. That she clearly had no idea how attracted he was to her or how enticing she really was only added to her refined allure.

She glanced at him a shade anxiously as she went about the task of filling the wine glasses. He doubted Lady Caroline had ever invited a man up to a hotel room before. In fact, he was pretty positive she was secretly regretting her rash decision. What would her old headmistress think?

He felt his throat tighten. This Lady Caroline DeBarry was a rare and valuable thing. He saw a damp breeze from the terrace send some of the rose gold of her hair streaming like threads of raw silk. It made him homesick for some reason.

YORKSHIRE, 1750

Elizabeth's head was bowed over embroidery when he came into her father's library. He had a brief moment to appreciate how the flickering light from the fireplace cast a shimmer over her thick tawny hair and at her unconscious grace as she pulled a silk thread through the linen square.

"Good evening," he said from the doorway.

"Robin!" Elizabeth exclaimed in delight. "What brings you to Manwaring? Did Father really summon you all the way from Hawkesmoor to see his new horse?"

"I came to see you, you perfectly silly creature." He settled on the Moroccan ottoman at her feet. "How have you been keeping, m'dear?"

She shrugged prettily. "Thank you for inquiring, sir. Mother believes my chill will soon be gone."

"That ought to give you an excellent lesson about coming in out of the rain."

"Piffle." Elizabeth made a sour face. "I was enjoying my gallop on Jupiter."

"Evidently." Robin raised an eyebrow.

"As if you did not fancy a good country gallop yourself." She reached out to playfully tap his shoulder.

He caught her hand and kissed the palm. Elizabeth gave a small gasp at his sudden effusiveness.

"I have missed you, madam." Robin said in a low voice as he kissed her hand again. "Do not be long from me and Hawkesmoor, I beg you."

"Robin," she said in wonder, staring at him with wide eyes, "it is difficult to imagine you could see me as anything else but that bothersome little girl who has followed you about since she could walk."

He held her hand to his cheek. "It has been some while since I viewed you, Elizabeth, as a little girl."

"Then you truly do not mind this match between our families?" Elizabeth gently intertwinᴇd her fingers with his.

"Madam," Robin gazed up at her. "I yearn for it."

"Robin?" Caroline's inquiring voice drove Elizabeth from his mind. "Are you all right?"

He reached up and rubbed his temple tiredly. "It's just been rather a long day. I'm sorry."

"Perhaps another night? No worries. My re-telling of castle ghost stories have bored many others before you."

Robin shook his head. "I love eerie tales and I'd much prefer to stay."

He managed to push vegetables and Dover sole about his plate for almost an hour, listening to Caroline's restoration plans for Hawkesmoor. He was saddened to learn how much the old place needed re-roofing, rewiring, new plumbing and antique refurbishment. It shouldn't have surprised him. Even in his day Hawkesmoor had required one or two major maintenance projects. Somehow, since he'd left Hawkesmoor, it had existed in his head as a sort of static dream. It never changed or deteriorated. Just as he had pretended the people he had loved had gone on to live flawless lives. The truth was like a dull blade gouging open old wounds. He had to work hard to appear neutral to Caroline's tale.

His admiration for the DeBarry family grew as she told him of their lives at the castle. He learned from Caroline that the line had jumped from Westmacotts to their cousins the DeBarrys in 1865 when Ambrose Westmacott's grandson William had died without issue. The hardworking DeBarrys inherited an enormous job. The Hawkesmoor estate had been gutted by Ambrose's greed and gambling. Five generations of DeBarrys had fought to save his keep from utter destruction.

Hawkesmoor by all rights had been his responsibility. His to protect and pass on to his sons. Sons Elizabeth would have given him. He had failed them all: Elizabeth, his parents but this girl — this Lady Caroline — had picked up his sword.

"Anyway," Caroline was saying over her wineglass, "we still hope to avoid the theme park route."

Robin almost jumped at her words.

"Theme park?" he repeated severely.

"Some British estates have incorporated a fun fair motif with rides and elaborately staged costume days. An American corporation has offered to take on Hawkesmoor if they can use it as a kind of conference center. You know, so they can send all their executives out to play Lord of the Manor." Caroline sipped her wine. "We would still be allowed to live there, sort of, in rooms at the top."

"The servant quarters?" Robin's elegant jaw dropped open. "The Earl of Hawkesmoor?"

"We could get used to it." She shrugged with a rueful grin. "Well, Peter, Hannah and I could. I don't know about Dad. He hates anything remotely modern and by modern, I mean electric typewriters. He's currently pretending smart phones and tablets don't exist."

He grinned back at her. "And who are Peter and Hannah?"

"Peter — my brother, Lord Merritt. He's at Oxford reading history. Hannah's our younger sister. She likes horses and boys in exactly that order. She's quite good at the aforementioned hated computers as well. Runs our little website about the castle."

"What about you, Lady Caroline?" Robin pretended to sip his Cabernet. He inhaled a strong draft of the rich woodsy aroma. "Starting from childhood."

Caroline glanced up from her meal. "Typical childhood."

"In a castle," he observed, saluting her with his wineglass.

She nodded with another one of her contralto laughs. "Typical childhood in a castle with lots of dogs, horses and school uniforms. I plowed through school with the usual dreams—ballerina, world famous pop singer, respected brain surgeon."

"Then," Caroline laughed at the memory, "then I was dutifully taken to the theatre in London where I discovered I really, really wanted to be a Shakespearian actress. I practiced monologues all over the castle and threw myself with terrifying tenacity into the drama clubs at school. Only one issue."

"No talent?"

"Not a shred!"

"You recovered, though." He had another faux sip of wine.

"Yes—by then the noble atmosphere of the Anglican school I was attending had seeped in. I decided I'd accept a nun's habit and devote the rest of my life to helping others."

Robin laughed out loud. "How long did this phase last?"

"Not long," she admitted. "Helping others—all the time—had an appallingly short sell-by date. I went on with my riding, finished school, traveled Europe in my gap year and went to university just like most of my friends. Very dull."

"Don't know about dull," he said. "I have a fondness for universities myself. Let me guess. Art history?"

Caroline giggled. "You'd think that, wouldn't you—given Hawkesmoor's issues. I'm actually a large animal vet. Took my training at Leeds and had hoped to specialize in three-day horses—you know, traveling to the fixtures and all that. I've been arguing with the FEI about their decision to scrap the long format in favor of more technical questions. The amount of rotational falls in the cross country phase is a scandal."

"I can't imagine you are anything less than brilliant," he said. "So it must be … Hawkesmoor?'

She threw up her hands in a cheerful pretense of frustration. "The castle reached critical mass just as my FEI duties were starting up. So put the career on hiatus until Hawkesmoor gets sorted. I make calls for our local vet when he's overbooked which is often by the way. When he retires in a few years, I will probably take on his practice."

"No special man in all of this?"

Here was the question that really intrigued him.

"Well," Caroline stammered, all the humor draining from her face. She polished off the rest of her wine in a single swallow, "there's no one really. Okay, not completely true. There's Mark."

Robin cocked his head to the side quizzically. "Is he the one?"

Caroline pushed away from the table as if the subject made her uneasy. She wandered to the open sliding door that led to the terrace and leaned on the door jamb, enjoying the cool breeze.

Robin stood up, drinking in Caroline's fine Northern English handsomeness and the flawless translucence of her skin in the soft light. This defender of his birthright was his bride by proxy, by noblesse obliges.

"Is he the one? The one that you want?"

Caroline didn't answer. She stared out at the New York skyline beyond Central Park and wrapped her arms about her ribcage protectively.

"Caroline," Robin moved with his cat quiet vampire's stride until he was directly behind her. He laid his long hands on her shoulders.

She took in a short nervous breath at his touch. Robin felt her pulse quicken in anticipation. He could sense both her want of him — and her fear.

"You have every right to ask me to stop," he murmured, gently pushing her hair to one side and dropping a kiss onto her shoulder, left bare by the pretty French dress.

"This isn't me. I don't just invite men up to my rooms," Caroline whispered as he kissed her neck. She gasped as he slid his arms about her waist and pulled her tightly against his tall frame.

"I know that," he said in her ear. "I know the kind of woman you are."

It was like the blood hunger. It had possessed the same urgency and the same ruthlessness. He had to have her. She was his past, his present and his future. He wanted to drink her in and make her part of him forever.

"Robin, please," he heard her voice dimly through the roar in his head when she had turned around in his arms and he kissed her with the full force of his revenant passion.

Caroline's hazel eyes searched his frantically once he had finally drawn away. She tried to step back but the door jamb pinned her in.

"This is very intense," she whispered hoarsely. "Please — I feel like I am drowning in you."

Robin froze at the desperate quality in her tone. It cut through the roar like a shrill whistle. He dropped his arms immediately and moved away, clasping his hands behind his back.

He stared at her, his green eyes stricken with regret. What had come upon him? He had frightened her — the one woman he wished above all others to please.

"Please accept my sincerest apologies. I have," his jaw tightened, "behaved very badly."

"No," Caroline pushed off the glass door and came towards him. "You just seem to care so deeply. It took me by surprise."

Robin crossed to the chair where his raincoat had been laid out to dry and picked it up.

"I will never see you again if you go now," Caroline exclaimed in real distress. She didn't understand how she knew such a thing but it seemed absolutely clear he would vanish forever.

"Don't be silly, my dear," Robin murmured. "I teach at NYU. Anyone could find me."

"You won't let me find you again," she said with a certainty she was unable to explain.

Robin offered her only a sad smile, folding his raincoat over his arm.

"Could we," Caroline couldn't bear the prospect of never catching sight of his breathtaking face or hearing his soft reedy voice again, "could we possibly have another go at this?"

He hesitated, his green eyes narrowed as he considered her words.

"I promise you won't be frightened again, Caroline," Robin said as he came towards her.

She placed her hands in his. "I know."

5

Robin sat up as the watery gray of a rain-soaked dawn filtered through the damask drapes of the hotel room.

"Caroline, my love." He leaned over to kiss the side of her face. She stirred at his touch. "Caroline, I must go."

She slowly opened her eyes and turned to look at him with a bleary smile.

"You lovely, lovely man," she said, reaching to smooth back a few of the copper-colored strands that fell into his eyes.

"I must go," he repeated with real regret.

"You are leaving?" Caroline began to truly wake. "So soon?"

"I have a class to teach." Robin bent to kiss her forehead. "My annual lecture on medieval guilds. A thankless endeavor."

Caroline slipped her arms up and around his neck. She pulled him into a deep kiss. He returned it with equal feeling, shifting his weight over hers as his desire intensified.

"Love," Robin let out in a hoarse breath once he could, "I really do have to go."

She ran her hands down his spine. He shivered with pleasure and found himself kissing her again with increasing passion. His physical body seemed at complete odds with his cool vampire mind. He felt like a mortal man again. All awkward nerves and misfiring energies. It was alien, familiar, unsettling and exhilarating all at once. What was it about this girl that rattled him to the very essence of his revenant structure? He had made love to humans over the centuries — affectionately, hungrily, sometimes bittersweet and sometimes with something akin to love but never like this. He belonged to this girl. She possessed him.

Robin untied the pale rose ribbons of her nightgown and pushed aside the muslin. His long fingers drifted over the soft, full curves of her breasts. She sunk her hands deep into his hair, relishing its thick silken texture.

"I can't defy you," Robin whispered before pressing his cool mouth against her lips and then an erect nipple. "Use your power over me wisely."

"Just don't," Caroline gasped as he suddenly pushed deep inside, "vanish."

He shook his head, unable to find his voice. Drowning in Caroline's exquisite rhythm, Robin fought to keep his external form from disintegrating. He felt the silvery spider web of molecular change drop over his nervous system, warning of an imminent phase change. He was literally coming apart as if his vampire molecular structure —instead of preparing to absorb Caroline's essence — was trying to reorder itself to bond with hers.

Last night he had been anxious to please Caroline with his considerable skill as a lover. She had been quite shy at first — her upper-class reserve perplexed by sexual intimacy with a virtual stranger. It had been a pleasure to slowly draw Caroline out. He explored her intoxicating curves, discovering how she liked to be kissed and that she had very sensitive breasts, acutely aroused at his touch. She was a passionate creature underneath the social restraints. Focusing so intently on Caroline must have held him together.

Now he was dangerously close to a kind of vampire meltdown. Pain, pleasure and panic surged through him with equal abandon. Unable to pull back, Robin moved inside her with increasing urgency. A white-hot noise — a chant, a roar — in his head threatened to overtake him. He wondered just how horrified she'd be if he shattered into a million pieces.

Caroline gasped as he became more aggressive. She wrapped her arms about his shoulders, shivering with her need of him.

Pain, panic, pleasure. The electric incantation rose in his system — perhaps he had already disintegrated. He just couldn't know with her. She was different from any other.

Pain, panic, pleasure. Perhaps she already knew. Just don't vanish! Perhaps she knew. Just don't vanish! Perhaps she knew. Just don't vanish! Just don't vanish!

The pressure was unbearable. He began to break apart — pain, pleasure panic. He had to ground himself. Robin dropped his head and sank his teeth into Caroline's straining neck. She cried out, shuddering down the length of her body. He collapsed in her arms, replete.

"Bloody hell," whispered Caroline, stroking his hair.

Robin slid a hand up to caress her damp neck. He had to make sure he hadn't drawn blood — that he hadn't tried to feed.

She shivered and pulled him closer. "That was different. Brilliant though."

"All right?" He moved up slightly to kiss her neck where a bruise would be forming.

"Bloody hell," Caroline repeated. She exhaled slowly. "Yes. Yes. Yes."

"About what you said before," he asked. "Just don't vanish? Did anything happen last night that would make you ask that?"

She was shy again. "It was," she said, "silly."

Robin kissed her quickly. "No, it's not. But just don't vanish?"

"You know, as in don't ever go. Don't ever leave me. Can't live without you." Her voice broke a little. "All the things you're not supposed to say right away. You must think I'm such a…"

"Caroline," Robin drew back to look at her, "I belong to you."

A glimmer of surprise flickered across her face, quickly replaced with relief and then a bright smile. "Seems we're equals then."

"Equals?" He grinned at the thought and pulled her to him.

The subway car jostled and hummed its way to Washington Square. Robin sat by a dirt-encrusted window watching equally filthy walls flash by.

He half smiled, thinking of the long night with Lady Caroline. It was one of the sweetest encounters of his hellishly long existence. He'd made love to someone who brought Lord Merritt back to life, even if it was only for the hours spent in her bed.

Robin laid his head against the window frame. Rather like an afternoon so long ago.

Yorkshire, 1750

They met at the Roman Copse, not too far from Elizabeth's ancestral keep, Manwaring. It was called the Roman Copse because it contained dilapidated remains of an ancient stone circle that had once served as a cooking pit for Roman soldiers during their conquest of Britain. Local legend claimed the little clump of trees was haunted. No specifics were given for who or what walked the copse but its sinister reputation made it an ideal location for secret meetings.

Elizabeth was having a wretched time while her family made preparations for their marriage. Her mother, a genteel invalid, had insisted on a long separation between them until their wedding day. An exception would be made for the betrothal ball at Hawkesmoor but for the most part, vibrant outdoor-loving Elizabeth was kept sequestered in her mother's sick rooms embroidering linens for her new household.

The draconian measures were designed to protect Elizabeth's reputation from the keen sexual appetite of an older, experienced man. He was thirty-two years of age. She was just sixteen. It seemed to be expected that he would happily take advantage of her if given any opportunity.

All fairly silly as he had known of Elizabeth since she had been a baby in her nurse's arms and if he had wanted to deflower her, he could have done so long ago.

Indeed, Elizabeth suggested the clandestine rendezvous. She had sent a pleading message via her French maid. She missed him awfully and would go mad if he did not agree to meet. She just needed an excuse to give her mother and her indomitable Aunt Pross the slip.

"If I do one more pillowcase," Elizabeth said as they sat in the summer grass, their backs resting against one of the ancient stones, "I will lose what little mind I have left. Do we really need so many? "

Robin's eyes followed the lazy movements of their horses as they grazed a short distance away. He would hate it if either of them stepped on a rein and broke it. Such a bloody nuisance to have repaired.

"You will be well-looked after at Hawkesmoor," he replied without taking his eyes off the horses, "so you may cease all linen work immediately."

"Mother will be furious with me," Elizabeth grinned with delight, "even if she thinks I rode off to see my friend Jane. I just do not understand why I am not allowed to see you. The wedding is only two months away, after all."

"Your mother is deeply concerned for your well-being." Robin reached over and patted her hand. "She has the good sense to worry that I will not behave like a gentleman in light of your exquisite beauty."

Elizabeth broke into a giggle and kissed his cheek. "You always know just what to say, Lord Merritt, sir."

He looked away from the grazing horses and raised an eyebrow. "That is why your mother is worried."

She sat back against the old pitted stone and thought for moment. An Englishman's dream in a pearl gray riding habit with her gold curls caught under a dashing tricorn hat.

"Robin, have you known many women?"

He coughed, "Elizabeth, really."

"I would like to know." A stubborn look rose in her clear blue eyes.

"Madam, I am a gentleman. I will not discuss my past affairs with you or anyone else."

"You are being very disagreeable." Elizabeth crossed her arms in defiance. "I have to be trotted out like a broodmare."

"Elizabeth —" he began in surprise.

"You, sir," she continued, interrupting him, "are made very fully aware of my background! Fortunately, my parents are very attentive so it is absolutely stainless."

Robin threw his head back and laughed at her vexed expression.

"I do adore you, Elizabeth Gwayr," he said with great affection.

"And I you, sir." She shivered despite the warmth of the summer afternoon. "I do not like this place. I am sure it is haunted."

"The superstitions of farmers, my love." Robin ran his fingers down the side of her face, marveling at the silken texture of her skin. "But it is growing late. I should see you safely back to Manwaring."

Elizabeth's lovely oval face crumpled in disappointment. "But I have not seen you for ages, Robin. Please not yet. Let us stay a while."

"We will see each other again at the ball." He tugged at one of her curls. "You do not want your father out scouring every hill and sheepfold in one of his tempers, do you?"

"No," she allowed glumly.

"Good girl."

"Robin," Elizabeth asked in a small voice before he could rise to give her a hand up, "do you not worry sometimes that all is too well? Do you think we are too happy?"

"I do not think it is possible to be too happy," Robin leaned over and dropped a lingering kiss on her cheek, "but if anyone could produce such an exalted state in me, it would be Lady Elizabeth Gwayr."

"Oh, Robin!" She flung her arms about his neck with sufficient force to send them both tumbling back into the grass. "I could not bear to lose you."

"And you will not, my sweet," he sputtered, recovering from the sudden change in position. "I promise."

Elizabeth rested her hands on his shoulders and looked down at him. Her eyes were filling with tears. "Aunt Pross has told me you will die long before I. She says I should prepare to be a young widow."

"Your Aunt Pross is an envious crow," he said, suddenly understanding why Elizabeth had so wanted to see him. The spinster sister of Elizabeth's father had taken delight in terrifying her niece with dark tales. He wondered if Elizabeth was afraid of her own wedding night. It would certainly explain her interest in his attachments with other women. He did not doubt Elizabeth's mother would fail to properly inform her daughter about the marital bed.

"Elizabeth," Robin said, praying he was not about to make a dreadful error in judgment. But where was the harm? They would be married by harvest. "Would you like it if I really kissed you?"

She wiped a tear away from her eyes and nodded, speechless.

Robin shifted his weight, pulling her down onto the grass beside him. He swept the dashing little tricorn hat from her head and threw it a distance away. Elizabeth watched him with huge anxious eyes. Her expression warned him that the Gwayr household understood the marriage bed to be a place of sacrifice and duty.

"Have I ever hurt you, my love?" he asked, unhooking the smart Hessian tassels which held together her riding coat.

She shook her head. The boning of her fashionable bodice rose and fell very rapidly with her agitated breathing.

"I am going to make love to you, Elizabeth," Robin said in her ear after he kissed her neck, "and when it is all over, you will know you have nothing to fear in me."

"Robin," Elizabeth whispered as if she were chanting a powerful word to ward off evil spirits. "Robin."

And indeed, when it was over and she lay in his arms while he stroked her hair, he had the odd thought it might have been an unwise choice to consummate his love for Elizabeth in the haunted grove. Bad luck, the locals would claim.

Robin's throat ached with the memory. If only he'd known how right the farmers were. The Roman Copse had been haunted that day in 1750 and the evil there had consumed them all.

6

Caroline and Beryl walked the exhibit route searching for any signs of visitor damage to the pieces — accidental or otherwise.

"Tell me about this Robin Dashwood. All I know is that he blithely sits in other people's priceless Venetian chairs."

Caroline grinned and moved forward to take a closer look at Queen Anne's immense traveling trunk. She knelt by its side, running her fingers over the brass studs.

"How did you know Ian was the man you'd eventually marry?" she asked in place of a direct answer to Beryl's question. There was not a great deal she could tell her assistant about Robin Dashwood. He was a British-born historian who taught at NYU and quite the loveliest man she had ever met.

Beryl's brown eyes widened in appreciation. "It has gone that far already? You mean, you might actually want to marry some bloke you just met in New York City?"

"Pretty crackers, eh?"

"Pretty crackers? Your father will be running to the gun cabinet." Beryl put her hands on her hips, her round face wreathed with disapproval. "Do you know what a magnet you are for Anglophile nuts?"

Caroline made a dismissive groan. "Don't be daft, Beryl."

"You are the daughter of an earl! A real English lady with a splendid castle to call home."

"That will belong to Peter," she interjected quickly.

"That belongs to the DeBarry family. Do you have any idea how many men would sell their own mothers to become associated with an earldom?" Beryl's voice rose slightly. "What do you really know about this man?"

"Robin Dashwood is kind and intelligent." Caroline returned to her feet, brushing off her knees with a briskly. "That is all I have to know for now.

Robin's walk was light and free as he headed down West 10th towards his old dowager aunt among the buildings, the Bailey. His was an incredibly long life punctuated with unique experiences but nothing had affected him like the night he had just spent in Caroline's arms. He felt changed as if she had reordered the very molecules in his blood. Transformed although he knew that was impossible. He was what he was — a three-hundred-year old vampire. He felt almost obliged to whistle.

He would contact his American solicitor Geoffrey Dunbar and have him wire thirty million pounds or so from the Swiss bank to Hawkesmoor's account. He would fetch his mother's emerald ring from the safe deposit box and give it to the woman he planned to make his wife. He was going home at last to the North Country, to Hawkesmoor Castle.

"Why, if it isn't Lord Merritt," said a voice from the cover of an alleyway.

Before he could react, Robin felt a massive figure grab the lapels of his coat, pick him up and shove him against the wall of an apartment building.

Robin coughed on impact. The powerful blow knocked the air from his thin frame. A vessel broke somewhere in his chest and blood began to drip from the corner of his mouth.

"Hello, Nate," he said as best he could through the pain. "It's been some while."

"You gotta stop with the druggies," the other commented, slamming him against the wall again. "You're so weak. It's embarrassing."

Nate Watkins. A vicious White Chapel pimp and murderer from the Victorian era. He was a brutish, ugly man with a prominent swordstick scar across his right cheekbone. A man so evil in his own time that a vampire had turned him so that Watkins' pure unadulterated aggression could be directed in useful ways forever.

Robin coughed up more blood. "What the hell do you want?"

The former White Chapel pimp grinned. "It ain't personal, mate. I got me orders."

7

Robin lifted his head, his mind coming back online like an old computer rebooting. He didn't know how long he'd been unconscious. Although he could see it was pitch black wherever he was and that he was hungry.

He tried to move forward but couldn't. There was a dull rattle of chain at his wrists. He was pinned. Pinned like a butterfly to what seemed to be a cold brick wall against his back.

Where the hell had Nate brought him? And under whose orders?

Robin winced. His head and body was beginning to protest the beating he'd taken.

Vampires, he thought as he gingerly tested the strength of the metal cuffs at his wrists, were condemned to walk the Earth forever but it was just another annoying myth that they couldn't be hurt. Vampires healed much faster than humans because they were physically and more perfectly stronger. Unfortunately, vampires could be hurt and hurt badly.

Robin tasted his own blood on his teeth and lips. Nate hadn't been the top Whitechapel thug for nothing. He obviously kept all his old back alley skills honed and sharpened.

"Nate!" he called out and knew it was useless all the same. The gentle drip of water somewhere out in the dark seemed to tell him he was completely alone.

Caroline. Damn. Robin rested his head against the damp brick. Caroline. She would be waiting for him. Lacking a certain confidence in herself, Caroline might assume he'd avoided her by design. She would leave — without him.

"Damn. Damn!" He tried to rise but the chains prevented him.

He didn't have time for Nate's vampire society machinations. He had to get to Caroline. She desperately needed him. Hawkesmoor needed him.

Where the bloody hell was Nate?

Robin rocked gently back and forth, trying to forget the hunger that was beginning to lick his thin frame. Cruel punishments meted out by arrogant vampire kings to disobedient indentured slaves or the masterminds behind attempted territorial coups were the stuff of legend. Tales of vampires imprisoned for a nightmarish eternity in tiny underground crypts or lead lined caskets in the sea. Vampires who would have been driven completely mad with the suffocating small darkness. Seared with the flames of the hunger, perhaps they even devoured their own flesh and drank their own blood. All that would be left was a shriveled sick consciousness.

Robin sucked in air to calm his nerves. He was neither disobedient servant nor would-be vampire king. To his knowledge, he had upset no one in the New York set. He stayed away from other revenants, preferring to avoid the labyrinth of political intrigue that always seemed to surround vampire courts. It was a perfectly valid decision. Many American vampires chose to go a solitary path. Unless one was an indentured slave or lacking the financial wherewithal to stand as an independent, one could do as one wished.

Max Aosta, the acknowledged vampire king of New York City and formerly Prince Amadeus dal Pozzo della Cisterna of Italy, had no quarrel with him. Max had always pleaded sadness at Robin's reluctance to fall in under his banner but he had never forced the issue or seemed to take exception to it.

So who would order Nate Watkins to chain him up somewhere in the dark to starve? Nate never acted on his own. He was always a hired gun for somebody.

Robin shuddered slightly as the hunger pangs slipped up a notch. Soon he'd be unable to focus on anything else but the hunger.

Where was Nate? Where in hell was he?

Robin lifted his head with a sharp gasp. He'd been dreaming of it again. The ghastly dream riddled with petty cruelties and many deaths. The horrible rattle shimmy of tumbrel carts and the hideously shrill voice of power-drunk people rising in triumph each time the bloody blade was hauled up and dropped.

He thought suddenly of Winnifred and wondered how the cloistered life she had chosen was treating her. If indeed she still existed in a recognizable form.

Dear Winnifred. If it wasn't for her great kindness he might still be an indentured slave.

Winnifred Turchil, daughter of one of the largest landowners in Saxon England. Married to the legendary Earl of Arthgal in 914 A.D., she became a powerful symbol in the continuing struggle against marauding Danes. A woman of keen intelligence and courage, Winnifred helped her less mentally agile husband devise ingenious methods to fend off the Danish warlords. Indeed, so well-traveled was the tale of Winnifred's brilliance that it attracted the notice of an even more powerful figure. A creature that had roamed the world long before Jesus Christ gave his life for all humans.

How he remembered that humiliating night in Paris in 1790 when his bored owner suddenly held an informal auction and Winnifred glided into his life.

Paris, 1791

It had been another winter evening of obscene waste and unrepentant frivolity in a city where most of the freezing inhabitants were slowly starving to death.

The glittering salon of Madame St. Cere was populated by both the most decadent members of Louis XVI's court and a coterie of vampires attracted by easy prey in the Parisian streets. It was always the same claustrophobic nightmare. Overindulged wine and drug addicts milling around, trying to out-clever each other in loud bleary voices.

He was pacing like a caged animal by one of the enormous French doors. He longed to throw open the glass and let a blast of cool air sweep over the sweltering ballroom. But he would be severely punished by his master for such a flagrant act. After all he was only a servant — the dogsbody of a vampire named Sir Anthony Fortesque.

Robin stretched his long fingers over the glass entreatingly. He could just sense the little winter cold allowed by Madame St. Cere's roaring fireplaces. How he envied the common streetwalkers out beyond the gilded townhouses. At least they could die of exposure and go on to whatever rewards they had earned in the afterlife. He had to spend his eternity with Sir Anthony Fortesque.

Sir Anthony — on the surface a powdered, effete fop. In reality, a ruthless predator with the ethical standards of a ship rat. Robin saw no way to escape him. As a relatively new vampire indentured to a well-known figure like Sir Anthony, he'd be tracked down like a dog.

"DuPlessis," came Fortesque's affected drawl behind him.

Robin stiffened slightly and knew his brief moment of freedom was over.

"DuPlessis!" The fey tone darkened considerably.

Robin clenched his jaw as he slowly turned away from the glass. Sir Anthony stood in all his exaggerated finery, glaring. His master was a true dandy. A lover of intricate diamante on his evening clothes, cascades of lace, powdered wigs and heavy grease paint. By contrast, he was quietly attired in a servant's black frock coat. His long auburn hair free of powder and pulled back severely with a black ribbon.

"Yes, sir?" He cast his eyes downward. Fortesque did not care for servants looking at their betters directly. Robin had learned that particular lesson the hard way.

"I. Had. To. Find. You," he said, emphasizing each word to make clear his complete displeasure.

Robin kept his eyes averted. "I am sorry, sir."

"The hell you are, you incomparable jade!" Sir Anthony's voice twisted with anger. "Fetch me a glass of champagne and be damn quick about it."

Robin steadied his temper. Fortesque held the complete deck of cards and taking on Sir Anthony was not really an option he cared to chance. He probably still had some family at Hawkesmoor. Sir Anthony had the power to reach out and hurt them.

"Champagne." He stepped forward obediently. A liveried footman carrying full glasses on a silver tray was just across the way. "At once, Sir Anthony."

Fortesque impatiently tapped his silver-buckled shoe against the polished wood floor as Robin passed him. Suddenly, with his vampire strength, he struck Robin with both hands and sent him stumbling forward. He crashed into a plump Parisian lady in apple green silks and a gilded cage of live finches woven into her tall powdered hair. The birds shrieked, and the lady cried out in displeasure as her wine spilled hopelessly across the costly green silk.

"Idiot!" she snapped as the hired musicians came to discordant halt. The entire ballroom stopped and previously bored hedonists shifted to watch the altercation.

"F-f-forgive me, Madam," Robin sputtered, righting himself.

The lady slapped him sharply across the face. One of her rings cut his lower lip and blood began to drip from the corner of his mouth. Most of the crowded salon let out a roar of laughter at the sight.

"Stupid boy."

Sir Anthony struck him from behind again. This time he fell to his knees from the force of the blow.

"Worthless wretch. I want you to fetch my champagne on your hands and knees."

Still feeling the hot sting of the slap, Robin shook his head and climbed back to his feet. He took another step towards the leering footman who backed up a pace, enjoying Robin's predicament. He held out the tray teasingly.

Feeling the amused eyes of the entire salon upon him, Robin lifted his chin and walked on with as much dignity as he could muster.

Fortesque struck him once more with explosive fury. Robin stumbled to the wood floor with a gasp of pain and this time Sir Anthony placed his exquisitely shod foot on Robin's back.

"I said crawl." His voice was low and dangerous. It reminded Robin how vulnerable his family could be to a powerful vampire.

Robin crawled. He made his way across the floor on his hands and knees, following a giggling servant who always held the tray just out of reach.

The drunken guests of Madame St. Cere adored his travails. Some urged him on like a favored racehorse while others made loud bets on the eventual outcome. He was showered with empty glasses which shattered upon impact with the floor and cut his hands. Women proclaimed him the 'pretty pony" and knelt to pat his head. Men preferred to kick the nag.

At last Sir Anthony reached down for a fistful of Robin's coppery hair and jerked him to his knees.

"Still I have no refreshing drink of champagne," he pointed out to the salon. Madame St. Cere's friends laughed appreciatively. "You see I am most indecently served. Fa! I shall sell the nag!"

Robin wondered if his hearing had been damaged by the repeated blows. Surely not even a rake like Sir Anthony would dare sell a contract of indenture in the presence of humans. Already he could see the vampires he knew in the group begin to recoil at Sir Anthony's announcement. Warily they backed off a pace to watch what would happen next.

"Up on that table, DuPlessis," Fortesque commanded and pointed with his quizzing glass to one of the gold gilt serving tables.

"Sir?" Robin asked in bewilderment.

"Stand on that table."

The room watched with keen interest as Robin reluctantly approached the table and awkwardly climbed onto its surface. As he rose to his feet, the Parisians cheered his effort.

"This is my indentured servant, Mr. DuPlessis." Sir Anthony came forward to tap Robin's hip with his quizzing glass. "Who will buy his contract? He is

English. Thirty-two years of age — give or take. Good looking enough if you fancy tall willowy types."

Robin saw the vampires narrow their eyes. They were beginning to realize how neatly Fortesque had boxed them into outbidding humans for the contract. They were not pleased.

"I will gladly sell Mr. DuPlessis to anyone who wants him."

"Four gold Louis!" sang out a giddy woman from the rear of the ballroom.

The vampires looked at each other in consternation. One of them, a dark Spanish gentleman in a gold and cream frock coat, sighed and bid ten Louis.

"Twenty Louis," shouted a human.

Robin chewed his bottom lip; nursing the cut the lady's ring had dealt him. He clasped his trembling hands behind his back and wondered which one of the vampires would be forced to claim him.

"Twenty-four Louis!"

"Thirty-five Louis!"

"Ladies, gentlemen," Fortesque shook his head disapprovingly, "thirty-five Louis for this pretty Englishman? Imagine what he could do for you."

"Fifty Louis!" The giddy woman bid again. "Oh, do let me have him! My husband is such a bore."

"Fifty-two," the gold and cream vampire grudgingly counter offered.

"Seventy-five Louis," another male vampire spoke up prompting a breath of relief from the gold and cream.

"Seventy-five." Sir Anthony began to nod his head.

"Most generous."

A woman with lovely violet-colored eyes stepped out from the vulgar crowd. Robin had not seen her before. He would have remembered her if he had.

Although she was richly dressed in aubergine velvet, diamonds at her throat and in her unpowdered sable brown hair, there was none of the Parisian excess about her person. What was such an elegant lady doing in one of Madame St. Cere's notorious salons?

"One thousand English guineas," she said in an English accent.

Even Sir Anthony gasped. Applause and catcalls broke out as he nodded his agreement. Robin anxiously scanned the vampires. They seemed both relieved and pleased. The lady in aubergine was a revenant.

"Winnifred, dear girl," Fortesque was saying as Robin climbed down. "I did not know you were in Paris."

"Only business would bring me to this vile city," she replied briskly. "I trust you will accept my note? The Sterling will be sent to you in the morning."

"Of course, dear lady."

"Have the young man collect his things and come to my address immediately." Winnifred flicked her violet eyes over Robin briefly and reached into her reticule. She retrieved a cream-colored card with an address engraved on it and handed to Robin without a second glance.

He accepted it tiredly, wondering if he'd been pushed from the pot into the fire. His new owner didn't seem any warmer a personality than the detestable Sir Anthony. Maybe he ought to let the vampires hunt him down. They'd tear him to shreds—put the pieces and what was left of his consciousness into a little dark box.

"As you wish, Winnifred." Sir Anthony bowed with fey politeness. "If you will heed my advice, dear girl—this creature is both arrogant and stubborn. He needs breaking."

"Thank you, Sir Anthony." She turned to give Robin one last glance. "I am mindful of what you say but I doubt he will prove much of a problem for me."

Fortesque's face flashed with annoyance but he bowed again with a cascade of flawless lace.

"You, sir," his new owner said curtly to Robin as she glided away, "I will expect without delay. Do not fail me."

Robin watched with growing dread as she disappeared into the chattering crowd. A feminine version of Sir Anthony Fortesque. Just his luck.

The original model gave him a push.

"A word with you, DuPlessis, before you leave me," he said ominously.

It was nearly dawn when Robin finally arrived at the doorstep of his new owner. He was a bit surprised by her address. For a lady able to toss around huge sums of English money, she possessed a small townhouse in a not-quite-yet fashionable district of Paris. He was even more surprised when she answered his knock herself, ushering him upstairs to a warm red and bronze sitting room.

"You look cold to the bone. Please go next to the fire."

"Thank you, madam." Robin gratefully crossed to the blazing fireplace and stood with his back to the crackling flames.

How comfortable and reassuring the room was. Unlike the hollow Baroque style so loved by the French court, it was a room one could actually enjoy. Moorish tapestries hung on the walls, thick Persian carpets lay under simple dark furniture and an exquisite clavichord resided in the corner next to a wall of fine leather bound books. He felt a heavy wave of homesickness for his rooms at Hawkesmoor.

He wondered suddenly if all his belongings had been disposed of by his grieving parents or if they kept them just as they were until the current Earl took the castle.

She studied him with her clear violet eyes for a long while without a word.

"What is your name?" she asked finally in a soft voice.

He looked downwards as Sir Anthony always required. "Richard Robin Francis DuPlessis. I was Lord Merritt of Hawkesmoor Castle."

"The Earl of Hawkesmoor," she mused. "A very old and noble keep. No wonder Sir Anthony delighted in tormenting you. What name do you prefer to be called? And do you really find my ancient carpet all that intriguing?"

He looked up to cautiously meet her gaze. "Robin, actually."

"So, Lord Merritt, what can I expect from you?"

"I did many… things… for Sir Anthony," Robin replied simply.

"I fancy you did!" She almost smiled at that.

He glanced around a bit desperately and found the clavichord. "I play music. Tolerably. Would you like me to play for you?"

"Please." She inclined her head with its gleaming sable hair towards the instrument.

Robin went to the smaller version of a harpsichord and sat on its chinoiserie embroidered stool. He laid his long fingers on the keys; beginning to play a melancholy air from the 16th century his mother had loved.

He would have gone on but in reaching for one of the stops to change the action, he felt a jabbing pain in his ribs. He held down the cry that rose to his lips but mashed the chord instead.

"Lord Merritt," she said in dismay. "Come here at once!"

Remembering the abuse meted out by Sir Anthony for such lapses, Robin jumped to his feet despite the pain in his chest. He came out from behind the keyboard a bit more hesitantly. In his present condition, he couldn't take another round. Didn't Sir Anthony tell him that Winnifred was a very old and very powerful vampire? Didn't he say she would use him up like firewood?

"I am sorry, madam."

"Lord Merritt, remove your coat and shirt." She was frowning darkly.

And here it began all over again. She was either going to hurt him or demand he make love to her.

"Lord Merritt?" She raised an eyebrow.

Slowly as to avoid aggravating his injuries, Robin slipped off his coat and unbuttoned his shirt. Reluctantly, he shrugged out of it and stood, awaiting her next command.

His new owner's eyes widened at the sight of him. She stood up with a quiet rustle of velvet and moved towards him.

Robin gasped slightly as she touched a gentle hand to one of the more serious of darkening bruises. So — she would have him in her bed.

"Do not fear me, Robin," Winnifred said as she examined his battered rib cage, running her cool steady hands over his skin. "I neither wish to harm you or use you. You have been badly done, sir."

She stood back with a displeased expression on her handsome face. "Go lie by the fire. I will clean your wounds."

"But," Robin frowned in puzzlement, "I am your servant, madam."

She crossed her arms. "Nonetheless, I will tend your injuries. Please call me Winnifred."

Winnifred proved to be a skillful nurse as she applied warm compresses to his cuts and bruises. It had been so long since he had any peace even the treatment of his wounds seemed like a rare pleasure.

"Sir Anthony did this?" Her voice hardened a little. Not so much a question as a statement of fact.

Robin almost smiled in the glow of the fireplace. "A fond farewell to a much loved member of his household."

"You had one dear to your heart in your human form?"

He closed his eyes as she probed a particularly nasty area, in more ways than just the physical injury.

"I knew," Robin breathed, "what it was to love."

"Ah," Winnifred returned the cloth to the hot water to soak, "I as well — a husband I miss greatly."

"Thank you, Winnifred." Robin reached up a hand and laid it on her alabaster forearm. "I had given up hope."

"One must never do that." Winnifred smiled down at him. She was so youthful with her clear white skin and glowing sable hair that it was hard to conceive she had been born in 900 AD. "When I saw what they did to you in that horrible house, I knew you were the one to help me."

"I'm bound to help you. I belong to you," he pointed out without bitterness.

"We have frightful work ahead of us here in France." She ignored his comment. "Terrible times are coming for the many."

"Vampires?"

"Humans." Winnifred retrieved the cloth from the bowl and returned to her work. "When it is all over, I will tear up your contract and set you free. I swear it."

"Oh," Robin paused as his voice grew thin, "I am bound…" He paused again. "Forgive me. I find I am not quite myself."

Winnifred placed the warm compress against his ribcage. "I have seen your courage, Lord Merritt."

Robin tried again to find his voice. "I am bound to help you with your cause," he propped himself up on an elbow a little awkwardly, "with or without my contract of indenture."

"And why is that, Robin?" She gazed at him in interest.

Robin met her violet eyes with a searching look. "It has been long since anyone touched me in kindness."

She gracefully rose to her feet and picked up the bowl of water. Without another word, Winnifred left the room.

Robin rubbed his bruised jaw. Would Elizabeth expect him to swear eternal loyalty to her memory? Would she turn from him in disgust if she knew all the things Sir Anthony had forced upon him? Perhaps he should be locked away in a little dark box. He was not very good at being a vampire.

When Winnifred returned, Robin was watching the fire. He heard the silken rustle of her gown as she knelt behind him but he did not turn away from the flames. Another laceration to tend, no doubt.

A chill ran down his spine when Winnifred brushed his copper hair away from his neck and bent to kiss his throat.

Robin didn't dare move. He felt disappointment like a dull ache. Nothing was going to change.

"You wish me to be your lover?" He failed to keep a hollow sound from entering his voice.

"We are both lonely." She dropped her arms down over his chest. "Like you, Lord Merritt, I only wish to be touched in kindness," she said. "Let loneliness be barred from this place if only for a few hours."

He turned to look at her: a flawless Saxon queen of milky skin and sable hair who was offering to throw friendship and comfort at his feet.

Robin raised a hand and ran the back of his long fingers down her exquisite cheekbone.

"And if Sir Anthony has made it impossible for me to oblige your request for such kindness?"

"You should have no fear of me, Lord Merritt. I place great value on freedom."

He slid his fingers into the heavy hair at the nape of her neck and pulled her into a gentle kiss. He liked the soft taste of her perfect mouth and the smell of orange blossoms on her skin. For the first time since his change into revenant form, he felt genuine desire catch at his heart. It was a giddy sensation. He had learned stomach-turning revulsion and pain as the way of the vampire. Wasn't it why revenants like Sir Anthony became such experts in delivering anguish?

Robin released Winnifred just long enough to draw her down onto the floor beside him. Then he kissed her again, more passionately this time. She ran her cool gentle hands down his battered back. It was like a salve.

"Give me your horrors, Robin DuPlessis," Winnifred said in his ear. "Let me take them for you."

Robin couldn't force words from his lips. He felt as if his blood had turned to champagne. He could only respond with greater sexual intensity as the discovery that he still possessed sensations of pleasure overwhelmed his ability to think.

Winnifred wrapped her arms about him, meeting his desire with equal force. She cried out softly as he moved his body weight urgently over hers.

"Vampires don't love, Robin. We only hunger."

"You're wrong!" Robin cried hoarsely into blackness, pulling against the chains. "I do love! I love Caroline DeBarry!"

The silence was deafening. He fell against the damp wall, doubling over as a racking pain tore at his stomach lining. The hunger was beginning to eat him alive.

"Caroline," Robin managed to force out in a dry whisper before another wave of pain crushed his ability to speak. "I do love you, Caroline. Real love. I promise, I promise, I promise."

8

Caroline stood at a rain-splattered window at JFK airport. She watched dully as a British Airways jet taxied away from its gate. She felt numb, anesthetized and unable to perform any task beyond carefully scheduled plans.

Robin Dashwood was dead. When he failed to appear as promised, she had called the university and a weeping secretary informed her that Professor Dashwood had been murdered. Stabbed in an attempted robbery and left to die in an alley.

Suddenly she understood what had happened to her over the past twenty-four hours. She loved him, and with that love and passion came grief, too. A terrible icy grief she'd not experienced since her mother died in a fox hunting accident. She'd only been fourteen then. Now the world seemed smaller. Her options fewer and her expectations hemmed in from all sides by duty. Magnetic Robin Dashwood with his long coppery hair and graceful ways had seemed like a bright streamer of rescue in a heavy sea of worries.

How exactly was she going to forget him and go on to a life in Hawkesmoor's servant quarters?

Caroline winced and crossed her arms to ward off some of the terminal's chill. How frightfully self-absorbed she sounded. It was Robin who was lying dead in the city morgue. She thought, as she had about a million times, how frightened he must have been in that alleyway as he slowly bled to death. A stab of sorrow caught her and she forced back tears. She was not going to weep in front of strangers at JFK International.

"Got you a cup of tea," said Beryl as she hurried up. "You really ought to sit down. You've had quite a shock."

Caroline accepted the paper cup gratefully. "I don't know, Beryl. Perhaps I should stay. I mean, somebody's got to see to it that Robin is looked after properly."

"Somebody will see to it," Beryl replied briskly. "I told you, I called the University this morning—this NYPD detective, Lieutenant Watkins, is handling the whole situation."

"A policeman, Beryl?"

"Believe me, this one can manage." Caroline's assistant reached out to pat her shoulder in the awkward way the British sometimes had when they tried to comfort each other.

"British Airways Flight 798 to London Heathrow is now available for boarding of First and Business Class passengers only," interrupted a clipped English accent over the loudspeakers.

Robin woke again with a start.

"Not the whole family!" he cried before realizing he was light years away from revolutionary France.

The darkness reminded him that he was still somebody's prisoner. He wished he could see in the dark. Some vampires could. Winnifred could. Of course, she had a truly formidable array of vampire traits that included telepathy and materializations.

Some vampires could just glance at the metal cuffs at his wrists and they would melt away or fly off. Sure, he could become a shade. He could even levitate as a shade and take to the air currents like an ice crystal. In theory, he should be able to dissolve and zoom off to a meal and bed without a backward sneer. In theory.

In reality he had never really learned to control his vampire traits and could not summon major matter transformations just any old moment. If he had just fed and fed well, he could manage it. He was not a powerful vampire like Winnifred, Max Aosta, or the creature that had made him. He had never possessed the desire to develop his few talents any further. He wasn't interested in the shadowy lives of vampires. Most revenants thrilled to the idea of virtual immortality, believing it evidence of their innate superiority. Robin saw vampires as no more permanent than acrid smoke drifting about the human battlefield. Everything that was vibrant, real and meaningful existed within the short human lifespan. They had an instinctual drive to leave a mark — something that proved that they lived and mattered. Vampires left no mark — save fleeting terror and pain.

"Still," Robin murmured weakly, "it couldn't have hurt to practice a little more often."

It did mean, however, whoever had commanded Nate Watkins — New York's most unusual cop — to lock him up was fully apprised of what he could and could not accomplish as a vampire. It meant he and his life in the Village had been carefully studied. But why? He wasn't out to claim anyone's turf and he hadn't stolen away anyone's immortal beloved.

He thought again of Winnifred and all her abilities. She would have been out of the black hole he was in faster than quicksilver. As his mind drifted with the pain of the hunger, he remembered the last time he saw her. 1794, outside of Paris, in the pouring rain.

Paris, 1794

Just as Winnifred had predicted, social inequity unleashed a terrible bloodletting in France. Not long after he'd been bought by the English Countess in what was to become Madame St Cere's final salon, Louis the XVI and his family were caught attempting to flee France at Varennes. The beautiful Princess Lamballe — a German friend of Marie Antoinette — was arrested with them. She was viciously raped and murdered by the mob upon the royal family's return to Paris. Her head and body parts paraded on pikes under the queen's prison window.

The carefree days of the highly raised and the highly born were over in France. Even Sir Anthony Fortesque found reason to amble to Italy for a course of study in sculpture.

Within months the Legislative Assembly was suspended and France declared a Republic. The dreaded Committee of Public Safety came into being, allowing the Reign of Terror to devour men, women and children.

Victims of the Committee's justice went to meet 'Madame La Guillotine' as the monstrous creation was called by the mob. After trial, they were taken by tumbrel cart through jeering crowds to the Place de la Guillotine where they watched each other die.

Except for the ones Winnifred and he managed to snag from the prisons and send off to new lives in England. If the stakes weren't so heartbreakingly high for the humans, it was quite an amusing game outfoxing the Committee for Public Safety. With their vampire strengths, it wasn't completely a fair match but the Committee had condemned far more aristocrats and their unlucky associates than they could ever rescue. Of course, the feeding was excellent. Who would miss a few ardent revolutionaries in all those ugly mob scenes?

Out of Winnifred's estimate of forty thousand who would go to the guillotine, they liberated less than two hundred. No more than a ripple in the blood bath.

He was surprised when he saw her arrive alone like a phantom in the cold rain.

Winnifred galloped towards him on her favorite gray gelding and drew up, mud sloshing about the horse's hooves.

"Where are the Corneilles?" Robin asked stepping out from the tree he'd been waiting under.

"The Marquis Corneille and his family went to the guillotine this morning," Winnifred said grimly. "Hours before the information we had. The Committee had other pressing concerns and wanted to clean house so to speak."

Robin's eyes widened in sorrow. "The girl was only nine years old."

"Yes. I am sorry." She swung off the horse — a beautiful Republican soldier in her red and blue uniform.

"And they would call us monsters," he said bitterly, turning to indicate his modest shelter under the trees. "I've a bit of a fire and some food for the horses."

"Sadly, we haven't the time for it," came Winnifred's odd reply.

"Where to next, then?"

"Wherever you would like to go, Lord Merritt," she said. His owner reached into one of the saddlebags and retrieved a roll of waxed parchment. "I'm setting you free."

Robin cocked his head to the side. "Set me free?"

"It's over, Robin." Winnifred held out the indenture contract she had bought from Sir Anthony. "Robespierre and his Jacobins have been arrested by their Committee for Public Safety. Madame La Guillotine is now eating her own."

He reached out for the contract, feeling elated and hollow all at the same time. For several years he had had a purpose, a part to play in the human world. Now what would he become? Another Sir Anthony?

"I will miss you," Winnifred said with regret. "But where I am going, you cannot follow."

"Where would that be, Winnifred?" His voice was strained. He walked the few steps to his fire and tossed the heavy parchment into the flames, watching as his years of servitude turned to ashes.

"I am entering the cloister in England. It is what a lady of my time would do when she wished to retire from the world and that is what I am going to do." Winnifred joined him by the fire, slipping an arm about his waist. "St. Sophia in the North country. Not so very far from your Hawkesmoor Castle."

"How the hell are you going to exist in a convent?" Robin asked sharply. "Why would they let you in?"

Winnifred shrugged. "I can only hope they will allow me to serve God as I am — 'I have come into the world as a light so that no one who believes in me should stay in darkness.'"

"Don't quote John at me." Robin shook off her touch. "It's a ridiculous idea. God isn't interested in vampires."

"You say that with such certainty, Lord Merritt," Winnifred replied. "Still you will pay my dower to the convent every fifty years and be careful you don't forget."

Robin bowed graciously. "Madam, you say that with such certainty."

"I am leaving you all my worldly goods, Robin DuPlessis." She returned the bow with a regal curtsy. "After nine hundred years I am a vastly wealthy vampire. It will hold you in fine style for as long as you care to roam the world."

"I'd rather roam the world with you." He held out his hands to her. "Please, do not leave me yet."

"We should be off." Winnifred spun on her boot heel. "You must escort me to London like a proper gentleman. There I will introduce you to my bankers and sign the papers."

"I will worry for you," Robin said bleakly in the fading light of a late afternoon.

Winnifred laughed as she remounted her gray. "You will be the one who needs the concern."

You will be the one who needs the concern. Winnifred's words echoed in his head like a mean-spirited joke.

9

"You know, Lord Merritt, sir," said Nate's Whitechapel dialect in the darkness, "the main reason I works in homicide is to help explain away some of Max's better known bodies."

"Nate!" Robin's voice was hoarse. "What is this about?"

"Now Max doesn't drink his targets dry," Nate switched on an electric light, "like you. He only destroys those who displease him."

Robin let out a sharp cry as the light seared his sensitive eyes. He covered his face with his hands, cowering against the brick wall.

"I've given Max no cause to be displeased."

"Lord Merritt, sir, you are a sad excuse for a vampire," Nate ignored his comment, "and that's a fact. Teaching school. Singing in Anglican choirs. A bleedin' choir!"

Robin slowly pulled his fingers from his eyes. They had studied him. He did belong to the St. Mark's choir. It was a blissful way to spend Thursday evenings, rehearsing the gorgeous musical phrases of Handel, Purcell, and Bach. He liked being included in choir Christmas parties and potlucks. He was the perfect guest: decorative and he didn't eat anything.

"I like Church music," he whispered. He was in some sort of basement, an older building by the brick walls and wood beams. He scanned the brick surfaces for any sign of a blocked out window.

"Feeding off the dregs of the street — and the occasional corporate shill." Nate looked disgusted. "You're not much stronger than a human."

"Is this what all of this is about?" Robin asked wearily. "Max is irritated about my choice of food supply?"

"It's dead grot, mate. All that heroin, crack and meth."

"Don't forget bath salts, Nate." Robin sighed knowing he was about to make a foolish move. But if Max wanted to scare him into better vampire habits, he'd give Nate a reason to get on with it. He cocked his head to the side quizzically. "Or maybe you don't know about that one yet. Been in the newspapers a lot lately. Did you ever learn to read?"

Nate's scarred face recoiled in anger. He came across the dirty cement floor and aimed a kick at Robin's hip. It connected with a sickening crack as the joint collapsed under Nate's steel-toed boot.

Robin cried out in anguish, crumpling to the damp surface of the cement. He vomited up stomach acids and mucus, unable to lift his head from the cold floor. The pain from his hip rolled over him like a relentless tide.

"You toff types are all alike!" Nate spat at him. "So bleedin' clever. Listen, you long-haired freak, I've told them all you're dead."

"Dead?" Robin wheezed. This sounded like more than a warning to take better care of his nutritional health.

"Dead as in Professor Dashwood was murdered. He's dead and gone. He don't exist anymore." Watkins sat on his heels to peer down at Robin. "They told your new girlfriend — the posh one. I bet she took it real hard, mate."

"You're still just a Whitechapel pimp, Nate," Robin said with a cough.

"And you still believe in a benevolent squirearchy, don't you, Milord?" Nate actually grinned and stretched out one of his powerful paws to pat Robin's head.

"Why, Nate — those are awfully big words." He retched again, bringing up more stomach acids. Just as vampire lore predicted, he felt as if his body was beginning to turn in on itself, atom by atom, like a collapsing star.

"I've been learning myself up proper these days," Nate replied in an exaggerated accent. He pulled at his forelock. "Milord Merritt, Sir."

"Not," Robin half smiled despite the hunger, "just a Whitechapel pimp after all."

"Ah, them were the days, mate. Real freedom. None of this smart phone, electronic tablet, computer rubbish."

"So where do we go from here?" Robin asked simply.

Nate reached out again to ruffle Robin's hair. "Mate, you got bleedin' bad luck and that's a fact. I'll be back in a couple years to collect what's left of you and stick it in a plastic bag."

"You tell Max I'm the one who'll do the collecting."

"Yeah, right." Nate stood up with a short harsh laugh. "I am going to offer you a choice, your lordship."

He strode back across the cement to the industrial strength metal door and flung it open. The policeman disappeared into whatever lay beyond the basement for a few moments. He was back promptly and leaned against the door jamb with a vicious grin.

"This is my particular twist," Nate pointed out proudly. "If you're not too noble and virtuous, Lord Merritt, you could feed on this!"

He pulled at something in the hallway beyond the door. Kate Ashby, disheveled and frightened, stumbled into the room. Nate ripped the gaffer's tape roughly from across her mouth and shoved her towards Robin.

"R-Robin!" Her face, a blur of tears and mascara, betrayed her horror at the sight of him, "Who a-are these people? What do they want?"

"Nate!" Robin found the strength to raise his voice to a ragged cry. "For god's sake!"

"God is for choirboys, Lord Merritt." Nate threw him a glare of disgust. "You're a friggin' vampire."

He disappeared again and slammed the metal door closed behind him. Robin could hear him locking it from the other side.

"Nate!" he cried, knowing it was useless all the same.

Kate was sobbing and struggling to help him sit up from the awkward position Nate's attack had left him in. He could hear the blood pounding in her veins — singing a siren's song — demanding his attention. It would take so little to pin her down and rip into her throat even as weak as he was now.

"Why are you chained up?" She squeaked in her frightened child tones. "What have they done to you? Robin!"

"Kate, love," he said as she wrapped her shivering arms around his waist and clung to him. The desire to drain her dry was nearly crucifying. "Please — get out of my reach. Do it now."

"I don't understand."

"*Do it now!*" Robin demanded with such savagery Kate flung herself backwards in fear. She flailed on all fours, stopping finally to stare at him with huge wounded eyes.

"Robin," she said timidly, "you have to tell me what's happening."

"Love, I don't know how."

"What is wrong with you?" Her eyes widened as she really looked at him under the brutal light of the naked bulb overhead. "Your hair — it's got lots of gray in it now. You're old! But you're only thirty-two."

"I'm over three hundred years old," Robin relented. What difference did it make? She was going to die and he was going to live out his eternity as an amusing little paperweight on Max Aosta's desk. "So I expect a few gray streaks are in order."

"We're not going to get out of this if you lose it," Kate said sternly. She was an optimistic American girl brought up on a steady diet of plucky heroines from animated Disney films.

"What makes you think we're going to get out of this?" He collapsed in his chains again.

"Let me help you."

"Stay the hell away from me! I mean it, Kate. I'm dangerous."

"Robin Dashwood, you're about as dangerous as my old Aunt Irene." She made a face and came closer.

"I'm a three-hundred-year-old vampire. I'm on the point of starvation and if you get near me, I'm going to tear out your throat." He pushed back against the wall to create a little more distance between them. It cost him something. The hip was not repairing itself the way it would if he were square with his feeding.

"Robin, try and stay with me on this." Kate's tone was less frightened—more and more her usual bossy style. "Vampires do not exist. You are a professor at NYU."

"Vampires have existed since the Fall."

Soap opera star Kate blinked. "What?"

"Since time began," he amended tiredly. "Now go away to the farthest corner and don't come near me despite anything I may say later."

10

Caroline glanced at her watch and returned her gaze to the window. The endless gunmetal gray of the Atlantic was far below. Only a few hours and she was closer to England than to him. What was left of him anyway.

"Robin?" came Kate's American whine. "How are we going to get out of here? I'm really hungry. I'm cold."

"My dear, we aren't going to get out," he replied in the kindest tones he could manage despite the almost overwhelming yearning he had to kill her.

"Why won't you even try?" She broke into a high-pitched sob. "Why are you being such a stupid coward?"

"Cowardice suits me." He smiled wanly at her through the fog of pain and desire.

"I hate you!" Kate hissed and scrambled to her feet. She went to the door, checking the doorknob for the fortieth time.

"Still locked?" he asked.

"Oh, shut up. You're such a jerk." She turned around to glare at him and then her livid face mutated into a stare of disbelief. "You're all gray now! You look awful."

Robin turned his head to look at his left hand cuffed and chained to the brick wall. It was the skeletal alabaster hand of an ancient creature — fingernails like glass. The motion of moving his head caused a heavy lock of his hair to fall across his face. It was bone white. So this is what happened to starving vampires. Either he was especially frail as revenants went or the aging process occurred much faster than he always imagined it would. Rather fascinating in its way.

"What is happening to you?" Kate wailed. "It's not possible. Not even human!"

"Stay away from me!" He warned her again as she appeared close to advancing. "I'm enough of a coward that if you get near me, I'll kill you to save myself."

"You mean," her eyes grew very wide, "you really mean there are such things as vampires? That dude who kidnapped me is a vampire too?"

"Yes, Kate. Why do you suppose so many people disappear every year and end up on Facebook alerts?"

"Alien abduction?" she asked hopefully.

Robin lifted his chin and faced her squarely. "I kill humans for blood."

The stomach twisting revulsion that swept over her pretty features was like another one of Nate's blows. Robin glanced away from her and swallowed roughly. Perhaps this was all for the best. He never wanted to see that expression of disgust slip across Caroline's face. He couldn't bear that. She really was best off with a dull riding instructor.

"I'm going to sit way over here," Kate muttered, dazedly gesturing towards an old wooden crate in the opposite corner.

"It's all right, love." Robin said quietly. "I'm not going to last much longer. You won't have to worry."

She gave him another hard stare and retreated, without a word, to sit on the wooden crate.

Caroline emerged from the black hole of customs to find her brother Peter waiting for her with all the other expectant persons in Heathrow's international terminal.

None of them would have been able to guess he was heir to the Earldom of Hawkesmoor. Peter looked exactly like the Oxford University student he was: black leather motorcycle jacket over a ragged sweater and jeans, a silver thumb ring and artfully tousled blond hair. He grinned upon seeing her and waved.

"Peter!" Caroline was never so glad to see him. She almost ran the last few steps. "You're supposed to be at Christ Church!"

"Ah, yes. Well," he gave her a quick kiss on the cheek, "Dad asked me to come home. Big family meeting. The Americans and all that. Thought I might as well fly up with you."

"What a lovely idea." She glanced at her wristwatch. "We haven't much time to catch our plane to Middleborough."

Peter looked down at his own watch. "Crikey, you're right! We'll have to make a dash for it."

As they set out for the run to the domestic terminal, Caroline reached out and tugged at his long hair. "Dad's going to love this."

"When I'm Earl of Hawkesmoor, I'll go in for your basic Tory cut," Peter said over his leather shoulder. "I keep promising Dad but then he always grumbles about not being around to see it."

"Robin?"

He heard Kate's voice like the thin whine of an insect over the pounding in his head.

"Robin, are you really a vampire?"

Kate was closer now. Almost within reach.

"Get… get away," Robin whispered hoarsely.

"I have an idea," Kate said. "If you're really a vampire, it might work."

He didn't answer. Talking was too hard. Soon he wouldn't exist anymore. He'd decay into dust and his disembodied consciousness would haunt the room forever or alternatively, one of the jeweled snuff boxes on Max Aosta's desk.

"Listen to me!" She stamped her foot in annoyance. "I'll give you some of my blood if it'll help you get us out of here. You don't have to kill me, do you? In the movies the girls don't always die."

Robin forced his head to move. Slowly he lifted his face so he could see Kate. She was staring at him rather wildly: her breathing was rapid and frightened. He could hear her heart pounding. The valves opening and closing with a soft chime like a child's toy. How cruel that some of his senses actually were improving with his body's destruction. Was that how eternity would be? Ultra-fine hunting senses that could find a victim a mile — maybe a hundred miles — away but no tools for the actual job? Never a drop to quench the enduring hunger?

"I said I'll give you some of my blood if you promise not to kill me."

Kate's voice of command. How had he lived with it? It had been different when she'd been a student at the university. Maybe he could kill her and then emerge to kill all neophyte actresses. There were so many and surely the world would thank him.

He could just imagine the pools of blood fanning out from behind their carefully coiffed heads. An ocean of blood on the white tiled floor of a dressing room. A wave of thick sticky blood crashing into the door jamb and then seeping out to run down the hallway.

"Robin!" Kate was shouting now. "Neither of us is going to get out of here unless you listen to me!"

He tried to hang on to what was left of his reason.

"Can't." Robin croaked. "Can't do small. Drinks. Always kill."

"Then," she replied, "you'll have to make me a vampire too, won't you?"

Robin made a monumental effort to concentrate on what she was saying rather than the alluring sound of her beating heart.

Make Kate Ashby a vampire? Give this life to another? But he had sworn an oath. Robin tried to remember. After Winnifred had galloped off to serve God. The rain was cold, relentless and barren, like him — he was a killer. A private resolution — never blood from the worthy. It was a way to exist. A way to survive in the human world.

"I have never made another," he said, barely to whisper. "I am not even sure I remember how it is done."

"Try to remember." Kate softened the strident tones in her voice. "I know it's all a bad choice but I'd rather leave here a vampire than in a box. We can get out if you'll just try."

Not be in a box. Not be in a box.

Robin nodded weakly.

"Promise not to kill me instead?"

"I can't promise that." His voice was as frail and thin as gossamer.

"Okay." Kate shrugged miserably. "What do we do now?"

Make Kate Ashby a vampire. Give her this life.

Peter snapped off the cap of a little airline bottle. He poured out a generous glass.

"What would our illustrious ancestors think of wine in plastic cups?"

Caroline looked away from the window.

"I'm sorry, Peter. Did you say something?"

"Nothing very interesting." Peter poured her a glass as well. "Missing New York already? It'll all will seem very dull now after America."

"Don't be stupid." Caroline frowned at him. "I can't wait to get back to Hawkesmoor."

Peter raised both eyebrows at the sharpness of her tone. "Well, America is coming to Hawkesmoor after all. I understand from Dad that they've already been out to measure up."

"What in heaven's name for?"

He shrugged eloquently and had another sip of wine. "Oh, lots of big plans. Apparently American corporate retreats require media centers, pools, cabanas — why the bloody hell they'd need those in England eludes me — steam rooms, car parks and," Peter switched into a broad American accent, "car maintenance facilities."

"But we haven't even agreed to let them have Hawkesmoor yet!" Caroline cried indignantly. "The bloody nerve of those people."

"They know we're stuck, Caro," Lord Merritt said. "We've got no real options. If those roof repairs don't start this year, we might as well write off the state rooms."

"I am out of ideas, Peter."

"We could always go in search of Lord Merritt's treasure." Peter laughed, referring to their old childhood game.

"A chest full of jewels and heavy with gold coin hidden in the mysterious walled-up room." Caroline joined in with a laugh.

Peter lowered his voice dramatically. "And Lord Merritt's skeleton — still poignantly clothed in his elegant velvet coat — draped over it!"

"How we need that treasure!" Caroline sighed. "Lord Merritt, *where are you?*"

Robin felt as if a billion atoms were going off in his body. Kate's blood was like a rare champagne. Rich but delicate — full of vibrant life. It vanquished all his suffering. Pain was fleeing his damaged frame like a bat from sunlight. He was better than his best. Newer than new.

It was all he could do to keep from stealing every drop. He had to stop. He didn't always have to kill when he fed. Other revenants could manage the small drinks.

Then it occurred to him that Kate might already be dead. He had taken so much blood. Her small cries of pain and pleasure had long since dropped away.

Startled, he pulled his mouth from her wrist. A scarlet flume of blood coursed down her limp arm. Kate was barely conscious. She stared at him dazedly with frighteningly large black circles under her eyes. She would die soon if he didn't act.

He willed himself to evaporate — to mix with the cool damp air of the basement. For one thrilling moment he floated with the dust motes, his survival instincts telling him to continue soaring until he was far from this place and safe.

The next moment he forced himself back. Free at least from the chains, he knelt by Kate.

"You," Robin said as he rapidly unbuttoned his shirt and pulled it open, "have to drink."

He glanced about for a moment and seized a spent rusty nail from an old packing crate. He plunged the sharp edge into his chest and made a crude incision over his heart. A crimson stream welled up in the jagged groove, spilling over his skin.

Robin slid his fingers into Kate's hair and pulled her face against his bleeding chest.

"Drink," he said roughly, "and be one of us."

11

Kate was still dazed as Robin helped her outside. After his wound had healed, it had only taken him a few moments to vanish to the hallway beyond and open the door.

They had been locked up, he noted grimly, in one of Max Aosta's many warehouses somewhere on the New Jersey waterfront. Probably one he reserved for the settlements of old scores. So few modern storage facilities came equipped with iron restraints worthy of a medieval dungeon.

It would be dangerous to attempt to go home to the Bailey. Max's spies would report his reappearance and he wasn't ready to see the former prince — yet.

Fortunately, he kept all his real financial affairs under the name Francis DuPlessis and not his mother's maiden name of Dashwood. Even if Nate had proclaimed him dead, only Professor Dashwood's relatively meager university earnings would be affected. Even a vampire could be thankful that all his credit cards would still work.

Robin picked up Kate and carried her towards city lights that glimmered like sanctuary candles through the marine mist. She was weak and feverish. He had to get her someplace safe and tend to her properly. An incomparably lonely sound of a fog horn came across the filthy dockside water, reminding him of earlier eras when it was easier to keep a secret. He decided that modern Manhattan was not the place for a neoteric vampire.

Nearly two weeks in the Hudson River Valley did them both good. He took Kate to a Colonial era inn he recalled from a trip he'd made in 1928. It was isolated from Max's New York vampire court and yet close enough to the center of a bustling little town called Windham so he could hunt effectively.

He quietly rid Windham of its annoying town drunk, a fundamentalist Christian who regularly beat up his stepchildren and an unprincipled land developer who preyed on farmland. Never had he been so hedonistic about feeding. But then he needed the strengthening effects of a good blood supply. There was much that needed to be done once Kate was ready to be on her own.

"How are you, love?" Robin asked as he let himself into the handsome set of rooms the inn had given them.

Kate looked up from the fashion magazine she was reading. She was resting by the cheerfully burning fireplace — pale and beautiful in a thick flannel robe purchased from the inn's tiny gift shop.

"Finally starting to feel okay. Thanks to you." She looked at him with genuine gratitude.

"Ah, nothing to it." Robin crossed the space between them and dropped down next to her on the rug. "This artificial gas fire is brilliant. So real."

"Really cold all of a sudden," Kate said with a shiver. "More like winter."

"Weather report says a big electrical storm is on the way." Robin held his long hands up to the warmth of the gas flames, watching as they pretended to devour the artificial aspen logs. Rather like when he pretended to eat human food in public.

"Next time," she moved closer, slipping an arm under his and resting her glossy blond head on his shoulder, "I have to do it on my own, don't I?"

He nodded. His eyes never leaving their study of the flames. "You have to be able to feed quickly and secretly. We depend on each other's skill to survive in this human world. Don't imagine for an instant just because we steal their blood we're safe from humans."

"What if I can't do it?" Kate asked dryly.

"Then other vampires will be forced to step in and remove your threat to our existence." Robin forced himself to shrug nonchalantly. "Rarely it happens. As I've told you, we are faster, stronger and endowed with various powerful traits. If you have a shred of common sense and you do," he turned to give her a reassuring smile, "you'll be just fine."

Kate pushed a lock of blond hair behind her ear and wet her full lips nervously with the tip of her tongue.

"But we can't stay in Windham forever," she said regretfully.

"It ought, probably, to be our last night here."

Kate drew back a fraction and kissed him briefly but sweetly.

"All this time together," she brushed her hands across his face and into his copper-colored hair, "and you haven't come into my bed. You haven't touched me. You always wanted to, before."

"Kate," he reached up to pull her hands away, "that part of our relationship is over."

"You could come with me to California. We could start fresh."

"You bored of me long ago, love." He released her wrists. "I may be a vampire but I'm still the Robin Dashwood you lived with in New York. I write history books and sing in a church choir."

"I loved that about you!" Kate insisted. "You were always different from all the other guys — old-fashioned and sweet."

"You liked it at first." Robin got to his feet as heavy rain began to pelt the window glass. A deep roll of thunder announced arrival of the promised storm.

He wandered to the restored window frame and gazed out at the curtain of silver rain falling over the village. A jagged fork of lightning cut across the storm clouds with sharp authority.

"You've never gone celibate before," she said behind him. "You always liked it."

Robin traced a raindrop down the glass with a fingertip. "Oh, Kate. Don't."

A lamp crashed into the wall. He turned to see Kate glaring triumphantly at him — an invitation to a real fight. Instead he stepped over the lamp shards and settled on a window seat without comment. She swept off into the bedroom, slamming the door behind her.

Volatile, ambitious, self-absorbed Kate supercharged with vampire magnetism. There were wolverines roaming out in the wild, pleased to be able to rip the throats out of other animals, without Kate's level of tenacity. She would gut Hollywood and watch it fall at her feet. Vampires had always thrived in Southern California.

Robin settled against the seat cushions, content to watch flickering shadows stipple the wet window glass.

Kate was right about his tastes. He enjoyed sex. Many vampires did not. They found complete erotic fulfillment in the act of feeding. But he had discovered sharing someone's bed could occasionally yield those precious moments when he almost forgot what he was.

His night with Caroline had been extraordinary. Different from any other. He had felt like a man in her arms — not just some shrewd revenant copying the form for its own advantage. He had felt his cool skin warm to her body's temperature. His heart rate sped up to match hers. Her blood did not sing. Only her desire excited him. The atomic structure of his alien being had tried to shatter and merge with hers. Caroline had the power to transform him.

He had to be with her. He would love and care for Caroline all the days of her life. *Surely that was worth something.*

Caroline shivered despite her flannel-lined anorak. The stable aisle was cold even for a spring night in Northern Yorkshire.

She watched intently as Evan, Hawkesmoor's head stableman, expertly slipped the soft rope about the distressed mare.

"All right, young lady," Evan said quietly. "I'm ready. In three, shall we?"

Caroline nodded. Firefly, her sister's new Irish thoroughbred had cast herself against the wall again. It was almost impossible for a horse to trap itself in any of the ten remaining loose boxes in Hawkesmoor's massive stone stables. They were big, airy loose boxes with magnificent wooden aisle doors carefully maintained since the 18th century. With the modern additions of automatic watering cups and overhead heat lamps to ward off the worst of the Yorkshire weather, horses seemed to approve of the Hawkesmoor equine accommodations.

All except for the green four-year-old from Ireland. It was the third time she had cast herself since her arrival a month earlier.

"One. Two. Three!"

Caroline and Evan firmly guided the mare off her back and over onto her side. With a startled grunt, the exquisite red bay scrambled to her feet and snorted nervously.

"Silly girl!" Evan chided as he watched the mare wander over to her feed bin to check for any bonuses. "She grew up rough in an Irish field and nary a problem. Poor sow doesn't know what to do with a fancy stall."

The stableman looked pleased as he pushed open the stall door and waited for Caroline to slip out before he followed.

"Good to have you home, Lady Caroline."

"Home," Caroline said, sticking her hands deep into the pockets of her jacket. "It's good to be back. Thank you, Evan."

But even home seemed different now, she thought, glancing about the tidy stable aisle she'd worked in since early childhood. Strange — Robin Dashwood had never been to Hawkesmoor Castle but it still seemed to miss his presence. He felt present like some well-reported phantom one always half-expected to come upon. She could almost imagine him standing at Dragon's big gray head, stroking the horse's neck and talking to him in that soft reedy voice.

Caroline wondered if it were possible for a ghost to haunt a spot it had never known in real life. It was just the damnedest feeling.

Robin sat up on the window seat with his arms wrapped around his knees and watched as lightning snaked down from a black sky.

Despite his lengthy sentence on Earth, he rarely felt so completely alone. All that he'd seen, done and been — he was alone in a rented room. Lost somewhere in America.

12

The Hawkesmoor stable was a short distance from the castle itself. Once, the stables along with other fixtures of a permanent garrison, had been in timber and brick buildings abutted to the interior of the castle's gray stone walls. They had long since disappeared. Relocated in the late 17th century to the end of a straight walk from Merlin's Tower.

Caroline wandered up the path towards the 14th century circular tower with its ancient square-cut merlons and embrasures. It was called Merlin's Tower because the legendary magician was said to have chained the white dragon, Saxon, to that very spot before its final confrontation with Cymru, the red dragon of Wales.

As she had a thousand times before, she paused to drink in the castle's stately beauty. The gray stone gleamed like pewter in the starlight. Its design too formal for the wildness of the land like a silver ring found among thistles and grass. A wraith in the moor country. No wonder Queen Victoria had reportedly called Hawkesmoor the fairy castle when she consented to pass the night in it on her way to official duties in Newcastle-upon-Tyne.

Hawkesmoor was not a massive border castle built to secure a mark in major historical events of the time. Instead Hawkesmoor was quite a small keep, created to defend the area from Viking intrusions.

Its elegant curvilinear symmetry seemed really too lovely to strike dread into any bloodthirsty Danes. Hawkesmoor might well have been built by Merlin — cast down into the wild Yorkshire moor for purely ornamental reasons.

Thank god it was a small castle, Caroline thought as she continued on her way. Off the radar of many tourists, Hawkesmoor and what remained of its once vast acreage lay along the border of the rugged North York Moors National Park. Its size and relatively remote location were the only reasons Hawkesmoor had been able to remain in private hands. All the big convenient ones belonged to the National Trust or theme parks.

"Evening, Lady Caroline," called a cheerful voice from Merlin's Tower's wide walk above her.

"All quiet, Tim?" Caroline waved up at one of the two security guards the insurance company insisted they have at night and on tourist visitation days.

"Right you are. Another slow night." He leaned over the stone to salute her with his coffee cup. "No Vikings, no Willie Wallace and no ordinary thieves."

"No corporate Americans in sight?"

He grinned. "Not yet, Lady Caroline."

Caroline waved again and pushed off. Actually, it did seem fitting to have the guards wandering the old stone. Certainly Hawkesmoor had always possessed security people of some description or another. Somehow the current uniforms just didn't seem as nice as the ones of medieval issue.

She strode across the grass of the courtyard towards the main building that the castle walls surrounded and protected. In the center was the original 14th century keep, DuPlessis Tower, and fanning out on either side of it were the brilliant additions designed by the Tudor architect Sir John Thynne, completed in 1567.

Since the death of the twelfth Earl — her grandfather — in 1964, the DeBarry family had occupied apartments in the west wing. The rest of the castle was maintained for its historic value and not lived in on a private basis. Here was the magnificent medieval great hall, the breezy Elizabethan gallery with its family portraits and numerous other lovely state rooms — one or two renovated as late as 1811.

She slipped through a modest side entrance and bid good evening to Sean, the other guard, who sat inside having his coffee.

Hawkesmoor's kitchen was still located in the west wing where Sir John had placed it in the 16th century. Caroline headed there to make a pot of tea. All she wanted to do was sip some Earl Gray, take a hot bath and think about what the hell she was going to do.

Upon her return to the moor country, she had thrown herself back into her duties at the castle — including taking calls for John Gilpin, the local vet. He had been overtaxed by a big outbreak of blackleg in county sheep flocks. She had hoped the work would push away gloomy thoughts and allow her to get on with things as her father liked to call it.

So far, just getting on with things was failing to address her grief. She felt utterly gutted by Robin's murder. No amount of self-chastisement in which she sternly pointed out to herself that one dinner date could not possibly merit genuine bereavement made it any better. She was not his wife nor his fiancée. She was not even an official girlfriend. She was nothing. Not one of Robin's friends or acquaintances knew about her. She didn't even know if he had family or friends. There was no one to share memories or commiserate with over his sudden death. Caroline had never felt so inexorably alone.

Robin sighed and left the window. The hunger was suggesting that he might like to feed. It liked frequent meals and could become quite greedy and demanding. He absolutely didn't need to feed again and could manage for a while longer, as he always had before.

But he needed to be strong. There was much more afoot than just teaching history and rehearsing with a church choir.

"So," said Hannah throwing one of her waist-length blonde braids behind her shoulder, "have you replaced Fiona yet?"

Peter gave her an exasperated glance. "Fiona's not a light bulb or a pack of chewing gum."

"You could have fooled me." Hannah grinned. "Don't they select the stiffest types for mathematics?"

"Fiona's a brilliant statistician." Peter placed a steaming pot of tea on a kitchen tray and returned his younger sister's grin. "She can pie graph anything."

"When she visited last Christmas — I'll never forget how she figured the total BTUs in the stable's manure pile in literally seconds," Caroline said over her shoulder as she found some cups and saucers in a cupboard.

"That's right!" said Hannah, rolling her eyes. "Remember how impressed Dad was?"

"Oh, get off it," Peter groaned. "You two can be so boring."

"Speaking of the noble parent, let's get tea up to Dad before it chills," Caroline suggested before Hannah could frame a suitable retort. "Peter, you carry the tray and Hannah, you have the torch?"

Over the years, it had become their habit to use flashlights instead of electrical light for nocturnal trips. The castle was fiendishly expensive to light and heat so they tried to do as little of either as possible. It was difficult enough to afford both security men and the minimal day staff needed to keep up Hawkesmoor.

"Hannah, do keep the beam steady," Peter complained as they headed for the main staircase. "I've almost tripped three times."

"It's not my fault Dad always insists on barricading off the back stairs for puppies."

"Quiet, you two!" admonished Caroline, putting a restraining hand on Hannah's shoulder. "Can't you feel it? The cold?"

In the greenish-gold of the flashlight Peter threw her a dubious look.

"We live in a castle, Caroline."

"No, she's right," broke in Hannah, "It's that cold. Haunted cold. Ghost cold."

"That cold indeed." Peter shifted the tea tray uncomfortably.

"You know," Hannah said jiggling her light up and down in excitement, "this is the Gray Lady's territory!"

Caroline had already moved off towards the main staircase. Hannah darted after her, leaving hapless Peter to follow as best he could with the tray.

They clattered over the stone floor with Hannah's flashlight revealing glimpses of magnificent 16th century linen-fold woodwork, the occasional flash of an oil painting and gleam of silver.

A moment later, the DeBarrys plowed to a complete halt. Peter lost a spoon off his tray. It fell with a surprisingly loud rattle to the floor causing all present to react with startled jumps.

All present with the exception of Hawkesmoor's legendary Gray Lady.

She was a well-known figure of the castle appearing with much more regularity than either the Black Monk or the fabled Moor Monster.

Caroline felt her throat go dry at the sight of Hawkesmoor's elegant will-o'-the-wisp. Without a sound, without even a whisper of a satin slipper or rustle of silk, the lady gracefully descended the staircase as she usually did. The shadows of night never marred her appearances. She seemed lit from within like a breathtaking spirit lantern. The Gray Lady's demeanor was always somber: her oval face drawn with worry or regret. A petite frame held up with funereal dignity as she floated down each step.

The Gray Lady glided to the base of the staircase and looking slowly from side to side as if scanning for a particular person. For one instant it almost seemed possible that she saw them.

All three DeBarrys unconsciously shifted backwards out of her possible sight line. Caroline felt a drop of perspiration roll down her cheek despite the cold.

Then the Gray Lady began to fade away. She became an indistinct column of pale light, then a vague swirl and finally nothing. She had returned to the night air.

"Bloody hell," said Peter after a very long minute. "What did we do to deserve an audience?"

Caroline wiped at the perspiration, surprised to find that her heart was pounding wildly. She suddenly felt exhausted as if the Gray Lady had usurped their energy to achieve form and direction.

"Maybe she knows the Americans are putting in a steam room," Hannah suggested brightly. "You know how the story goes! The Gray Lady always appears before a great change at Hawkesmoor — and Dad's pretty healthy."

"Hannah," Peter sighed.

"The Gray Lady," Caroline said with a shiver, "knows something bad is coming our way."

13

Geoffrey Dunbar pushed a sheaf of papers across his gleaming mahogany desk and looked perplexed.

"That's an awful lot of money," he said bluntly, "for a restoration project."

"I've got an awful lot of money," Robin replied, leaning forward to scrawl his spidery signature on the top page. "This doesn't even make a proper dent."

"Seventy million dollars is a proper dent."

Robin grinned at his old friend's slightly sour expression. "I could spend that sum every day for a year and still not feel it. All thanks to you, my friend."

The honorable and conservative Dunbar firm had managed his affairs since his arrival in New York in late 1918. Geoffrey's great-grandfather Aloysius Dunbar had shrewdly cared for Winnifred's ever-expanding fortune even avoiding the ruinous '29 crash by keeping the principal abroad in Swiss banks.

Geoffrey thought Robin was Francis DuPlessis, the polite, rather eccentric grandson of the polite, rather eccentric Richard DuPlessis his father had known. He didn't know Professor Robin Dashwood at all. Robin kept his academic identity completely separate from his DuPlessis affairs just in case difficult problems like the one he currently faced with Max Aosta surfaced to haunt him.

"So the Swiss bank will transfer this sum immediately?"

Dunbar nodded. "I'll see to it. Don't worry."

"Thank you, Geoffrey." Robin rose to his feet. "I will contact you from Europe."

"I'm very gratified you have decided to stay with Dunbar despite your relocation." Geoffrey held out a well-manicured hand. "Thank you, Francis."

"Changing management was never an option." Robin shook the proffered hand firmly. "Now I'm off to say good-bye to some other old friends."

"Renovations could be complete as early as fall," said one of the two corporate Americans as Caroline was leading them through the gallery.

"Bob, I've got to hand it to you," said the other — a jowly blob named Cliff. He gave his associate an assertive nod. "Your state room incentive program is top drawer."

Caroline paused in her step and fixed her eyes on the portrait of the missing 18th century Lord Merritt. She had always thought his large green eyes looked rather kind and today Lord Merritt seemed to be telling her to take heart.

"State room incentive program?"

"Our top-producing guys would get one of the state bedrooms for a weekend," Bob explained and then added in a patronizing tone, "You know, like a reward system?"

"I see." Caroline reluctantly pulled her gaze away from Lord Merritt's painted eyes. "I don't think that will be possible, Mr. Turner."

"Call me Bob, please," Turner gave her a condescending wink. "I believe you will find that part of our contractual agreement, Caroline."

"Lady Caroline," she returned in her most polite manner, "if you don't mind. My father has yet to sign that piece of paper, Bob."

"Caroline!" Peter's anxious voice called from the other end of the long gallery. "A word, Caro!"

"Incentive programs can be the heart of any executive superstructure and I'm positive Bob's incentive program will be a hot feature of our fiscal year," Cliff began in his flat Midwestern drone as if he would simply overcome her objections by crushing them with the mighty weight of his Chicago corporate needs.

What a perfect thicko, Caroline thought before Peter distracted her again.

"Caroline!"

"Excuse me, gentlemen." She disengaged herself rapidly and strode towards her brother.

It would have been nice if her father was better able to talk to these sorts of people but he couldn't. It was all Peter and Hannah could do just to stop the old school Earl from grabbing one of his inherited Purdey shotguns and shooting over the heads of the Americans. She'd never forget the infamous visitor day incident in which the Earl drove off a group of tourists called Clowns for Christ when they decided to treat the castle to an impromptu performance. Thinking on it, she'd never seen clowns run so fast.

"Caro!"

"Those bloody twits!" she snapped, *sotto voce*. "They actually want to dole out state rooms like prizes at a fun fair."

Peter took her by the arms. "Dad got a phone call from Coutts."

"A bloody incentive program! Who needs an incentive program for executives? Are they not ambitious and acquisitive by nature?"

"Caroline, listen to me!" Peter shook her gently. "Our account at Coutts. Well… there has been an anonymous donation."

She tried to focus on Peter's words. "An anonymous donation? Is it enough to make a start on the roof?"

Peter's handsome face lit up with a huge grin. "More than thirty-five million pounds!"

"Thirty-five million pounds?" Caroline felt as if the sky had opened. She threw her arms about her brother with a sob of joy.

"There, there, old girl." Peter patted her back. "You've been terribly weepy of late. Look ye, one of us has to put a halter shank on Dad. He's preparing to drive off the enemy and I'd hate to lose all our repair money in lawsuits."

Caroline drew back and wiped at her eyes. "Please let me be the one to tell them. Please."

"Go ahead." Peter bowed in deference. "Hog all the fun."

She winced. Hearing her father bellow "Down with the bloody Huns!" from the main staircase.

"Off I go!" Peter turned to dash to their father's side.

Caroline waved cheerfully at the two executives who looked both startled and apprehensive at the loud sounds beginning to emanate from the Great Hall. Apparently Dad had knocked over the dinner gong again.

"Gentlemen — about Bob's incentive program. Could I have a word?"

Robin didn't imagine there was a vampire in New York who would give him a second glance. Some had the ability to detect another vampire's energy pattern but such a scan took some exertion and he very much doubted any passing revenant would find him worth the effort. He looked like a tall, slightly stooped Catholic priest making his dignified way with the other pedestrians on Fifth Ave. Almost anyone else on the Upper East Side sidewalk would seem a more promising drink than a frail anemic man of the cloth.

He decided he rather liked the long black frock coat and wide-brimmed trilby hiding his long hair. It reminded him pleasantly of the elegant clothes men used to wear.

Max Aosta, the Vampire King of New York, was currently the powerful head of his own multi-national corporation. He could have easily become the head of the Costa Nostra given his glittering Italian pedigree and canny business sense but Max shunned the Mafia as lowbrow and they were frightened of him. Persons who irritated Max had a way of ending up dead or missing. A rumor still persisted that Jimmy Hoffa had picked up the wrong salad fork at one of Max's dinner parties.

Like the arrogant Princes he came from, Max liked to live in an opulent palace high above the unwashed where he could wander out onto the balcony and gaze upon his land. But instead of a medieval fortress dwarfing the vineyards, Max built himself Cathedral Tower. Sixty floors of steel and glass — a haven for the ultra-wealthy who paid upwards of forty million dollars for the privilege of keeping a flat in Max's palace.

Robin touched the brim of his trilby as the Cathedral's liveried doorman pulled open the glass entrance gate to the plush lobby.

"Evening, Father," he said pleasantly.

"God bless you, young man," Robin murmured as his eyes scanned the glittering lobby. No obvious vampire drones hanging about to protect Max from any possible danger.

The Cathedral was really a village tucked into a gleaming modern tower, Robin observed on his way to the huge onyx information desk. The lobby, for all its Baroque-adjacent pink Italian marble floors, custom-made gilt furniture and massive floral arrangements, was just a jumping off point for the Cathedral's impressive amenities. Cathedral dwellers could visit their own boutique shops, work out in a world-class gym, catch the latest film in its private cinema or dine at Cathedral's five-star restaurant named, unsurprisingly, Max's. Cathedral residents never had to leave the building if they didn't wish to. Max had quite successfully turned a corner in America into his private fiefdom.

Robin thought gaining access to the Cathedral's roof could require a bit of doing. Max might possess appalling taste but he wasn't stupid. Random humans or vampires weren't going to be able to simply ascend to the lofty heights of the prince's kingdom without censure. He made a dignified exit through the main doors but doubled round to where he figured there was a freight elevator. There had to be a properly dingy staging area for all the drudges who toiled to make life special for the fortunate few.

He found a metal windowless entrance door about where he supposed it might be and pushed the buzzer.

"Yes, sir?" came a tinny voice over the intercom speaker.

"I'm Father Tim from St. Felicitas. Here to see… Jose," Robin replied, inventing a name.

"Jose? Jose Hernandez?"

"That's correct. Jose Hernandez."

The buzzer sounded and he dutifully stepped into a spartan cement and white tiled vestibule. Max didn't waste any pink marble or roses on the lowly. He didn't even issue the staff a genuine security guard at their door.

A young woman in a neatly pressed Cathedral Tower uniform and a name tag that read Courtney directed him towards the staff elevator. She told him that Jose worked as towel manager for the fifty-eighth floor fitness center and that she had to accompany him on the trip. Courtney also gave him her best Team Cathedral smile and apologized, explaining that the building's protocol never allowed non-residents to wander without an escort.

Courtney was pretty when she smiled. He felt his hunger rise a notch. She'd have a delightful taste. Of course, so would have had Windham's best innkeeper if he'd actually allowed himself the delicacy. Instead he'd grabbed a trucker at a comfort station on the way to New York. Not even in the same league.

Robin rode with Max's pretty young employee up to fifty-eighth floor. She asked him one or two polite questions about the life of a parish priest that he endeavored to answer in friendly but simple terms so she'd find them completely unmemorable. He also noted a security camera in the elevator and realized he would have to access the upper level of the Cathedral in a very different way. He was going to have to test his vampire mettle.

The vast hall of fitness encompassed the entire level. If Louis XV had thought to install a gym in the Grand Gallery at Versailles, it would have resembled Max's tribute to 21st century wellness. Every surface from the peach colored marble pillars to lavish Baccarat crystal chandeliers shimmered with reflected light. Even the rows and banks of exercise equipment gleamed aggressively with polished chrome. The Cathedral's regulars who dutifully toiled at the machines seemed subdued. There was a kind of a hush to the place as if they were exercising in a museum or perhaps the glittering temple just overwhelmed its inhabitants. Max's cheerful employee was happy to give him a lot of memorized blather about the fitness center's world class indoor tennis courts, gym equipment that included everything from treadmills to mechanical horses for polo practice, indoor/outdoor pools, climate controlled decks and a luxury spa that featured Beluga caviar facials.

They stepped beyond a wall of glass doors to a heart-stopping view out over the cantilevered structures of the city and up to azure skies dotted with spring cloud. This was a Manhattan only the very rich and their minions were allowed to enjoy on a regular basis. The massive deck, spare and elegant for Max's taste, surrounded the entire fifty-eighth floor like the promenade on a magnificent ocean liner. He inhaled the sweeping panorama of skyscraper canyons and scanned the setback sides of the building. Sleek glass and steel relieved by dramatic balconies.

He knew from a cocktail party he'd attended a couple of years earlier that Max's lair took up floors fifty-nine and sixty at the very top of the Cathedral. He needed to access the roof where he would wait for Max to come home. Providing he survived the confrontation, he'd be on a plane for London in the morning.

Feeling fortunate that Jose had not been a worker in the parking garage, Robin pondered his options. He needed to divest himself of the helpful Courtney first.

It proved to be simple. Humans with uncomplicated mental processes, those whose thoughts rarely strayed far from acquiring goods, food, sleep and sex, were reasonably easy for a clever vampire to reprogram. Courtney was just such a human. With a little concentration and his long fingers pressed against the pulse in her wrist, he was able to suggest that she had long ago escorted a blandly uninteresting priest to the main floor. But now she was famished and needed to go find a sandwich immediately. Without a glance back in his direction, Courtney dutifully trotted off in search of food.

Free of human interference, he found an abandoned corner away from any of the fitness center's clients who were jogging or walking on the track that followed the deck around the building and evaporated into shade. He could have tried it to gain covert entrance to the Cathedral but being a shade was difficult to maintain and he couldn't afford a mistake.

Robin began the ascent to the Cathedral's summit, using the balconies of the next two floors as his touchstones. His superior revenant strength and reflexes allowed him to spring from ledge to ledge until he finally threw himself over the lip onto the roof. Exhausted, he fell against the wall and reassembled. Just one more night and he'd be on his way to England.

I'm coming, Caroline. I'm coming home at last.

14

Caroline rested her head back on her favorite chair, wearily shut the book she'd been reading and closed her eyes. She exhaled slowly and in spite of feeling flu-ish, savored the sensation of quiet. All she really wanted was to feel the way she had with Robin Dashwood. She wanted her heart to rush with excitement and pleasure when he touched her. She wanted the silken weight of his hair to fall against her cheek again when he kissed her. Nothing — not even Hawkesmoor Castle — seemed to mean as much without him.

Her sensation of quiet was short-lived as a soft rap came at the bedroom door.

"It's Peter," came his muffled voice through the fine old wood. "Brought you a hot chocolate."

"*Entre tous.*"

Peter carried in a pair of cups and grinned as he gently pushed the door closed with his foot.

No wonder the Oxford girls thought her brother was lovely, thought Caroline, admiring Peter's gentle good looks with his longish blond hair and silver earring.

"Everyone's packed it in," he said referring to a small gathering of close friends who had come to the castle to celebrate the anonymous donation. He offered her one of the cups which she accepted gratefully. "I told them you weren't feeling very well."

"Bit of a flu thing, probably," Caroline said as he settled on the ottoman in front of her. "How is Mark?"

Peter shrugged. "Slightly miffed that you didn't come down to find out how he crushed old Squeaky Miggins at the Manwaring show with one of his school horses. Said he'd ride by tomorrow."

"That's nice." Caroline rubbed her temple. "I think I shall take an aspirin."

"I'll fetch you some if you'll finally come clean about New York," Peter countered swiftly. "Come on. You've haven't been yourself."

Caroline looked annoyed. "I should have known the delicious hot drink was just a bribe."

"No, the enticing beverage was an underhanded way of gaining entrance. The aspirin is the genuine bribe."

"Really," Caroline sighed, "I'm all right."

Peter shook his head. "Pull the other one. When you're not snapping at us, you're off having a cry."

"If you're going to be disagreeable — shove off."

"See what I mean?" Peter leaned forward in interest, propping his sweater-clad elbows on his knees. "As the old gangster movies say — what's your beef?"

Caroline relented, too tired to hold up the facade. "I met a man in New York."

Peter's eyes lit up. "A rich Texan? Is that why we have all this money?"

"Shut up," she snapped. "It's not funny and it's not a joke."

"What about him?" Peter looked at her in genuine concern. "Did he treat you badly?"

Caroline felt tears rise to her eyes. She shook her head. "No, he was lovely, absolutely lovely. He was… killed. His name was Robin Dashwood."

"Oh, Caro," said her brother coming to drape an arm about her shoulders. "I'm sorry. That's rotten luck."

Caroline dissolved into sobs. She hadn't seen Robin in weeks and it wasn't going to be possible for her to ever see him again.

She just had to learn — had to accept the fact that whatever sweet and fragile thing had been beginning between them was lost. Robin Dashwood was gone. All their possibilities had run out with his blood into the New York gutter.

Robin blew out a short breath of cold night air. He crossed his arms and continued to wait for Max Aosta to return. He scanned the living room below him with wary interest.

Max's penthouse had the additional luxury of massive skylights. They hogged most of the roof space to give Max the illusion, Robin supposed, that even the moon and stars were within his mighty grasp.

"Excuse me." Caroline suddenly pushed away from her chair. "I'm going to be ill."

She barely made it to her little bathroom, retching up champagne, hot chocolate —seemingly everything she had ever eaten in a series of violent surges. It was odd. She was seldom sick with flu or colds and even more rarely prone to losing her meals.

"Sorry," Caroline groaned from her spot on the tile floor.

"Caro, I don't mean to be indelicate," Peter knelt next to her and held out a clean towel, "but did you — forgive me for asking — did you sleep with this Robin Dashwood?"

Caroline's eyebrows shot up at the directness of his question. Blushing, she nodded.

"Dearest sister," he squeezed her shoulder sympathetically, "I think the Grey Lady came to announce a big change in you. I bet you're pregnant."

She stared at him in horror over the edge of the towel.

15

Robin watched as Max and his inner court arrived home after an evening spent stealing small drinks from New York's sleek and chic.

He scanned the main room through the skylight. Yes, he knew most of them. A very elite group indeed. Rough-hewn Nate Watkins wouldn't be found among this clique. After all the homicide detective was just hired help. Robin wondered as he shifted position slightly to gain a better view, how quickly Kate would join such a court.

Robin glanced at a tall racehorse of a blonde as she laughed at something Max said and collapsed onto his white velvet sofa. Joslyn Merriweather, a vastly successful clothes designer and owner of the Merriwear label. She had been Pansy Merrimac. The daughter of a pre-Civil War plantation owner in the deep South until a vampire gave her the hunger. Famously fast, loud and competitive, Joslyn had used every vicious revenant tool at her disposal to further her company. Designers who dared copy her ideas or had better ideas mysteriously disappeared. Some died in grisly accidents. No textile union ever managed to organize in her factories. Not that Joslyn cared for American workers. Still feeling entitled to slaves; she had taken her manufacturing to Indonesia and Africa where children could produce her products for pennies a day.

He looked across at a very thin olive-skinned girl wrapped in pale aquamarine-colored silks. The teenager sat upright and regal in one of Max's gilded chairs — the personification of exotic elegance. Despite her adolescent exterior, Sita was one of the oldest vampires known to the modern courts. Once a princess of ancient Ceylon where she had been worshiped as a living goddess, Sita had become something of a traveling diplomat in the 20th and 21st centuries. She mediated territorial differences between courts and often stayed as Max's honored guest during her tours of the North American continent. Even sitting quietly and observing the other guests, Sita radiated power. A subtle energy distortion rose from her slight figure like heat off desert sand.

The fey Broadway musical star, Grant Ashby, was devotedly hanging on every word of Joslyn who created him. Robin wondered if poor Grant would ever get over his mental enslavement to the Southern vampire. He was both sophomoric and clingy, easily miffed. Legend had it a frustrated Joslyn tore up his indenture contract and threw it in his face years ago but Grant never seemed to notice. One of the few examples in which a vampire really regretted the right to indenture.

Robin almost smiled but shivered instead. He couldn't imagine possessing Kate as indentured slave. She wouldn't take very well to the Sir Anthony treatment.

He shifted his line of vision to take in another figure lounging about Max's main room. This vampire, still affecting a thin black mustache from the twenties, was handsome in way no longer fashionable. Nico, of course. Lovely old Nico Steffanopoulos, a Greek shipping executive who used to be one of Isadora's rent boys before Max found him.

And of course, Max himself. Descended from mountain bandits who had forced the beleaguered populace to make them princes, Max was loud, arrogant and lacking in the subtle. This reflected itself in his physicality which was robust and well-muscled like a hearty Chianti. He always looked upholstered in his five thousand dollar bespoke Italian suits. Robin had often mused in the past that the phrase to gild the lily might have been coined after a visit to one of Max's houses. To Max's mountain bandit soul, an object was good if it glittered and shone.

Hang on, thought Robin, moving again for a better view. One was not a vampire. A nervous young man with creamy skin and thick charcoal-colored hair. He was small but lithe and handsome despite the appalling Italian silk suit Max had made him wear. The boy was hanging about in Max's big, gaudy shadow, anxiously eyeing the other guests. This must be the Carlo he'd heard rumors about. The boy with whom Max actually seemed to have fallen in love. Most of Max's pretties ended up in the East River as gruesome floaters as Nate probably termed them. They were like moths existing for a few days, maybe even only hours, before burning up in Max's hot flame. But Carlo had lasted.

Caroline reached down into the sink and gathered up some of the steaming water. She swept it onto her face, relishing for one brief moment the comforting warmth.

"Right then," she said, reaching for a towel. "We'll drive to Middleborough and get a pregnancy test."

"What do you mean we?" Peter protested with a shake of his blond head. "I've got to get back to Oxford tomorrow. I've missed heaps of tutorials. I'll never be ready for my exam."

"Peter, you're dangerously close to whining," Caroline warned him as she patted her dripping face. "One day isn't going to make much difference, is it?"

"Oh," he let out a resigned groan, "I suppose not."

Once Peter had left, Caroline thought she might be able to exist without the security of the bathroom. She made a tentative return to her chair.

Pregnant. Caroline instinctively laid a hand over her abdomen. Her head reeled faintly as a fresh wave of nausea rushed through her system. Pregnant and Robin Dashwood the father. If the test results were positive, a mess of spectacular proportions was in the making.

Move, Carlos! Robin thought. The room was nearly empty now. Nico, Grant and Joslyn had all departed, leaving only the regal Sita behind to chat with Max and his boy toy. He readied himself, watching for the instant when Carlos would step free of Max's orbit.

Robin sprang as the boy wandered away from Max. He crashed feet first through the skylight, sending shards of glass splintering down with him to Max's thick white carpet. The vampires, armed with superior reflexes, dove for cover until they could assess the situation.

Carlos tried to scream as Robin wrapped an arm about his throat. It came out as a hoarse rattle. The boy struggled but was no match for Robin's strength.

"No!" cried Max plaintively coming out from behind his bar. "No violencia. Don't hurt Carlo."

"Why, Max?" Robin tightened his hold on Carlo's neck. The boy gasped painfully for air. "I was never a threat to your court."

Max held up his hands in a submissive gesture. "Robin."

"That's Lord Merritt to you—a prince from some tin pot Italian principality." Robin kept backing up, taking the straining Carlo with him.

"This is most unlike you," said Sita standing up from her spot of momentary refuge. "You are not given to attacking others of our kind."

Robin ignored her, concentrating all his energies on Max. He picked up a large shard of glass from a table top and drew it across Carlo's cheek. Blood spurted from the jagged incision. Carlo let out a horrified rasp of pain.

"Lord Merritt, please," Max begged. "I'm sorry. It was all a simple misunderstanding."

"Quite a big misunderstanding for you and little Carlo here." Robin held up the blood-smeared dagger of glass. "The next one scars him forever."

Max's glittering dark eyes seemed to be searching desperately for an answer that would work.

He shrugged eloquently. "You were the wrong one. A tragic mistake."

Dispassionately, Robin drove the glass point into Carlo's chest, pulling it through tendon and muscle. Not quite enough to kill but certainly enough to cause great pain. Carlo sobbed soundlessly, sagging in Robin's grip.

"Nate Watkins doesn't make tragic mistakes, Max."

"Of course not. I was stupid to think you would believe that."

Sita listened with great interest to Max's hedging. She took a seat on one of the rococo chairs — content to watch and evaluate the situation.

"I had a life that I liked, Max. I taught my classes. I lived down in the village far away from your bailiwick," Robin said bitterly. "Why lock me up in a box to starve?"

Sita raised both eyebrows and looked at Max.

"Carlo," Max murmured, gazing helplessly at his creature. "Lord Merritt, please. Accept my apology. I was only doing as I was asked. Don't hurt Carlo anymore. He is just a boy."

"Doing as you were asked?" Robin repeated incredulously. "Max Aosta, the vampire king of New York?"

The former Italian prince shrugged again. "Even Max Aosta has debts."

"Who do you owe, Max?" Robin's voice darkened in warning.

Max threw Carlo a look of real regret. He sighed and turned away.

"I cannot tell you, Lord Merritt," Max said with flat conviction.

"Even for Carlo?"

Max's broad upholstered shoulders rose and fell as he sighed again.

"Even for Carlo."

Robin registered the finality in Max's tone. The vampire king had decided to close the circle. Well, thought Robin bitterly, he could up the stakes. But only if he was strong enough to pull it off.

"Say farewell to Carlo." Robin closed his eyes and willed his body to rise. He'd seen other vampires do it. He was now well fed and angry. He had to learn how to channel his darkness.

Robin felt himself lift off the floor. He rose towards the shattered skylight, carrying the limp Carlo with him. Opening his eyes, he could see Max and Sita's startled reaction to his feat. Robin Dashwood was not supposed to be a strong vampire. All the vampires knew him as a frail failure. He felt an incalculable sense of power surge through his system.

"Carlo!" cried Max, grief-stricken. Obviously Aosta had hoped to save Carlo by giving him the hunger.

"Too late," Robin spat before disappearing with Carlo into the night sky.

Air work in full three-dimensional form was like gliding through water Robin decided as he carried the young Italian to the rooftop of a nearby building. Not at all like melting into a shade and traveling with the air currents. Of course, being a shade was safe. Zooming about, clearly visible in New York, was not often going to be possible.

He dropped down next to a large air ventilation outlet and laid the groaning Carlo in its shadow. Max would already be combing the immediate area with his people.

Carlo was a bloody mess. Robin knelt at the boy's side and shoved open the crimson-stained shirt. He pushed down the desire to drink from the dripping wounds. The jagged chest injury was worse than he had intended. Carlo was losing too much blood. He'd die if some sort of help didn't arrive soon.

Robin tore at the priest's collar, ripping the front of the black frock. He laid his long hands on either side of Carlo's blood-smeared face.

It only worked on humans. He had discovered the talent after a terrible carriage accident in 1898.

Using much the same thought process that allowed him to turn to shade, Robin made a mental bond with Carlo. He pulled Carlo's pain and Carlo's dreadful damage into his own frame. He took over the wounds, etching them into his own flesh.

The electric pain threw Robin back. He fell onto his elbows with a sharp cry. The deep incision on the chest pulsated violently from searing cold to hot and his face throbbed as it spilled more blood.

Robin felt tears come to his eyes. He slid off his elbows until he was lying flat on his back, willing the terrible pain to go away.

Inhaling and exhaling deeply, drifting with the tide of the pain, he watched his breath stream up into the cold night air and dissipate. Robin had a sudden memory of another night in 1942 when he lay badly wounded during a lull in the British battle of El Alamein in North Africa.

The icy starlight above him was much the same as that hideous night in the desert long ago. Disgusted by Hitler and Nazi plans for Europe, he had left New York for Canada, taking an officer's commission with the British Army in 1939. He saw firsthand the devastating sting of Rommel's forces as Britain suffered massive casualties and bitter defeats. His own luck had held until the decisive push at El Alamein.

Legs shattered and blind in one eye, he had waited on the cold ground with the dead and wounded men of his group. All night bathed in agony. The throbbing tedium broken only by the chilling sounds of distant tank movement. He had envied the British lads who stopped their cries and slipped away in the desert darkness to join the other war dead. At least they had finally found release.

Carlo's Botticelli face suddenly appeared above him. El Alamein dissolved into mist. The pretty Italian boy stared down at him in fascinated horror.

"You've got my cuts." He touched his now pristine cheek with his fingertips. "You must be an angel."

An alien metallic sound came from behind Carlo. He pivoted with a frightened cry. The sound had come from wide gold cuff softly striking another on the long elegant arm of Sita. She was standing not far from them — regal and exotic in the gentle folds of her pale green silks.

Sita held up a long serpentine hand. "Run, Carlo. Do not let Max find you. Leave this city tonight and never come back."

Carlo threw Robin one last panicked glance and scrambled to his feet. Robin watched, unable to speak or move, as Carlo frantically scuttled into the rooftop shadows. A few moments later, he heard an access door banging open and Carlo clattering down the steps.

With her vampire swiftness, Sita moved closer and stared down at him as if he were a new species of insect.

Not long after Carlo's flight, the pain began to lose focus and direction. Once begun, it faded rapidly like a boiling kettle removed from heat. Robin sat up after a few minutes and let out a relieved breath. He was back to rights. Tired but back to rights.

"What kind of vampire are you?" she asked in a low voice.

"Sita," Robin said politely. "Forgive me if I don't get up. Max isn't with you, is he?"

"It is only I." Sita did not break off her stare as she dropped down next to him, rich silk rustling with quiet elegance.

She wrapped her thin arms about her knees.

"You healed that boy. You are a true empath."

Robin offered her an exhausted smile. "A handy device sometimes."

Sita frowned. "You joke. I have heard of no other vampire with this gift." She frowned even deeper. "Even I do not have this gift. It is for humans?"

"I can't make it work for our kind. Tried once."

The Princess of Ceylon, perhaps the noblest, most aristocratic vampire of them all, moved to bow at his feet. She bent forward and touched the ground with her forehead in genuine reverence.

"Please stop that," he begged, embarrassed.

"I honor you, Lord Merritt, and what you are." Sita replied rather cryptically. "Find a safe refuge, Lord Merritt."

The Indian vampire rose to her feet. "I shall tell Max I found you by the side of the boy, Carlo. I shall tell Max the boy is dead. I will then say I destroyed your three-dimensional form and scattered your consciousness in the streets."

Sita brought her hands together in front of her chest and bowed again. She vanished with the exquisite skill of a vampire queen.

16

Robin handed his passport to the clerk at Heathrow immigration. The middle-aged man flipped it open, scanned it briefly and thumped his ink pad with a stamp.

"Welcome home, Mr. DuPlessis," he said politely, stamping one of the pages. "It's been awhile, I see."

"Much too long," Robin replied, holding out a slender hand for the passport. "I hope I can still find my way around."

The clerk gave him back the book. "Dear old Blighty never changes. Good luck, sir."

Robin slipped the passport back into his leather shoulder bag, glancing about the modern airport terminal with its humming baggage carousels and brightly lit moving ads for duty-free perfumes and cigarettes.

Blighty never changes, he thought with a laugh.

"No," said Peter looking up from his book as she approached his table in the Middleborough tea shop.

Caroline nodded and slipped into one of the chairs. She smoothed back a loose strand of her strawberry blonde hair.

"You need some Earl Gray," Peter decided, reaching for the chipped brown pot. "It's way past tea time. Should I fetch you a cake?"

"I'll just be sick again."

"Right." Peter winced. "Dad's going to love what you've done to the Rover."

Caroline shrugged miserably. "Tell him one of the dogs did it."

He pushed a cup of tea across the table to her. "So — when is your appointment?"

"Appointment?" She jerked her head up in alarm. "But I haven't made up my mind about it yet."

Peter's blue eyes grew worried, "Caro, you can't be serious. This could be disastrous for you. Dad will be horrified."

"It's a baby, you big lout," Caroline said fiercely. "Not a pair of shoes."

"You're going to have it, aren't you?" His jaw dropped.

Suddenly her direction seemed very clear. Suddenly she just knew.

Caroline lifted her chin. "Yes, Peter. I am."

Robin slid behind the wheel of the indigo blue BMW roadster with real pleasure. As lovely a low-slung two seat roadster as any he could remember from the 1930s but happily, unlike the spartan earlier models, these came equipped with heated tan leather seats, satellite radio and GPS navigation.

He had a brief flash of how long the journey once was from London to Hawkesmoor. Four days at best with good horses but even longer if one was forced to travel by river.

"You're going to love driving this one, Guv," commented the satisfied salesman, interrupting Robin's memory. He held out a leather folder. "She's cherry. You've got a girl to impress?"

"You know, I really think I might." Robin accepted the papers, tossing them on the passenger seat. He turned the key in the ignition and the little roadster obediently came to life.

The BMW man grinned widely and gave him the thumbs up. "*I'd* marry you for this car."

"Oh, god!" groaned Peter. "You're not going to be sick again?"

"Sorry," Caroline replied dejectedly as she searched her pockets for any spare Kleenex.

"Okay, I'm pulling over," Peter tugged at the steering wheel. "Dad's going to hate this smell in his Rover."

"I'm not wild about it myself," Caroline said just before she leaned out the Rover's side window and was violently ill.

It was twilight as Robin smoothly shifted the little indigo car into a higher gear and left London behind him. He headed north towards Cambridge, intending to exit the motorway there and follow back roads up to Scarborough. He wondered if he would even be able to locate the village of Beckdale near Hawkesmoor Castle. Beckdale had been a very small spot on the landscape in his day. Perhaps it didn't even exist anymore.

An aria from Handel's Rinaldo was drifting out from the roadster's sublime little speakers. It reminded him of the days when he traveled regularly to London to see opera and theatre.

The DuPlessis of Hawkesmoor Castle were a musical family. They had all mastered various instruments and filled many winter evenings by playing chamber music or accompanying his mother as she sang popular art songs of the day. Oliver Tupin, their young music master, had become his best friend despite their initially awkward social gap and most often went along with him to hear the new music in London.

Robin smiled as he adjusted his back slightly in the buttery leather seat. It didn't matter how one traveled from North

Yorkshire to London — horse, coach or canal — every method left one feeling pummeled. Even in the superb private equipage his father insisted upon, one could expect the inevitable dull backache from a four-day coach trip.

Of course, it was also true that the journey was worth the discomfort. London was a marvelous place in the 1740s. It was the Age of Enlightenment. The Church had lost ground to reason and the notion of individuality. In every possible area of endeavor, this intellectual freedom had brought remarkable scholarship and artistic achievement into full efflorescence.

For a titled young man with a bit of brain and money, London was a glittering and witty playing field. He had explored it with a giddy abandon, wiling away daylight hours in crowded coffeehouses arguing philosophy and scientific investigation with the likes of Lord Kames, Edmund Burke, and the intolerably smug Nicolas Fatio de Duilles who was notorious for even offending the normally genial Sir Isaac Newton. Then when night fell and oil lamps lit the streets with guttering gold, he frequented theaters and opera houses to drink in all the new plays and music.

And like most young men of his set, he kept a mistress in London to make the trip even more palatable.

Corisande Belfield. Robin sighed a little as her name came back to him. A singer with Handel's opera company, she had risen to become one of the master's most gifted sopranos and real favorite with London audiences. Part of Corisande's popularity could be attributed to her rare ethereal beauty. She had been so slender and pale with huge dark eyes dominating a small oval face. Corisande's rich red hair was her only slash of color and it fell in luxurious curls to her waist.

When he met her for the first time in one of Handel's salons, Corisande was already dying of consumption. She was trying to finish her final season with the company before the cough forced Handel to let her go. It hadn't been difficult over the next few weeks to fathom out what the future held for the singer. In the middle stages of the illness, Corisande could expect to live for some while before the disease destroyed her lungs. But without an income from the opera, the singer would be unable to keep her physician or a roof over her head. From serpent tongued society wags he learned the beautiful Corisande had a history of "putting on airs" as they deemed it. She had famously refused lucrative offers from many a powerful opera patron. The result being that as her health declined, Corisande had become a liability. None of her would-be protectors wanted her anymore and she would face utter ruin.

It hadn't been easy to win Corisande's affections. She had been a proud woman, confident of her magnificent talent and unused to accepting favors from anyone. He had triumphed in the end. Robin sighed again, more deeply this time. As the disease stole more and more of her voice, Corisande had been grateful to settle into the handsome house he'd bought for her. She had humbly relinquished her iron resolve to live only for the opera, exchanging stage costumes and paste jewels for the real articles. While she was still well enough, Corisande even seemed happy to accept his passionate attentions.

Robin changed lanes to get around a truck and wondered how he would treat the same situation in the present era. He'd been a man of his time in the 1740s. Perhaps not so brutal as many but still, he had seen nothing amiss in essentially forcing Corisande into his bed. If she desired protection from the horrors of an 18th century poorhouse, she understood perfectly what her end of the bargain would entail. What seemed so odd to him now was how completely rational and ordinary such an arrangement was considered in Georgian England. He had triumphed all right — over a frail woman with no options.

Still, he reflected, catching a glimpse a green field scattered with fat dappled ponies, Corisande had made something out of the arrangement. Gifted with intelligence as well as talent, Corisande gathered the best and brightest about her in the airy Georgian townhouse. Musicians, poets, painters, philosophers and acknowledged wits attended her salons and kept her keen mind from dwelling on her illness.

Robin shifted up again and the BMW obediently zoomed ahead with well-engineered verve. He remembered the night they had gone to hear Farinelli sing.

Corisande's health had been in serious decline for some while and her physician expressly wished her to remain in the sickroom especially during the damp evening hours. She had begged Robin to take her to Farinelli's performance and though he tried to distract her with promises of other evenings listening to the legendary castrato, Corisande was adamant about attending that particular performance. Unable to deny her anything, he had reluctantly agreed.

Robin took in a deep breath of the English air — even the motorway couldn't completely destroy the wonderful odor of fresh earth and rain that Britain always seemed to possess.

It had been difficult for her. All eyes had been trained on his box the moment they had entered it. Everybody, especially visiting rustics from provincial counties, wanted a glimpse of Corisande Belfield, the dying DuPlessis whore. With most of her extraordinary beauty drained away by sickness, Corisande was no longer a diamond of the first stare. She was just a very thin and frail lady. Despite the hum of a modern motorway, he could still hear the disappointed murmurings from the main floor. There had even been a few anonymous boos thrown out by dismayed provincials with rough manners.

LONDON, 1750

Corisande closed her jeweled fan slowly and turned to raise a bemused eyebrow at him.

"Do you suppose I ought to ape Nell Gwynne and cry 'I am only the Protestant whore'?"

Robin reached out to lay a hand over hers. He raised Corisande's hand to his lips and kissed it with great affection, a demonstration of his respect and loyalty. He did it not just for Corisande but for the entire opera house.

"They are not fit to brush the dirt from your shoes, Corisande."

"You are very kind to me, my Lord." She smiled back at him.

"Madam knows I adore her."

Corisande coughed. She bent over with the pain, hastily pressing a bloodstained linen handkerchief to her lips.

Robin threw a worried glance at his friend Oliver Tupin, who was moving promptly to shield her from the audience.

"Shall I take you home, my dear?" Robin asked quietly as he stroked her back. He could feel the terrible cough rattling her chest through the heavy plum-colored velvet of her gown. "Surely this is too great a strain?"

"Please, Corisande," echoed Oliver softly, "Robin is right. Allow us to."

"No, no." Corisande straightened her back and gave them both a tired smile, her eyes bright with pain. "I want to hear Farinelli. I must hear Farinelli."

"Sweet," Robin's voice dropped even lower, "I will bring Farinelli to sing at your pleasure."

She reached out to tap his cheek with her delicate fan. "I am very well now, thank you both — and see? The footmen are dowsing the candles. We will away soon enough."

The opera house's attentions now went to the legendary Farinelli as he took to the stage. They gasped audibly at his lack of fantastical costume.

Like all castrati, Farinelli was known for his elaborate depictions of Greek Gods and other notable mythic beings. He never appeared as a simple man on stage as his incredible three-octave-spanning voice was deemed too unnatural to portray mortal men. Somehow it was considered quite all right for him to become ethereal creatures of the dream realm but a great insult to humanity if he chose the stage mantle of a mere man.

It was common knowledge that Handel had refused Farinelli the honor of singing certain pieces of his work. Handel had remarked unkindly that he wrote most of his music for human voices, not mutilated freaks.

Yet here was Farinelli, his long ebony hair pulled severely back with a black ribbon and dressed simply in a wine-colored velvet frock coat, confronting his audience as a mortal man.

Robin marveled at Farinelli's courage and stole a glimpse at his own mistress, who sat forward engrossed in the other singer. He thought that courage must be a hallmark of theatre folk — for in her way, Corisande's appearance at the opera house had taken about as much bravery as Farinelli's daring transformation.

The superbly handsome Farinelli who had caused women across Europe to swoon at his appearances, strode to center stage and nodded at his concertmaster, Nicolas Porpora.

The music began. The slow sweet strains did not belong to one of the ingenious showpieces Farinelli usually sang to demonstrate all the remarkable things his strange voice could manage. The music most decidedly had come from the hand of the master. The music was Handel's *Lascia ch'io pianga*.

Handel had relented at last to Farinelli's request? Robin flicked his eyes off the stage and over to the box where he knew Handel himself was occupying. The old man was gripping the box railing, staring down at Farinelli in stunned anger. Farinelli had obviously pirated some of the forbidden pieces and was defying the master for all of London to see.

To say later that Farinelli had made a good go of it would have constituted a gross misstatement. The opera house was filled with a sound it was likely never to experience again. Stripped of his mythic beings, Farinelli found his human voice. It soared through the bittersweet phrases, sure and rich, carrying his audience along to the giddy heights of artistic accomplishment. No capricious Greek god here, no mutilated freak, either. Just a man pouring out his sorrows in simply the most beautiful voice God had granted to any mortal being.

The opera house went mad with joy when at last his pure tones faded away and Farinelli took his bow. So lavish and wild was the ovation that, at first, no one noticed Handel's reaction. Weeping, the master staggered to his feet and collapsed, overwhelmed by Farinelli's vision of his work.

"But where," asked Oliver, mystified, "did Farinelli get the sheet music? Everyone knows Handel hoards his work like the gods guarded fire."

Robin watched as the tall slender figure of Farinelli turned in the direction of his box. The singer bowed deeply and when he straightened, his dark eyes radiated gratitude.

"I think I could hazard a shrewd wager," Robin said in wonder, gazing at his mistress as she nodded her head at Farinelli.

"Corisande!" Oliver breathed. "You!"

She opened her fan with a short expert motion. "I assure you gentlemen I am far too indisposed to have smuggled documents to a creature of the stage."

They watched as Handel's limp body was carried from the opposite box. Farinelli was still accepting the crowd's roars of approval, standing in an endless shower of flowers.

"Nicely done, madam," Robin murmured, reaching out to stroke her cheek with back of his fingertips.

"Fa!" Corisande said as she fanned herself. "I had a notion this performance ought not to be missed."

Robin saw the sign for Cambridge and began searching ahead for the exit. She died shortly after Farinelli's triumph. The year he was to marry Elizabeth Gwayr and set about producing an heir for Hawkesmoor. It had been a ghastly way to die.

Corisande's lungs had collapsed like spun sugar. Fevers so intense that her eyes wept blood instead of tears. Blind and in anguish, Corisande had clung to him until her frail body shattered like a sparrow in the talons of a hawk.

Farinelli sang at Corisande's service. Robin still remembered the words: Death always returns but life is fleeting.

He followed the curving arch of the road towards Cambridge. Speaking of which, Robin thought, even Cambridge had to possess a few bullies they were anxious to be rid of.

17

"Caro," Mark greeted her cheerfully as she and Peter came in through the kitchen door, "I came by to show you that new mare."

Mark and her father were sitting casually about the kitchen having cups of tea. The Earl seeing Caroline's stern face, removed his leg encased in a muddy hacking boot from the tabletop. He pretended suddenly to find his pocket watch fascinating.

Caroline masked a grin. That was her Dad, secretly terrified of the domestic wrath of women.

"Hello, everybody," she replied, throwing a pointed look at Peter that begged him to interfere on her behalf. "Sorry we've been gone so long. Terrible…"

"Terrible thing," broke in Peter artfully as he helped himself to a biscuit. "We picked up a stray and took it to John. Poor old thing was sick all over the Rover."

"All over the Rover?" The Earl looked up from twirling his pocket watch. "God, it'll be wretched for weeks."

Caroline threw Peter a harder look. "Yes," she said, "Sorry."

"Still it was for a sick dog," her father allowed and patted the head of his old black lab who soberly offered his paw for the Earl to hold. "Why thank you, Harold."

"Come on then, Caro," Mark rose from his chair, "The mare's in the stable. You've got to see her."

Caroline shook her head. "I can't, Mark. I'm sick as…"

"A dog?" chimed in Peter, exactly on cue as if he'd rehearsed it for a play.

"Ha ha. But it's true, Mark. I've got some kind of flu thing."

Mark's handsome face registered disappointment. "Poor darling. You ought to go straight to bed."

"My thoughts exactly," she said in relief.

"Why not stay over yourself, Mark?" suggested the Earl. "Your mare's too green for night riding anyway. Hack back in the morning after Caroline's had a chance to take a look at her."

"Super idea." Mark beamed at the Earl and then directed his brilliant smile towards Caroline. "In fact I was planning on having some time off tomorrow. I could spend the day."

"Splendid! Then it's settled."

Caroline held back an annoyed groan. She saw Peter wink wickedly at her over Mark's tweedy shoulder.

"Good night, Mark." Caroline patted his arm lightly and hoped he didn't notice that she was grinding her teeth in frustration.

The winding English country roads were much more familiar to him than the modern motorway. He found the velvet black stretches of rolling farmland and moor country, scattered occasionally with the warm glow of small villages, not so very different from his own time.

Robin was pleased to see many of the places of his day still existed in one form or another — most improved much for the better. People of the current era always tended to dismiss thoughts of just how filthy life could be in 18th century England. The open trenches near every common area defied description especially in light of the modern world's passion for tidy, antiseptic indoor plumbing.

He was suitably impressed to find Beckdale a thriving little community. Once just a church, a few cottages and a rather miserable posting inn, Beckdale had reconfigured itself into quite a respectable collection of Victorian buildings. It was pretty obvious that the mid-1800s with its bustling interests in northern textiles and coal, had created a sort of mild renaissance in the area.

Robin parked the roadster. He slipped out from behind the wheel and took in an unsteady breath of the cool night air. Victorian improvements or not, it was still the sharp, wild air of his moor. He was home again.

He looked around, taking in what he could of the gray buildings in the yellowish glow of the rewired antique street lamps. A pub he didn't remember from his day, The Shattered Lady, seemed busy with local traffic and a quite appealing inn was just across the high street. It certainly wasn't the grim establishment from his 18th century. A disheveled hovel that provided a mean bill o' fare to local ruffians and unwise or unlucky travelers. Modern Beckdale's inn, the Hawkesmoor Arms, was a much more inviting affair in every respect. Its florid hand painted sign promised *the charm of yesteryear with all the comforts of today.* Just the place for a weary vampire to lay his head.

Caroline sat, curled up in a chair, writing a description of Robin Dashwood and how they had met at the exhibition in New York. Something she thought the baby might like to have one day. She wanted to get it down before the clarity of his face and the sound of his voice faded from her memory.

"Come in," she said when a knock came at her bedroom door. If it was Peter, as she suspected, she'd let him have it for the sick dog story.

"Darling!" Mark stepped inside. "I was hoping you were still up. How are you feeling?"

"Better. Thanks." Caroline shut her notebook reluctantly. Robin's urbane essence flickered and died with the gentle thud of the cover.

"You don't look as green," he admitted, crossing the room to join her. "Jolly good to have you back. I missed you while you were away."

"How nice. Thank you," she said, noting with dismay he seemed intent upon settling in for a good old chinwag.

"You should have seen Claret go at the Manwaring show!" Mark collapsed in the opposite chair. "She didn't wonk out her corners and took the triple combinations like an old pro. I really think she could win at Windsor or White City."

"That's why you're a professional, Mark—and I'm just a lowly amateur," Caroline replied cheerfully.

"There's nothing lowly about the way you ride a line of fences, Caroline," Mark said, gazing at her fondly.

"Oh, stop! You'll spoil me."

"Darling," Mark's voice dropped, indicating the seriousness of what he was about to impart, "with Hawkesmoor saved from ruin, let's get on with it!" He leaned forward to take her free hand. "Let's set a date with St. Michael's and get married."

"Always happy to accommodate a late traveler," said the cheery proprietor of the Hawkesmoor Arms. He glanced at Robin's registration form. "You have number 7, Mr. Dashwood. It's up the stairs and to the right."

"Thank you," Robin replied, picking up the key from the dark oak counter.

"The Shattered Lady will be open for a bit longer if you should require a drink. Otherwise, there is a bottle of sherry in your room. We do have Internet but it can be a bit dodgy out here."

"Just a hot bath, I think." Robin gave the man a tired nod. Even vampires grew weary at time changes.

"You in to see our castle?"

Robin looked at the innkeeper in mild surprise. "I beg your pardon?"

"We have a very pretty castle here about. Quite a few people drive this way to see it," he explained genially. "Hawkesmoor Castle. The Earl lives there with his children. Occasionally they even dine here. We have a very good French chef, Mr. Dashwood."

"I shall have to try him." Robin half-smiled and turned away.

"The castle is private," the innkeeper called after him, "but the Earl is very generous in allowing interested persons to look around the grounds at certain times."

Robin paused for a moment as he caught sight of a lit window from the pub across the street and slowly returned to the reception desk.

"The Shattered Lady," he asked with a frown. "Is there a story behind that peculiar name?"

The round face of the innkeeper was wreathed in delight. Obviously local lore was his particular interest.

"Just so, sir!" The proprietor cocked his head and concentrated for a brief time before breaking into a childish rhyme *"Poor little Elizabeth Gwayr, her one true love left her here. She broke all her bones tumbling down Hawkesmoor's bloody stones."*

Robin felt the room spin around him. His throat went dry. "What a ghastly little song," he managed to force out.

"She was the seventh Countess of Hawkesmoor and shattered her skull falling down the castle's main staircase in the 18th century." He peered at Robin in concern. "Are you all right, Mr. Dashwood?"

18

"Caro," came Peter's voice as he opened her door and looked inside. "Oh, sorry. I didn't realize you were busy."

Caroline swiveled in his direction anxiously. "No, no, it's all right. Do you need something? Is it about something *really important?*" She hoped her brother would pick up on how much she wanted him to stay and shield her from Mark's line of inquiry.

Peter stared at her blankly for a moment and then widened his eyes as if some sort of internal light switch had just flipped on.

"Ah, yes. Weighty matters." He cleared his throat and went on in a deeper, more serious tone of voice, "I wonder, Mark, if I may bend my sister's ear for a bit. It's about one of my," Peter sighed eloquently, "many, many duties as Lord Merritt."

Mark frowned in annoyance and lifted his hand from Caroline's.

"Bloody hell. I'm trying to pin down your sister on an actual wedding date."

"Gosh!" said Peter in surprise. "I wasn't aware Caro had even agreed to marry you yet."

Mark's blandly handsome face brightened with a wide grin. "You have a point there. So, Caro — you *are* going to marry me, aren't you?"

Both young men turned to look expectantly at her. She shifted uncomfortably, really disliking Mark's confident smile.

He thought it was all so simple. Of course she would want to marry him. He was *the* Mark Halsey. The bold show jumper who was the heart's desire of every young woman in the area.

Caroline tried to choose her words carefully, "I don't think just now is the time to discuss marriage."

"What can there be to discuss?" Mark asked. "We just lack a date to give our friends so they can run out and stock up on wedding gifts."

Caroline felt herself weave a little. A memory of the night in New York when Robin had made love to her suddenly washed all around. The silken weight of his long hair against her cheek and the lovely coolness of his alabaster skin as he pressed against her.

She could never settle for anything less ever again. Even if she never found such passion again, it would be awful to attempt a bland sort of contentment with just a pleasant and socially acceptable man. Besides, it wasn't fair to Mark. She'd always be thinking of Robin. Always pretending it was him in the dark.

"I'm not going to marry you, Mark Halsey — or anyone else for that matter," she announced flatly. "I just want to go to bed and get a little sleep. Now clear out — the pair of you!"

Mark's jaw dropped open at the severity of her tone.

"Caroline…" he began with genuine confusion.

"Go on, shove off!" Caroline waved her hands at them.

"About those weighty matters," Peter said in his deepest voice. The corners of his mouth threatened a wicked grin.

"Out, out!" She pointed to the door. "I don't feel well and I want to be left alone."

Robin closed the door of his room and leaned his back against it as he tried to order his thoughts.

Poor little Elizabeth Gwayr, her one true love left her here. She broke all her bones tumbling down Hawkesmoor's bloody stones.

The horrible children's song rattled through his head with the same grisly echo of the tumbrel carts and WW2 tanks in the African desert. One more hideous shred of human cruelty to add to his collection.

Elizabeth Gwayr, his golden girl. The young beautiful creature had loved him to distraction. She'd have been proud to tear her body apart in childbirth for him and for Hawkesmoor. She would have raised his children with kindness and made his keep a sanctuary against the cold moor. She'd have worn dignified widow's black when at last he died and would keep a pretty miniature of him until the day she finally joined him in the family crypt.

If things had gone along the way they had been intended. Instead, Elizabeth had been forced to endure Ambrose Westmacott and a brutal death. But *why*? What could have possessed Elizabeth to accept Ambrose as husband? She could have had any number of other perfectly acceptable young men with pretty estates to their names.

Ambrose Westmacott. Robin tightened his jaw, remembering.

YORKSHIRE, 1750

"God's blood. Another dreary country ball at Manwaring—still, you have done well," drawled Ambrose, saluting him lazily with a glass of wine. "Well done, sir."

Hating to look away from the brilliantly colored satin and velvets as the minuet reached its elegant peak on the ballroom floor, Robin forced his head to turn in the direction of his odious relation.

"I am afraid your point escapes me, cousin," replied Robin.

Ambrose guzzled more wine and then gestured with his glass at the delicate swirl of dancers out on the floor.

Robin followed the movement, noting Ambrose's fingernails were, as always, filthy. The man really was a swine in human clothing. Only thirty-three years of age, Ambrose was already fat from rich food and lack of exercise. He drank to excess and squandered his father's money in London brothels.

"Your lady." Ambrose's red-rimmed eyes feasted hungrily on the slight figure of Elizabeth Gwayr as she gracefully completed a difficult transition in the minuet's pattern. "'Upon my soul, she has become a pretty little trinket."

Robin didn't answer. He sat back in his chair and crossed his arms, choosing to ignore Ambrose altogether. It really was a shame Ambrose was considered socially acceptable. In actual fact Ambrose Westmacott was one of the least presentable people he had ever known and yet, because of his family connections, he was impossible to exclude from society.

"'Tis a pity I did not speak for her first," Ambrose continued almost wistfully. "My mother yearns for grandchildren. Have you yet bedded your brood mare?"

Robin turned his head again to take in Ambrose's puffy features. "I beg your pardon?" he said in an icy voice.

Ambrose took another swallow of the wine. "Why, Cos—surely this slip of a country girl is just for breeding more DuPlessis? God knows she would be hopeless in fashionable circles."

"Ambrose," hissed Robin through clenched teeth, "keep a civil tongue in your head. I warn you, cousin or not — do not cross me."

Westmacott saluted him again with the glass. "I just speak plainly, dear cousin. I meant no offense."

"You will excuse me." Robin rose to his feet and strode away from the dancing.

He slipped through a set of heavy green velvet drapes to one of the new French doors Elizabeth's father had just added to Manwaring's ballroom. It was suddenly all the rage to possess them. Everyone wanted the airy and expensive expanse of glass overlooking one's gardens.

The cool night air outside felt like a balm to his senses. He leaned against the stone ledge that encompassed the newly constructed terrace and gazed out over the shadow-shrouded grounds. A slivery edge of a crescent moon hung in the sky, drifting in and out of wispy clouds. It would probably rain later and keep some of Manwaring's further afield guests from attempting the trip home.

Robin swallowed roughly. It did not seem right somehow. Corisande dead just a week and he was politely attending to his social engagements as if she had never existed at all.

He'd never forget her burial in the little churchyard of St. Giles. Sheets of hard, cold rain hammering the plain oak coffin as the yardmen lowered her none too gently into the muddy ground. Just he, Oliver, and a tired old priest standing by the grave edge.

Better to make the actual burial a simple affair. Too much fuss and bother, too elaborate a coffin would attract the grave robbers. Corisande had gone into the ground dressed only in a white cotton shift: the single splash of color came from a flower he pressed into her icy hand before the lid was nailed shut.

"Lord Merritt, sir," came Oliver's voice behind him, "I have been commanded to play that new violin work from Germany. Would you be so gracious as to accompany me on the harpsichord?"

Oliver never called him Robin except in private. After all, despite Oliver Tupin's widely acknowledged mastery of music, he was only a paid servant of the Earl of Hawkesmoor. Just as Corisande Belfield had been only the kept mistress of the Earl's son.

Robin pushed off the stonework.

"I am alone, Oliver," he said dully. "No need to pull your forelock."

"You are thinking of her, are you not?" asked Oliver, instantly shedding the servant's demeanor like an ill-fitting coat.

Robin glanced away from his friend. "It is difficult not to. I cannot imagine London without Corisande."

"Her life was too short," Oliver agreed, "and I miss her too but this night is for Elizabeth's birthday. Let us go make it merry."

Robin gave Oliver a slow nod. "Perfectly correct as always. The future Lady Merritt deserves all my attention."

"Besides she is trying desperately to be polite while your cousin Ambrose pulls her about in the gavotte. He is not an accomplished dancer."

"Damnable cur!" Robin said angrily as he swept past a somewhat startled Oliver.

Robin slid down to the floor, hands over his ears as if it could muffle the shrill children's voices in his head: *Poor little Elizabeth Gwayr. Her one true love left her here.*

He should have gone with Kate to Los Angeles. He could be pretending to drink lukewarm champagne at all sorts of tedious events, watching her butcher her way to the top of the film world. Even L.A.'s entertainment industry couldn't dish out anything worse than the guilt he felt pressing down on his thin frame like a soul crushing vice designed by Astaroth.

Elizabeth's entire life reduced to a banal and pathetic end. Frail, exhausted, and defeated by those who conspired against her, she had finally bowed to their greedy conviction and allowed them to destroy her. Ambrose hadn't even granted her the dignity of a staged riding accident or the privacy of poison. He had simply smashed her head in — the crude way he might have dispatched an unwanted cur dog.

Robin wrapped his arms about his knees and pulled them up against his chest. She who had trusted him above all others, was only remembered now as an abandoned woman. Just another senseless victim. The shattered lady of Hawkesmoor. A creature of pity and grim jokes. Honored only by a gaudy painted sign over a pub anxious to snare curious tourists.

Robin bent forward, his forehead coming to rest on his knees. A sob rattled through his chest.

"Elizabeth," he whispered into the darkness as if she could hear him wherever she wandered now, "I'm here at last to put things to right somehow. I promise you. I promise you I will."

But the Victorian room didn't shift and failed to reveal any comforting secrets. Elizabeth failed to drift in with the pale moonlight and relieve him of his burden. It seemed her life force had fled the moor country and if she did walk through its cold heather, she did not deign to hear his voice calling her name anymore. She was beyond him — long past caring.

19

Robin skipped the charming breakfast buffet that other lodgers were happily attacking with gusto and slipped a brochure the innkeeper had given him into his brown leather satchel. It was a modest little offering entitled *A Handy Guide to Our Castle.*

He emerged from the inn into the cold crisp air of a Northern spring morning. It was one of the remarkably clear, wind-whipped mornings he had loved as a child. The moor was rich with fine earthy odors, promising all sorts of wondrous possibilities to a well-rested child. He remembered dashing away from the inevitable breakfast tray his Scottish nurse Mrs. Martin would bring in and out to meet the bright cold morning. There would be house dogs to throw sticks for, invisible armies to fight with a wooden sword, stablemen to pester for more information about horses and new secret hiding places to discover.

Robin almost laughed as he crossed the street to the gleaming BMW. All to be done before afternoon lessons began with old Mr. Pitt — the man who had inspired his centuries old love of history and teaching. He could still hear Mr. Pitt pacing around the schoolroom's polished wooden floor in his squeaky leather shoes with the enormous silver buckles of which he was inordinately proud. "Shall we now pass over the terrible bloodletting of the Huguenot Rebellion?" Mr. Pitt might inquire on a typical afternoon. "Oh no, Mr. Pitt," he would reply immediately, "as I am quite sure 'tis the best part!" "Well then, young Merritt," Mr. Pitt would always return, with a smile threatening to pull at his craggy features, "imagine, if you will..."

Mr. Pitt's voice faded in his head as he unlocked the car door and slipped in behind the wheel. He was on his way to Hawkesmoor Castle. A shiver coursed down his spine. It was all waiting for him to discover like the secret places of his childhood. They were all waiting too. His lost family and his friends, long waiting for him to return and learn of their fates. He would put a real end to their stories and set them free.

Caroline squeezed her legs against Dragon's gray sides and the big gelding obediently broke into a canter. She allowed him to find his own way on the long stretch of soft ground she knew from experience to be free of holes. They had put in many such miles together over the years.

"Remember Gatcombe Park three years ago?" Caroline said, leaning forward to pat his dappled gray neck as they sailed along. "You really showed them how to handle banks, you old Irish lad."

She often wished the Irish fairies had gifted Dragon with speech. Caroline suspected he would have quite a pithy sense of humor and far more intelligent conversation than most people she knew.

Dragon shifted up into a hand gallop and they flew down the path towards the old Roman Copse. She laughed and for the moment all of Caroline's worries spun away in the brisk morning air.

There it was, Hawkesmoor Castle, far across the wild expanse of moor country claiming the horizon like some imperial gray ghost. Robin felt his throat tighten painfully at the vision. He slowed the car to a stop by the side of the road and got out to gaze at it. Robin smiled as he made out DuPlessis Tower rising from the center of the graceful gray stone battlements. He shifted his view slightly and caught a glimpse of the magnificent 14th century Merlin's Tower with its twelve sides and deceptively elegant machicolations. Just how many of Hawkesmoor's ancient enemies, the Vikings, had perished in a scalding flood of boiling pitch and quicklime poured from those handsome embrasures?

He failed to see how much had changed from his day. Hawkesmoor looked exactly as it had when he used to return home from various journeys. Once inside he was sure he would see many changes: modern plumbing, electrical lights, kitchen appliances, telephones but from where he stood time had stood still.

The muffled roar of a jet engine caught his attention and glancing up, he spotted an RAF Tomcat streak across the brilliantly blue sky and disappear from sight.

Robin inhaled the crisp spring air and turned back to the little indigo blue sports car. He could be such an idiot. Time hadn't stood still at all.

"Sorry about the long way round, Mark," said Peter as they came down the main staircase in the Great Hall, "but Dad's insisted on barricading off the west stairs for Daisy's puppies."

Mark shrugged his broad shoulders indifferently. "I can't believe Caroline being so dodgy. Did I do something to offend her? I don't think I did."

"Give the old thing some time." Peter patted Mark's back in sympathy. "She has a lot on her mind. Caroline's still exhausted from America."

"It's almost like she has another chap but I know all the chaps here about and that can't be it."

"Peter!" came Hannah's anxious voice from above them. "Come quick! Daddy's dropped his studs again and we think a puppy swallowed one!"

Peter peered up at Hannah who was leaning over a landing rail. "What is a puppy doing up there anyway? The insurance men don't like that."

Hannah threw up her hands. "As if that means something to Dad. You know how he is about puppies. He's got six of them."

"And how many do you have in your room?" Peter called back as he began to climb the stairs. "Sorry, Mark — have to help on this one. Good ride home and all that."

Robin took a deep breath for courage and stepped into the Great Hall of DuPlessis Tower. He had a moment to let his eyes adjust to the slightly darker lighting and absorb the massive room. He glimpsed the pewter-colored glow of Hawkesmoor's fine collection of arms and armor and sensed rather than saw the Beauvais tapestries hanging against the cold stone of the walls. Inhaling the rich musky odor peculiar to ancient places, he could just make out the pale shadows of spectral servants as they hurried across the polished stone floor. He heard the familiar squeal of metal as one of the great iron chandeliers was lowered to have its thick candles lit.

He felt momentarily stunned as if his nervous system was having difficulty adjusting to the highly charged atmosphere. He was home at last. In this magic place he could actually sit near the dust and bone that had been his parents.

Then the sound of a girl's voice calling out, "I only have a couple of puppies! I'm not like Dad!" broke the memory force field about him.

The phantom servants spun away and suddenly Robin was staring at a reasonably handsome man with very blond hair.

"Good morning," Robin said, offering the unamused young man a pleasant smile.

"And just who the hell are you?" snapped the young man. "This is privately owned, you know."

"Yes, I…" Robin began politely.

The blond cut him off immediately. "You'll just have to go back to Beckdale or wherever you came from and wait for a tourist day."

Robin gazed at the bully in benign interest. The young man was discomforted by his failure to be impressed by angry tones.

"I am a friend of Lady Caroline, actually," Robin said before the man could start blustering again. "Is she about?"

"No," the blond replied abruptly.

"Mark, who are you harassing?" inquired a cheerful voice from the stairs.

Bully boy Mark turned to look and allowed Robin a view of another young man dropping down the last couple of steps. This one possessed the distinctive strawberry blond coloring of Caroline and the same clear-featured intelligent face. The DeBarry boy's eyes widened in surprise as he clattered across the polished stone floor and then he beamed in genuine pleasure. Mark's expression mutated unattractively between utter bafflement and annoyance.

"Mr. Dashwood!" The DeBarry boy cried warmly, extending a hand. "Excuse me for seeming startled. We'd heard sad news about you. Obviously untrue. Thank god!"

Robin took the young man's outstretched hand and shook it. "Thank you …?"

"Peter, Caroline's brother."

Robin held back a smile. "Lord Merritt, sir — an honor."

"Call me Peter, please." The new Lord Merritt turned slightly to include the bully. "Mark, this is the historian Robin Dashwood. When Caroline told me she'd met him in New York, I realized I'd read his book on Disraeli! Mr. Dashwood — this is Mark Halsey, one of our neighbors."

"Mr. Halsey," Robin inclined his head politely, "a pleasure."

Mark's jaw tightened. "Mr. Dashwood." He flicked his eyes away quickly as if Robin was only mildly less interesting than a bowl of old porridge. "I've got to get back to the school. Tell Caroline I'll be back to take her off to dinner somewhere."

"I'll let her know." Peter didn't look pleased with his neighbor. "But I'd ring by first if I were you."

"Is Caroline about?" Robin asked quietly once Mark had clumped away.

Peter's cool expression warmed instantly as he forgot about Mark. He reached out to lay a hand on Robin's forearm.

"No," he said in an equally soft voice, "she's out riding. Mr. Dash-"

"Robin."

"Robin," Peter said in almost a whisper, "She's been very sad. Thank you for coming."

"I'm afraid the NYPD got a bit overly zealous in reporting my demise. They've been sloppy lately."

Peter grinned. "I'm glad. Would you like a cup of tea?"

20

Caroline heard the voice as soon as she led Dragon into the stable aisle. A low and gentle voice talking to one of the horses — reassuring it, telling it what a lovely creature it was.

Not Evan's familiar tones nor her father's or even Mark's. A stranger was in their stable. She crept forward somewhat cautiously to investigate. Perhaps a very bold tourist had a liking for horses.

Caroline came a bit closer. Dragon followed obediently at her boot heels. The stranger was in Firefly's stall, she noted in distress. Firefly didn't like unfamiliar people in her stall. She didn't even like the concept of stalls very much. The idiot would be lucky if the skittish mare didn't kick him in the head.

"What a lovely girl," murmured the quiet voice in Firefly's stall. "Oh, you like a bit of carrot, don't you?"

Caroline could now make out a figure through the iron railings. A man by the cut of the handsome russet tweed hacking jacket. Firefly was happily nuzzling the man's long pale hands as he fed her a carrot. The mare obscured his face by arching her neck over his shoulder. Caroline paused to frown at the notion. Firefly seemed utterly content, even delighted, with the stranger in her stall.

"Can I be of some help?" Caroline ventured finally in her most businesslike voice.

She watched as the man seemed to freeze behind the shield of Firefly's glossy neck. Then the spidery fingers slipped up to grasp the leather nose band of Firefly's halter. Almost, Caroline thought suddenly, as if he wanted the big Irish mare to hide him.

"Sir," she tried again, a strand of anxiety entering her tone, "if I can be of any assistance?"

"I don't wish to frighten you," he replied quietly. "Please don't be frightened of me, Caroline."

She took an instinctive step backwards. Her boot-heel scraped the stone floor and she stumbled. Surprised, Dragon danced sideways, pulling his reins out of her hands.

"Who *are* you?"

The long fingers released the halter reluctantly and Firefly obligingly stepped away to operate her watering cup. The man slowly lifted his head to meet Caroline's eyes.

"I am no ghost," he said.

Caroline opened her mouth to speak but words wouldn't form into real language. Shock, joy, profound relief, fear of the unknown rose up like rogue waves and slammed into her. She did something completely out of character. Something that her entire life's experience as her father's daughter had trained her most carefully not to do. She fainted.

When Caroline opened her eyes, she recognized the softly glowing lamp on her bedside table. She was in her own room. But what had happened? She tried dizzily to remember. The stable… someone in Firefly's stall…

"You're awake, Lady Caroline," said their local doctor as he came into her visual range. "Quite a knock on the head. Edge of a tack trunk, I believe."

As the doctor spoke about rest and ibuprofen, Caroline remembered the face she had seen in Firefly's stall. Robin

Dashwood! He had been there. Clearly there. He had spoken to her. *I am no ghost.*

"There's someone — someone I have to see." Caroline struggled to rise up on her elbows. She had to get out of bed and find him.

"Your friend?" Dr. Peaches stooped to pat her shoulder reassuringly. "Rather pale young man with longish hair?"

Caroline felt tears of relief rising to the surface. "Yes," she breathed while simultaneously praying that she was not in the middle of a particularly spectacular dream.

"He's been pacing up and down the halls with the rest of your family. I'll send him in. But," Dr. Peaches wagged an old arthritic finger at her, "if he riles you up too much — I'm packing him off with no reprieve."

It seemed an age with Dr. Peaches gone from the room. She anxiously smoothed her hair and listened as the murmur of voices in the hallway came closer. Her hands began to shake when the enameled knob rattled and the beveled door gave its little squeak as it was pushed open.

Then he was actually in the room. Robin Dashwood. A man she had never expected to see again.

"It was not my intention to give you fright," Robin said urgently as he quickly strode across the floor. "I'd never have come if I thought."

"You came. That's all that matters now." Caroline tried once again to sit up. "I can't believe this is not just some wishful daydream."

Robin sat on the edge of her bed. "Your doctor is quite right, you know. You really must rest."

Caroline gazed up into his green eyes, allowing Robin's concerned expression to wash over her like some sort of opiate. She lifted one of her still trembling hands to tentatively touch his highly planed cheek.

"They told me you were dead," she said in wonderment. "Murdered in an alleyway."

"A bit of an exaggeration," Robin said as she continued to trace his cheekbone with her fingertips, "as you can see. I was injured. They thought I wouldn't survive. I was completely out of it for a while in a ware… a ward — an intensive care ward. When I was finally able to leave, you had returned to England."

Caroline found words leaving her mouth before she could weigh them properly.

"Why? Why did you come here?"

She immediately regretted her choice. It had sounded so brutally blunt — suspicious as if she was wary of Robin Dashwood's intentions.

Robin glanced away from her and down at his pale hands. He laced and unlaced his fingers for a long uncomfortable moment.

"I came," he said in a slightly strained tone, "because I love you, Caroline. I discovered my life in New York meant very little without you in it."

It had to be a fantastic dream. She'd wake up to find Mark had booked St. Michael's for a fortnight away, purchased a ready-made morning suit and tickets for a dreary trip to the Pan-European show jumping finals in Brussels.

Robin still looked down at his hands. "I can't hope you feel the same way about me — we only just met but I…"

"Robin, will you marry me?" Caroline asked, ignoring his last comment. "You see; I so desperately need you to marry me."

He was silent for an awkward moment. Caroline had the distinct impression he was actually shocked by her proposal. Not the speed of it really but simply that *she* had been first to speak of marriage.

Robin turned his head away from the examination of his long fingers and gazed down at her, a smile beginning to ghost his angular features.

"You're a forward lot, you modern women," he said in a wry tone.

"I live out on a moor." She winced slightly as her headache increased a notch. "Over the centuries we have learned to snap up handsome strangers from a different gene pool with alacrity."

He leaned forward to massage her aching temples with gentle skill. His soothing touch seemed to reassure and relax. Caroline felt her eyes closing. A lovely long sleep was only a few moments away.

"You won't leave me?" she murmured as he slipped his fingers into her hair and continued to smooth away her pain.

"Not forever and ever and ever," came his soft, somewhat cryptic reply. He sounded a world away now as she finally surrendered to the hypnotic sleep his touch seemed to induce.

Pretty odd was her last thought. Drifting in the tide of sleep, her headache was disappearing like a tendril of sea mist.

21

Caroline's headache pounded fiercely at Robin's head as if angry at being imprisoned in another, stronger host. It would take his body a few minutes to destroy the pain. The exchange always cost him something and he would need to rest awhile before feeding again.

A late afternoon breeze riffled through Robin's long coppery hair as he pulled open the door of the roadster. It tried to smooth his jangled thoughts but even the clear, sharp wind off the moor couldn't shake the sadness. He took a long look around, noting with distaste some typically hideous Victorian *improvement* to the East lawns. How his mother would have hated the cloying style of the late 19th Century.

Robin sighed. It was a lot to manage all at once. At least Caroline's banging headache had finally left him. He inhaled some of the rain-scented air and thought of another time long lost to him.

Yorkshire, 1750

The betrothal ball at Hawkesmoor attracted guests from throughout Britain. Many parties arrived as much as a fortnight in advance hoping to avoid bad weather and long delays on the journey. England was having a season of unpredictable and powerful storms that swept down from the North. Some sustained enough force to rage down to busy London and bring it to a soaking standstill.

Hawkesmoor's hardworking servants were stretched to their limits trying to attend to the needs of so many discerning visitors complete with their own sets of traveling ladies' maids, valets and grooms.

In such a taxed environment, it had proved difficult for Robin to have any contact with Elizabeth. Hawkesmoor grooms were simply unavailable to take a note to Manwaring. They were all far too busy managing the crush of horses into Hawkesmoor's straight stalls. Even when Elizabeth's party arrived two days prior to the ball, it was impossible to communicate with her in any way. Elizabeth's mother and her Aunt Pross were determined that not a hint of scandal would waft about the wedding of their dear girl to infamous Lord Merritt, the lover of opera whores.

In accordance with such a policy, his most gracious mother had given them sets of rooms in another wing far away from DuPlessis household. These were guarded as if Elizabeth were some vitally important foreign queen many malcontents wished to see dead.

He decided a little sleight of hand might work better than entrusting a note to the Gwayrs' nattering chit of a ladies' maid.

Hence Lord Merritt of Hawkesmoor Castle came to intrude upon the ladies' circle after the midday meal. He ambled into the Green Salon and found himself momentarily distracted from his task by the ladies who represented some of England's more impressive families. They sat, very precisely poised on delicate furniture and sipped a sugary brew of hot lemon water and honey from flawless bone china cups rimmed in gold like angelic visions from a country vicar's fever dream. Speaking in soft refined voices of modest matters and only vaguely aware of the music Oliver was so diligently producing on the harpsichord, they nonetheless flew their families' standards with as much verve as their rougher medieval ancestors. Their loyalty no longer simply waved on a castle battlement or on a pike outside a field tent, it was shouted in the splendid afternoon gowns — discreet day dustings of pearls and precious metals — the up-swept cantilevered hair arrangements only clever French maids could manage and stage whispered in the murmur of a politeness or a gracious tilt of a head.

Robin clasped his hands behind his back and continued to wander towards them as if he was trying to fight the boredom of another rainy day.

Yet, he thought, as the ladies lowered their bone china cups to the saucers at the sight of him, they were all present at Hawkesmoor to participate in an essentially clannish rite to pair the chieftain with a healthy local girl for breeding purposes. An event that might have been celebrated long ago by burning to death a few unlucky members of a rival clan while the chieftain publicly forced himself on the frightened girl in an attempt to make the crops grow again. And for all the ancient history of the role he was to play, he, Richard Robin Francis DuPlessis, Lord Merritt of Hawkesmoor Castle, could not have a brief private word or two with his intended to learn how she fared.

Ironic, Robin thought, his jaw tightening slightly, given that on his wedding night, at least one chambermaid would manage to accurately report back to the servant quarters just how many times Lord Merritt had proven his love to his new wife. He couldn't remember the number of times he'd overheard one servant tell his or her counterpart about wedding details at other large holdings: "'Tis really a shame, I tells you. My friend Betsy in service at Blandings, says all the young Marquess could muster up was twice 'fore dawn. No love match there, poor girl! Still she'll have all that pin money and gowns, won't she?" By Christmas every great house in Britain would know how Lord Merritt had mustered up to the challenge.

"You look positively vexed, my dear," said his mother as he came to a halt near her chair. "Would a cup of hot lemon improve your distemper; do you think?"

Robin pushed away the distressing vision of a kitchen full of servants exchanging all they knew on the subject of his virility. He gazed at his mother blankly as his mind attempted to slip into another stream of thought.

"Dear heart," murmured the cultivated voice of his mother, "are you really quite yourself this day?"

"Uhm," he cleared his throat, "yes, thank you."

"And, to what do we owe the honor of your presence this afternoon, my son?" His mother's voice had a tinge of reprove in it. She didn't care much for gentlemen barging into gatherings of ladies without an invitation.

Robin quickly scanned the circled gold gilt chairs. He was annoyed to find Elizabeth absent from the cloister.

All the women stared back at him as if they suspected he was tainted with the plague but were too polite to inquire directly as to the state of his health. Well, there he was, the patrician faces said without a single actual utterance, Lord Merritt who had fallen at the feet of a dying opera singer.

He could hear varying pitches of their soft voices rising in a kind of relentless concerto in his head.

"Everyone knows perfectly well those miserable creatures exist to lure in the ton and ferret away the family money."

"Not a jot better than the chits on those squalid streets in Whitechapel."

"Worse in fact. At least street whores scurry away, happy with fourpence."

"Certainly Lord Merritt has demonstrated great weakness of character."

"Dear Augusta—the pain she bears for his willfulness."

"He was very publicly seduced, wasn't he?"

"The perfect idiot did not even attempt discretion!"

"I have heard Lord Merritt still keeps the house in London just as she'd left it."

"Lady MacKinley told me in strictest confidence that he still visits her grave and leaves arm loads of flowers. All, of course, bearing his engraved card without the slightest care for his family's feelings."

"I came," Robin cleared his throat again softly; why not dazzle them with half-truths? "to seek out my lady and fulfill her wish to see my new gelding. Perhaps even to take her riding while the weather holds."

His mother raised her eyebrows and he saw her quickly suppress a smile. The Countess of Hawkesmoor pretended to study her four-strand pearl wristband as if the diamond catch was not altogether secure.

"What a lovely thought," she said, "but I'm afraid Elizabeth has retired to her rooms to continue her course of study in Christian thought. Really, I had not the slightest idea she was such a devout and studious girl."

Robin saw a few of his mother's really close friends roll their eyes slightly at each other over the shimmering rims of their china cups or the perfect pleats of their exquisite fans. Some of the other ladies feigned interest and a scattered few — most from a particularly dour Scottish contingent — evinced sincere approval of the Gwayrs' bridal preparations.

"My own Father Blacknell is with her now," Elizabeth's thin spider of an aunt replied in grand tones her background did not suggest. Indeed, her brother, a proud Yorkshireman, spoke a thick local brogue without apology. "At my request, he is instructing her in the proper ways of a dutiful wife."

Robin felt his jaw clench in anger. How dare this cruel crow make his future wife miserable?

"The ways of dutiful wives, madam," he said in icy tones, "is surely one subject we can rest contented knowing is in the hands of you and your priest. You can both claim such vast experience."

The never married spinster jumped at his words and narrowed her small brown eyes. She hadn't expected a direct challenge to her authority. A collective intake of breath produced a silken ripple of female voice. Then a few giggles escaped from behind painted fans and prompted Aunt Pross to rise to her feet indignantly.

"You will pray excuse me, Augusta," Aunt Pross said in her most brittle tones, painstakingly copied from the excellent English governesses Thomas Gwayr brought to the moor country to educate his daughter. "I find I must attend to my dear niece."

Augusta nodded her head with circumspect sympathy, tapping her ivory fan against her opposite palm thoughtfully. A bad sign, Robin knew from past experiences. His mother was most irritated.

"Lord Merritt." Aunt Pross barely tilted her head in acknowledgment of his social superiority.

"Oh, do not rush away, Miss Gwayr. I beg you," Robin protested with an overly elaborate bow that clearly mocked her station. "You are always at the zenith of your particular charms when discussing with authority topics about which you know absolutely nothing."

"My good will towards your family prevents me, Lord Merritt, from informing Elizabeth's father of your unspeakable insolence," she hissed and spun on her heel.

"Thank you, Oliver," said Augusta with a curt nod of dismissal for the wide-eyed music tutor. "Excellent as always."

Oliver made a polite noise in the back of his throat and scrambled to gather his music. He shot Robin a veiled look of puzzlement.

"Ladies, perhaps you would all care to seek some rest before the evening's entertainment?" Augusta continued to tap her fan against her pale palm.

The other women murmured their politest agreements and rose like a scattering of butterflies to heed the Countess' suggestion.

"That was most poorly done, Robin," Augusta said severely once the Green Salon emptied of guests. "You have brought me copious quantities of unwanted pity and curiosity — not to mention shaming a guest under our protection. I am appalled."

"Come now, mother," Robin replied, clasping his hands behind his back with the resignation of a sailor about to be flogged by his ship master. "Surely 'tis nothing compared to the dishonor I did you with the opera whore."

"Do not ever speak of Miss Belfield in that disrespectful manner," his mother countered sharply. "She was a kind little soul. It is not her fault you could not behave in an acceptable manner. Imagine — a future Earl of Hawkesmoor so lacking in discretion and good breeding he is capable of expressing his affections for his mistress publicly."

Robin swallowed roughly. He bowed his head at his mother's stinging censure. Corisande had warned him to expect a backlash from a few thoughtless hours spent at an opera supper or a play.

"A handful of outings could hardly qualify as …"

"We are not the demimonde," she interrupted curtly. "An Earl's son does not require his mistress to be at his side in open society. If that lovely Miss Belfield — God keep her — is now regarded far and wide as an opera whore then you, Robin DuPlessis, are the one guilty of betraying her."

Robin flinched at her indictment. Words with the skin-shredding power of the cat o' nine tails.

"And now, you are actually surprised to find Elizabeth's family wary of your intentions? Why should they expect you to behave with any better judgment towards their daughter?" Augusta snapped open her fan with a sharp clack and fanned herself as if his very presence created an annoying hot blast of summer sun. "Given a free rein, would you not expose Elizabeth to cruel rumor and sly wit as well?"

He jerked his head up angrily. "No, madam. I would not."

Augusta raised her delicate eyebrows quizzically. "How very reassuring to find you so certain of yourself."

Robin had the grace to wince. "I know," he said in a very bitter voice, "because I have been made to learn."

The countess' voice softened a little. "The Gwayr line is a very old and noble one despite its lack of gaudy titles. They, as a family, have very deep ties to the land here. You know such a connection will only serve Hawkesmoor well."

"Yes," Robin said.

"It is surely our fault," she sighed, leaving the window with its gray views of a rain-whipped landscape. "We should have seen you married years ago. I made a case for the Duke of Roxburghe's third daughter, Evangeline—an exquisite creature with such style and manners, but your father wished a connection with the Gwayrs very badly."

Robin lifted a hand to interrupt her. "I have never objected to marriage with Elizabeth Gwayr."

"Still, it is not an ideal match." Augusta looked older as disappointment settled across her fine features. "Elizabeth is a delightful child but far from being able to hold her own in real society."

He half-smiled at that. "The very qualities I admire in her. Ease your mind, Mother. I go to this marriage without cares. Indeed, I welcome it."

Augusta returned his smile with a bright one of her own, erasing the aging effects of her earlier mood. "'Tis fortunate then your father chose not to honor your marriage bed with the elder Miss Gwayr."

Robin coughed violently. "Pross Gwayr—my wife?"

"But, of course. You were nearly twenty-four years of age. Elizabeth only eight at the time and Miss Pross Gwayr, an unmarried lady of twenty-five. Much thought was given to extending an offer to Pross."

A vision rose up in his head of what marriage might be like with Pross Gwayr. The tedium of trying to make polite dinner conversation, the horror of being constantly exposed to Father Blacknell and his pompous ill-informed opinions, the duty to produce a male heir for Hawkesmoor and why did he know Pross would frustrate his efforts with four or five girls before finally relieving him of his burden?

A warm reassuring hand on his forearm pulled him out of the unsettling reverie. He focused his eyes again and found his mother gazing at him affectionately.

"Before the ladies appeared en masse, the good Father Blacknell was quite desperate to find his spectacles," she said lightly. "Poor fellow is hopeless without them. I do hope Oliver has not make it impossible for someone to find them — eventually."

"Mother," Robin raised an eyebrow, "what have you done?"

His mother playfully tapped his shoulder with her fan.

"Elizabeth was dragooned into the hunt. She seemed quite anxious to speak to her intended husband so I suggested she might undertake a search of the third attic.

"The third attic?" Robin's dismay was real. "You might as well have sent her to Moscow in winter."

Augusta turned away, a graceful swirl of rustling skirts followed after her.

"I lent her a wrap, of course. Pray excuse me, dear one. I really must attend to your father as he will have grown bored of card games."

"The third attic?" he repeated incredulously.

"Well, I doubt even the envious Miss Pross would think of the third attic," came his mother's reply as she swept into the hallway. "Have a mind, Robin — I envision a brief and wholly appropriate conversation between a gentleman and his intended."

"You do not trust me?"

"No," her voice radiated back over her shoulder. "Not a whit."

Robin winced at the memory of her stinging words. How well she had known the 18th century aristocratic man. The Whig Oligarchy had produced vibrant men of invention and education. The same men could easily and often confuse charm with genuine kindness and cruelty with social necessity,

He had thought himself a good man in 1750. Fair of manner, face and mind, he had never intentionally brought harm down upon any living soul. Had he not even volunteered to be the official overseer of the Elizabethan Poor Law in Beckdale? Had not the village been grateful for his example of Christian duty and aristocratic fealty to his land and people? Had they not marveled at God's intricate order of natural laws that had produced such a creature of innate superiority?

It had all been such a bloody awful lie.

Robin started up the BMW. It hummed to life instantly and responded with catlike instincts when he asked it to swerve out of what once had been the place for waiting coaches and carriages.

He roared out into the castle's long drive, grateful for the cold blasts of Yorkshire air coming through the car's open windows.

Had he not — the perfect 18th century Lord Merritt — met all his mother's worst fears about him in spades? Had he not plundered Corisande Belfield's dignity and ruined the only thing that really meant anything to her — that her name might be remembered entwined with the great art her voice had produced? Had he not left young trusting Elizabeth Gwayr to the brutal attentions of Ambrose Westmacott? Had he not left his father without an heir for the estate he had seen through much thick and much thin? Had his father not been made soul sick by the prospect of Hawkesmoor going to the greedy money-squandering Ambrose Westmacott? Had he not condemned his own mother to a much lower station as a widow whose presence was to be suffered at Hawkesmoor only by the charitable kindness of the new Earl, for whom she could claim no blood ties?

Robin leaned his head back on the leather rest. The really tragic bit was that his intentions had always been honorable. He had only meant well by his actions.

What was he doing back at Hawkesmoor? Would his best intentions towards Caroline and her family only serve to bring more unhappiness to Hawkesmoor Castle?

He was hungry. Very, very hungry.

22

The village of Worsdale had been Beckdale's biggest rival in his day. Everything about it was just that much better than hard living 18th century Beckdale. It had a collection of well-stocked shops, two posting inns, a proper jail, a quite respectable Norman church and an excellent yearly horse sale. All in all, a fine place for people of quality to stop for the night and safely find a comfortable bed with a hearty breakfast to look forward to in the morning.

Robin slid the car into a parking slot and stepped out from behind the wheel. He looked about as he locked the BMW and activated its alarm system.

Even draped in twilight, Worsdale seemed to have proved its earlier promise and become a bustling metropolis. Worsdale had carefully mended and restored its lovely Tudor shop fronts to snare its fair share of Britain's tourist wealth. The typically twisted and narrow old village streets miraculously boasted modern, gleaming stores like Marks & Sparks, Boots, Mothercare, and Selfridge's. Sainesbury and Tesco were also in evidence, offering everything from shepherd's pie to Mexican taco sauce from America.

The old town center where the Norman church still stood and now offered views from its bell tower for a pound, was a lively place. A lot of the farm land surrounding Worsdale had gone to rings of increasing newness: late 18th century near the center, Regency to Victorian/Edwardian in the middle and post World War II developments in the last. Each ring filled with British consumers anxious to have all the options larger cities could offer.

It was no surprise to find Worsdale's variety of restaurants, pubs, New Age and traditional bookstores all doing sharp trade. Hip coffeehouses and clubs were also packed with young people from the various technical track colleges in the area

Ah, wherever students gather—wunderbar! Easy hunting. Robin remembered a vampire named Ernst Von Draemar saying to him in 1962 at a dinner party in Scottsdale, Arizona.

He shivered, strolling up the high street. Von Draemar. A decadent Prussian butcher. He had nightmarish fondness for torturing his prey the way cats toyed with their kill. A weird variant from typical vampire urges, Von Draemar craved human flesh, too.

Last Robin had heard, Von Draemar had been removed from general circulation by a sect of publicity-shy vampires concerned that the Prussian's flamboyant kills might lead to serious human interference. But rumors held the Prussian was still taking down victims in remote points of South America or the Middle East.

Wherever students gathered—students were safe from Robin Dashwood, he thought as he returned a smile from a passing young girl in art student black and a cheerfully faux platinum blonde 20's bob.

Robin didn't know the area well enough anymore to track down the underclass—if indeed Worsdale had a suitable pool of drug addicts, nearly dead tramps and violent youth. A polite question to a clerk in a chemist's shop and he was directed to where he found the supply of potential victims almost inexhaustible: the emergency ward of any hospital.

In the style of English towns and villages where nothing was ever too far from the center, Worsdale Hospital was a few streets away in a rather tired collection of government sponsored buildings dating from the 60's heyday of benevolent socialism in action.

Although modest in size compared to a New York hospital, it was obvious Worsdale did the major medical treatment for most of the surrounding countryside. Such a place was a gathering point for all sorts of people. He just had to find a quiet spot to watch, listen and wait.

A relatively busy night allowed Robin to slip into a chair in the emergency ward and scan without seeking a more covert location.

Three women were in different stages of labor, a boy had swallowed his father's small pocket watch on a dare from schoolmates, another youngster had taken a fall at her gymnastics practice and broken her left tibia, a car accident brought in seven victims, none very seriously hurt, and a teenager was in having her stomach pumped after a botched suicide attempt.

Slim pickings indeed thought Robin as he pretended to read a newspaper. So far the anguished teenager was the best bet but he hated to prey on the young. Maybe he ought to simply do his vanishing trick and raid the blood supplies but again his sense of fair play really disliked the idea of stealing something useful.

He carefully folded the paper and wondered about the sad little girl that had passed him on the stretcher. He was no stranger to mental illness, having survived his own revenant version of a severe breakdown.

He had imploded after Winnifred had disappeared behind the stone walls of St. Sophia. Gone mad like a brain sick dog. All time stretched before him like an endless ribbon gored with relentless human and revenant atrocities.

He became a creature of the night, joining the vast nocturnal culture of London's most dissolute slums. He was a dangerous scarecrow in tattered clothes that had once been very fine and his long red-gold hair fell in tangled shreds to his waist, surrounding an ashen angular face often smeared with what appeared to be blood.

"'E belong to some toff family," declared Katie O'Connor confidently at the Flag and Coin before she vanished forever one night. "Mad as a 'atter and they just let 'im loose 'cause they be shamed. We all ought to chase 'im down and 'ave 'em lock 'im up in Bedlam, we ought!"

No one took Katie's advice. Slum toughs and poor working people alike avoided him at any price. Common streetwalkers dreaded to see him shift his cold green-eyed gaze in their direction. He even frightened the gray learned heads of crime families specializing in hired murder and grave robbing.

He walked like a brain-damaged king through ruined lives, invading even their diminished capacities to dream of the dark and monstrous things, evolving into legend.

They gave him the name "The Prince of St. Giles" or "Prince Ice" for those in a hurry to tell a bit of news around a pewter cup of gin black with ever-present coal dust.

Both titles were fit for short sniggers and to hide unmanly shivers of primordial fear. The Prince of St. Giles was no mere wisp of moonlight and coal smoke: he had an unsettlingly bad habit of suddenly appearing in public houses, doorways, poorly lit street corners and all manner of black byways.

It was rumored in the pubs and public houses that Prince Ice protected the dead in St. Giles' churchyard. Didn't foul terrible things happen to Bill Watford and Elton Eddowes when they tried to dig up that grave? Hadn't Prince Ice been seen there often, sitting on a headstone like a raven? It became common enough said that only heaven could help the poor grave robber who wandered into his territory,

But then the graveyard Prince himself never spoke. He only stared with dead green eyes that seemed to dilate with some kind of terrible excitement when they centered on someone specific. Usually that someone disappeared.

The Prince of St. Giles reigned over and protected the filthy churchyard until modern urbanization swept away the worst of the muck and he sank into the oblivion of a minor footnote in a dust-choked book on London city lore.

In reality, Robin had literally broken down into air molecules and ghosted away on a northwestern wind. It was the first time he had discovered his ability to dismantle his physical body and he had given himself up gladly, hoping England's cold winds would tear him apart and it would all be over.

But, no. That would have been too simple — too elegant.

Robin pretended to sip coffee from a plastic cup and allowed his gaze to sweep over the waiting room. The perfect candidate had yet to arrive. He went back to mulling over the teenager as the final solution. She was swimming in starlight and seductive whisper now. He had been there.

England's air currents had refused to pull his essence apart that night. His molecules had been swept northwest to Welsh mountains where human time had no meaning.

Up in the gray, greens and golds of Cader Idris, the great Welsh mountain, he had spun and drifted with capricious winds. Rising with a sharp updraft breeze to purple peak or starlight, he could then soar downwards again to ride gentler breezes through mountain meadows. Occasionally, as if he was jerked back into three dimensions by sheer accident, he took human form again for brief moments. Haunting Cader Idris' lonely pathways, he spoke with a Welsh shepherd driving his flock or even a poet seeking a vision. He felt no urge to steal their lives. The hunger had left him. Blood no longer sang to him.

Instead he knew the talk of birds, following raptors as they scanned for prey and gulls as they headed for the sea. He heard the deep melodic rhythms that emanated from Cader Idris and recognized it as the intricate blood song that bound the Welsh to their land. He saw that only a fraction of Great Britain could be charted in human geography: most of it existed in other, far more haunting forms.

Lands, times, inner and outer dimensions crossed and crisscrossed Britain like lyrical ley lines in a universal mandala. To wander its supercharged air was to be swept away to where Saxon the English dragon still fought Cymru the Welsh, to where fairies danced and Merlin slept. Britain was the joining place — a still point for all worlds great and small.

It was there that the Fair Ones came to him — the Tylwyth Teg with their strange alien songs: *We balance your hunger with healing. We, who have called you to this place, anoint you as the chosen one — the forever king. Built from the mortar of your strengths and sorrows, you become both bridge and barrier.*

Robin stared into the coffee's reflecting pool in his cup. The Welsh and their cauldrons — always trying to catch a glimpse of hidden lands. He shook his head slightly to push away the dizzy memories.

Besides, he had gone mad. All his memories of Cader Idris were the ravings of an insane entity. None of it was real. One day he simply came back to his senses. He found himself wandering down a footpath to a drovers crossing; mysterious Cader Idris wrapped in the regal purples of spring was far behind him. A passing pig drover told him the year was 1843. He'd been lost more than forty-five years in the Welsh mountains.

A bullying voice grew louder as it came nearer. A strident voice telling the doctors, nurses, everybody that his wife was just a clumsy woman. Always running into things. Small wonder she always had black eyes.

Robin looked up sharply. His favorite brand had just arrived.

"Vin d'Ambrose Westmacott," he murmured, rising to his feet with all the coiled grace peculiar to predators targeting their prey.

23

Caroline shifted uneasily in her bed despite the deep sleep Dr. Peaches' medication had imposed upon her. She heard voices calling. A woman's voice reminding her about the third attic. *Robin and the third attic.*

"Poor old Caro," said Peter to his father as he closed her bedroom door. "She looks wretched."

The Earl nodded with a sigh and reached out to stroke the big head of his ever-present dog Harold. A true countryman, he used dogs like worry beads, rubbing their heads or pounding their sides affectionately while he sorted out a problem or two.

"She hasn't been the same since that trip to America," he said. "Bloody silly idea in the first place! Our household goods on display to anyone with a few greasy coins in their pocket."

"Dad, don't pretend you've forgotten how important that trip was," Peter countered. "You know we had to do it and thank god we did! We both know that huge donation had to have come from a wealthy American."

His father's face tried to rearrange its aquiline features into an expression of hope. "It might have come from HM, you know. She's always been fond of Hawkesmoor, God keep her."

"Dad," Peter said with a theatrical groan, "the Queen did not— Oh, for god's sakes."

"Ware puppies!" cried the Earl in a mixture of dismay and delight as a herd of black and yellow Labrador puppies suddenly thundered up the long hallway. "Ware puppies! Harold, into the breach!"

Harold let out a series of excited barks and bounded forward to mix it up with an equally enthusiastic batch of little retrievers.

"One day we are going to have a nasty-tempered replacement for one of our security men and he's going to tell the insurance company all about these things," Peter observed as his father scooped up a pair of plump black pups who were wiggling and urinating simultaneously with the pure joy of it all.

"A regular puppy is a happy puppy," the Earl announced with a contented shrug.

Robin cornered the domestic bully in an empty room. A large ugly man in a filthy Manchester United shirt, he swiveled as Robin closed the door with a gentle clink.

"Sod off, ya berk. Me wife ain't 'ere. Gone to x-ray."

Robin advanced on him without hesitation, an apex predator moving in for the kill.

The bully's heavy face twisted into an aggressive snarl and he raised clenched fists. "You a bleedin' queer? You're dead."

"You first," said Robin.

He hurled himself at Robin who deflected the ungainly attack without losing a beat and spun the man into shoulder lock.

"This be about the wife?" he sputtered desperately. "She's clumsy…"

Robin crushed the man's voice box and jerked the chin up, exposing a thick, pulsating artery. He sank his teeth into it without regret.

Wife. An image of Caroline came into his mind. If not quite the modern world's concept of beauty, handsome in a patrician way. She really had mourned his supposed death in New York. She loved him. She had asked him to marry her.

He pulled his dripping mouth from the straining man's ravaged throat, twisted the head efficiently to the left in a horribly unnatural angle and punctured a fresher vein.

Unbidden, a memory came to him of another lady who had loved him. Elizabeth Gwayr. Had she not held such hopes for herself? Had she not placed herself in Lord Merritt's way, trusting he would honor her above all others and bequeath her a life of peaceful purpose?

YORKSHIRE, 1750

Elizabeth was sitting in a high backed chair he vaguely remembered as having once been in his grandmother's apartments. A carved wooden box rested on her lap and she was turning it slowly from one side to the other in great interest.

"My old Chinese puzzle box," he said from the doorway. "I have often wondered where it had got to."

Elizabeth looked up in surprise. Her eyes glittered with relief and joy at the sight of him.

"Robin!" She clapped her hands together. "I would rise to greet you, sir, but I am rather pinned under this box of yours."

He quickly crossed the floor and knelt in front of her to lift the intricately carved box from her knees.

"Please know that I have been trying desperately for a glimpse of you."

"I know," she replied and her voice wistful. "Oliver has told me this. And I heard you speaking sharply to Father Blacknell yesterday."

"How have you been keeping, madam? In reasonably good spirits, I trust?"

She chose her words carefully. "They mean only the best but it has been difficult."

"I shall take you off to the Continent once we are married. We will have weeks and weeks alone together, I promise you." He moved the puzzle box to the floor beside him.

Elizabeth rewarded him with a bright smile. "I should like that, Robin. Will you allow me excessive amounts of champagne too?"

"I would lay all of France at your feet if you so wished it, madam."

Elizabeth blushed shyly at the admiration in his tone.

"What is a Chinese puzzle box?" she asked in an effort to change the subject.

Robin reached out and ran his pale fingers over its wood and mother of pearl surface.

"There are three secret steps to opening the box," he explained, gazing up at her and taking pleasure in the way her graceful neck dropped into pretty shoulders of dark green velvet. "It keeps one's treasure safe from pirates."

"Will you show me how to open it?"

"Of course — later," Robin said and placed a hand tentatively on her knee. He traced the embossed pattern in the heavy fabric up to hard boning at her waist.

Elizabeth let out a small gasp at the boldness of his intent.

"Robin," she protested in a near whisper, "this is wrong of us, surely?"

"It is only wrong," he murmured, slowly stretching his long fingers across the stiff velvet bodice, "if you do not want me to touch you, Elizabeth."

She gasped again and pulled back a little as his fingers drifted over the green damask covering her left breast.

"Please," she begged. "I cannot bring shame to my father's name."

Immediately Robin lifted his hand away from her bodice and laid his forearm in a loose, affectionate manner across her knees.

He grinned. "I fear you have already been fully compromised. If you recall, I had you very completely in the Roman copse not very long ago."

Elizabeth's young face colored. "Robin," she chided quietly.

Robin rested his chin on her right knee and looked up at her in good-natured interest. "Does the good Father Blacknell know you haven't any maidenly virtue left to protect?"

"Really!" Elizabeth exclaimed with something like her old spirit, "you are most inconsiderate."

He laughed at her vexed expression. "But you do care for me, do you not, Elizabeth Jane Gwayr?"

Her shyness returned and she glanced away from him. "You know right well I do."

Robin picked up her right hand, kissing the back of her fingers. "And I burn at your touch, madam."

She turned her head to stare at him in astonishment. "My touch? But everyone says you loved only your …"

"Forget what everyone has said. Everyone is an absolute idiot." Robin moved closer, his hands sliding slowly up her arms to the hooks on the front of her bodice. "I do not see you as a little girl any more, Elizabeth. These past days have been torture. I am half mad with wanting you. Sleep deserts me. My thoughts are scattered. "

"Surely they will come soon looking for me." Elizabeth gingerly dropped her arms down about his shoulders, taking a sharp breath as he leaned in to kiss her collarbone. "Even here in the attics."

Robin freed the last of the hooks and the green velvet slipped down her shoulders.

"You are so beautiful." Robin's voice grew hoarse with desire. He pushed aside the delicate muslin under gown to find the pale beauty of her upper body.

"Robin, are you quite sure we are safe?" Elizabeth shivered as the attic chill found her exposed skin.

She let out a small guttural cry as Robin's arms fiercely encircled her bare waist and his mouth found her breast. She slipped her fingers into his glossy red gold hair and surrendered completely to the masculine sovereignty of his touch. Whatever the misgivings her native instincts might possess, Lord Merritt of Hawkesmoor Castle was master of the present and owner of her future. It was not her place in the scheme of things to deny him anything.

Robin felt Elizabeth's slender frame bend towards him. All resistance borne of social edict ebbed away in his embrace.

Just as Corisande had, the night she'd taken residence in the elegant townhouse he had given her. One night was all London society needed. When Corisande stepped outside the handsome Doric columns of her new residence she would never again be known as the finest singer in Master Handel's company. She was only Lord Merritt's opera whore.

Robin drew back from Elizabeth in regret.

"Forgive me," he said.

"Oh," Elizabeth's voice was a soft whisper of dismay, "I know I am not very experienced in such things."

"My dear, it is not that," he replied unhappily.

She dropped to her knees in front of him and laid trembling hands on his shoulders.

"Is it that I am not Miss Belfield?" Elizabeth asked carefully. "It has been impressed upon me that you valued her above all others."

Robin glanced away from her worried eyes. There was a long silence before he spoke.

"Madam, I will offer you no pretty speeches begging your forgiveness."

"And why should you, pray?" Elizabeth gently smoothed back a lock of his amber-colored hair. "Many gentlemen keep mistresses in London, I am told."

He clenched and unclenched his jaw. "Those gentlemen pay their respects to their creatures in a discreet manner. I did not. It was thoughtless — for you and for Corisande."

"Many men keep mistresses, Robin," she repeated and rested a soft palm against his left cheek, "but I imagine few love them as you loved Miss Belfield."

Robin lifted his eyes to meet hers. He was stunned at her graceful generosity of spirit. How had such a wise child emerged from the confining strictures of her religious Yorkshire family? The very same bloodlines that had produced bitter condemning Pross.

"Aunt Pross has told me how you used to take Miss Belfield to the opera and for rides in the London parks. She said it was a very public insult to me as the future Lady Merritt."

Robin swallowed roughly. "And so it was."

Elizabeth tilted her head and smiled at him. "I do not see it as an insult to me or to your Miss Belfield."

"You do not? "He sighed a little. "You will find yourself among a very select group indeed."

"I would hazard a guess more English women than you might believe secretly admire what you did for Miss Belfield."

"I did nothing, save to cast her name down into the mud." His voice sharpened with reproach. "Do you not fear I shall do the same courtesy for you?"

Elizabeth gazed back at him and allowed her hand to drop away from his face. "No, Lord Merritt, sir. I believe that if I could inspire such devotion, you would cast me up into the stars."

Without speaking, he pulled her roughly against his chest and kissed her with an intensity he dared never loose on the frail Corisande. She responded in kind, wrapping her arms about his ribcage and returning his kiss with happy abandon. He could felt her body quicken with desire and anticipation.

Robin forced himself to take his mouth from hers.

"God's blood," he said hoarsely, "We must stop."

Elizabeth unhooked a final fastening from the muslin under gown. She threw the gown completely off her shoulders despite the chill of the attic.

He let out a ragged breath and stretched out a hand to trace his fingers down the creamy skin between her full breasts. She gasped in pleasure and Robin responded by bending to kiss her neck. He felt her inexperienced hands fumble at the buttons of his waistcoat.

"Upon my soul," came the loud deliberate drawl of Ambrose Westmacott. "Why, here she is!"

Robin pulled his mouth from Elizabeth's quaking body and turned sharply to see his awful cousin standing in the third attic doorway, idly twirling a quizzing glass round and round on a thin black ribbon.

It could not have been worse if Jesus Christ himself had returned to join the search party for Elizabeth. Ambrose's corpulent figure was surrounded on all sides by a nightmarish panel of witnesses: a small contingent of servants, Elizabeth's father, Aunt Pross, his parents and Father Blacknell. Each — save Ambrose who was content to leer at them in mean triumph — wore a paralyzed expression of horror.

Aunt Pross collapsed against Father Blacknell and broke the hideous silence by emitting a mind-bending shriek of dismay.

Robin rose to his feet and pushed a trembling Elizabeth behind him so she might attempt repairs to her velvet bodice.

"Is there no end to the efforts this household will take to frighten and humiliate my future wife?" Robin's voice was low but very angry. He flung his hands up in exasperation at the lot of them.

Suddenly they all began at once: Five voices in strained counterpoint.

"Rakehell!" screeched the reviving Aunt Pross.

"By god, ye' will answer for this, Lord Merritt," thundered Elizabeth's father in his thick Yorkshire brogue. He was a massive moor chieftain of the old sort who used to cleave unfortunate attackers in half with a single stroke of the broad sword.

His own father, a tall willowy man like himself, shook his head in grave disappointment. "God's teeth! What have you done? Thoughtless. Thoughtless."

"Lord forgive us our trespasses," droned Father Blacknell as he tended to Elizabeth's weeping aunt.

"Forgive me," his mother cried in dismay. "I should have known you would not be able to…"

Robin picked up a weather ruined brass tray from on top of a trunk next to him and hurled it at one of the wooden beams. The metal tray cracked against the solid beam with such force that it silenced the voices.

"I want them *out*" he said indicating the servants who were staring at him in spellbound fascination. There would be much to tell at cook's table that night.

His mother immediately turned to the footman and maid, waving them away.

"Elizabeth!" her father commanded furiously, "Go tae ye rooms, ye wretch of a girl. Pross, she'll have nae food nor comfort 'til I bid it."

The aunt gave a martyr's nod and stood up straighter. "Come, Elizabeth," she said, the imperial tone returning.

"I think not." Robin moved to stop Elizabeth as she obediently moved forward, her head bowed in terrible shame, to join her aunt. He laid a gentle hand on her forearm. "Elizabeth will stay until I decide she may retire."

"You Norman cur!" roared Gwayr, surging forward like the Saxon warriors he was descended from. "Who are ye tae speak such?"

"Father!" Elizabeth cried out fearfully. "No!"

Robin stepped forward to meet him, effectively blocking Gwayr's access to his daughter.

"Who am I, sir?" asked Robin crossing his arms indifferently at the oncoming parent. "Lord Merritt, sir — your social better."

"For god's sake, Robin," groaned his father.

Gwayr struck Robin across the face hard with the back of his hand. All three ladies let out cries of dismay. The younger man stumbled back two steps at the force of the blow and then righted himself, blood dripping from the corner of his mouth.

"Very civilized," Robin observed, lifting a hand slowly to wipe away the scarlet rivulet running down his chin.

"You claim to be civilized? You who have so coarsely insulted my only daughter?" Elizabeth's father began to raise his fist again.

"Insult Elizabeth?" Robin's voice was incredulous.

He stretched out a hand to her. Hesitantly and staring at her irate father with wide anxious eyes, she took Robin's hand, allowing him to draw her nearer until he could wrap a protective arm about her trembling shoulders.

"Nay, Gwayr," said Robin quietly. "I worship Elizabeth. I will be proud to call her wife. I will be proud to know she is Lady Merritt of Hawkesmoor. I have shown no dishonor for her today—only the weakness of a man before love."

The room was silent. Gwayr, his chest rising and falling rapidly with the exertion of defending his daughter's virtue, seemed at a loss for words.

In truth neither he nor the Earl's household wanted a break between Elizabeth and Lord Merritt. Surely a sensible father would take some measure of relief that his daughter's arranged marriage would also be a love match. Surely the intimate scene they had witnessed only pointed to the happy prospect of many children to carry on two noble bloodlines. After all, there was no doubt Lord Merritt would marry Elizabeth. It wasn't as if he was spoiling her chances to make a good match elsewhere.

A moment later, Gwayr's hot anger splintered and began to fragment.

The large Englishman raised his arms questioningly as if inviting verbal support from the others present. "'Tis true you both shall be wedded before the month is gone."

Ambrose applauded dryly. The sarcastic sound eradicated the rest of Gwayr's intended words of rapprochement.

"Oh, well spoke, Cos," he drawled. "A pretty speech indeed. I suppose opera whores might even believe it."

Robin stiffened at Ambrose's implication.

"That will be enough out of you, sir," said the Earl in a low warning tone. "Retire at once and have your man pack your things. Your coach will be made ready."

"At your service, uncle." Ambrose bowed with faux courtesy. "I simply call attention to our dear cousin's penchant for making whores out of ladies."

Before the Earl could answer, Robin pulled away from Elizabeth and flung himself at Ambrose. He shoved the plump figure backwards with a growl. Ambrose bleated at the indignity like an injured ewe. Robin rounded on the cowering Westmacott.

"I demand satisfaction." Robin's voice was deadly.

Ambrose's eyes widened in an unattractive combination of fear and surprise.

"You are mad!" he cried. "No one fights a duel for the likes of Corisande Belfield. I refuse to do it!"

"My second will call."

Robin turned on his boot heel.

"Cos, you make too much of a simple jest — a playful parry."

"I believe my husband asked you to retire, sir," said Augusta coolly. She indicated the attic door. "Please remove your person from the other ladies. I may have to suffer your presence because of a family connection but they, surely, are not required to do so."

Ambrose's heavy face lost its panic at her words. A deep wellspring of hate seemed to rise and take light in his eyes. He gazed at her and at Robin beyond with unadorned malevolence.

"Good aunt," he replied with another bow and strode from the attic.

"Father Blacknell, if you would take Pross to her rooms for a restorative," directed the Countess firmly.

"But I ought to be with Elizabeth." Pross looked confused.

"Off you go."

"As you wish." Pross' chin wavered for a moment and then she too swept from the third attic, followed by her anxious priest.

"Elizabeth," Robin was saying. He dropped down to his knees before her. She gazed down at him with shy affection tinged with worry.

"Elizabeth," he held up an open hand, "before your father and mine, I swear my devotion to you. I swear you shall never be less to me than beloved wife and future Countess of Hawkesmoor. Will you forgive me for having so thoughtlessly put you at disadvantage?"

She smiled at the pleasure his words brought her and accepted his hand. "Of course I will."

Robin let out a short breath of relief and dropped a light kiss to the back of her hand. Afraid to let his lips linger on her skin, he drew back to look up at her with an intimate intent that begged her not to worry, promising her a lifetime of passion in the years to come. Elizabeth's large blue eyes regarded him kindly. Then she looked quickly away as color rose to her creamy skin. He gave her fingers a final gentle squeeze.

"And to you, Thomas Gwayr," Robin stood up and faced Elizabeth's father. "I swear Elizabeth shall never have reason to regret accepting me as husband. Can we part this place as friends?"

Gwayr looked down at his feet as he shuffled uneasily from foot to foot. He cleared his throat and pulled at his thick salt and pepper beard.

"Part of what Westmacott says 'tis true; you are a clever, fancy lot, you DuPlessis. Your Norman line's outlasted many a true Yorkshireman." He glanced at his daughter and then at Robin. "You are good wit' words, Richard Robin Francis and my daughter loves you. I say we part as friends but if ye ever do harm to my Elizabeth wit' your fancy ways, I'll make ye wish your people stayed clear of these moors."

"Understood." Robin nodded curtly in agreement and turned to his dumbfounded parents. "I beg your leave, Mother, Father. I find I have a head-ache and would keep to my rooms awhile. Please give my regrets to your guests for my absence at dinner."

The Earl waved him away with a sigh. "I shall join you later for a cognac, Robin." Robin bowed slightly and left the third attic.

Had he known he would never see Elizabeth Gwayr again, he would have looked back over his shoulder just once and memorized every detail of her face.

24

Robin felt mildly ill as he exited the hospital. It wasn't the usual junkie flu he picked up from terminal heroin users. He just felt very tired as if it were possible for him to have an energy leak somewhere in his system. Highly unusual given the recent infusion of healthy blood even if it had been sweetened with cocaine or amphetamines.

He walked back along the high street, weaving unsteadily through students who were gathering near various coffee bars and pubs. A sharp stab of pain struck his right temple followed by the dull throb of a headache that clearly planned on settling in for a while. Where was it coming from? Caroline's headache couldn't have doubled back. The empathic touch never worked that way.

Robin found the car and managed to pull keys from his coat pocket. He wondered if he ought to take a room for the night in Worsdale. He might not be able to drive the narrow country roads in his current state. He was feeling distinctly dizzy now. A small knot of footballers surged out of the pub in front of him, their boisterous shouting telescoped to a high-pitched whine in his head.

Robin let out a small cry and raised his hands to his temples, dropping his car keys in the process. They clattered to the cobbled walk with a dull jingle. It was like someone was applying a vice to the head of his voodoo doll somewhere. White-hot pain ran the length and distance of his neural net, crisscrossing his brain hemispheres, ripping up circuits with extreme aggression.

A moment later he fell against one of the celebrating pub-crawlers who had come over to admire the sport scar.

He was blind.

"Eh! Watch it, mate!" He was good-naturedly shoved out of the way. Others in the group laughed at him and then ignored him, replaying the football match in bleary voices.

Robin swerved around unsteadily, arms outstretched to protect himself.

"Please," he said trying not to let his rising sense of panic cripple his ability to think rationally, "I need help."

Robin felt his legs give way under the assault of another razor hot stab of pain. He sank to his knees on the cobbled walk, his mind spinning out into bright wheeling colors. He needed some sort of doctor but who could be trusted to look at a vampire's chemistry?

He felt rough hands on his shoulders. "Christ, mate. You look dodgy."

"Winnifred T… Turchil," he managed to force out. His throat was beginning to lock up as the brain disconnected itself from his body. It wouldn't send his commands to his nervous system. "Please… I need you to take me to her. Please."

"Bloody hell, man." The voice sounded distant as if his ability to hear was being overwhelmed by the frantic rattle of his brain preparing to go off-line. "You need a proper doctor."

Robin reached up to grasp his Samaritan's wrists. "It… It has to be Winnifred. I have money — take it all. I have a car."

"Where is this Winnifred?" The fading voice was hesitant but the allure of driving the glittering roadster was powerful.

"St. S… Sophia. St. Sophia C… Convent." Robin threw his head back as a cerebral hatchet hacked at his system and succeeded in tearing apart nerve endings. He felt hot blood begin to pour from his ears, his eyes, his nose. He dimly heard the Samaritan yell to someone.

"Caroline," he said, blood dripping from his mouth.

Robin felt his body give way. His brain deactivated and he knew nothing except the dark.

"Caroline!" said Robin's voice urgently. "Caroline!"

She sat up in bed, startled.

But she was alone. There wasn't even one of their collection of dogs sleeping at the foot of her bed.

Caroline brushed a thick strand of hair from her damp forehead. But she had heard his voice so clearly, as if he been in the bed next to her.

An unmistakable sense of dread crawled over her skin. Caroline shivered and crossed her arms protectively over her abdomen. Something was just terribly wrong. The universe was not in sync. Things were out of kilter. She felt it with the same clarity as she had the November morning her mother had gone hunting on her new black and white dappled gelding.

"Bad luck color for a horse. Bad luck horse. No good will come of it," Evan had pronounced dourly when the big gelding had come down off the horse box straight from the yearly sale near Manchester.

Her mother had laughed at his Celtic doom-making and said the horse's bold splashes of color were quite dashing.

She remembered the same odd shivery feeling and how she had left her breakfast to look out the nursery window at all the local fox hunters hacking away from the castle. Her mother was in the first flight with her new dashing black and white gelding. It — the eerie sense of foreboding — had whispered into her head that her mother would never see Hawkesmoor Castle again.

And so it went. The bad luck gelding had taken a ghastly dive at a stone wall near the Roman Copse. As if, one of the Whips had said, the horse had seen something that no one else could see and had tried to compensate for it. Both the dashing black and white gelding and the Countess had gone down in one of the worst accidents in local hunting memory. Her mother was killed instantly. Right hock completely shattered, the horse was destroyed shortly afterwards.

She shuddered and looked around to see if Robin had mysteriously appeared in any of the corners that quiet way he had sometimes. To her sharp disappointment, the room was still empty.

"I know it's highly irregular," said Sister Clare. "St. Sophia is a school."

The Abbess looked up from the books and papers scattered across the ancient refectory table she used as a desk. She regarded the other nun kindly. "We have also been a hospital order for five centuries."

Sister Clare clasped her hands together in a gesture of gratitude. "Thank you for allowing me to care for him. I promise you he will not hurt… interfere… with anyone or their duties."

"Sister Clare, you, of all of us, should know we would not turn him away."

The nun bowed her head, moved by the Abbess' words. She knew it to be true and of no small consequence.

"I am much more concerned," said the Abbess, returning her attention to a pile of recently graded essay papers, "that the energetic youths who brought him here are encouraged to hop it before they discover we have a lot of pretty seventh form girls about the place."

25

"Good morning, my dear," said her father as Caroline came into the kitchen. "You look much improved."

"Dad's right," agreed Peter, lowering his cup of coffee to the long narrow wooden table that had resided in the Hawkesmoor kitchen since Elizabeth, the doomed seventh Countess, had it made for her fussy French chef.

"I feel much better," she replied, reaching for a cup of her own. "That sedative produced some pretty amazing dreams."

"I've had one of those nights. Remember that time I got whacked over the head at the school games day?" Peter asked as he buttered some toast.

Caroline paused to reflect. "You were the only boy at school to get knocked out cold during an egg and spoon race."

Peter bit into his bread. "It's still talked about."

"Probably because you were pummeled by a girl from St. Sophia. The bitter shame follows us even today." The Earl had a swallow of tea before going on. "What are you plans for the day, Caro?"

"And does it involve Robin Dashwood?" Peter interjected quickly. "I'm absolutely dying to talk to him some more. Do you think he'd look at a few of my papers? The one on Lloyd George is pretty good."

"The old goat," observed the Earl with a laugh.

"Robin seems to like students." Caroline shrugged. "Bet he would."

Her father cleared his throat. "About your day?"

"Well, I do want to catch up with Robin." She sipped her tea. "I want to enlist his help in cataloging Hawkesmoor's holdings properly before we bring in the restorers. It'll give us a better idea of what we're up against."

He frowned and stroked Harold's silky black head thoughtfully. "What about the catalogue we already have? The one those wretched insurance people insisted we produce."

"It's all right for the recognized stuff in the staterooms. But Hawkesmoor has a Mt. Everest of objects our generations haven't even seen up in all those attics. Then there are the lesser known portraits in the Gallery and all the slightly less important period furniture, china, silver, etc, etc."

"Dad, he'd be brilliant help," added Peter with real enthusiasm. "His book on Disraeli is considered definitive."

The Earl made a sour face and reached for a piece of buttered toast to give his Labrador, Harold. "What I really want to know is just how you plan to hand Mark his hat. That is what you plan to do, isn't it, Caro?"

Caroline felt her face warm with color. She hadn't realized her interest in Robin Dashwood was so clear.

"Dad," she sighed, "I know how fond you are of Mark, and so am I, but I can't marry him. I can't spend my life passionately discussing bran mash."

"And Mark can go on about it for at least twenty minutes," Peter grinned at her conspiratorially. "I've heard him! You know, he has a deep, perhaps unhealthy interest in the regularity of his horses."

"Thank you, Peter, for another keen insight." The Earl threw his son an exasperated glance. "No wonder we sent you down to Oxford."

"No need to get all tetchy, Dad," Peter countered good-naturedly. "Just because Caro wants to marry Robin Dashwood."

"Peter," Caroline groaned, "put a sock in it, would you?"

The Earl turned to her in something like amazement. "Is this true? You want to marry this man? But you've only known him for a few days at best."

"Well," Caroline said too brightly, "he is British!"

"I shall expect him to ask my permission, of course." The Earl got to his feet, followed immediately by the faithful Labrador, Harold. "Things haven't completely gone to blazes around here."

She beamed at him. "Thanks, Dad."

"A village church affair, I suppose," he mused thoughtfully, more to himself as he headed out for his morning ride. "Big breakfasty thing back here."

"You've got about six weeks before the big breakfasty thing turns into a quick sausage roll after the registrar's office," Peter said once their father had clumped outside in his riding boots.

Caroline swallowed hard. "I know."

Robin was far away. Further even than the purple spires of Cader Idris. He was more than elemental and yet less than nothing. Stranded beyond even the fairylands, hearing many faraway voices in rituals he would never be sophisticated enough to see. It was so lonely here. Well, except for the girl.

She had held his hands for a while and stroked his hair with her cold fingers, tracing a crown, she said, about his head.

"Who are you?" he had asked not unreasonably.

"The Seer of Dulmen," she replied rather to his surprise.

"Anne Catherine Emmerich?" He had been impressed. "You made Gerard Manley Hopkins weep. I remember it clearly at a retreat in England. The Dolorous Passion was read and he wept with grief at your description of Christ's passion."

The frail, sickly girl had just stared at him in mystification.

"I know not of these things. I am here to comfort you. You, like I, can walk on many complex levels through ribbons of time.

You make dark choices, selecting who will live and who shall die, yet you change blood to life as ordinary wine transforms into the blood of the King."

"But I am a vampire," he had said simply. "I prey on humans to survive."

Anne Catherine Emmerich bent over to press her equally cold lips to his forehead.

"Butterfly," she said as she drew away. "Butterfly."

"I'm afraid I don't understand you at all," he had whispered.

"In the last twelve years of my life I ate no food save the Eucharist. You, Richard Robin Francis DuPlessis, who will become both bridge and barrier, will take this gift from me."

"It's all very, very odd," said an inordinately handsome man in a white lab coat. He spoke to Sister Clare who was listening intently while he jotted down some notes.

"Explain," she said moving a step forward to gaze down at Robin as he lay on a hospital bed attached to many wires and electrodes, "if you would be so kind, Dr. Candlethorne."

The doctor glanced up from his writing. "Winnifred … I'm sorry." He smiled briefly at his mistake. "Sister Clare, you say you have known this vampire a long time?"

"Robin and I are old friends." Sister Clare reached out to lay a hand on Robin's cold forehead. She looked like a walking anachronism in the order's full-length black habit and wimple.

"Do you know when he became one of us?" Candlethorne tapped his silver pen restlessly against the clipboard.

"1740s, maybe 1750. I'm not exactly sure. He was indentured to Sir Anthony Fortesque when I met him."

He grimaced. "Poor wretch. I heard Sir Anthony's in Brazil these days. Best chums with the Nazis, I suppose. Tormenting the natives."

"As you may recall, some of our kind were very committed to the Nazi party."

Dr. Candlethorne nodded and shifted his gaze back to his clipboard. "Monsters."

"Tell me what is so odd about Robin's condition." Sister Clare changed the subject. "I assumed he ingested diseased blood and was having an unusually bad reaction to it. "

"You were quite right to call me in. Tainted blood, as you know, is the main focus of my research at Cambridge. More vampires than you might imagine have nasty reactions to the 21st century blood supply." He made another quick note with his silver pen. "Vicious new immune diseases like AIDS, recreational drugs, pollution, toxins in the human diet from pesticides to added hormones have all made our kind very prone to debilitating illness. It's going to be crucial for us to find a way of coping. It'll only take a small epidemic of desperately sick vampires turning up at human hospitals to start the witch hunts."

"Yes, yes," said the sister impatiently. "But why is Robin different?"

"Your friend here," Dr. Candlethorne looked up again from his pages, "has had a major hemorrhagic stroke."

Sister Clare took a step backwards in surprise. "A stroke? Humans have strokes — not our kind — and even if he had sustained an injury, his system should have healed itself by now."

"Oh, his vampire systemic healing process has been working on this problem for some while now." The doctor offered her a reassuring smile. "I ran a line of human coagulants into him. I'm guessing he'll be all right in a few hours."

"Human coagulants?" She stared at him. "Now you have me quite confused."

"Then you're keeping pace with me. I'm pretty confused myself." Candlethorne shrugged with the tired but happy quality of a scientist faced with a deeply baffling mystery. "I examined a few samples of Mr. DuPlessis' hair, skin and blood when I arrived.

The results were typical — just what I'd expect of a vampire. But there's a slide of his current cell structure in that microscope over there. Take a look. I cultured it less than an hour ago."

Sister Clare frowned and swept across the clean tiled floor to the lab microscope. She peered through the lenses, adjusted the focus and looked again.

"I don't understand," she said at last. "It's not vampire."

"And it's not human, either," Candlethorne finished for her. "Yes, it's a hybrid."

"Not possible!" She shook her head and returned to Robin's side, gently pulling back the white hospital sheet. "That's just not possible. You've seen he bears the mark of Morvidus?"

Sister Clare reached out with a finger and softly traced the black teeth marks that marred the skin above Robin's left breast. It was a rare thing. Morvidus, the oldest one of all — some vampire historians said the first vampire of all — always left a black mark to brand his brides forever. It was a scar the chosen few wore with distinction. It was a mark of nobility — the closet thing vampires had to a royal bloodline.

"Mr. DuPlessis must have been one of his last," Candlethorne mused, joining her by Robin's bedside. "1750 was about the time the old one disappeared."

"What's happening to him?" she asked pensively.

"I don't know. I've never seen anything like it before in the many, many decades of my work." He leaned sideways to check a monitor. "My best guess? He absorbed a massive stroke from his last victim. I put out the hypothesis that Mr. DuPlessis' victim, under strain from the attack, had a stroke, and for some reason, DuPlessis took on the human's distress and allowed his superior vampire system to begin making repairs."

Sister Clare glanced at the plain wristwatch on her thin wrist.

"I must see to my geometry class," she said regretfully. "Will you keep an eye on him?"

"Wild horses couldn't drag me away from Mr. DuPlessis," replied Candlethorne emphatically.

"You know we must keep his condition a secret between us." Sister Clare bent over Robin and kissed his forehead. "No other vampires must learn of this."

Dr. Candlethorne nodded in grim agreement. "I have colleagues out there who would take the greatest of pleasure in dissecting your friend like a lab rat."

"And I know any number of vampires who would do literally anything to suppress such information," she said, her jaw tightening at the thought.

"Well, change usually means a shift in someone's power structure."

Sister Clare raised an eyebrow. "Vampire Kings simply hate change."

<h1 style="text-align:center">26</h1>

Robin opened his eyes and found himself gazing at the beautifully chiseled features of a man with a stethoscope. Fear immediately knotted up in his chest, making his lungs ache with the pressure. Where the hell was he? Had he been taken to the Worsdale Hospital? A doctor meant human tests providing odd results, followed by intense human questions. Questions he would have difficulty answering properly.

"Welcome back!" the man said jovially. "How do you feel?"

Robin searched for his voice. "Okay. Thank you," he whispered cautiously.

"Dr. Hugh Candlethorne." The other man patted his shoulder. "You must be petrified. Would it help to learn I met our mutual colleague, Winnifred Turchil, at an archery contest in 1643? She won, by the way."

Robin breathed in relief and felt the anxiety in his chest fade away.

"You've known her longer than I," he said hoarsely.

"Perhaps, but she's so extra fond of you." Candlethorne smiled. "She'll be in later. Her name's Sister Clare these days."

"I'm glad she survived here." Robin said gratefully. "I was always worried about her."

"Apparently Winnifred existed entirely on small drinks from the convent farm animals until the advent of modern blood storage. A remarkable story, really."

"I… I was in Worsdale," he remembered suddenly. "I went blind."

"You had a very bad reaction to your last food choice." The doctor's smooth voice was very reassuring. Hypnotic even. Robin half closed his eyes. "It's getting more common these days. Rest for a bit and then you can actually go home."

Robin felt sleep demanding his surrender. He closed his eyes all the way and began to drift down into peaceful darkness.

"It won't be a problem anymore," he heard himself whisper to the kind vampire doctor. "She told me I don't have to drink blood."

Robin had no idea what the bloody hell he meant and wondered what Dr. Candlethorne would make of his tired rambling.

"You look grieved, Sister Clare," said Mother Abbess, an imposing figure in ecclesiastical black. She had come across the other nun sitting on a bench near the school chapel, lost in thought.

"I was so happy here, serving God," Sister Clare said. "I do not wish to be in the dark, separated from Him."

Mother Abbess laid a gentle hand on Sister Clare's head, a blessing. "Remember that Jesus said *Nothing can snatch you from my hand.*"

"Yes," Sister Clare swallowed hard.

"So," the Abbess took a dignified seat on the bench, "I gather you are leaving us?"

Sister Clare nodded in sadness. "Things have changed for my … kind. Many may die unless I go."

"No one within these walls has served God as long as you, Sister Clare. And you have served well with humility and grace."

"You are my family," she replied with a break in her voice.

Mother Abbess regarded her with great affection. "This is your home, Sister Clare — always — but you have a new mission field now. Go and serve God."

"Hello, Beryl!" Caroline came into what was once the old servant dining room. It now served as an office in which everything from castle tourist days to the Earl's sheep breeding schemes were managed.

Beryl looked up from paperwork she had spread before her on the long wooden table. She beamed at Caroline. "So? Where's Himself?"

"Dad's out walking sheep with George." Caroline peered down at Beryl's pages. "Wow. We spent that much on silver polish last month?"

The ever-efficient manager of many jobs at Hawkesmoor gave her a funny look. "Peter's packed himself back to Oxford. He decided to drive this time and took his Renault. He's dropped Hannah at St. Sophia."

Hannah, like many well-bred modern girls, went away to board at a good local school and came home at the weekend. Caroline had been a St. Sophia's girl, too. The school was part of a very old and beautiful 14th Century Abbey run by dedicated sisters who also maintained a small but highly regarded hospital order.

"*Help, Health and Happiness,*" Caroline said, quoting one of St. Sophia's school mottos. She plunked down a file on the wooden table. "The minutes from Dad's sheep club. Can you have them transcribed?"

Beryl nodded. "It'll be the highlight of my day. And just so you're up to speed: security off on their hourly patrol, village staff busy cleaning and polishing — it's brass and silver day again, you know."

"Again?" Caroline sighed. "Where does the time go?"

"Right, then. Let's start again. So?" said Beryl pointedly with a wide expectant grin.

"So?" Caroline raised her eyebrows in puzzlement.

"So! Peter told me Professor Robin Dashwood turned up yesterday!" Beryl exclaimed. "Peter said it had all been a big misunderstanding by the NYPD. Peter said I ought to start looking for just the right spring dress."

"Peter says a lot when he feels like it," Caroline replied dryly. "But I'll be happy to let you know about the dress if and when Robin ever asks me to marry him."

"Of course he will!" Beryl waved a hand at her. "Why else would Professor Dashwood come all the way to Northern England? He must be mad about you. I think it's terribly romantic."

"You read too many novels, Beryl."

The staffer howled. "Oh, really? And I suppose you always flit about in a frothy little dress?"

Caroline gave her frail concoction of silk and velvet a guilty glance. She had the notion that if Robin fancied sophisticated New York women, she'd try to bring some fashion to Hawkesmoor. A pity that the Ana Sui dress didn't seem quite up to the hale and hearty climate of Northern England. Caroline had the mildly disconcerting notion that one good stiff blast of wind would simply shear the dress into tatters.

"You look like a lovely dewdrop fairy." Beryl added helpfully.

Since dewdrop fairy existed nowhere near chic, Caroline headed up to find a sensible pair of trousers. She carefully gathered up the wispy hem of her New York dress and began the athletic process of climbing over the intricate system of tall stools and chicken wire her father had placed lengthwise across the back stairs to keep puppies from coming up. One had to be a savvy combination of Olympic gymnast and mountaineer to successfully navigate the complicated vortex of stool legs and wire. The Earl always insisted that nice, sensible ready-made dog gates were too pricey and satisfactory ones could be made with things around the property. She always suspected he just enjoyed creating masterpieces of nuisance as a passive-aggressive way of getting his own back when they wouldn't let him to shoot at tourist coaches.

Caroline winced midway, hearing a muffled tear in the silk georgette — almost as if the milquetoast fabric had let out a soft cry of *oww*. The expensive boutique dress had failed to meet the standard required of clothes needed to clear her father's current puppy barrier.

Funny, she thought as she pushed over the remaining stool to the relative safety of a clear step. The back stairs had been built as a convenience for servants who needed to zip up and down on errands for their betters.

Hawkesmoor itself was quiet and contented as she clomped up the rest of the stairs. It had never been a scary sort of castle. Even Hawkesmoor's most famous ghost, The Gray Lady, was hardly frightening. She kept her visits few and far between, and never attempted to scare anyone.

Well, Caroline corrected herself as she crossed the landing onto their private floor, there had been Rosie Dunway, the castle needlewoman on the night the unlucky seventh Lord Merritt had disappeared. The sixth Countess, Augusta, who had always kept voluminous notes on ordinary life at Hawkesmoor, had written about her.

Until her dying day, Rosie Dunway had claimed to anyone who would listen that she knew exactly what had happened to the missing Lord Merritt. She said she had wandered away from the frantic, hot servant quarters that night to get some air and had come across the terrifying sight of Lord Merritt being devoured in the arms of some hideous ghoul.

Since the seamstress also had a reputation for being over-fond of cooking sherry, no one, including the sixth Countess, had given Rosie's tale much credence.

How she and Peter had relished that diary entry in Augusta's clear firm hand. As children, they had stayed up long summer nights, wandering the castle grounds outfitted with flashlights and candy bars. They were positive that they'd eventually get a spectral glimpse of Lord Merritt's frightful fate in the bloodstained claws of the ghoul.

Lord Merritt's ghoul never did present itself. Caroline laid her hand over her abdomen, where she assumed the baby might be holding court. She had never really thought about it before but it must have been terribly difficult for Augusta to record Rosie Dunway's story for her descendants to read. While the seventh Lord Merritt was to them simply an elegant figure in a rather unimportant painting, he had been her flesh and blood son. Rosie's horrid tales of toothy ghouls must have been shattering to hear in the wake of his mysterious disappearance.

Third attic flashed into her head like a polite cough reminding her to do something. The third attic is very important for Robin. She remembered that from the dream she'd had.

"Let's go have a look," Caroline announced to the silent hallway and turned on her heel to return to the staircase. "Wish I had a few of those candy bars right now."

"He knows nothing," Dr. Candlethorne said as Sister Clare sat studying his file of notes. "But he wants a cup of coffee. He's far from stupid, Sister. He knows right well something has shifted."

"If only we knew what to tell him," she replied, still scanning the page. "You write here that Robin demonstrated telekinesis?"

"He lifted a book off a table surface for a moment with the power of his mind. It was very brief and not very controlled but he seemed surprised — not one of his usual tricks."

"Robin never was a strong vampire," she said thoughtfully. "Actually, his great strengths lay in what remained of his humanness: courage, intelligence and a real sense of kindness. Your notes seem to indicate that despite his new hybrid state,

Robin has kept his vampire characteristics and indeed, he's added to them."

Candlethorne raised his eyebrows and nodded. "If he can develop telekinesis, he can develop mental weaponry and take on any of the vampire kings."

She closed the file cover. "Robin doesn't want to be a king. He never did. It's part of his charm. Despite the mark of Morvidus, kings and kingmakers have left him alone."

"They'll track him down and cut him up for firewood if they find out what's happened," the doctor said grimly. "How many of our kind yearn for a new direction? A return, if you will, to a more human-like state? If word gets out one of our kind has evolved — and I use that word very pointedly — evolved into a sort of superhuman vampire, utter chaos is going to ensue."

"There has to be a meaning to all this." Sister Clare shook her head in annoyance that an answer wasn't immediately presenting itself. "I cannot believe this is simply a random event."

"Surely this isn't your vocation speaking?" Candlethorne grinned.

She ignored him. "Research. Hugh, do you think Gabriel is safe?"

The grin faded. "I don't think any vampire beyond these abbey walls is safe and Sister Clare — Winnifred — we both go down with Robin if they come after him. You know that?"

"I do." Clare stood up and lifted the black nun's wimple from her head. "Hugh, will you join with me? Whatever change Robin DuPlessis is to bring to our kind must be allowed to take place."

"I'll go to London and start looking for any historical references." Hugh stood up as well. "Gabriel's been expecting me to do some background work on one of my projects anyway. You'll go with him?"

"Yes. Robin has just gained a minder." She put the wimple on the desk. "He won't like it but he'll get used to the idea."

"From nun to bodyguard," Candlethorne sighed. "It's a funny old life."

27

The third attic was part of an interlocking series of rooms located at the very top of the castle's central 16th century structure. Unlike many large houses, where an army of servants had been billeted in the uppermost rooms, Hawkesmoor's attics had been used for storage since the new structure was completed in 1567. Hawkesmoor's servant class had been housed down below ground, in the castle's vast former armaments and supply areas.

Caroline thought of Rosie Dunway as she pushed open the heavy oak door. The sixth Countess had not seen fit to describe Rosie in any way, except to note that the woman's fitness for duty notably deteriorated after the incident with the so-called ghoul. Caroline imagined the needlewoman was probably a cranky old crone, mean-spirited enough to say anything for a bit of attention.

She wondered what Rosie's life must have been like in her few hours away from embroidering household linens and mending mountains of clothes. A few stolen glasses of wine and a fitful nap on a small hard iron bed. Probably in a horridly cold and claustrophobic closet of a room she shared with another servant woman. Caroline switched on the light. Small wonder that after several strong cups of demon drink, Rosie could eagerly imagine her master's son being torn apart by vengeful ghouls.

A few naked light bulbs hung on cobwebbed cords from the attic ceiling. In the 1970s her Grandfather had finally installed electrical lighting in all portions of the main house, but the work done to the attics had been quick and cursory at best. She wouldn't even be surprised if the bulbs hanging from the rusty metal sockets were the original items.

The crude lighting was somewhat augmented by the last of the afternoon light coming through a rather nice octagonal leaded glass window. Caroline scanned the large room and noted that it looked much like all the other attics full of old trunks, boxes and mysterious pieces of furniture long shrouded in grimy drop cloths.

"God only knows what's up here," said Caroline aloud. She had never been through the third attic. In her childhood — after an unfortunate incident involving Peter, a large navel orange and a rather valuable musical score of the aria "Ev'ry joy that wisdom knows," signed *In deepest gratitude, your most humble servant, George Frederic Handel* — the attics had been kept strictly locked by her grandparents' ferocious head butler, Wilson.

"God only knows why I'm up here," she added, at a loss as what exactly she ought to do with her whim to visit the attic in the first place.

Caroline listened to a light afternoon rain as it gently pattered against the leaded pane of the window. Why did the dream think there was anything of interest for Robin Dashwood in an attic? She allowed her gaze to follow the light shaft from the window to a grouping of some seriously old leather and brass trunks.

He was an historian. Maybe there were some intriguing items — Roman coins or Egyptian tomb masks locked away somewhere. She wondered idly if her dream heralded a new phase of her life in which she would be some kind of archeological psychic, and then laughed out loud at the ridiculous notion. There were sheep wandering her father's fields with more psychic ability.

Caroline crossed the floor and knelt at the base of one of the dust-smeared trunks to assess how difficult the fastenings would be to open. They seemed to be old but fairly simple brass latches. She shivered. The attic suddenly seemed very cold, as if a not inconsiderable draft had torn through some ill-fitting window joint.

She brushed away dirt from a brass plate on the decaying leather lid.

"E.J.G." Caroline read aloud from the engraved lettering. "E.J.G?"

She heard the whisper like the clatter of dry leaves shuffled by a capricious breeze and even then, Caroline would never be sure she really heard a voice at all. Perhaps it just came to her as wind rattled through the grove of apple trees outside: *Elizabeth Jane Gwayr.*

Robin leaned against one of St. Sophia's stone pillars and gazed out at playing fields beyond the small hospital annex. A rugged band of schoolgirls was darting and dodging across the grass, wielding hockey sticks in a frenzy despite the drizzle. He liked their cries of excitement and carefree laughter as a lively counterpoint to the constant tapping of the rain.

He took a long drag from the cigarette, his first taste of tobacco since 1750, and closed his eyes, letting the soothing rainwater course down over his features.

"Richard Robin Francis, Lord Merritt of Hawkesmoor Castle," came a familiar woman's voice near him.

Robin opened his eyes. Winnifred Turchil, not in heavy black habit as he expected, stood next to him. She looked much the same as he remembered her, save the shoulder-length hair and modern clothes.

He held out his free hand to her and saw that it was shaking.

"Sorry," he said, clenching his trembling fingers together and lowering his arm. "I'm a bit of a wreck these days. Good afternoon, old friend."

Winnifred's intelligent face regarded him in real affection. She came closer, took his clenched hand in hers and pressed it to her cheek.

"Dear Winnifred," Robin murmured thinly. He pulled her into his arms and rested the side of his face against her silky dark hair, inhaling the orange blossom fragrance of the perfume she had always worn. "I've so missed you all these years."

"As I have missed you." She stroked his back in the comforting way he remembered.

"You're dripping wet, Lord Merritt."

He pulled away with an embarrassed laugh. "Not bright enough to come in out of the rain, I'm afraid."

"You always liked rain." Winnifred reached out to lay a cool palm against his wet cheekbone. "Dear Robin. Thank you for all your long and interesting letters from New York. I drove our postman mad asking if another one had arrived."

Robin drew his head back from her and took a final drag from the nearly spent cigarette.

"You might have answered one," he said with a catch in his voice. "At least one to let me know you were all right. I worried."

"And still you wrote every week."

He threw the cigarette butt down to the wet gravel and ground it out impatiently with his shoe.

"Candlethorne found me cigarettes. I'd forgotten how much I liked tobacco and these modern ones are so bloody smooth in comparison to…" Robin stopped and walked a few anxious paces beyond the covered walk.

He turned back suddenly. "What the hell is happening to me, Winnifred? I can drink coffee. I ate a tea biscuit. I don't hear blood song but I can become shade, I can—"

"Robin, you really mustn't panic."

"Just what am I?" he asked in real horror. "Has it happened before — or am I just some kind of freak? Oh, god," Robin ran a hand through his hair as heavier rain began to hammer down in sheets around him, "a freak among freaks."

Winnifred stepped out from the sheltering stonework. "Whatever is happening to your body chemistry has only made you stronger."

Robin shook his head miserably. "You don't understand. I have spent three hundred years learning to live as this revenant thing!" He struck his chest with a fist. "Now I belong to neither our kind nor to the humans?"

He slowly dropped to his knees in the dirt and gravel of the hospital's tiny courtyard. "Winnifred," he said in a dazed tone, "she is all I ever wanted. I just wanted to be with her through the days of her life. Is that asking so much after so long?"

"You're in love with a human?" Winnifred asked, disappointed. "Robin, you know that is never wise."

Robin lifted his head to stare at her, his large green eyes narrowing in anger. "Ask your human God just why he hates our kind so much. Ask your God why I, Richard Robin Francis DuPlessis, have only the right to bitterness."

"Revenants bring ill fortune to the humans they toy with," Winnifred said with a terrible certainty. "It is selfish of you to want this girl. You know that."

"I love Caroline," he replied simply.

Winnifred cocked her head to the side and thought for a moment. "You don't mean Lady Caroline DeBarry of Hawkesmoor Castle, do you?"

Robin smiled at the sound of her name. He felt very dizzy, as if the coffee and cigarettes had charged up his system like champagne used to. Champagne — perhaps he could drink champagne again. He dropped his head back, feeling the cold rain dripping onto his eyelids and running down his face.

"Robin," said his old friend, "are you feeling all right?"

He outstretched his arms with the palms up.

"You are where the light is poor," Robin murmured as a picture of Caroline began to form in his head like a complex graphic on a slow computer. "The light is gray."

"Robin!" He heard Winnifred warn him, "Please, don't!"

Caroline let out an awed breath as she shook out another gown from the creamy tissue paper it had been beautifully wrapped in.

The first trunk and two others with the same E.J.G. initials on the brass plaques were filled with a collection of exquisite ladies' clothes from the mid-18th century. Caroline could only hazard a guess that the trunks represented what had been Elizabeth Gwayr's trousseau when she came to Hawkesmoor imagining she would shortly marry the seventh Lord Merritt.

Odd that they had been put away so decidedly. It was obvious the gowns had been worn very little if at all. Some still had the wrappings from the London and Paris houses where they had been painstakingly assembled for the bride of Lord Merritt. The incredible expense alone would seem to justify their use even if her first bridegroom had vanished under mysterious circumstances.

The gown she held between her hands was marked by a ribbon that read *For Miss Gwayr's ceremony of marriage*. It was absolutely breathtaking. A day gown of celadon green in yards and yards of heavy satin with lavish pale peach trimmings dusted with pearls. A wedding dress for a lovely young girl hoping — Caroline corrected herself, *expecting* — to find happiness in her new life as Lady Merritt.

Elizabeth might have been unable to bear the thought of wearing it to wed Lord Merritt's much more ordinary cousin. Caroline wrinkled her nose, thinking of Ambrose Westmacott's ill-tempered looking portrait in the gallery. He had such an unsavory face, puffy from excess and centered by small suspicious eyes that looked down upon the viewer with derision.

Caroline sat down to digest her vast find. As soon as she caught her breath, she'd dash downstairs to let everyone know what she'd discovered. Her father would be over the moon — he adored anything to do with Hawkesmoor's past. The wardrobe was going to be of tremendous historical interest. Besides the extraordinary dresses, there were underclothes, shoes, hats and gloves to complement any costume change the new Lady Merritt might have in mind.

She bent forward to examine one of the more intriguing items: an elaborately carved wooden chest encrusted with ivory and mother of pearl. The chest didn't seem to have a visible way to be opened and Caroline found herself sighing with exhaustion. The excitement of the trunks' contents combined with the extreme care needed while gingerly unpacking them had taken a toll on her taxed system.

"Lord Merritt," Caroline said with real regret to the empty attic, "if you can hear me. I just hope you were there to meet Elizabeth after he shoved her down the stairs."

Suddenly, unbelievably, in front of her, Robin Dashwood simply appeared. He was on his knees, arms outstretched and dripping wet.

Robin lowered his arms, staring back at her with about the same level of disbelief as she. Water was already beginning to pool on the floor from the sodden cuffs of his white shirt.

"Caroline," he said, his voice hoarse with wonder.

She felt her body weave slightly. Somehow there would be a perfectly rational answer to how and why Robin Dashwood had magical powers. At the moment nothing very scientific was presenting itself.

"This can't be real."

Robin gave her a slightly giddy smile and shrugged. He started to laugh.

"And what is so bloody funny?" Caroline demanded just before a laugh of her own escaped to join his.

"Life, my love, life," he replied, shaking his head at the apparent nonsense of it all.

"Oh, very easy for you to say!" She pulled up one of the annoying Anna Sui straps. "You could have beamed in and startled Dad at his ablutions."

Robin just looked at her and laughed again. Caroline found herself giggling too, despite the fact that she was sure she was having some sort of psychiatric episode. The kind that would be whispered about for years to come at local Women's Institute meetings.

One their laughter had died down, he eyed the torn dewdrop fairy frock. "What a very pretty dress," he said, raising an eyebrow. "Though it seems to be completely lacking a right panel."

It was enough to start them both off again. Robin pulled Caroline into his arms. She buried her face in the damp folds of his shirt, her shoulders shaking with laughter.

"You know you are absolutely soaked," Caroline commented once she'd caught her second breath.

He turned her slightly so he could drop a kiss on her forehead.

Robin ran his right hand down the side of her face and slipped his long fingers into the soft reddish blonde hair at the nape of her neck. "Will you do me the very great honor of marrying me?"

"Now I know this is a symptom," Caroline said gazing up at him wistfully. "I've bumped my head again, haven't I? You're really some dream symbol, aren't you — masquerading as Robin?"

He half-smiled at her baffled tone and let out a short sigh. "No, Caroline. I'm really here. I'll explain it all to you one day."

She drew back and refocused on him. She felt she had to take in his presence again for the first time.

"But you just appeared out of thin air. I saw you materialize in an empty space. How can you explain that? So I know this can't really be happening."

He met her anxious eyes calmly and held out a hand. "I am flesh and blood, Caroline. Touch me."

She reached out and took his hand. It was definitely real. She could feel the delicate bones under the cool skin.

"Does it matter how I got here?" Robin asked. "I'm here."

"I'm glad of that," she admitted, glancing away as she felt the slight blush peculiar to shy British girls rise to her face.

"Do you love me, Caroline DeBarry?" The question was quiet.

For a long moment, she could not find her vocal chords to speak. No one had ever asked her that question before.

"Because if you don't," he continued with a slight edge to his voice, as if her silence had caused him some disappointment, "I have no reason to stay."

Caroline's head spun in a frustrating collage of inner voices. Some urged to find her tongue, some told her to beware of men who demonstrated strange abilities, others cried out that the entire situation was just a figment of her imagination, and old hurtful ones reminded her she was just a rather plain girl who had just enough inherited social stature to attract the wrong sort of men.

"I see," Robin said very quietly. "I beg to be allowed to take back my ill-advised declaration from yesterday. I would not burden you with it."

"No!" she blurted, as her voice finally emerged. "I won't give those words back. They mean everything — to me."

He raised his palms in an entreating gesture that begged her to release him from an untenable position.

Caroline threw her arms around his neck with a kind of reckless abandon that before she had only been able to express through the dangerous rigors of equestrian sport.

"I love you!" She kissed his cheek several times. "Of course I love you. How could I not love you, Robin Dashwood?"

Caroline tightened her embrace, wrapping her arms down around his chest. She shivered with dizzy happiness at his rapid breath. She felt his intense sexual interest as a fierce electrical aura that was absorbing her into its particle beam.

It was an amazing thing to be wanted, desired so much by someone. She wondered at the pure force, the liberating ruthlessness of it. None of her previous sexual experiences had ever led her to believe a man could want to physically possess her in the way Robin did.

Robin let out a murmur deep in his throat as he slid his hands up her back. She felt his long fingers sweep over the thin fabric of the dress until they found the zipper.

He loosened it in one downward movement and pushed her gently away so he could look at her. Caroline's throat ached at the affection she read in his green eyes. Robin reached out to grasp the thin straps in either hand. He lightly pulled open the ruined Anna Sui dress so it fell off her shoulders and gathered in folds of silk about her waist.

Caroline swallowed roughly. It was hard for her to be studied in such a stark way. She lowered her chin and glanced away from him.

He laid a hand against her face and forced her chin to rise where she could see him.

"You are," Robin said to her astonishment, "almost too beautiful, Caroline. Your strength… your tantalizing flaws… your humanness."

He bent forward, kissing her deeply while lowering them both to the ancient attic floorboards.

A wondrous spider web of intoxicated feelings and electric nerve endings settled about her as Robin made love to her. It created a barrier against the outside world. She was oblivious to how much time passed between them.

How different a lover Robin was from what she could bear to remember of previous interludes. Ordinary to extraordinary.

She laughed at the thought. Robin paused and lifted his head from her neck.

"How are you, my love?" he asked kindly.

"Wonderful," she whispered. "Are you positive you aren't just some lovely dream?"

Robin smiled and began to move again inside her with exquisite slowness. "I might well ask the same of you one day."

28

Robin threw the sleeping Caroline an affectionate smile as he pulled himself up to a sitting position. What a passionate creature she was under all the English schoolgirl insecurities. Rather like Corisande once uncertainty and fear had been stripped away, but there was even greater physical pleasure with Caroline because — Robin smiled at the thought — because he loved her madly in a way that was unique in his experience.

"Caroline," Robin said to nudge her awake. "Caroline, love."

She stirred with a groan and opened her eyes slowly.

"I ought to go back to my room at the inn," he said as he slipped an arm into a sleeve of his now dry shirt. "Your family will be searching high and low for you by now. I genuinely doubt the Earl will welcome the notion I arrived unannounced to bed his favorite daughter behind his back."

"I *did* tell you I *would* marry you, didn't I?" Caroline asked in a tired voice. She looked very pale and unwell in the bad light. Dark circles that had recently formed under her eyes gave her a haunted quality. "I did say yes, didn't I? Because I will. I will marry you."

"You did, love. I must arrange to speak with your father next," Robin replied and looked back at her in concern. "Caroline, are you all right?"

She closed her eyes as she massaged her right temple. "I haven't been feeling very well lately. Still knackered from America, I think."

"I should have shown more restraint. You're still recovering." He returned to lay a worried hand on her forehead. "My god, Caroline, you're burning with fever."

"I'll be all right in a little minute." Caroline opened her eyes again.

Robin noted the fever-dulled quality in them with alarm, and began to put her thin little silk dress back to some semblance of respectable order.

"We've got to get you out of this damnable attic and into a warm bed," he said, slipping up the straps of her dress. "Let me help you sit up."

"What about the unamused parental?" she asked faintly, as Robin put his forearm about her shoulders and eased her forward.

"I've been in worse spots," Robin murmured, much more interested in getting her downstairs quickly. "Here, put your arm around my neck."

"Did I tell you I would marry you?" she repeated with a dazed smile. "You're wonderful! No one's ever carried me off to safety before."

"Try to let yourself rest, Caroline." Robin gathered her up in his arms and rose to his full height.

It was just the state of his current fortunes to descend the Hawkesmoor staircase with a very ill Caroline and confront the glowering face of Mark Halsey.

"Just what in god's name do you think you're doing?" Mark demanded hotly as he took in the sight of Caroline crumpled against Robin's chest clad only in a thin ravaged looking dress.

"Caroline has taken ill," Robin informed him briskly. "Could you point me in the direction of her room?"

Mark practically growled as he stepped towards them. "I'll take her. Give her to me."

"I don't think so," said Robin dangerously.

"Caroline and I appreciate your concern but we can manage very well without you." Halsey raised an arm to begin shifting her over. "Come on, Caro. I've got you now, darling."

"Mark," Caroline put in irritably, "get the bloody hell out of Robin's way. I'm going to be terribly sick in a moment."

The blond jump rider stared at her, stunned. "But, Caro — I ought to be the one who—"

"Good lord!" boomed a voice of concern. Robin glanced up to see the Earl hurrying down the hallway. "What's wrong with Caroline? Dashwood, you look like a good man in a crisis. What has happened?"

"Sir, she's very feverish and nauseated. If I can get her to her bed, I think you ought to ring for the doctor." Robin ignored Mark, focusing his entire attention on the approaching Earl.

"Right! Caro's third door on the left. If it is of any assistance, all of our private rooms are here in the west wing." Her father pointed down the wide hall. "I'll ring Peaches now. It's about time to get to the bottom of this. Caro hasn't been herself for weeks."

"Perhaps I should take Caroline," interjected Mark quickly as Robin began to move away.

"Don't be a bloody fool, man," replied the Earl. "Go home. I'll ring you later if there's news."

"But…" Mark began, his face incredulous.

Caroline's father waved him away. "On your way out, get Mrs. Gates to put the kettle on, would you?"

"Sir," Mark muttered resentfully.

"What do you mean he's *gone*?" came Hugh Candlethorne's incredulous voice over the cell phone.

"I told you," sighed Winnifred from her small room in St. Sophia, "Robin focused on where he wanted to go and off he went."

"You mean he can manage teleportation?" Hugh sounded awed. "He really has come a long way for a weak vampire."

""I have an idea where he might have gone."

"Let's hope you find him before any other vampires hear of his evolution."

"You are really committed to the thesis that it's an evolutionary step for our kind."

"It has to be," he replied with the fervent belief of a scientist determined to prove a treasured concept.

Winnifred leaned back in her desk chair. "I'll just stay at a discreet distance and keep a look out."

"Be careful." Hugh didn't seem convinced. "Check in with me daily. If your Robin's rattled, he may do something foolish and get us all in quicksand."

"Robin's not rattled. He's in love with a human."

"Oh, brilliant!" Hugh said flatly. "This reminds me of the day I bought a first class ticket on the Lusitania. Well, I'm back to the stacks, checking out all vampires with the Morvidus brand first. Maybe there's a precedent way back in time."

29

“Come in and partake of an adult beverage,” said the Earl pleasantly as Robin quietly knocked on his half-opened door. “Sherry?”

Robin realized with a bit of a start that the idea of a glass of sherry was enormously appealing. He actually longed for a sherry. Indeed, he was quite hungry too, and wondered if he might be given a bit of dinner as well.

“A sherry would be well received,” he admitted, stepping inside and glancing about a little warily.

The Earl of Hawkesmoor stood pouring the amber-colored fluid into a couple of small-stemmed glasses. He looked up and took in the black sweater and American Levis borrowed from the household.

“I see you found something of Peter’s you could bear to be seen in.”

Robin smiled as he let his gaze trace the gentle Edwardian sprawl of the Earl’s study. Now it was all comfortable, overstuffed chairs, threadbare Persian carpets, hunting accouterment and dog-eared copies of *Horse and Hound*. Robin felt his throat tighten as memories laid claim to his thoughts. Once it had been a private music room.

Yorkshire, 1748

His nimble fingers deftly coursed over both of the harpsichord's keyboards as he neared the end of Couperin's little 1717 piece, *Les Barricades Mysterieuses.*

"Excellent, sir!" called out Oliver happily. "You have it to a fare thee well."

Robin set down the last chord and pulled his hands away from the intricately painted instrument. He laughed out loud at the sheer pleasure of it.

"Well done, Robin!" echoed his mother, rising to her feet to applaud in genuine excitement. "I do not think you have ever learned a piece so quickly before."

He shrugged modestly. "'Tis a lovely effort from the composer. It would make even the clumsy seem inspired."

"Sir, I doubt I could manage it half as well," said Oliver as he removed the heavily engraved music pages from the keyboard and began to sift through a small collection of other works, looking for his next assignment. "But, if we are to win the Duchess of Mexborough's wager we must practice. Her salon is only a fortnight away."

"Odd's fish," the Countess sighed, "I will never win more applause than that marvel of a singer from Master Handel's company. Georgianna has set a very unfair task."

"Your own fault for losing to her at cards, Mother," said Robin with a fond glance in her direction. "You ought to know better than to try to best Aunt Georgianna at Faro."

Augusta threw him back a sour expression. "As if you are pained by the very idea of spending an evening surrounded by members of Handel's opera company."

He laughed again. "I admit I have long wished to make the acquaintance of the beautiful Miss Belfield."

"Careful, sir," interjected Oliver as he selected a sheet of music and placed it on the stand. "I hear Miss Belfield is very reluctant to make the acquaintance of young gentlemen. She is truly dedicated to the opera."

"I am sure she will be right pleased to make my acquaintance," Robin grinned at them both. "After all, my mother will have just put her voice to shame in the musical portion of the evening. Miss Belfield will, without doubt, be pondering the wisdom of proceeding with her career."

"A daydream, I fear," replied Augusta wistfully.

"Especially with your regrettable tendency to swoop notes in your higher range, my lady," murmured Oliver, tapping the heavy cream-colored parchment with his forefinger. "Let us begin with this small aria from Purcell."

Robin thought he almost could hear Oliver's beautifully manicured finger rapping the stiff parchment as memory faded.

It was the Earl's boot heels on the wood floor as he stepped off the ancient Persian rug to deliver the sherry.

"You look almost as pale as Caro," he commented, as Robin accepted the glass gratefully. "Collapse into a chair and keep me company if you would. Hate these bloody medical emergencies."

"Yes," murmured Robin, following the tweedy back of his host to the rather ugly green marble fireplace he didn't remember from his time. It seemed as good and right a time as any, just now, to ask if he might have Caroline's hand.

He lowered himself into a dark oxblood leather chair and took an initial sip of the sherry. The warm rich flavor reverberated in his senses and almost brought tears to his eyes. He had thought never to know the singular pleasure of sipping human wine again.

Caroline's father caught Robin staring at the green marble. He smiled wryly.

"Hideous, isn't it?" He found a seat opposite. "That old scoundrel the seventh Earl had it put in. Apparently he went on a wild and ill-considered campaign to leave his mark on the castle."

Yes, thought Robin sadly, of course. My music room. He had to destroy it.

"He wasn't bred for the job, you see," added the current Earl. "He came to it unexpectedly."

"The missing Lord Merritt? Yes. Caroline told me about him."

"He caused no end of trouble for everyone I can tell you." He sipped his own sherry. "Probably nothing the poor devil could do. Little doubt now that Ambrose Westmacott had him murdered or shanghaied to a slave ship in the Far East."

"Oh?" Robin leaned forward in interest.

"Westmacott had all sorts of seedy connections. He was a foul man, fond of gambling and drink. Lucky we have a castle left at all — despite the entailments."

"So you think it's possible this Ambrose sold his own cousin to a merchant vessel?" Robin asked. It was almost amusing to hear the logical explanation of his disappearance because — he suppressed a shudder — because they could not even imagine what had really happened that night.

"Ambrose was deeply in debt and needed money badly. It's not difficult to imagine he arranged a method of clearing the path to a rich Earldom," Caroline's father said with a small regretful shake of his head. "I imagine for a couple of gold coins, Ambrose hired some London thugs to do the job."

"But wasn't Lord Merritt a skilled swordsman?" Robin cleared his throat in order to choose his words more carefully.

"I mean Caroline told me Lord Merritt had been a skilled swordsman. He couldn't have been easy to overpower."

"In a direct attack, no. Ambrose wouldn't have been so sporting. He'd have murdered by stealth."

There followed a silence in which the older man toyed with the rim of his sherry glass thoughtfully. Finally, he spoke again but it wasn't about the mysterious disappearance of an 18th century nobleman.

"My Caro seems awfully keen about you, Mr. Dashwood," he said. "I'd be remiss as a father if I didn't ask what your intentions were. Despite her poise, Caro possesses a sensitive and compassionate spirit. She could be hurt very badly, you know."

Robin met the Earl's gray eyes squarely. "I ask your permission for Caroline's hand, sir," he said simply by way of reply. "She has given me reason to feel I would make her an acceptable husband."

The Earl of Hawkesmoor stared back at him for a long moment. Then he took a quick sip of sherry and seemed about to enter his views on the subject when the door to the study swung open.

"Ah, there you are," said Dr. Peaches. "Good. I've completed my examination of Lady Caroline, my Lord."

They both stood up anxiously as the elderly surgeon made his way across the study. He glanced at Robin with some interest and then refocused on the Earl.

"Your Lordship," he said. "Your daughter is resting comfortably."

"That's all very well," the Earl frowned at the older man, "but what the hell is wrong with her? She's not been right for days."

Dr. Peaches looked at Robin again. "Might I have a word in private, my Lord?"

The Earl waved a dismissive hand at Peaches. "You may speak freely in front of this young man."

"Your Lordship," the doctor demurred, "Medical confidentiality protocol suggests otherwise."

"None of that modern prattle. Spit it out, man!"

Peaches cleared his throat sharply as if he didn't agree with the Earl's transparency but went on in a crisp professional tone.

"I've advised a rest and good food — fairly standard advice for a young woman who is in the first trimester of a pregnancy."

A stunned silence dropped over the study. Robin felt his heart pound at the news. Caroline — pregnant? But he was not able to sire children. It was a vampire law, a tenet of the hunger. Vampires could not create a bloodline — they only destroyed them.

Various emotions stabbed at him. He experienced hurt like a hot poker stabbing him in the chest. That Caroline could have let another touch her — and most certainly the other man had to be Mark Halsey, the self-absorbed oaf. He was also angry — and painfully jealous.

Dr. Peaches and the Earl both stared at him and not in a manner especially friendly. Robin thought his legs were going to go out from underneath him. He took an unsteady step backwards.

"Mr. Dashwood, Lady Caroline assures me you are the father of her child."

The Earl rose to his feet at the words, his aquiline face wrestling with dueling natures. It looked as though most of him wanted to take his hunting whip and flog his daughter's seducer while a small portion fought for calm and clear-headed thinking.

Robin tried to find his voice. He did not think it was in Caroline to manipulate a situation. He couldn't imagine her trying to trap him into marriage with claims of false paternity as a mathematics professor he had seen occasionally — before settling in with Kate — had tried unsuccessfully to do.

But he couldn't have children. Nothing altered that. He was a three-hundred-year old vampire. It was a revenant law of nature. He couldn't produce living sperm.

But it was also true that Caroline was simply incapable of duplicity. He knew she loved him. Caroline could not commit such a cruelty to someone she loved. That too was a law of nature, just as irrefutable as a revenant's.

"My Lord," Dr. Peaches made a polite bow of retreat. "I will leave you to your family. I'll check in again tomorrow."

"I… I," Robin's voice was strained. He sat down heavily in the leather chair. "Sir, I never meant to put Caroline in such a mortifying position."

The Earl shifted his attention from the departing doctor to Robin. His voice was cool. "I would suggest that you would follow up on your marital plans with some alacrity."

30

Robin carried a dinner tray into Caroline's room. No easy feat as it had taken a bit of doing to convince her unamused father.

She was sitting up in a pretty Regency bed that must have been acquired by the second Westmacott Earl at Hawkesmoor. The girl looked lost in unhappy thoughts, her forehead pulled with strain.

"Oh," Caroline's face blanched at the sight of him, "it's you."

He carefully readjusted the silver platter and pushed the door closed with the heel of his shoe.

"Darling," Robin replied affectionately, putting the tray on her night table and sitting on the bed's edge. He wasn't going to make it any easier on her. He wanted to hear her voice when she told him. He had to know if she was completely certain he was the father. He smiled at her benignly.

She crossed her arms anxiously. "It's just that… I mean, I must seem so unsophisticated to you. I can't believe I was so thoughtless. I mean, I ought to have been more careful."

"Forgive me, love. I'm not following you." Robin pretended to be baffled.

"Didn't Dr. Peaches tell you?" Her voice was thin and dry.

He shrugged in the negative and took one of her hands in his. "But you're all right?"

"Something happened the night we spent together in New York," she began in an embarrassed and repentant tone.

He reached out to playfully brush her cheek with a forefinger. "I remember."

Caroline shook her head miserably. "You see, I never expected to meet you. I never expected to meet anybody except old codgers and anglophiles so technically, I wasn't prepared for — you know — what happened between us."

Robin raised an eyebrow. "I think I understand. You're…"

"Pregnant? Yes!" she jumped in, radiating relief that the news was now between them. "I'm so glad that you finally know. It's been very difficult all on my own."

Robin coolly withdrew his hand from hers, hating the puzzled expression that crossed her face. "I think you should know," he despised himself for what he was about to say, but he simply had to gauge her reaction and know for sure, "I'm not capable of producing children."

Caroline's face lost all traces of color. She stared at him in disbelief, dark circles of worry beginning to pool under her wide eyes. She was also beginning to breathe too quickly and too shallowly, her chest rose and fell rapidly in almost a wheeze.

"What do you mean you can't father children? But that's not possible," she said in a razor thin voice. "You're the only one. Well, it's just not — did a real medical doctor tell you that you couldn't have children?"

Robin studied her intently. He felt a mixture of elation and panic rise in his system. Caroline was telling the truth, as she knew it: he was the father of the child she was carrying. That was for certain. He could see it in her eyes, hear it in her voice and feel it in the wavering electricity of her aura.

Yet, if he was the biological father — what the hell was happening to him? He was neither human nor revenant but some sort of hybrid freak. Was it possible he could produce live sperm like a human?

He took a sharp intake of breath and sat up straighter. That extraordinary first night he had barely held on to his outward form. Had it happened then? And if he was capable of making Caroline pregnant, just what sort of genetic material had he implanted in her human system? Was it a human infant or monster? What had he done to the woman he wanted so badly to care for and look after?

"I'm pregnant, Robin," Caroline said lifting up her chin, her eyes flashing with both stubborn pride and vulnerability. "I am going to have a baby."

Once he had decided to accept the incredible notion that he was the actual biological father, Robin's mind raced to choose a course of action. He had to stay, of course. She would need him and what he knew of his kind. If he had learned of his ability to produce a bloodline in another fashion, he would leave Caroline forever rather than subject her to the unknown. But staying had its problems, too. If any revenant learned he had made Caroline pregnant, she and the child would be mortal danger. There were vampire kings who would stop at literally nothing to prevent a live birth. Almost the only thing vampire kings feared was change. Change could mean catastrophic shifts in the balance of power. Images of one such bloody purge in the London court more than a century earlier flickered across his mind.

He gazed across at his Lady Caroline. She and the child depended on him completely to protect them from harm. He had failed his parents. He had failed Elizabeth Gwayr. He would not fail Caroline DeBarry.

"If I am to be a father," Robin said, "then I suppose I ought to dart into the village tomorrow at the crack of dawn and secure a marriage license. I must say I am very irritated at the medical profession in general. No children indeed!"

Caroline burst into tears and then laughed out loud in relief.

"I'm surprised Dad hasn't fired a shotgun at you over the banister yet."

Robin handed her a linen napkin from the dinner tray. "I think I can guarantee he is not be best pleased."

She wiped at her streaming eyes. "Dad will get over it. His new lambs are doing well."

"In the morning I'll collect my things from the inn. I brought a ring of my mother's for you."

Caroline beamed at him over the tear stained napkin. "So you knew all along you wanted to marry me?" Then her face turned thoughtful. "Your mother won't mind you giving it to me?"

He half-smiled and brushed a long strand of his auburn hair back behind his shoulder. "My mother's been dead for centur… many years… but I know she would be very pleased to see it come to you.

Robin thought his mother would be ecstatic to know her magnificent emerald ring had returned to Hawkesmoor. Since the mid-Victorian era, after he came down from Cader Idris, he had bought pieces at auction he recognized as belonging to his family. He had managed to acquire nearly all his mother's jewels. Quite a few of his mother's jewels had come up for sale over the years because much of her collection came from her own family and therefore was not entailed to Hawkesmoor. He now knew, thanks to Caroline's excellent sense of history, that desperate DeBarry Earls had needed to sell off pieces to keep the place solvent after Ambrose Westmacott had ravaged the coffers.

It would give him great pleasure to give all his mother's jewels to Caroline. As his wife, they would rightfully belong to her anyway. He wondered if much was intact of the plate and jewels entailed to the castle and wouldn't be at all surprised to learn Westmacott had managed to break it up piecemeal and sell off the pieces to support his gambling obsession.

"Father?" inquired Caroline. "Aunts? Uncles? Brothers and sisters?"

"Dead. They're all dead." He made a dismissive gesture. "I never had any brothers or sisters."

Caroline gazed at him, her blue eyes widened in sympathy.

"Then you've been very lonely," she said it more as fact than question. "You must miss them terribly sometimes."

"There have been moments," he replied quietly, and realized it was the first time he'd ever admitted to a human he occasionally felt less than cheerful.

"Well, you've got a great lot of family now," Caroline leaned forward to squeeze his hand. "You'll find us all dreadful nuisances and pests — and that's not when Daddy's taking off after a coach load of German tourists with a shotgun."

Robin lifted the hand she held and moved it to her slightly thickened abdomen. He stretched his long fingers over the soft cotton of her nightgown, taking pleasure in the steady pulse pounding through her arteries.

"Mine?" he murmured for the last time.

"Yours," Caroline said without edge.

"Imagine that." Robin breathed and sent up a brief private prayer to the ether: *Please grant this child light, peace and all that is human. Grant me the strength to keep this child safe from any harm.*

Maybe his plea would rise to meet the night breeze and drift far away to Cader Idris. Maybe the ones who had spoken old Welsh to him in wise gentle voices would capture it like a firefly and remember.

Laying his head against Caroline's chest, listening to her heartbeat while she stroked his hair, he could still hear their soft singsong:

We balance your hunger with healing. We, who have called you to this place, anoint you as the chosen one — the forever king. Built from the mortar of your strengths and sorrows, you become both bridge and barrier.

31

Robin was given the Japanese Room because, he gathered, it was pointedly a goodly distance down the hall from Caroline's.

It was a very pleasant set of rooms that in his day had been used exclusively by his mother as a seamstress closet, accommodating a cutting table, bolts of rich fabrics imported from the finest textile merchants in the world and several dress forms in his mother's slender size. His mother had a weakness for exquisite clothes, employing two expert needlewomen just to care for her personal wardrobe and create the less complicated day-to-day gowns. Important clothes were entrusted only to the deftest of the London or Parisian dressmakers.

He poured himself a stiff whiskey from the decanter that had been kindly placed, along with a selection of other energized beverages, on an ebony side table in the sitting room.

Certainly the rooms were much more handsome under the current reign. Quite acceptable pieces of antique Japanese decorative art had been arranged with care throughout the two rooms. Robin wondered if it had all been collected in the late Victorian period when Japanese things were all the rage. He had a great fondness for Asian aesthetics. Its spare elegance and sweeping uses of the single line reminded him of Georgian design sense at its serene best. He even admired the courage it had taken for one of the DeBarrys to strip the walls of ornate color and whitewash them in homage of the Japanese preference for utter simplicity.

Not that all was simplicity itself, he thought, eyeing the large four poster bed where a ground level mat ought to be resting.

A grandfather clock out in the vast hallway joined with several other more distantly located pendulum clocks, to solemnly announce the hour in their variously pitched chimes. They told him it was three o'clock in the morning.

He took his whiskey over to the window and leaned his forearms against the broad ledge to look out over the silvery stone of Hawkesmoor's ancient castle walls.

Sleep had deserted him. He had tried to read one of Peter's books, which attempted with a heavy hand to dissect the life of Chesterfield.

"Here's to you, Philip Dormer Stanhope, Fourth Earl of Chesterfield. You incredible old bore," said Robin, lifting his glass up and taking a drink. The rich liquid burned his throat and created a warm path down through his chest. He felt the lovely detached hum that strong alcohol ignited flare up in his system as if it were carbonating his blood.

"An old bore, but" Robin shifted his weight slightly, moving so he could sit on the window ledge, "for a human, a shameless predator."

He rested his head back against the wide window jamb and sipped a little more whiskey, hoping it would blot away his thoughts.

Winnifred and her friend, Hugh Candlethorne, the revenant doctor, had to know something. They both understood that something very strange was happening to him. He had to get back to St. Sophia and talk to her. Winnifred would never wish him harm even if he could establish a bloodline. She carried no allegiances or debts to vampire kings. She was a very old and powerful vampire so she knew things, had heard ancient tales of revenant lore. Such arcane knowledge might make all the difference to keeping his new family alive.

Robin's eyes narrowed in thought. Then there was Gabriel Addington, the scholar.

Gabriel had been a contented monk in 13th century Shropshire before he acquired the hunger. Since 1698, he'd been a very successful rare book dealer in London. Currently he owned and ran perhaps the best antique occult bookshop in Britain, in an extremely handsome location in Charing Cross.

Addington's possessed an additional feature of interest to intelligent vampires worldwide: a secret subterranean floor housing a vast vampire library. Gabriel, with his meticulous monk's mind, had over the centuries collected every scrap of written documentation regarding revenants he could locate. He himself wrote as well, carefully noting down the creation of new vampires and the three-dimensional destruction of others. Gabriel's 'family tree' of revenants was a masterwork of historical research and of priceless value. Vampires from around the world made the trip to Charing Cross to read their dark and fascinating history. Many, who had come to the hunger in remote or lonely circumstances, came to register themselves with Gabriel so they too would be noted down in his tidy pages.

But if something very strange was happening to him, Robin mused as he swallowed some more whiskey, Gabriel might have a precedent hidden away in his massive collection of bound books.

Maybe it wasn't really so unusual. Perhaps some vampires did mutate, as he seemed to be doing. It would be a relief to learn other revenants had passed through a similar change and survived.

He exhaled slowly and gazed out over the old stonework of Hawkesmoor, watching the flashlight beam from one of the security guards as he made his rounds. Gabriel Addington fell under the watchful eye of Garnet Petherbridge, Lord Scyon, the current vampire king of London.

Robin shuddered involuntarily, remembering 1878 when Petherbridge made a very violent and bloody bid for the job, destroying a legion of revenants loyal to the Marquess of Southbrook. Petherbridge personally lit a pyre beneath his old mentor's feet and watched him burn at the stake for days as Southbrook's powerful revenant form refused to dismantle its three-dimensional aspects.

THE COTSWOLDS, ENGLAND, 1878

He had been in London himself then, working as an aide de camp to Disraeli and knee-deep in the preparation of briefs for the Berlin Congress. As usual, he had stayed completely out of vampire circles, preferring to remain in service to humans. He had a lovely little house in Mayfair run by an Irish housekeeper named Mrs. O'Hare, a mildly diverting affair with an opera dancer named Lisette, and fascinating work to do for a superb intellect like Disraeli. Like most pleasant things, his London life was too good to last.

But as luck would have it, Petherbridge's bloody coup occurred while he was spending a fortnight fox hunting in the Cotswolds. He was staying with human friends at their hunting box; thoroughly enjoying sleeping alone while Lisette's opera company was away on tour. She was a sweet-natured little thing but not terribly bright, and rather common despite her delicate pale blonde appearance.

The pack had drawn covert near a wood. He had found a spot by himself, letting the reins fall to the buckle over the neck of his favorite horse, a big chestnut mare named Sonnet who could be difficult and had a regrettable tendency to show a hoof to another horse. Politely, he kept the mare at a reasonable distance from other horses while the field waited to see if a fox would break and run. Sonnet was pawing the cold ground irritably, snorting steam into the frosty air. A rider in visitor black like himself trotted his very handsome gray horse across the snow flecked ground in his direction.

"Lord Scyon would like ye to take tea with him in a fortnight," the rider said in an Irish brogue, as he pulled up his gelding. "He has taken a fancy to the notion ye might make a useful creature."

Robin picked up his reins with his right hand in case Sonnet took a dislike to the gray.

"Have we been introduced?" he asked coolly.

The other horseman used the bone handle of his hunting whip to push back the brim of his hat so it sat at a rather jaunty angle on his head. He was a handsome Irishman with thick dark Celtic hair and big chiseled features.

"Now we don't hunt so formal in Galway," he said in his lilting tones. "I am Sean Ian O'Neal. Pleased to be makin' your acquaintance, Lord Merritt, sir."

Robin threw the Irishman a sharp glance. He didn't use his title anymore, hadn't since his indenture with Sir Anthony Fortesque.

"You can tell Lord Scyon I have less than no interest in becoming his creature."

"Pity for ye, Lord Merritt," O'Neal shrugged eloquently. "Ye must know Scyon has taken London from Southbrook this very day."

"I don't care if Scyon becomes the next King of England. Tell him to leave me out of his plans." Robin shortened his reins quickly as the hounds began to bay in excitement along the covert's western edge. Sonnet's ears perked up at the hound cries and she began dancing sideways in anticipation of a good gallop.

"A goodly hundred lost their physical bodies today," Sean Ian O'Neal informed him with another one of his sunbeams of a smile. "Lord Scyon thinks ye are too pretty to put in a snuff box, sir. I think ye too intelligent."

"I don't give a damn what you think," Robin snapped and spurred Sonnet's side irritably. The surprised mare gave a start, crow hopped and then lurched forward into a canter.

"More's the pity," O'Neal called after him, "Scyon ain't afeared of strong poison, sir. He'll have ye if it pleases him."

The hound cries changed abruptly and Robin could see the hunt staff beginning to dismount. He wondered if the pack had just chopped a fox. If so, and given the late morning hour, the field would probably be dismissed and after wishing the master of foxhounds the traditional "Good night" he could hack home to the hunting box.

"My god!" he heard one of the Whippers-in exclaim as he drew near on a very nervous Sonnet.

"Chopped fox?' Robin asked Lady Darnley, who scanned the undulating pack of hounds intently.

"Most likely, Mr. Dashwood," she said, her eyes following the feathering sterns of the tricolor hounds.

"Good lord, man!" the master of foxhounds exploded in frightened tones. "Get it away from them!"

"That doesn't sound like a chopped fox," Lady Darnley said in real surprise. "Let us take a look, Mr. Dashwood!"

"Your servant, madam."

He followed her the few hundred yards to where the hounds were congregating. Huntsmen were on foot threading their way through the large pack trying rather desperately to get at something.

"Oh, god," the florid-faced master of foxhounds sputtered upon seeing Lady Darnley ride up. "Dashwood, for heaven's sake, do not let the ladies near."

Robin watched one of the huntsmen make a grab down in the pack, but he obviously missed as a large bitch proudly carried the trophy out of his reach and into the view of the field.

Lady Darnley, a hell-for-leather horsewoman, screamed. Many of the horses spooked. Robin stared in sick disbelief.

The bitch carried the severed head of his French opera dancer Lisette by a ravaged section of her blonde hair. The one blue eye that hadn't been devoured by the hounds seemed to be looking about wildly in a kind of frigid horror.

Robin wheeled Sonnet around and spurred her into a gallop. Blindly, he allowed the mare to careen away from the rioting hounds, finding her own path. It wasn't until he dimly realized another horse had lit out in pursuit that he finally pulled up the big chestnut near a small copse of apple trees. The furious baying of the hounds could still be heard in the distance.

"Lord Scyon — he ain't afeared of a little strong poison," repeated Sean Ian O'Neal's voice on his right side.

Robin jerked his head around to stare dumbly at the Irishman. He felt a hot tear drop from his eye and course down his wind-chilled cheekbone.

"You know, Lord Merritt, sir," O'Neal said, gesturing casually back at Lisette's ghastly head. "I had the little bitch three times before I sliced her head off. Oh, she begged me not to — you know, in that funny froggy accent."

"You tell Lord Scyon," Robin said in a low dark voice, "I will see him in a fortnight."

The Irishman beamed good-naturedly. "So, ye'll be a whore again, will ye? Sir Anthony brags about breaking ye to bridle, you should know that."

Robin expertly threw out and snapped his hunting whip. The thong flicked across Sean Ian's grinning face, biting deeply into the flesh of his cheek and ripping off a thick stripe. The Irishman cried out, as blood geysered from his cheek in a scarlet spray. He covered his face with a choked sob of dismay and agony.

"Tell him I'll bring him your head in a burlap bag," Robin said as he backed off Sonnet.

He'd done it too, Robin reflected, having the last sip of his whiskey. He had dumped O'Neal's head on Garnet Petherbridge's Regency desk, with all the contempt it deserved. The gesture seemed to convince Petherbridge that he really did not care for Robin Dashwood as his creature after all.

But then Petherbridge would also not care to have his vampire librarian, Gabriel Addington, give any assistance to one Robin Dashwood either. Indeed, Garnet Petherbridge could be counted on to be the first revenant to act and act violently on any whiff of information concerning Caroline's pregnancy.

Robin looked away from the window when a quiet knock came at his door. He pushed off the ledge and crossed the room.

"Yes?" he said as he pulled open the door. "Caroline, love."

She stood in the hallway, wrapped in a heavy blue woolen dressing gown and raising a finger to her lips to beg for quiet.

"I was up and saw your light under the door," Caroline said. "I hope I'm not disturbing you."

"Don't be silly." Robin quickly glanced up and down the massive hallway. Everyone else seemed to have taken to their beds. "Come in, please."

She obediently stepped inside and seemed relieved when he closed the door after her.

"I know it's ridiculous, but after this afternoon — I had to check and make sure you were real. I've been having the most vivid sort of dreams."

Robin cocked his head to the side and smiled at her. "I'm just having a whiskey." He held up the empty glass. "I could make you a cup of tea."

"Yes, please. Earl Gray." Caroline almost blushed and glanced at the bed tapestries, appearing to find the silk Japanese crane print fascinating. "Could I stay here with you tonight?"

He widened his green eyes slightly, returned to the sideboard where the tea things were kept and switched on the electric kettle.

"I would be happy to have you with me, my dear — but I suspect your father would rather we slept apart."

"Oh, I'll go before he gets up in the morning," Caroline promised, sitting on the edge of the four-poster. She leaned back against the headboard. "This particular dream was just so incredibly realistic."

"Dream?" Robin picked up the electric kettle as it started to whistle. He poured some of the steaming water into a squat brown teapot.

"Yes. Elizabeth, the seventh countess. She came and sat on my bed to talk to me."

There was a sharp clatter as Robin dropped the spoon he was using to measure loose tea.

"The seventh countess?" he breathed.

"She wanted to tell you something." Caroline stifled a small yawn. "As if an 18th century ghost would know you were in and about the place."

Robin forced his long fingers to continue the tea process. He kept his voice light.

"Does she haunt the castle?"

"We only have two really consistently documented ghosts and we've all seen them at one time or another." Caroline pulled her legs up onto the bed and wrapped the heavy dressing gown about her knees. "Every now and then, a gray lady drifts down the main staircase until she fades away. We always imagine it's Elizabeth because of how she died but we haven't a clue, really."

He turned and wondered if his attempt at a gracious smile looked as frozen as it felt. "Sugar?"

"Just black, actually." She smiled back at him.

Robin swung back to the tea things and poured a cup from the brown pot. Then he poured a stiff whiskey. "So, did this dream frighten you?"

"It's eerie, but she hardly seems scary or anything." Caroline accepted the teacup from him gratefully. "I don't know why I find myself thinking you're just going to fade away too."

Robin sat down on the bed, leaning against the opposite post from her. He gazed at her thoughtfully over the rim of his whiskey glass.

"I'm not going anywhere, love," he said.

"You do seem a bit down though."

Robin stared down into the amber liquid sloshing about the crystal. He couldn't admit to Caroline how much the thought of Elizabeth's shade wandering the castle for centuries upset him. How could he tell her vampires who possessed that particular ability to dissolve their three-dimensional forms and roam the air currents as he did occasionally met up with ghosts? What poignant hollow beings they were. Not human, and not spirit. Just endlessly drifting fragments of human emotion trapped between one dimension and another. They were like lobotomized mental patients wandering the ether. Not by choice but because, somehow, a portion of their molecular structure, their essence, didn't make the transference to wherever it was humans went when they died.

To learn that it was possible Elizabeth, in the terrible fright of her death, hadn't completely made the jump and now wandered the halls in that mindless pain of the human shade.

"Robin?" asked Caroline in concern. She moved across the bed. "Are you all right?"

He lifted his head, forcing his facial muscles to assume a cheerful expression.

"I'm not used to good Scotch whiskey anymore."

Robin pushed off the foot board and pulled off Peter's black sweater, tossing it onto a nearby chair.

"Can you tell me," said Caroline as he approached the bed, "about the scar on your chest?"

Robin's fingers automatically went to Morvidus' mark. He'd answered this particular question many times before for inquisitive lovers — always with some easy lie about an accident — but now it seemed genuinely an evil thing to hide such a hideous truth from someone he loved as intensely as he loved Caroline DeBarry. It just wasn't the time, if it ever would be just the time, to tell her he was the long lost Lord Merritt of her childhood adventure stories.

"Uhm," he murmured running the tips of his fingers over the hard edges of Morvidus' brand as if it still pained him, "it's an old thing. A car wreck. I apologize if it offends you. It's not very pretty."

"You're so beautiful. It's a bit of a relief to discover you have a flaw."

"I'll tell you the whole story one day," Robin promised with a tired smile.

He ran his long fingers over her soft strawberry blonde hair and bent to kiss her shoulder, then dragged his mouth up to kiss her neck.

"You ought," he whispered hoarsely in her ear, "to remember your father's intent in exiling me to the Japanese room."

She kissed him, with a tentative vulnerability that unlocked a very aggressive side to his sexual nature. He was still, in some ways, a man of his times. A man who had kept an opera whore and thought of attractive women as creatures who existed almost exclusively to please him.

Robin pushed her back against the pillows and lunged after, kissing her fiercely. He pushed open the blue wool robe with a heavy hand and entwined his long fingers onto the edge of gown underneath. With a sharp jerk, small pretty buttons popped and the pale blue cotton tore with a soft cry of distress.

"Robin," Caroline gasped when he pulled his harsh kiss away from her mouth and down to her breast, "You're…"

Robin covered her mouth with the hand that was not throwing aside what was left of her nightgown, completely cutting off what she was trying to say. He didn't want to talk. He didn't want to listen. He wanted Caroline like he once wanted human blood — and he always killed when he fed.

32

Caroline woke to the gray drizzle of a Yorkshire morning. She felt warm and comfortable under the heavy quilts.

She lifted her head slightly from the curve of Robin's shoulder where she had been nestled and looked across at the aquiline features of her future husband's face.

Asleep, Robin's elegant face possessed none of the wary, haunted quality it almost always had. He had a dark side, her Robin Dashwood or rather, he possessed what the Spanish Gypsies called *duende* — a kind of dark passion.

It hadn't been *lovemaking* at all. Robin had made love to her before and had tempered his passion with gentleness and skill. This had been pure, undisguised sexual aggression. He hadn't ripped apart her favorite nightgown in order to prove his deep care and love for her.

She laid her head back against his chest, deciding to wait just a little longer before the big shift onto the cold floor. Robin frowned in his sleep and murmured something. He moved his head slightly from side to side.

"Corisande Honoria Belfield," he said in the slightly slurred speech of sleep, "I plight thee my troth and take thee as lawful wedded wife."

Caroline drew up in surprise. It had never occurred to her that Robin may have been married before. But, of course, it was entirely possible. Had he and this Corisande divorced in

America? And if this Corisande had once held his heart, how could she bear to let him go?

Robin shifted again, reaching for her in his sleep. He pulled himself across Caroline and kissed her longingly.

"Corisande," he said again before opening his green eyes and focusing rather incredulously down at Caroline's face.

"Oh," Robin frowned in some puzzlement as if his mind was not yet fully operational, "Caroline, love. You're still here?"

She nodded. "I haven't yet the courage to leave this lovely warm bed."

He turned his head to take in the drizzle beading on the bedroom windows and narrowed his eyes as the gray morning light stung his sensitive retinas.

"Don't blame you," Robin said, returning his attention to Caroline. "You don't mind your very old-fashioned father knowing you slept here with me?"

"I'll go soon," she promised, sliding her arms up around his neck. "He'll be at his morning coffee, reading the *Times*. Oblivious to all but the racing results."

"You've been got with my child," Robin replied in one of the oddly old-fashioned phrases Caroline had noticed he tended to fall into when he was tired or worried. "I suppose it's occurred to him that you welcome my attentions."

He abruptly pushed away from her and got up, reaching for Peter's discarded clothes on a nearby chair. "I'm going to take a walk," he said as he pulled on the jeans. "Don't you dare move from this bed until I return with your breakfast."

Caroline shook her head. "I ought to get dressed. Mark will be over soon to talk about next month's jumping clinic."

"I hate the idea of him touching you," Robin said with real edge in his voice. "Over-reaching farmer's son."

She widened her eyes at his words. He had sounded just like her paternal great-grandfather, the eleventh Earl who had been very much an aristocrat of a different era. An era filled with huge staffs of house servants; nearly complete isolation from the middle classes and an unshakable belief in the benevolent squirearchy. Even her own father wouldn't write Mark off as only a farmer's son.

Robin jerked on Peter's sweater and ran a hand through the untidy jumble of coppery hair.

"God's teeth," he swore taking several steps back, "what the hell have I done to you?"

Caroline was puzzled by his despair but before she could frame a reasonable response, Robin was gone.

He walked the castle battlements in the rain, smoking stale cigarettes from a package he'd found in Peter's room. Everywhere he looked was some sort of spot where as a child he'd played soldier or had sat in the summer sun reading. In another few years he'd have a child of his own to discover those very same places, probably for much the same things.

Caroline greatly worried him. She was pregnant by a non-human. He didn't know how such a pregnancy might affect a human but she was obviously not doing well. He had human friends who had produced children and they hadn't been at all liable to collapse with intense fevers. He remembered them, in fact, as having seemed extraordinarily vibrant. Caroline, alternatively, already looked as if she were being slowly drained dry by the process. It was not difficult to imagine a half-vampire child could do that. The idea that the baby, by force of its half-breed nature, was siphoning off Caroline's life panicked him like nothing else had in his long existence as a vampire.

He couldn't stomach the idea of Caroline destroying herself to have his child. The journey to producing a full-term pregnancy was already fraught with grave danger without the very child itself turning in on its own mother.

Robin paused under the slight shelter of what had been a soldier's post. He struck a match, out of the way of the light but persistent rain, and lit another cigarette.

He looked through the arrow slit, out over the wild moor country. Three hundred years later and he still could never tire of it.

Looking in another direction, he saw the simple elegant lines of Merlin's Tower where the great Welsh mage was supposed to have kept chained Saxon, the white dragon of England.

Merlin's Tower, where Hawkesmoor Castle kept its dead in crypts under the old Norman chapel. His father, mother and even Elizabeth would be buried there. He remembered how difficult achieving a consecrated burial place was in his day.

LONDON, 1750

"Corisande looked very unhappy after her priest left her today," said Robin with a slight frown as he played a game of cards with Oliver. He threw down the Queen of Hearts on the discard pile. "She usually seems so pleased to have confessed and done all that tedious, popish rattletrap. It is not like her to retire early when I am able to be in London."

Oliver picked up the discarded Queen and added it to his hand.

"You can be such a complete thickie sometimes," sighed his closest friend.

Robin scowled as he picked up a new card. "How very helpful."

"Robin — Corisande is a devout Catholic and she is dying."

Robin glanced up sharply from his fanned collection of playing cards. "She is not dying. She hardly ever coughs anymore."

"That is because the consumption has moved into her spine. Corisande will not live to see summer."

Robin's card hand jerked at Oliver's words and knocked over his glass of claret. The wine spread out over the white tablecloth like a huge bloodstain.

"Corisande is regaining her strength!" he snapped as he rose angrily from the table. "You heard what her doctor said — only last week."

"He said that because that is all you will allow him to say." Oliver rose as well. "You want to make believe Corisande will improve. Such selfishness ill becomes you, sir."

Robin threw his cards on the table with a short brutal gesture. "I will not hear this, Oliver!"

"You pretend all is well to avoid confronting the end of your arrangement here. You have deep feelings for Corisande, and who would not? She is a woman of extraordinary fineness."

Robin stiffened his back and eyed Oliver warily. "She is most certainly that, yes."

"Robin," Oliver's voice softened to almost a pleading tone, "you will go on pretending all is well and she will away — before you can be of true service to her. What a pity that would be, sir, for both of you."

"Explain," replied Robin, his jaw tightening.

"Corisande, as a Catholic, wishes to be buried in consecrated ground. *Holy* ground."

"I am aware of the definition for consecrated ground, thank you."

"As an unmarried woman known to be a kept lover, Corisande has been denied that most important rite by the Church. She will lie in an unmarked grave in some field."

Robin pounded the table with his fist. "May he rot in hell! I will not allow that pompous little pop-eyed priest to speak to her again! I will not have her frightened in this manner!"

Oliver held out his hands, asking for calm. "You cannot forbid Corisande to see her own priest, Robin. That is monstrous."

"I will do whatever the bloody hell I want to do in my own house!"

"It was my clear belief that you gave this house to Corisande."

Robin stared at Oliver Tupin with a black anger before he finally spoke. "Take these to that idiot priest from St. Giles," he said, picking up a handful of gold coins from the card table and tossing them at Oliver. "Drag him from his warm winter's bed. Tell Corisande's maid to wake her mistress and see to it she is handsomely dressed."

"Sir?" Oliver cocked his head to the side in puzzlement.

Robin crossed his arms. "I will marry Corisande Belfield this night."

"But the posting of banns has not been…"

"Petty edicts have no bearing on me," he snapped. "I will marry Corisande and then, by god, let no self-important priest keep her from holy ground!"

Oliver bowed gratefully. "Please consider it done — with no happier business have I ever been charged."

Robin's icy demeanor faded and he crossed the floor to embrace his friend.

"Forgive me, old friend," he said with a catch to his voice. "It is most unsophisticated for a gentleman to admit his mistress means everything to him. Ask Chesterfield. Only an uncouth rube falls in love with his opera whore."

"Only a social monster like Chesterfield could fail to fall in love with Corisande," Oliver said softly. "You will have the honor of calling her wife."

Robin's voice broke completely. "'Tis only for a brief time."

Robin blew out a stream of smoke. He gazed at Merlin's Tower through the shimmer of rain. A 14th century circular tower with a large subterranean store and meticulously planned embrasures; it had been a virtually undefeatable military position. Even the circling stone staircase inside the tower had been designed to force a potential invader to come up with his weapon side open, the shield arm awkwardly pushed against the wall.

He left the guard's rest and walked the battlement towards the tower's wide walk, which had been constructed in the 15th century to join it and its sister, DuPlessis Tower, to a new barbican, creating much of what would be called Hawkesmoor Castle. It would be yet another century before the brilliant Sir John Thynne designed the interior house, incorporating DuPlessis Tower as the centering great hall.

Elizabeth, he thought as he approached Merlin's Tower, would probably be entombed somewhere down below in the family crypt. The only wife of his entire wretched existence, Corisande, lay many miles to the south in a poor little churchyard in London — if St. Giles, as they had known it, even existed anymore. By right she ought to be here — but then, there had not been time to announce to his family and society at large that he had married. He became a widower a few days after the little midnight ceremony in Corisande's sickroom.

He remembered how he sat on the bed's edge and held her hand during the long recitation by her priest. Despite the ravages of the terrible consumption that had devoured her once much envied and emulated beauty, Corisande's happiness at achieving a rightful place in the eyes of her cold Catholic God made her pale and thin features radiate a genuine loveliness.

She had given him such a breathtaking smile of joy when he slipped his mother's emerald ring on her finger, he considered it a gift he would carry with him for all the days of his life.

Corisande would die in absolute agony about forty-eight hours later; as if her God wished to punish her for interfering in some carefully laid plan to preserve precious holy ground for the chosen.

He often envied humans their ability to die and go on to meet their Gods. He would give much to be able to seek out Corisande's imperious God and—

A pale and slender youth emerged from the stone archway into Merlin's Tower. About fifteen or sixteen, he stared at Robin with large worried blue eyes. A lovely mass of wheat-colored hair fell in thick spirals to his shoulders.

"Hello," said Robin flicking some ash away from his cigarette. "Not to worry. I'm a friend of Lady Caroline's."

The boy said nothing in return, but continued to stare at him in trepidation. Robin decided he looked fifteen — tall but thin for his age and very handsome in a fragile way. The white shirt and breeches he wore seemed to indicate he was involved in the equestrian side of the castle.

"Do you ride for the DeBarrys?" he asked in his kindest tones. "I hope I didn't disturb your coffee break."

The young man backed up a step.

"I'm Robin Dashwood," he offered, holding out a hand to the youth.

A shrill caw from one of the many moor birds that nested on the castle grounds distracted Robin momentarily. When he glanced back, the boy was gone.

33

"I think we should marry within the week," said Robin over the writing desk they had improvised to use as a breakfast table. "If you'll still have me, that is."

"You're a funny creature." Caroline picked up her fork and speared some of the scrambled egg gratefully. "How lovely! I haven't been served breakfast upstairs since Dragon and I fell badly at Badminton at the dreaded tier of Irish banks. I broke my collarbone in three places."

"Dragon?" he asked in genuine interest. "After Saxon of Merlin's Tower?"

She nodded, in the middle of chewing her scrambled egg.

"Speaking of Merlin's Tower… I met one of your exercise lads while up on the wide walk. A very shy blond boy, about fifteen?" Robin paused to savor the decadent taste of heavily buttered bread. "Seemed nice but I didn't catch his name."

Caroline stared at him incredulously. "I don't have exercise riders. We're only maintaining three horses and a pony at the mo. You saw a young man on the wide walk?"

"Very suitably dressed in breeches, boots and a clean white shirt." Robin frowned at her. "He certainly seemed to know his way around. You'd have to know him — long, heavy blond hair and very handsome?"

He saw a knowing look cross Caroline's face. She sat back against the pillows, letting out an amazed breath.

"You're in a very select group," she said finally. "My Grandfather used to see him now and again, as did Queen Victoria's husband Prince Albert when he was staying for a visit."

"You're telling me that perfectly clear three-dimensional teenager was a ghost?" It was Robin's turn to be incredulous. Every ghost he'd ever encountered had comprised of a few abandoned air molecules imprinted with a couple of sad memories.

"A famous one here, but a rare one. He doesn't come out very often. We don't know who he was. Probably a ghostly stable lad who had died tragically in some way," Caroline shrugged loosely, "while sneaking smoking tobacco."

He shook his head as if to clear it and changed the subject. "I'm going to go into Beckdale and collect my things."

"I'm having Dad talk up Father Hazelton this afternoon. We could manage something small here in a few days."

"I leave it in your capable hands, my lady." Robin raised a cup of coffee in salutation. "Just tell me when and where to stand."

Robin parked the Earl's ancient Range Rover near The Shattered Lady. He noted the very pointed presence of his BMW in front of the building. It certainly hadn't taken Winnifred long to track him down.

"Good afternoon," said Robin. He threw the Earl's car keys on the linen-covered table and sat down in the opposing chair. He picked up the menu card.

"And to you," she replied, smiling benignly at the inn's young waitress who appeared promptly to take Robin's luncheon request.

"The grilled vegetables and a bottle of Burgundy, thank you," he said to the girl, who nodded obediently and hurried off to place the order.

"I brought your lovely new car back," Winnifred began politely. "You must have missed it."

"It's a present," he murmured with equal civility.

"Thank you. I believe it rather suits me."

Robin looked across at her and thought how really handsome she was in a mossy green cashmere sweater and skirt — Hermes scarf tied rakishly at her long throat.

"You've left the order at St. Sophia?"

Winnifred nodded. "You're going to need me, Richard Robin Francis DuPlessis."

"But I'm just going to marry and restore an old castle."

"You must know as well as I," she lowered her voice and leaned forward, "if Petherbridge learns you have acquired telekinetic abilities and can even manage tele-transportation — he'll destroy you."

"Good luck to him." Robin sat back a little as the girl set a large wine glass down and then his plate of steaming vegetables. Another anonymous waitress followed with the bottle of Burgundy and a very light salad for Winnifred to push around in a shrewd approximation of eating.

He very pointedly picked up his fork, speared a grilled section of Italian squash and ate it.

"It's almost as if I could live as human or vampire," Robin said, reaching for the glass of Burgundy that one of the girls had poured out for him. "The idea of drinking blood doesn't appall me as it would have in my human days. I know I could do it if I had to."

"Like some kind of survival feature you have in your arsenal." Winnifred chewed her bottom lip thoughtfully. "You're a superhuman vampire."

"Cheers to that." Robin drank some of the dark red wine and then gazed at her over the rim of his wineglass. "Also, Caroline is pregnant."

Winnifred jumped at his words, a fork from her table setting clattering to the floor.

"Mine," he said quietly before she could form the question. "I have no doubt of that."

"Sweet Jesus," she fell back against the chair, almost in a daze. "You've placed that girl in harm's way — in terrible danger."

Robin's voice took on an edge. "You think I don't know that? You think it doesn't haunt my every move?"

"Petherbridge will kill them both — and you if he discovers even a tiny fraction of what is happening."

"Garnet Petherbridge is the least of my concerns at the moment. I can deal with him if I have to," he said with a small sigh. "It's Caroline. I don't believe she is doing well. I think the alien nature of the baby is too much of a strain on her human structure."

There was a very long pause before Winnifred spoke and when she did, it was with very carefully considered words.

"Hugh Candlethorne must become Caroline's doctor. He's the only one who can oversee her pregnancy with any degree of wisdom."

He nodded. "Done."

Winnifred rapped her tea saucer with her fingernails just as he remembered her doing while plotting out a daring rescue of aristocrats from the guillotine.

"And, Robin," Winnifred looked across the table at him with great seriousness, "You must tell your future wife and mother of your child just who and what you are."

"Winnifred—" he began in a warning voice.

"You cannot wed this young woman who is carrying your half-revenant child without giving her the complete picture of what she has gotten into. Not only is it the decent and honorable thing to do but such information just might save her life in the bargain."

Robin stared at her. "You can't be serious."

She pushed back from the table and stood up. "If you don't tell her, I will. I'll do it for you."

34

Robin tightened his jaw in annoyance.

"You know I don't take well to threats, Winnifred. Even from you."

"And I never thought you for a cruel man," she replied pointedly.

"Explain." He reached for his wine glass.

"It's cruel to let this lady you claim to love face danger even we can only partially appreciate," Winnifred said in her quiet but firm way, "without the slightest idea what she's up against."

Robin swallowed a sip of the rich deep-bodied wine and considered Winnifred's words. He could see she was right — but he failed to see just how he could even begin explain to Caroline that he was a three-hundred-year old vampire and because of him, she was carrying a potentially dangerous being within her human body.

"You'll find a way to tell her, Robin," Winnifred said in that uncanny way she sometimes demonstrated of knowing what he was thinking. "You must."

He had another drink of wine. "What if she shrinks away at the sight of me? What do I do then? Disappear forever?"

Robin felt his throat ache at the idea of leaving Yorkshire until the day it could be said all who had known him that wet spring had long disintegrated into ash.

Winnifred moved to where she could lay a hand on his shoulder. She squeezed it reassuringly.

"You've certainly moved with your usual speed and deftness," Robin commented before he had another sip of the Burgundy. He'd really forgotten how much he had liked wine.

"So beautiful! You're a vision," exclaimed Beryl in genuine wonder.

"I had to try it on," Caroline admitted as she slowly turned around in the castle office. "It's lovely, isn't it?"

The seventh countess' pale green and peach gown was magnificent. The beautifully seamed and finished lines enveloped her in the subtle shimmer of truly fine satin.

Beryl picked up an edge of the right sleeve and examined the exquisite pearl embroidery on the peach-colored piping. "Well, you ought to wear it too."

"Oh, I couldn't!' Caroline shook her head. "This dress belongs under glass. The insurance people would lose their minds …"

"What the insurance company doesn't know about yet," said Beryl sensibly, "can't hurt 'em. This dress was made to be worn at a wedding."

"Elizabeth's marriage to Lord Merritt." Caroline ran her hands gently over the heavy, gleaming satin.

"Speaking of which," commented her assistant as she returned to a pile of notebooks on her desk, "have you ever noticed how much Robin Dashwood actually looks like the portrait of Lord Merritt? Crikey, it's eerie."

Caroline paused and conjured up a mental image of the small portrait of the missing Lord Merritt in the gallery. Lord Merritt had been tall and willowy — supremely elegant in his simple black frock coat, his gleaming auburn hair unpolluted by powder. She remembered his eyes — large, intelligent and almost an emerald green in color as the anonymous painter had depicted them.

Beryl was right in a superficial way. Robin Dashwood and Lord Merritt did share some physical characteristics but their countenances were so very different.

Robin Dashwood, for all the innate kindness in his nature, possessed a wary, edgy side. As if he were a seasoned resistance fighter or a world-weary MI6 operative who was always on the tacit watch for danger round every corner.

The Lord Merritt of the castle portrait gazed out with serene confidence. He was the entitled son of a wealthy Earldom — all that was best of England lay at his feet. Not only was Lord Merritt completely aware of such homage to his breeding, he expected no less. He may have been more artistic than many, more scholarly by nature, if his mother's diary entries and letters were to be believed, but the portrait still revealed a man of his times.

It must have been a dreadful shock to his system when someone abruptly changed the course of his ordered, privileged life forever on the night of the betrothal ball.

For about the millionth time, Caroline felt a stab of pity for Lord Merritt of the unknown fate. She refocused her eyes and found Beryl staring expectantly at her, expecting a reply.

Caroline held out the skirt of Elizabeth's pale green gown. "You really think I ought to wear it?"

Robin latched the final lock on his case and lifted it off the bed to set next to his other pieces of luggage.

He had taken what he could from the New York flat. The rest — rather unimportant bits of furniture and art had gone into storage. Most of his mother's jewelry collection remained in a safe deposit box in New York, with the exception of her magnificent square-cut emerald ring, and a lovely set of pearls with a matchless diamond clasp he wanted to give Caroline as an engagement present. When the child was born, he'd send for a few more items. Slowly Caroline would get the lot and they could be passed down to the next generation at Hawkesmoor as his mother would have intended.

A wedding. Robin sat down on the bed and let out a long breath. Not so very different from the morning ceremony he would have had with Elizabeth, followed by the wedding breakfast and day-long general entertainments intended to cheer the spirits of the locals.

The moor wind suddenly picked up about the inn — Robin heard it rattle over the roof and buffet the trees. He smiled, remembering his human life in Yorkshire. A storm must be sweeping across the moor from the sea and this first wave was announcing to the natural world that turmoil was on the way.

Then Robin had the odd thought that the wind carried a something like a song in its capricious eddies. He rubbed his temples as the song grew in intensity.

Voices — old Welsh. Voices he knew and remembered — even loved. Not simply the wind but the trees about the inn and the ancient elemental energies of rock and water adding timbre. Song threads were weaving together that spoke of the land, kings who had held it, battles and births, gateways and shadows. One song thread floated high and crystalline above the rest, begging his attention — Lord of Time, we who have called you to this place, anoint you as the chosen one — the forever king. Built from the mortar of your strengths and sorrows, you become both bridge and barrier.

Robin pulled his hands from his face, alert to a strange sensation deep within his frame. One he had not felt in centuries. He was splintering. He could feel his cellular structure coming apart as if the elemental song threads had penetrated his body and were tearing it asunder.

It was excruciating. It was exhilarating — sheer horror and joy.

Robin staggered to his feet, watching as his outer frame shattered and dissolved into nothing. He joined the blood song, rising with wind currents into the storm over Britain. Below, he could trace the golden ribbon of abandoned faerie paths that wound across and once protected human geography. Above, he saw shards of the past, present and future falling towards him like rain. Voices wove through and around him. He was a prism. He was the Lord of Time. He was alone. He was joined with all elementals — a sentience that permeated every aspect of the universe.

Growing electricity in the approaching storm brought him flashes of the treacherous Corpse Road and its gate. A gate — built of physics and metaphor — under constant assault from shadow and growing fatally weaker. On its far side, he heard voracious, hungry shrieks that demanded entrance to former killing fields.

Time and space was bleeding. It had to be staunched — but how? Elemental voices sang to him of bridge and barrier — but why? He was a vampire.

Thought limited by beginnings and terminations shattered the energy prism and he felt his essence begin to rebind. The voices grew indistinct from the roar of the storm. He began to fall.

35

Caroline paused on her way to the kitchen for a fresh cup of tea, the sound of distant piano music having caught her attention.

Someone was actually at her grandmother's concert piano in the west wing. This was not her sister pounding out a rudimentary Chopin waltz in the square and coarse manner of ordinary people who had been required to take music lessons. The deft and thoughtful interpretation of the second movement from Beethoven's *Pathetique* that drifted in from her grandmother's piano was the work of an extraordinarily gifted artist. The player lent it a sense of deep regret and an unbearable sadness, choosing to let the melancholy notes mist off the keys like a cold rain.

Caroline followed the haunting music down the hall. Her father couldn't play a musical instrument if armed terrorists threatened to detonate the planet unless he produced a reasonable version of Clair de Lune on the spot. Forced into lessons by her musically inclined grandmother, she had made it as far as Mr. Kangaroo before escaping to more field hockey.

She came to the doorway of their private reception and peered in, looking for the ebony grand piano by the windows. What she saw was jaw-dropping — her Robin sat at the keyboard, his long hands floating over the keys with unerring competence.

He hadn't seen her so he continued to play without a pause. His heavy curtain of amber hair fell over his shoulders as his body moved forward slightly as the second movement deepened in intensity.

Caroline felt an electric chill run through her nervous system, remembering that this extraordinary man claimed to love her and seemed to take real pleasure in her company.

Robin was beautiful, brilliant and kind. A pang of disquiet began to form in her mind. So why was his first wife Corisande no longer at his side? How could this Corisande bear to be without him? Was he one of those men she'd read about who seemed absolutely perfect until the left over wedding cake had been cut up and portioned out in take-away boxes for guests — then they turned into horrors. Caroline listened as Robin drifted through the *Pathetique*. No one who could play Beethoven with such sensitivity was a secret monster.

Robin returned to the central theme of the sonata. He managed to make it into a world-weary sigh, as if the span of musical notes reflected a small journey through a life.

She was about to enter the room properly when Robin looked up from his keyboard and stopped playing abruptly. He stared out the window. Caroline was astonished to see a heavy tear drop from his right eye and roll down his highly planed cheekbone.

Robin dropped his elbows heavily onto the keys, creating a blast of mashed chords. Caroline couldn't catch his face as he buried it in his hands, but she could see his shoulders were shaking. He was crying as if his heart would crack and shatter into pieces. She had never seen him so vulnerable. With the exception of his passionate approach to bed, he always seemed too watchful and cautious to be vulnerable.

Caroline left the doorway. Robin didn't even appear to know she was in the room. He was bent over the keyboard, grief-stricken.

She stood behind him and dropped her arms down about his shaking shoulders.

"It will be all right," Caroline murmured as she brushed her cheek against his soft amber hair. It smelled faintly of oatmeal shampoo. "You'll see, Robin."

Robin lifted his head from his hands. He looked up at her, his green eyes luminous with tears.

"No," he said hoarsely, "I'm not sure it can ever be made right again."

She stroked his hair and said nothing.

"Caroline," Robin rested his head against her. He closed his eyes. "There is much I would tell you. Things you should know about me."

"Is it about Corisande?" she blurted out without thinking.

Caroline felt his body stiffen under her touch. Robin's green eyes opened. He slowly turned on the piano bench so he could see her more directly.

"I beg your pardon?" Robin's voice was hushed with shock.

"Corisande… you know," Caroline fumbled for a way out, "you were once married to a Corisande Honoria Belfield."

He coughed violently, as if her words had caused his throat to severely contract its muscles.

"You were murmuring your wedding vows in your sleep," she interjected anxiously. "You hadn't told me you were married before. It just surprised me, that's all."

"Corisande." Robin's beautifully planed face shadowed with sadness. "It has been a day for ghosts, has it not?"

Caroline chewed on her bottom lip, cursing herself for falling into a big black hole of her own digging.

"Forgive me. Your past is certainly none of my business."

He shifted his gaze to her face sharply.

"I disagree. You have every right to know everything about me." Robin lifted a long hand to wipe at his eyes. "Ask me what you will."

Caroline shrugged, wishing fervently she had kept her bloody mouth shut.

"Ask," he repeated more strongly.

"Well, where is she now?" Caroline ventured awkwardly. "How long have you been divorced?"

Robin thought for a moment and then focused on her intently.

"What is left of Corisande occupies a grave in the churchyard of St. Giles, London."

Caroline wove a little on her feet. Perhaps the dreaded pregnancy nausea wasn't so far away after all.

"Oh," she said unhappily, wondering what had possessed her to bring up Corisande at all. She wiped at a bead of sweat she felt spilling down the side of her face before offering lamely, "I am so very sorry."

"Corisande was very ill. She died."

"Did you love her very much?" Caroline wiped at another rivulet of perspiration that had dripped into her left eye, making it sting.

Robin didn't drop his gaze and his eye line narrowed as if he were taking a more in-depth look at her. "Yes," he allowed. "I loved Corisande very much."

"I'm just so sorry," she held up her hands in a helpless gesture. "I'm sorry. I've never been very good at knowing what to say in perfectly awful moments like this."

"You know," continued Robin, as if he hadn't heard her at all. A faint smile played at the corners of his mouth. "When I first saw you at that opening, I almost thought you were Corisande. You look very like her. She came from the north, too. York."

It was Caroline's turn to be surprised.

"I remember you saying something like that," she said in wonder. "But I thought you meant the portrait of Elizabeth, the seventh Countess of Hawkesmoor."

"Oh, no," he replied, his large eyes gleaming at the memories playing out in his head. "Elizabeth was very small and pretty. Less an acknowledged beauty than a sort of exquisite tomboy."

"But, Robin," Caroline felt a wave of absolute nausea wash over her, almost knocking her off her feet, "how on Earth could you possibly know that?"

36

Caroline paused to keep her balance as her brain seemed to lose magnetic north, spinning counterclockwise and then upside down. She swallowed dryly, trying to ignore another somewhat wave of nausea.

"Please — I'm really curious. How do you know such detail about Elizabeth? You see, we know so relatively little about her here, and if you have come across any references in your university work."

Robin shook his head and turned to close the lid over the keys.

"I think I have a certain ability," he said carefully, "from my historical writing to draw conclusions about a person from their portraits."

Well, it was partially true, he thought. He did get ideas, even if they were really only memories.

"Oh," replied Caroline, wiping unconsciously at more rivulets of perspiration running down her neck, "of course, yes. Stupid of me to not have thought of that."

She took an unsteady step to the side and began to fall forward.

Only his superior vampire abilities allowed him to move fast enough to catch her before she smashed her head against the edge of the piano.

"Caroline, darling," Robin breathed as he swept her up into his arms. "My god, what's happening to you?"

She was burning with fever again and his sensitive hearing picked up the return of the Earl through the kitchen door. He heard the housekeeper answer his inquiries about the whereabouts of Caroline by indicating he might have a look in the reception room where, unusually, the piano had been playing.

God's teeth! Robin swore, looking about the room for another way out. If the Earl saw his daughter had collapsed again, he'd insist on taking her to a hospital immediately, and rightfully so. But hospitals meant awkward questions about odd blood test results, which would lead to more awkward questions and more invasive tests. Genuine danger for Caroline and the baby — perhaps even discovery by an alert vampire.

French doors — he swung that way as the sounds of the Earl's boot heels in the hallway grew closer. It was raining heavily — *no bloody good* — and the door to the hall was blocked by the quickly approaching Earl.

There was only one way out. Robin closed his eyes and tried to focus. Maybe he could do it. He concentrated on Caroline's room and could just see the outline of the Regency bed forming in his head. Then he felt the warm shiver of molecular breakdown coursing through his nervous system.

He heard the Earl call out his name expectantly in the distance and then heard faint rumbles of befuddlement about having just seen the damnedest thing!

Hugh Candlethorne leaned forward over the ancient Welsh text with a chill of excitement dancing over his nerve endings. Here was the first possibly relevant passage he'd come across and felt lucky he just happened to have had a Welsh mother who taught him the language.

"Pretty esoteric stuff even for you, Candlethorne," came the toff drawl of Garnet Petherbridge, the vampire king of London and the British Isles.

Hugh looked up to find the blond and imperially handsome Petherbridge leaning against the door jamb of the tiny reference room.

"Oh, I don't know about that." Hugh dredged up a smile for the icy figure of Lord Scyon. "I'm a pretty esoteric fellow."

"I always took you for a bubbling vials and hypodermics type — not really bookish." Petherbridge wandered towards him in his very elegant and modern black bespoke suit.

Hugh tried to appear casual as he laid his forearms deliberately over the Welsh words.

"May I ask, what induced you of all revenants to enter this place of scholarship?" Hugh asked, hoping the small barb had reached home somewhere behind the vampire king's cold blue eyes.

"I get the urge every now and then to do a bit of searching," Garnet said easily. He sat with his arms crossed, on the edge of the reference room's battered oak table.

"And what are you searching for today?" Hugh pretended to yawn and closed the heavy leather cover of the occult book. "Early works on earning confidences through the art of torture?"

"Hugh," Garnet made a disappointed clicking sound, "you have always underestimated the value of torture."

Hugh held down a sharp reply. He had too many memories of trying to mend some of Garnet's mangled and torn victims who had managed to hang on. He almost shuddered remembering the Marquess of Southbrook after he'd been burning on Garnet's pyre for days — more a tall blackened cinder of flame-seared flesh and bone than a revenant. A human, of course, would have died within the first hour. The Marquess of Southbrook had been a strong vampire. He survived for days — his body attempting constant repairs even while the greedy fire was in the process of destroying it again. Billions of exposed, raw nerve endings flared up again with unimaginable agony as the vampire's body tried frantically to heal. Finally, battling the pyre was no longer an option. Southbrook had been losing too much ground and there just wasn't enough three-dimensional body left to make any repairs at all.

Hugh remembered how Garnet had collected Southbrook's still lucid consciousness, locked it away in a tiny jeweled snuff box and carried it on his person so Southbrook's mind could suffer fully the frightful effects of the hunger gone unsatisfied. He wondered if Garnet had the snuff box in his breast pocket even now.

"So you would be down here searching for," Hugh made a questioning gesture with his hands, "an unlucky delivery boy?"

"No," Garnet raised an eyebrow. It made him look like a wolf. "I've heard Lord Merritt is back in England. I do want to see him. We have so many old conversations to finish."

Candlethorne feigned the bored body language of someone too polite to cut off another's repartee.

"Lord Merritt? I vaguely remember the name." Hugh pretended to search through his mental address book. "I don't think I've ever met him — 17th century cavalier poet?"

"No, no — a minor Earl's son. Just a north country rustic," Garnet replied with a careless shrug.

"If I come across such a vampire, I'll certainly relay the news to you," Hugh glanced at his wristwatch significantly. "Oh, the time! I've got a dinner engagement."

"Thank you, Candlethorne, for your aid in this matter." Garnet nodded his head briefly, a gesture of approval in the intricate social dance of the revenants.

"Say no more." Hugh picked up his leather-bound notebook and headed for the narrow doorway. "The singular joy of helping you, Lord Scyon, is all I require."

"But you might tell your old friend," came Petherbridge's languid voice behind him, "the vampire nun—"

Hugh froze instantly at the chilling words that followed.

"—that I still remember how she flatly refused to sell me Merritt's contract of indenture."

Hugh swallowed and put on a jovial expression. He turned around to face the king of British vampires.

"You wanted to indenture a north country rustic?"

Garnet's blue eyes studied him intently and without warmth.

"Lord Merritt may lack a fashionable address but he was the glittering prize among the indentured ones. Of course I wanted Merritt." The vampire king stood up from his place on the table edge. "Why should a dried up old medieval like Winnifred have the hedonistic pleasure of owning such rare beauty?"

"All revenants are magnetic," replied Hugh, pretending only a vague interest. He reached into his trouser pocket and pulled out his car keys so he could jiggle them to feign restlessness.

"I remember the first time I saw him," interrupted Garnet, running his large powerful hand over the ancient embossed leather of the occult book as if he were scanning it like a scientific instrument. "He was human then. Walking through Vauxhall's rose gardens with his dying opera doxie on his arm."

"Dying opera doxie?" Hugh rattled his keys half-heartedly. In truth he really wouldn't mind hearing a little of Robin's past. It might shed some light on the revenant's amazing metamorphosis.

"God, she was ghastly looking. Once very beautiful, I was told, but consumption turned her into a miser's bag of stewing bones with an appalling cough." Garnet grimaced. "Any reasonable man would have installed some bright young thing to assume her duties and had the wretched woman removed through the trade door."

"And this Lord Merritt chose to keep his mistress," Candlethorne made a theatrical gasp, "despite the appalling cough?"

"A patronizing tone ill becomes you." Garnet flashed him an irritated glance. "It was odd for those times. I remember following them through the paths, watching Merritt treat her with such exquisite manners as if the chit was his acknowledged wife rather than a theatre whore. I found it fascinating."

"You mean, Lord Merritt fascinated you?"

"Yes. I became addicted to their little human love story as it played itself out." Lord Scyon almost smiled as he paused to recall his memories. "I became their shadow. I followed them when they went out. I sat in the dark corner of their room at night. Towards the end, Merritt just held on to her while she vomited up rivers of repulsive black bile. She suffered horribly. Through it all, Lord Merritt loyally sustained her and after she died, he wept from missing her."

Hugh frowned and leaned against a yellowed wall. "I find it hard to believe you were entranced by human fealty. You wanted to own this man?"

Garnet's eyes went bright and cold at the same time. He did smile finally.

"I wanted him, yes. I still want him."

"But, why?"

"For the pleasure of turning the tables on his ordered life of privilege. I wanted to make Lord Merritt take her place."

Hugh was incredulous. "Living a privileged life seems a modest flaw to me."

Garnet Petherbridge looked vaguely disappointed at his response. "He just had to have her. She was a famous singer — but almost as renowned for never accepting any gentleman's patronage. Lord Merritt wanted to be the gentleman who finally caused the great diva's heart to melt. What a dashing stroke! He'd be the talk of the opera suppers."

"Well, I must say, I'm impressed," murmured the vampire doctor in genuine surprise, although he failed to blot sarcasm completely from his voice. "Lord Scyon has a tender spot for opera singers."

Petherbridge brushed the smallest speck of lint from the sleeve of his perfect suit coat. "She was a descendant of my dear sister."

"Did this," asked Hugh, secretly staggered by the vampire king's tacit admission of some familial feeling, "have anything to do with Merritt's becoming one of us?"

Petherbridge flashed him one of his brilliant and cold smiles. "Another afternoon, perhaps."

Hugh felt disappointment coil up in his senses. He had seemed so close to discovering something in Robin DuPlessis' background that might help with his research.

He made a point of looking at his wristwatch. "I can't be late for my engagement! Thank you for your entertaining tale, my lord."

"A trifle." Petherbridge walked gracefully across the little room. He paused just after exiting the doorway and looked back at Hugh, a disconcerting metallic sort of glint sparking in his large eyes.

"Oh, and Hugh — you won't forget to ask Winnifred about him, will you?"

"You needn't hover, Robin," said Caroline in a slightly frustrated voice. "I'm going to change clothes and come down for dinner. It's perfectly normal for pregnant women to feel light-headed."

"You've fainted again!" Robin fought to keep his temper and volume in check. "It is not normal."

"Then I shall see Doctor Peaches in the morning."

"No!" Robin spun on his heel sharply to face her. He was having sharp shards of memory: Corisande's physician Kendall insisting on more bleeding — *more bleeding* in his high-pitched bleat. She bled enough to soak the bed linen a ghastly Chinese red and had suffered through ice baths despite cold wet English weather in an idiotic notion that the treatment would clear blood clots in her lungs. "No physicians! I will not have it!"

She stared at him. "*You will not have it?*"

Robin stared back at her. The images of Corisande's torture at the hands of her physician stabbing at his mind.

"Forgive me," Robin said as he tried to regain control of his nerves. "Dr. Peaches… Dr. Peaches will advise plenty of rest and extra iron tablets. I would feel greatly relieved if you would agree to see a friend of mine."

"This is a doctor?" Caroline asked rather pointedly.

"Of course he's a doctor — a Harley Street specialist in obstetrics."

Caroline dropped her head against the pillows, looking very tired. "I don't want to travel to London to see a doctor."

"He'll come here!"

Her expression wavered between doubt and mild annoyance. "Why would a Harley Street specialist do that?"

"An old friend," Robin struggled. "An interesting case."

She widened her eyes. "You're being a bit of a…"

He cut her off. "You'll see this doctor? Soon?"

Caroline shrugged, now truly annoyed. "If it'll make you happy."

Robin collapsed onto her bed edge in relief. He bent forward to kiss her forehead.

"Thank you," he murmured, moving to kiss her cheek.

"Thank you, darling." Robin dropped lower to kiss her mouth but pulled back when Caroline gave him a gentle push.

"Enough out of you. I have to change."

""Would you take a walk with me after dinner?" Robin said as he rose to his full height. "There is much I would tell you — about me."

37

R obin sipped from his second whiskey and strolled down the elegant Elizabethan gallery, gazing up at the family portraits of various DuPlessis, Westmacotts and DeBarrys.

He paused, coming to the smallish portrait of himself in the plain black frock coat. It was the product of an exceptionally cold, wet and windy week long forgotten. Sheer boredom had propelled Oliver Tupin to his paints and canvas.

It was a creditable portrait despite Oliver's self-admitted status as an amateur. He was glad the music master had taken the time to do it. The great Jonathan Richardson had been commissioned to paint his first real portrait — a massive effort that would have hung next to his parents in the gallery with the express intent of reminding all their descendants just who had the run of the place in the 18th century.

But, Robin reflected with another drink from the heavy whiskey glass, Morvidus had chosen him before Richardson had been due at the castle. It had the result of making Oliver's smaller effort the only real historical marker of his presence at Hawkesmoor. Other than the rainy day portrait, Richard Robin Francis DuPlessis had no more shape or relevance than one of Hawkesmoor's dust motes spinning randomly in a sun shaft.

Robin toasted the clear-eyed unpretentious portrait. "Oliver Tupin — your health, sir. Wherever you wander now, old friend."

He swung slightly on his heels and gazed down the dark wood panels to where Ambrose Westmacott's grandiose full-length portrait hung next to the painting of pale tragic Elizabeth in her riding habit.

Of course. Ambrose had taken the commission with Jonathan Richardson. And why not? Ambrose was the new heir to all he craved — even Elizabeth.

"Christ!" he said out loud. "It didn't take Ambrose long to break your spirit, did it?"

"Why do you not leave this place?" said someone behind him. It was an eerie sort of hollowed-out voice, as if the speaker were uttering the words from a far distance beneath water. "You are not wanted here."

Robin spun around. The blond boy from the battlements stood, glowering at him, long elegant hands on the hips of his breeches.

"Just what sort of ghost are you?" Robin demanded, amazed at the clarity of the completely three-dimensional spirit.

"Dashwood — there you are."

One glance away to note the arrival of Caroline's father was enough. When he looked back again, the ghost had vanished. Disappointed, Robin turned to deal with the current Earl of Hawkesmoor Castle.

"Sir?" he nodded politely.

The Earl looked profoundly ill at ease. This was a man who liked to walk the sheep holds, accompanied only by his thoughts and his Labrador. A man not accustomed to family drama or forced intimacies.

"All set for tomorrow," he offered awkwardly. "It'll be hell, of course."

"Hell, sir?" Robin sipped his whiskey.

Caroline's father waved his hands in irritation. "Wretched catering people disturbing everything, bossing everybody and demanding perfectly pleasant dogs be kenneled."

Robin hid a smile behind the rim of his glass.

"Peter is driving up in the morning. He's fetching Hannah from St. Sophia on the way."

"It will mean a lot to Caroline," said Robin watching as the Earl ran an anxious hand through his graying hair. "Everyone has been very kind…"

"I don't know what to think," The Earl interrupted suddenly, "about you, Mr. Dashwood. You're charismatic and clever. I can see that Caroline is utterly mesmerized."

Robin has a moment to remember Elizabeth Gwayr's father: *You are good wit' words, Richard Robin Francis and my daughter loves you.*

Caroline's father shook his handsome head. "I suppose you'll take me for a fool but I would rather she was marrying Mark Halsey tomorrow. He might be dull but he's not a mystery."

Robin downed the last of his whiskey. He felt sadness flood his senses along with the warmth of the alcohol. Did nothing ever change?

"I promise," he replied, loathing the words he was about to utter because he had said them all before, "I will never give you reason to regret her choice."

The Earl assessed him intently and then let out a short breath. He held out a hand. "No father could ask for more than that."

"I do love your daughter," Robin said, as they shook hands — not warmly, perhaps, but with mutual respect.

"She is a kind girl, and a good sport like her mother. Excellent qualities in a wife. Well," the older man turned away, clearly relieved to have a difficult conversation over with, "sheep club business to finish before bed. Good night, Mr. Dashwood."

Robin watched Caroline's father head off to his paperwork and wished he had another drink.

38

Hugh gave Gabriel Addington, the keeper of the great vampire library, a wan smile as he passed the former monk's small office. The librarian languidly saluted him with a sherry glass filled with blood.

"Lovely fresh stuff," Addington said by way of an invitation. "Lord Scyon brought a bottle as a gift."

"Anyone we knew?" Hugh asked, leaning against the door frame rather limply.

Gabriel smiled and lifted the little sherry glass so he could eye the crimson contents.

"Yes, one does wonder if Lord Scyon hasn't made one a present of a particularly cherished human friend."

"Just his witty little way of saying *I care*," added Hugh.

The librarian laughed out loud and held out his free hand to indicate a comfortable-looking old leather chair. "Sit down, Hugh, now that the library is closed for the night, and talk to me about your research. You seem to be on the trail of a favorite subject of mine, if I judge correctly the books you've been poring over."

"And that subject would be?" Hugh tried to keep the wariness out of his voice as he collapsed into Gabriel's office chair. In the end, Addington answered to Petherbridge.

"Hugh Candlethorne — you're our greatest bio-chemist," Gabriel sipped from the sherry glass. "You seek to learn just how we revenants function. Surely you are dragging out old Welsh texts to chase down hints as to our earliest origins."

"As you know, I have long held a belief that revenants are a natural evolving species like humans." Hugh said carefully. "We should have creation myths like humans but we don't. Where is our brow of Zeus? Our Jesus Christ?"

Addington shrugged. "So you hope to find revenants among the ancient fairies of Wales?"

"I'm looking for," Hugh found himself whispering, "references to a specific place, actually."

The former monk held up a hand to silence Candlethorne. He stood up and took a very pointed glance round the library from his office doorway to make certain they were alone.

"Hawkesmoor Castle?" Gabriel asked softly as he turned away from the doorway. "Lord Merritt's keep?"

"Petherbridge carries an obsession about Lord Merritt," Gabriel was saying as he returned to his desk chair. "I do not pretend to understand it. Ever since Petherbridge found out the wretched creature might be back in Britain, he's been pacing back and forth."

Hugh felt vaguely ill. So Petherbridge was actively seeking Robin DuPlessis. He wondered just how the black-minded vampire king would dispose of them all.

"Lord Merritt is a very unusual revenant," Hugh replied frankly. There seemed little point in being coy — Addington seemed to know quite a lot about Robin's return to Britain. "I am studying him."

Gabriel's gray eyes widened a little. "My friend, I would leave London and not return until Petherbridge is finished doing whatever he wishes to do with your unusual revenant."

"Technically," replied Hugh with a small clearing of his throat, "Lord Merritt is no longer a revenant."

The former monk actually gasped.

"Beautiful night! Rain's passed," called out Tim from his patrol up on the great walk. "No sign of Willie Wallace and his bloody Scots!"

"Thank you!" called back Caroline with a wave. "Have you seen Mr. Dashwood? He said he was taking a walk on the grounds."

"Aye, your ladyship," he pointed with his lit flashlight towards Merlin's Tower. "Mr. Dashwood went into the chapel."

The Hawkesmoor chapel was a fine example of Norman design — strength and simplicity quietly reigned in the spare gray stonework. No sentimental and cantilevered displays of complicated woodwork and colored windows to gum up the sense of powerful and earnest belief. It was a chapel built for warrior Norman knights with little time for frivolous and fussy details. Their God was not a baroque trickster with grand designs on the infinite. Their God was a dignified, direct deity who expected to make a simple exchange of piety for power.

Robin pushed through the set of black iron gates that led to the chapel's crypt. He switched on his flashlight as the electric light from the chapel proper failed to provide enough power to find his family. Robin had a series of mental pictures from his human time when he had come through the same iron barricade. When his paternal grandparents and his infant sister had died.

The oldest graves were medieval, laid out in three tidy rows of stone sarcophagi. Robin laid his hand against the cold northern gray stone. He ran his spidery fingers across the carved breastplate of his ancestor Frances Guy DuPlessis, second Earl of Hawkesmoor. This was where what remained of his family rested, moldering behind stone.

Robin breathed in the stale damp air and held his flashlight up so that its beam illuminated the stone walls. He gazed round the crypt, searching for newer sites in the walls.

The flashlight dutifully revealed the silver plaque of his sister — *God keep this child, Lady Catherine Georgiana DuPlessis.*

Infant daughter of the sixth Earl and Countess of Hawkesmoor. Born December 1739, died February 1740.

Robin felt a sadness wrench at his heart. He had loved the delicate little Catherine. She had gurgled and cooed with joy so many times in his then 21-year-old arms. He had begun to anticipate the day when he would marry his neighbor Elizabeth and sire his own children.

All his human hopes and aspirations were entombed in Hawkesmoor's crypt as well. He could almost imagine the silver plaques for those, too:

Sensible estate manager died 1750.

Competent musician died 1750.

Dutiful husband died 1750.

Affectionate father died 1750.

"Robin?" came Caroline's worried voice. "Please say that's you with the light."

He swung round, his beam catching sight of Caroline as she waited cautiously just inside the black gates.

"Yes," he said quietly. "It's me."

"Thank heavens." She smiled back at him in both relief and genuine happiness. "You asked me to join you after dinner. You wanted to tell me something?"

"Perhaps I just wanted to get you alone—all to myself." Robin held out a hand to her. "I'm sadly lacking in 21st century scruples, you know."

"That's difficult to believe," Caroline said as she followed the light across the crypt to join him. "The family plot seems rather a spine-tingling setting for traditional romance."

"Ah! But who said we were having a traditional romance?" Robin slipped an arm around her shoulders and bent to kiss her temple. "Hello then, darling. How are you this evening?"

"Quite recovered, thank you."

Robin felt a shiver run through her body as he wrapped both arms about her, drawing her tightly against his tall slender frame. This brave defender of his birthright really did love him.

He remembered Winnifred's exhortation to tell Caroline who and what he was and shivered himself.

How could he bear to see a look of revulsion or horror cross her handsome English face? He rested his chin on the crown of her soft blonde hair and began to ponder his choices.

Surely Winnifred was wrong. Caroline was far better off not knowing he was a vampire. After all, as a three-hundred-year old revenant himself, his instincts could be trusted, too.

But Caroline's warm body in his arms produced a tremor of sexual interest that fluttered over his senses, overtaking his ability to reason a sensible course of action. With the awkward urgency of a first kiss, he moved his head down to press his mouth against hers. Caroline let out a low murmur of pleasure in the back of her throat and it encouraged him to become more demanding. The kiss deepened in its intensity. Robin ran his hands up her spine, anxious to find a button or hook to release so he could make love to her at the foot of his ancestor, the second Earl of Hawkesmoor.

"Darling," he whispered hoarsely as he pulled his mouth away momentarily.

"Robin," said a disapproving voice behind him.

Before he could extricate himself from Caroline, Robin felt a crushing blow impale his back between his shoulder blades. He arched up and back from the force of the attack. His nervous system began to overload and then shattered like cheap glass under pressure — he had been viciously stabbed. Hot, cold, hot, hot pain coursed along all his nerve endings and his right lung began to collapse from the penetration of metal.

He vaguely heard Caroline gasp out a horrified sob through a growing ringing in his head. He felt her grasp desperately at his arm as he sank to his knees, falling against his ancestor's stone coffin.

He was dying.

Robin caught one last glimpse of Caroline's anguished face as she tried to tell him something. But he was deaf now and she had become some frightened bird beating frantic wings against window glass.

Then he went blind and felt his head begin to fall heavily forward. He never felt it come to rest on his right collarbone.

"Robin! Oh, god! Robin, please!" Caroline cried as she pushed open his jacket and saw the spreading stain of blood across his chest.

She glanced up and saw him staring dully at her. A moment later, an inner light actually seemed to extinguish itself in his green eyes. His head fell forward to rest awkwardly on his shoulder.

"You can't leave me — not like this. Not ever!" Caroline reached out to grasp his face between her hands and lifted his head up. "Breathe, damn you!"

Robin's eyes were still open and they stared at her now without seeing. His pale skin was already colder to her touch — his body just an abandoned shell.

Caroline could only let out a strangled cry of disbelief as his head fell from her quaking fingers and dropped back to his chest.

"The King is dead. Long live the King," said a voice, not unkindly.

39

Caroline jerked her head up as she moved forward instinctively to protect Robin's fallen body. She caught sight of a woman, beautifully dressed in an aubergine velvet dress, calmly watching her from across an expanse of stone floor.

"What do you want? Antiques? Was it worth killing a man," Caroline demanded in a tear-choked voice, "in a *church*? We have professional security guards. You won't be able to steal anything and you won't get away!"

"I have no interest in your treasures, child," she said. "Your security men are no threat to me."

Caroline watched, dazed, as the flawless pale creature lifted an arm and the black iron gates obediently slammed shut on her command, without her taking a step towards them.

Then with the supreme control of a flamenco artist, the woman stretched her fingers towards Robin's discarded flashlight. The plastic and glass casing obediently flew up into the chapel's holy darkness, towards the high arching ceiling like a space-age distress flare to God himself. Like so many modern prayers, it seemed to miss its mark, and quietly hooked onto the ancient iron chandelier. It poured down a golden pool of light that better illuminated the crypt. The elaborate stone coffins and wall tombs came into clearer view. It was as if Robin's killer were pulling away heavy old velvet drapes and exposing the crypt to rays of sunlight.

Caroline saw her mother's plaque slowly emerge from the ancient dark of the wall, with its dying wreath of flowers from the Hawkesmoor gardens. Utterly mesmerized, she watched the woman who had so viciously stabbed Robin Dashwood step directly under the brightest shaft of light.

She did not wear anger and bitterness etched into her flesh as Caroline imagined a murderess would—indeed, if Robin wasn't dead at her feet, she might have taken her for a wraith out of the faerie realm. But no: this was the brutal intruder who had stabbed and killed the man Caroline needed like an addictive drug. Without Robin and without ever feeling the weight of his hair falling against her cheek again, she would die herself from withdrawal.

Caroline let out an animal-like cry of pure pain and anger before she could suppress it. She shifted forward onto the balls of her feet. Every defense mechanism bred into her from generations of a ruling house told her to destroy this cruel invader.

She pondered her options, as Robin's killer took a step towards her. The cool swish of the rich purple velvet was even more frightening than the woman's movement. It seemed to warn of massive occult power and danger like the soft pace of a hunting lion through dry grass.

The lady glanced down at Robin's still form and sighed a little. She began a graceful drop to the floor next to him.

"Stay back!" Caroline pushed forward and barred the woman from being able to get to Robin's head and shoulders. "I'm warning you. Just what are you? Some kind of magician?"

"Robin loves you very much, you know," replied his murderess not unkindly. "But you have no idea what winning his heart means for you and the child you are carrying."

"How," Caroline shook her head and prayed she was simply caught in another particularly nasty nightmare, "did you find out about that? Did Robin know you?"

"I, too, once loved Robin a very long time ago," she replied. "But I set him free."

Caroline allowed her arms to slip down as she studied the woman next to her.

"Corisande!" Caroline breathed and shifted slightly closer towards Robin, as if his corpse could still feel fear at the creature's proximity. "Are you some sort of ghost?"

"No," said the elegant killer. "I am Winnifred Turchil."

"Winnifred Turchil?" Caroline repeated, mystified.

"Robin and I are," Winnifred laid a hand gently on Robin's shoulder, "revenants — vampires."

Caroline felt a scream coiling up at the base of her throat. One composed of almost as much frustration as fear at this strange woman who had single-handedly destroyed her future.

"You're absolutely mad!" she shouted at Winnifred Turchil. "You're no vampire. Vampires do not exist!"

"If only it were so simple, my child. That's why I am here — to explain it all so you will understand what destiny has brought to you."

"Rubbish. I'll wake up soon." Caroline covered her ears with shaking hands. Maybe she could just push the nightmare away. "Just go back where you came from."

Winnifred leaned towards Robin's body and pushed open the jacket to press her fingers against the blood-soaked chest. Caroline lowered her hands as she saw an expression of deep concern settle across the woman's alabaster features.

"He should be breathing by now," she murmured, glancing down at a plain watch on her wrist. "Something's off."

"Yes. He's dead." Caroline reached out a restraining hand. "Leave him alone."

"My god," Winnifred continued, ignoring Caroline, "have I made a horrible mistake?"

She put her bloodstained hand under Robin's chin and lifted his head so she could peer into his unseeing eyes.

Winnifred let out a worried breath and her brow knitted together in thought.

"Robin's revenant healing process should be allowing him to breathe at least. I've got to get him to Hugh."

"For god's sake," Caroline interrupted hotly, "make some bloody sense!"

Robin was floating in a sea of mist and softly pulsating lights. He heard soft songs in old Welsh all about him, as if they were panels of a beautiful aural boat carrying him gently and surely to shore.

"Fascinating," said Gabriel. "Petherbridge has always maintained an interest in Hawkesmoor. I have actually done most of your research for you and come to some conclusions based on what I found."

"And *what* does Petherbridge make of your findings?"

Gabriel actually shivered and glanced away. "I have not told Petherbridge my own thoughts on Hawkesmoor. I'm too frightened of what he might do."

Hugh closed his eyes for a long moment before he could speak.

"What you're really saying is Petherbridge will track us down like dogs and destroy us all."

"I'm saying I believe there is more to Hawkesmoor and your poor Lord Merritt than Petherbridge can bear any revenant knowing." Gabriel took a sip from his bloody sherry glass.

Candlethorne began to say something when he broke off to wince. He pressed a hand to his right temple.

"I'm getting a pretty desperate call for help from Winnifred," he said with another wince. "I've got to go to her."

"Where is she?" Gabriel asked as he set down his glass.

"My teleportation powers are crude at best," Hugh replied, rubbing his temples. "I think she's at Hawkesmoor."

"Well, my talent for teleportation is well-documented. I'll come with you." Gabriel held out one of his slightly ink-smudged hands. "Let's go then."

Hugh hesitated. "Gabriel, you'll be destroyed like the rest of us."

The monk raised an eyebrow and made an impatient gesture with his out held fingers.

"So be it."

"But you don't even know Lord Merritt."

"I know Lord Merritt once had the courage to say a firm no to Garnet Petherbridge. That's more than any of us have been able to accomplish in our long lives." Gabriel gazed evenly at Hugh. "I would give my outward form for such a creature. I'd consider it an honor."

Hugh reached out and took a firm grasp of the other vampire's hand. "Right then," he said roughly.

He wasn't alone.

In the mist surrounding him were the many. He could feel their shadows pulsating through the curtains of gray. He heard their cries: tortured, mad and unbearably hungry all around him, circling him like hyenas around a dying gazelle.

DuPlessis, DuPlessis, DuPlessis became the chant, the howl and the vicious whisper.

Now Robin could feel them reaching out for him, touching him and latching onto him. For an eternity they had been separated from light. They were hungry to devour it.

Ah, Robin thought as they completely engulfed him with their desperate wants, *I am in hell.*

"Make some bloody sense," Caroline repeated.

Robin's killer stared at her a bit wildly.

"He should be breathing at least," she said pointlessly.

"You stuck a big knife in his back," Caroline found herself replying slowly and calmly as if she were talking to a frightened child

"God's blood!" came a new voice — a deeper masculine one. "What has happened?"

Caroline looked around to see two men running down the aisle towards them. Oddly — she found she couldn't drum up any more feelings of surprise at their added presence in the family crypt.

"Hugh! Thank heavens!" cried out Winnifred in relief. "Robin's revenant system isn't repairing him."

The very aquiline and handsome man who had spoken dropped down next to Robin's corpse and glanced warily at Caroline.

"Well, what in god's name happened to him?" he asked.

"She stabbed him in the back with a knife," Caroline pointed out in the same calm voice. At least if she was losing her sanity, she was keeping her dignity. No foaming at the mouth for her: A DeBarry of Hawkesmoor Castle.

"Jesus, Winnifred!" the man named Hugh snapped.

"But I had to show her what he is," Winnifred protested, genuinely rattled. "She had to know Robin's a vampire. How else could I show her?"

Hugh didn't answer. He was pulling Robin away from the tomb, laying him flat on the stone floor and exposing the blood-drenched chest.

"Your kit," said the second man, setting down a medical bag by Hugh's side. Caroline thought he was a little older than the fellow named Hugh but inordinately handsome as well, as if he and the other two belonged to a secret sect of physically perfect people.

"You see, Winnifred, my love, Robin is no longer fully revenant." Hugh was starting CPR on Robin's still chest. "He's more human than vampire. Superhuman, perhaps, but human nonetheless. I think you can kill him now. I think he's no longer immortal."

Winnifred let out an anguished cry. "Oh, god! What have I done?"

"I think you have destroyed the first truly important evolutionary step in vampire history, my dear." Hugh pounded Robin's chest without much success. "I'm afraid Lord Merritt is dead."

Startled, Caroline lifted up her head and focused on the seemingly knowledgeable man.

"*Lord Merritt?*" she whispered dryly. "But my brother Peter is Lord Merritt."

Hugh glanced up from his medical duties. "This Lord Merritt comes from 1750."

"Richard Robin Francis DuPlessis?" Caroline gasped.

She stared at Robin's dead face, with its high elegant planes surrounded by a mane of red-gold hair — just like the painting of Lord Merritt in the Elizabethan gallery.

Was she actually looking at the remains of their missing Lord Merritt? The body she and Peter had spent their entire childhood searching for — the sad skeleton clothed in a once elegant 18th century frock coat.

"Yes," said Winnifred. "That very same Lord Merritt."

"Was that very same Lord Merritt," Hugh threw her a look of frustration. "Really, Winnifred, this was very bad."

Robin's back suddenly arched up violently as he let out a hoarse gasp, just as if he had come up from an underwater ascent and was desperate for oxygen.

He threw his arms out wildly to ward off unknown, invisible assailants.

"Arianrhod," he cried in a thin rasp of a voice. "The Silver Wheel!"

40

Robin gasped again and cried out in pain. In his unconscious agony, he fought Hugh as the doctor tried to attend to his freshly bleeding wound.

"Gabriel," Hugh said urgently as he struggled to prepare a hypodermic needle, "I've got to use human drugs to calm him down, but without your help I'll never get it into his system."

"Right you are," Gabriel replied, obediently securing a powerful grip on Robin's shaking shoulders.

"I'll help." Caroline settled next to Robin, calmly avoiding one of his flailing arms.

Hugh glanced up at her pensively.

"Thank you, Lady Caroline."

"Robin, it's me," she said, bending towards him so she could say the words into his ear. "It's me, Caroline. I'm here. Please let us help you."

Robin's head swung from one side to the other, the beautiful bone structure contorting with pain and fear.

"Arianrhod," he repeated.

Hugh injected a needle into Robin's left arm and almost immediately the frightened flailing began to subside. Robin's face relaxed as Caroline spoke to him in a quiet, reassuring voice.

"Caroline," Robin murmured when she laid a soothing hand on his forehead. "Love Caroline — must protect her."

Caroline found herself beaming down at him despite the very strange circumstances. Whoever he had been. Whatever he was now, Robin really did love her. It had never seemed so certain to her before. She had kept waiting for the moment when he noticed she was a pretty ordinary girl and went back to a glamorous creature like Winnifred. But Robin wasn't going to retreat from Hawkesmoor. He did love her. He did belong to her.

"Well done, your ladyship," murmured Hugh as he opened Robin's shirt to take a real look at the wound. "He likes the sound of your voice. Keep talking to him, please."

"Thanks be to God," said Winnifred, peering over Gabriel's shoulder. "Robin's revenant system is finally up and running."

"He's healing now that the human drugs are taking away the panic." Hugh was placing his stethoscope gently on Robin's chest cavity. "Amazing, really — and quite unique in our scheme of things."

Caroline watched, mesmerized, as Robin's jagged exit wound, which she had just seen pumping out fresh blood, closed itself neatly. In another few moments she suspected even a scar would be impossible to detect.

But then why, she wondered, if he possessed such a remarkable talent for injury repair, was he marked over the heart with such a ghastly black-edged scar? The one he told her he got in a car wreck? Why hadn't that healed the same way?

"Your ladyship?" Gabriel broke into her reverie.

"I'm sorry?" she glanced up at him.

"Obviously Lord Merritt will have to rest somewhere else besides your family crypt." He took his hands from Robin's now peaceful shoulders. "Might I suggest introducing us to your household as Robin's rather eccentric …"

"Sister," said Winnifred from behind Gabriel.

"Brother-in-law," added Hugh, holding up his hand like a schoolboy.

"And I shall be his oldest chum from school," Gabriel decided. "Good old school. What lovely long days of cricket we enjoyed there."

"School… friend?" said Robin in a weak rasp. "Gabriel Addington, is it n…not?"

"Robin," broke in Caroline, leaning across his repaired chest. "You were actually dead."

"Oh, love," he murmured regretfully. "I never wanted you to see me like this."

She laid her hands on either side of his face, caressing the cool smooth skin that stretched over his cheekbones. Despite the impossible things she has just witnessed — and the sheer weight of the new reality, which had settled on her shoulders with all the subtlety of an archbishop's jewel encrusted cope — she found herself marveling at the capricious nature of fate that had allowed Robin to return to her.

Still, and in spite of that baroque mind warp, there was one question she had yet to ask him.

"Are you really Richard Robin Francis DuPlessis, Lord Merritt, who disappeared from this castle in 1750?"

Robin closed his eyes and said nothing.

"Gentlemen," Winnifred stood up, "would you be so kind as to escort me on a tour of this lovely example of early Norman architecture?"

Both Hugh and Gabriel made polite noises and all three simply vanished in front of Caroline's eyes like motes of dust spinning out of a shaft of light.

Funny, she thought, she didn't feel particularly shocked anymore, just incredibly aware that they had performed the showy magical feat simply for her benefit. All so she would be better able to absorb whatever Robin had to tell her.

"So," Caroline said, refocusing on Robin, "are you our missing Lord Merritt?"

He opened his large green eyes. A kind of unbearable sadness glittered in them now.

"I," Robin paused briefly to clear his throat, "I am DuPlessis, Lord Merritt — yes. I am also a revenant — a vampire. Many have died so I could continue to exist on this plane."

"Oh, my god," she breathed, staring down at him in wonder.

He had actually said it. He had actually admitted to being their Lord Merritt. The Lord Merritt who had vanished the night of his betrothal ball. The Lord Merritt who had caused so much pain to those he had left behind.

It was odd, Caroline mused in the brief space before Robin could reply, the fact that he had also admitted to being a mythical being who drank human blood for sustenance was far less interesting to her than his historical affiliation.

"I wasn't given a choice, you know," Robin said as he slowly pulled himself up to a sitting position. He leaned back against the stone tomb with a small out-take of breath. "That night in 1750. I would never have left my family or Hawkesmoor by choice."

"Or Elizabeth," Caroline found herself pointing out. "You loved her very much."

A faint hint of a smile ghosted his elegant features. He reached out with a loose tired arm to run his fingers through the jumble of hair by her left cheekbone.

"I love you, my dear," he replied fondly. "I held Elizabeth Gwayr in the deepest affection and respect. I'd have been proud to give her my name."

"Oh, my god," Caroline repeated, as another treasured Hawkesmoor myth crumbled into dust. "So what exactly did the old needlewoman see that night at the betrothal ball?"

"An old needlewoman?" Robin frowned. "I'm sorry. I don't understand you."

"Rosie Dunway. She was an old crone who did needlework in your time."

"Rosie — an old crone?" Robin almost smiled again. "Rosie Dunway and I grew up together at Hawkesmoor. She was the daughter of one of the stablemen. I taught her to read."

"Your mother's diary records that Rosie claimed to have seen you being devoured by a ghoul that night. Whatever she did see drove her to drink and despair."

Robin looked away from her, his eyes unhappy. "Poor Rosie"

"But," Caroline's voice rose a frustrated notch, "what did she see?"

Robin refocused on her and seemed about to say something when a low rattle, almost a growl, rumbled through the very stonework about them.

The black iron gates creaked loudly on their old hinges and lighting fixtures swayed with the rattling.

"It's an earthquake!" Caroline cried incredulously.

"No. Something different." Robin pulled her against him as centuries of dust swirled up into columns. He took in a sharp breath as his lungs fought against convulsion. The trip had cost him — they had forced entry by latching on to his energy.

Hugh, Gabriel and Winnifred ran towards them.

"We've got to get out into the grounds!" called Hugh. "The place is going haywire!"

"You should see the paranormals," added Gabriel, as he darted forward to help Caroline and a still very weak Robin to their feet. "Phantom dogs, black monks, lights and rappings."

"Look," said Winnifred, holding out a steady hand to Caroline, "all around us."

Shimmering through veils of ancient dust were many figures. Shadow figures — their physical features were indistinct but vague outlines revealed the entities as having human form — were heading towards them with unnerving certainty.

"It's incredible," said Caroline as various streams of Morse code-like tapping and rapping began to assail the crypt walls. There was a low persistent chant, too, underneath the noise.

"Out, out," cried Hugh as he slung an arm around Robin's waist. "We're being surrounded."

"But they're just ghosts." Winnifred glanced around; her anxious eyes giving lie to her offhand comment. "Just bits of directionless matter."

"Not ghosts," murmured Robin with a painful wheeze. "They came with me."

They fled the crypt. The night air revealed that the castle was in an uproar. Electrical lights went on and off as the power surged unevenly. The family dogs were madly barking, racing about the grounds after unseen entities. The two security men were running on the Great Walk, their torches bobbing with the same nervous energy of their shouting voices.

"Caroline," cried her father running towards them with a flashlight of his own. "The bloody power has gone mad! I don't know if it's us or the wretched Middleborough District …"

"You all right?" she asked anxiously.

"Yes, perfectly." The Earl surveyed the three strangers without a blink. He seemed content that they were not obvious representatives of the regional power company.

"Allow me to introduce you to Robin's family," Caroline interjected quickly. "Robin's sister Winnifred, and her husband Hugh. Robin's old school friend—"

"Gabriel, sir. Gabriel Addington." The vampire made a small and polite bow after Winnifred and Hugh had made similar responses. "An honor, sir."

"Let us not stand too much on formality during this siege," Caroline's father suggested, waving them after him. "Come along. We have to sort rooms. Everything's in a frightful muddle."

"Best to not rattle your father with new revelations, Caroline," said Hugh in a low voice. "Take Gabriel and give me a moment to stabilize Lord Merritt."

Caroline looked as if she would like to argue the point, not wanting to leave Robin's side. She hesitated, her face strained with worry and frustration. Finally, Caroline gave a tight nod. She and Gabriel ran to catch up with the Earl who was bellowing at the security guards to stop flitting about like old ladies at a boxing match.

"His breathing is very shallow," Hugh told Winnifred. "I'd like another look at him immediately."

But before she could assist the vampire doctor, Robin doubled over in pain, dropping to his knees.

"I must," he said in a rasp, his chest seizing with effort, "send them back."

Winnifred threw Hugh a puzzled glance. "Send who back?"

Hugh ignored her question as he worked furiously to prepare a hypodermic. "Adrenaline," he said tersely. "It should open his lungs."

Winnifred stood up and scanned the castle walls. The ancient grey stone flickered into view whenever the power surges allowed the artificial lights to function. "Hugh, look."

Hugh pumped the adrenaline into Robin's arm. "Winnifred, for god's sake."

"Hugh," she repeated urgently.

Hugh jerked his head up in annoyance, about to snap at Winnifred. Then he saw the shadows moving across Hawkesmoor's walls. Not products of the electrical surges, they were alive — intelligent. Entities such as he had never seen before. They emanated with malevolence as if they changed the very air they moved through.

"I promised to keep this world barred from your kind." Robin pushed away roughly away from Hugh and dragged his battered frame to his feet. He raised his arms towards the shadow beings as if he were literally pushing them back to wherever it was they had come. "When I no longer can, there will be another to take my place."

Silence answered Robin's words. In fact, all of Hawkesmoor had lapsed into quiet. The castle lights stopped flickering, all hammerings and chanting voices died and the shadow figures disintegrated, blowing away with the night breeze. It was over. The entities were gone.

Hugh cleared his throat. "Game, set and match to Lord Merritt."

41

The three vampires watched him in an intent combination of awe and envy as he took a long sip of whiskey.

"I realize now I've heard the voices all my life," Robin said from a chair by the fireplace. He gazed into the amber liquid and wondered what the morning would bring him: news that Caroline wanted him gone or hasty preparations for a hasty wedding. "Only after Winnifred stabbed me, could I hear them clearly."

"Them?" asked Gabriel from his place on one of the other Victorian Pseudo-Japanese chairs.

Hugh and Winnifred had gotten Robin to his rooms without eliciting much notice from the DeBarry family or its castle staff. Once Hawkesmoor had returned to relative peace, Gabriel left an anxious Caroline to prepare for her wedding and had come to discover how all was with him.

"Before I was vampire, I was faerie," Robin said. "I am Tylwyth Teg."

"Tylwyth Teg," breathed Hugh in wonderment, "the 'fair ones' — singers at the edge of time, watchers of dimensional gateways."

"Apparently, in my human time," he nodded at Hugh in appreciation of the vampire doctor's arcane knowledge, "I was the strongest genetic cross in generations of DuPlessis. My father couldn't hear their song — they use poetry and metaphor as their communicative language — although he had the affinity for music and certain intuitive abilities."

"*Caer Arianrhod*," Hugh murmured appreciatively. "I knew when I found connections to the white dragon in the Welsh *Barddas*."

Winnifred tilted her head in puzzlement. "The Welsh *Barddas*?"

"Ancient Welsh manuscripts thought to have been dictated by *Naddreds*," Hugh replied. "They're powerful Welsh bards. Far older than Merlin."

"I see," she said, raising a quizzical eyebrow, "of course — and the connection between pretty faerie folk and this particular castle would be.?"

Robin looked up from his whiskey and focused on the vampire who had once been his owner and lover. Funny, he thought as he ran his gaze from her lovely oval face and down over the body he had spent so many nights beside— she who had told him with such certainty: *vampires never love, they only hunger,* loved him deeply. He could sense it now, keenly, and see it reflected in her eyes. What a great stupid cosmic joke on them both.

"I am from the Tylwyth Teg, as was my father. All DuPlessis carry the bloodline." Robin reached over and squeezed her hand. "Don't you see? Hawkesmoor's legend of Merlin chaining the white dragon Saxon to this ground — it's all just a poetic metaphor for our family's gene pool."

"I don't think we are really understanding what Robin is telling us." Hugh waved his hands in frustration.

"And that would be?" Gabriel shifted in his chair towards the revenant physician.

Hugh leaned forward to emphasize his point. "*We are not alone!* There are other preternatural species besides vampires. It's a bloody amazing concept. It also proves conclusively that strands of human myth and revenants are inextricably intertwined!"

Gabriel made a sour face. "Oh, that old water into wine, wine into blood business." He made a dismissive gesture with his hands. "That was a creaky theory back when we vampires gathered around John Dee's library fire in the 15th century."

"And inadvertently you make my point for me," Hugh insisted. "Did not Dee proclaim Elizabeth R was the fulfillment of the Arianrhod prophecy? That the Queen was the promised lunar goddess — *the lady of the silver wheel* — who would keep the skein of time from unraveling?"

The former monk crossed his arms with a small sigh. "Well… yes, but he was only waxing poetical so Queen Bess would continue to issue his meal tickets."

"Poetical 'bout Elizabeth I, yes!" Candlethorne countered quickly. "I think Dee was off in his calculations. I think *now* — this new millennium — is the time of Arianrhod."

"Gentlemen," said Robin, standing up. He brushed Winnifred's cheek with the back of his fingers, "and dearest Winnifred."

She looked up at him with a smile and took his hand in hers.

"I do not have the answers to all your questions. I do know that other beings have walked the Earth long before revenant kind claimed it. I know that others with dark and terrible ambitions for this world are gathering, waiting impatiently for a portal to collapse."

"God's blood," whistled Gabriel. "So, in a strange way, despite all the colorful mythic language, it's as simple as that. You are to hold off…"

"An army," Robin said and took another drink of whiskey. He wondered if they could tell how frightened he was. "A dark and terrible army."

Winnifred kissed the back of his hand. "We've done that before, you and I."

"Love," he glanced down at her with admiration, "your courage has always humbled me."

"You'll need quite a lot of vampire help, I expect, to hold back such an army," Hugh pointed out. "You have three here in us."

Caroline stood at her bedroom window, wiping her brow with the back of her hand. The fever seemed to be abating but she felt sick and knew it wasn't just the pregnancy. The awful weight of what she had learned twisted around her like a mace and chain. The world was now a dark, uncertain place where supernatural creatures stalked ordinary people. Even Robin had stolen blood from, and perhaps even killed, innocent human beings.

A quiet knock came at her door. It startled her.

"Caroline," came Robin's voice, "could we talk. Please?"

"I'm really very tired," she replied. "No."

"Caroline?" He sounded surprised at the sharpness in her voice.

"Oh, why not?" she relented, feeling miserable. "Come in."

Robin opened the door and tentatively stepped inside.

He was so beautiful, Caroline thought instantly, with a catch in her breath. Tall and elegant in his black cashmere sweater and her brother's well-worn jeans. His red-gold hair had grown and now fell past his shoulders making the resemblance between him and the anonymous painting even more striking.

"Why do you bother with the spectacles?" she asked curtly, referring to the handsome tortoiseshell glasses he wore. "Surely an extraordinary predator like yourself has perfect sight."

Robin flinched and pulled them off his face. "Forgive me. I've become accustomed to wearing them."

"Back in the chapel," Caroline looked away from him as her voice broke. She paused to regain control of it. "Back at the chapel, I thought maybe I could handle all of this — all of this frightening, dark stuff. But you're asking me to accept a reality in which you have quite possibly killed …"

Robin stepped forward as if he would like to touch her but then stopped awkwardly in mid-movement, "I wish I was just a history professor but I'm not, Caroline, I'm not."

"But why didn't you tell me earlier?"

He threw his long hands up in frustration. "Yes. I can just imagine you accepting a dinner invitation from a gentleman claiming to be a vampire from the 18th century."

"A gentleman doesn't hunt his fellow man for blood." Caroline almost winced at her brutality.

"Caroline," he breathed, as if his vocal chords had become partially paralyzed.

"I mean — why would a glamorous vampire like yourself want to marry me anyway?" She interjected in a very brittle tone. "You wanted Hawkesmoor back?"

"Don't," he said, his back stiffening. A warning.

Caroline straightened her spine as well. She returned his cool gaze.

"I was fully human once," Robin replied, tightening his elegant jaw. "As much a part of this world as you."

"You're a vampire," she said, "and you didn't tell me."

His face shadowed with strain and he turned away from her, walking to the fireplace. Robin gazed down at the gas jets cleverly masquerading as a cheery Edwardian coal fire.

"Almost real," he swallowed hard, "like me."

"You swept in and changed everything — *everything*!" she continued, "Not just the direction of my life but everything. The world. Vampires exist! Vampires exist! Vampires exist!'"

The rest of her words were lost to a deep and raw sob that violently retched from her throat like bile. Caroline felt as if she were vomiting panic and despair. She stood and sobbed with a ferocity she hadn't experienced since her mother was killed in the hunt field.

He slowly pulled away from the fireplace and faced her. His face was drawn sharply with sorrow.

"You have my promise," his tone flat and dead. "I will leave tonight and you will never see me again."

She wiped furiously at her streaming eyes and tried to recover her speaking voice. "There's a baby now."

Robin held out a handkerchief he had retrieved from a pocket. "I will always protect you both," he said. "You can forget about me and my kind."

"Forget?" Another sob broke from her aching lungs.

He crossed to the door. "I can only beg you to understand that courage failed me. I should have trusted yours."

Caroline took a deep breath and felt her anguish begin to break apart. Turbulent, painful change had come when her mother had died. She had been devastated and frightened, completely unnerved by the realization that she would have to help her family in their grief and in their inherited duty to Hawkesmoor. She had straightened her spine, accepted the challenge and out of that initial misery emerged a worthwhile life of purpose and deep familial connections.

And despite this new reality with all its strange horror, she could do it again. Suddenly an old pop lyric skipped across in her mind: *I'd rather live with him in his world than live without him in mine.*

"No," she called after him, "don't go."

Robin paused and looked back.

"You really do love me?" she asked.

"Oh, Caroline," he said with regret, "that you should even need to ask."

"Because I will always love you." She came and wrapped her arms about his waist, laying her head on his chest. They stood together for a long time, Robin stroking her hair.

"My darling girl," he asked quietly, "are you quite sure?"

She nodded, tightening her hold about his waist. "I will try, Robin. I promise you I will."

42

Robin opened his eyes to the darkness of the Japanese room. He felt his extra keen vampire senses flare up registering that the room's atmosphere was now very different — charged as if the air molecules were moving at a faster rate. He sat up slowly.

Something was out in the dark. He felt an almost physical impression in the air like a silk curtain brushing against his skin.

"Who is there?" he said softly.

The night air seemed to shimmer towards him like a ripple on water.

"Can I do something for you?" Robin narrowed his eyes trying to find an image. "Is there something you want from me?"

He heard the sound of velvet and silk rustling, a slide of a leather-soled shoe over floor. Then a whisper, a faint thread of a voice he'd not known in centuries.

"Elizabeth?" Robin pushed off the bed and forward into the darkness. He reached about frantically, knowing that she ought to be within reach but wasn't.

Robin heard his room door swing open and shut. He heard what sounded like a woman's sob in the distance and the echo of light footsteps running down the hall.

He moved with his vampire swiftness but the dimly lit hallway revealed no glimpses of 18th century phantoms.

"Damn!" Robin said out loud.

He returned to the Japanese room and made a direct line for the drinks table, pouring himself a stiff whiskey.

What a terrible sadness.

Unlike the mysterious boy, what was left of Elizabeth Gwayr existed as a badly scrambled packet of molecules, fixated on some minor point from a lost life.

That was really the pathetic aspect of hauntings. Humans gave such relevance to the action of ghosts: *The old black monk must be trying to lead us to monastic treasure lost during the sacking of the brotherhoods by Henry the Eighth! — The Green Lady warns us of impending doom by pointing to the wall in just that spot!* In truth, ghosts retained so little of their original personalities that they tended to latch onto whatever insignificant actions they dimly managed to recollect.

Hence what remained of the old black monk might really be trying to find its way to the monastic loo and the Green Lady could be simply pointing to a spot where her broken personality thought she was instructing a servant to lay out hot drinks.

Robin drank the rest of the whiskey in one shot. His head felt like it was going to explode from all of the hideous revelations it had absorbed since he had walked into that New York museum.

But what else did he expect? He had lied to himself for decades: Elizabeth had married a kind young nobleman who had treated her as the gem she was, his parents had lived long contented lives and somehow, Ambrose Westmacott had lost out on the succession to a responsible person who understood the meaning of duty.

All pathetic lies. Robin pushed off the bed and went to pour himself another whiskey. He had abandoned them all — and now he was supposed to become some sort of faerie knight defending the earthly dimension from disaster.

He had even lied to Caroline, with reassuring murmurings about how he had never killed for blood. How he used modern blood banks and employed the elegant technique of stealing small quantities from humans when he had to go to a living source. All he ever did was lie and misdirect.

"So —your ladyship, where is that handsome groom?" asked the ever-cheerful Miss Cordelia Shaw, the region's most successful caterer to the ton. Her workers and specially kitted out vans had swept into Hawkesmoor's courtyard like an invading army.

"I don't know," replied Caroline wearily, watching as Miss Shaw's crew members began to disgorge a frightening amount of stuff from the vans. There had been so much happy interest in the castle wedding that her father, loath to hurt local feelings, had transformed her discreet family gathering into a major Yorkshire event. "I'm looking for him."

"Very good. If we could just go over the schedule." Miss Shaw held up her electronic tablet. "I don't think I've ever put together a wedding so quickly!"

"Beryl will show you where everything is and all that." Caroline indicated Beryl's little blue Metro as it arrived in the courtyard.

There was a time, Caroline reflected as she turned to begin her search for Robin, when Hawkesmoor would have had a much more satisfactory staff of its own to manage such affairs. Nowadays most of the smaller estates used professional caterers like the indomitable Miss Shaw — which wouldn't be so bad, Caroline admitted, nipping around one of Miss Shaw's neat little vans, if the insurance company would allow the DeBarrys to use their own silver and plate. Apparently it was all too valuable to be used for such purposes. Her mother had been the last Hawkesmoor bride to sit down to a wedding feast served on the family possessions.

After exhausting the usual places, such as the Japanese room and the kitchen where, unfashionably, the DeBarry family preferred to take breakfast, Caroline remembered how previously he'd walked the battlements and seen the ghost of the blond boy.

And there she found him on the Great Walk leaning against the its ancient stone, gazing out at miles of moor country that fairly sparkled under a bright clear sky.

"Robin?" Caroline ventured cautiously.

"Beautiful, isn't it?" He turned towards the sound of her voice and opened his arms expansively to indicate their surroundings, a nearly empty bottle in one hand. "Bloody bloody beautiful."

"Have," she stared at him in dismay, "you been drinking?"

"You'll be pleased to know," Robin lowered his voice to a stage whisper as he lifted the bottle to prove his point, "it's only whiskey."

"As opposed to what? One of the catering assistants?"

He gave her a dazzling smile, bowing rather formally given his simple costume of jeans sans any shirt or sweater.

"Very funny," he said. "Your ladyship possesses a quick wit."

"How long have you been out here?" Caroline shrugged off her favorite coat, an old baggy leather thing that had belonged to her father and had lovely big pockets in which to stick the odd mane comb or bit of wire.

"I'm a vampire, my love. You have noticed my body temperature is lower than yours." Robin looked at her with amusement. "The cold doesn't really affect me."

"Piffle!" she replied, holding open the coat so he could slip his arms into the sleeves. "Despite the summer weather — this is England."

He put the whiskey bottle on the stone ledge and obediently put his arms into the leather coat.

"I couldn't sleep," Robin admitted as she pulled the coat about his shoulders. "Came out here to sit in the dark and look at the stars."

"And forgot to come in once the sun came up, did you?"

He reached out and ran his long fingers over the gray stone ledge as if savoring the rough texture on his skin. "I played up here as a child, you know."

"Was it very different? Out there, I mean." Caroline peered over the wall at the lawns below. "We have some inventories of the interior — not especially great ones but they have allowed us some insight. The grounds, though, are a bit of a mystery."

"My parents," Robin picked up the bottle and to her continued dismay, took another long drink before answering, "had a preference for French formal design. The design for the lawns and gardens was elaborate and really very difficult for the English grounds men to keep up after the French landscaper had left. We employed thirty of them to maintain such high formality in the middle of the moor country."

"Thirty gardeners!" Caroline whistled softly. "Gosh."

Robin leaned against the gray stone and stared down. "Most of it is gone. Your Victorian ancestors, I imagine."

"I, for one, am sort of glad they did," she said. "Imagine how we would have to struggle to maintain such a massive design."

"You have plenty of money now." He had another swallow of whiskey. "It could be restored. I think I could even draw you a diagram."

Caroline turned away from the view. "You are drinking rather a lot, Robin. I had no idea vampires could suck down single-malt."

"You're beginning to sound a lot like Winnifred." He winced slightly. "Good old Winnifred. One of the best. She was my lover, you know, many, many, many years ago."

Caroline felt a jolt of pain at his admission and struggled to prevent the sudden emotion from taking over her thoughts and expression. She had to remain clear-headed in the midst of all the incredible events swirling around Hawkesmoor.

"It happened," Robin said, as if he had no concept that his previous comment could be hurtful, "down there off one of Monsieur Lavec's beautiful limed pathways." He scanned the green expanse below and shook his head slightly. "Gone, now, of course. Replaced by serviceable Victorian gravel."

"What do you mean by it?"

Robin didn't reply. He lifted the bottle and downed another draught of whiskey.

Frustrated, Caroline stepped away from the stone wall. "When you feel like getting dressed, there are a few things you might do before people start arriving."

"That day in 1750," Robin didn't turn away from the view below, "I had a few things to attend to as well. Nothing very crucial: just some minor estate matters with a few local farmers, and, of course, the long process of preparing oneself for an important social occasion. I sat for ages while my valet combed powder through my hair. Other manservants were taken up by readying my flawless costume."

"Your betrothal ball to Elizabeth Gwayr? The night you disappeared?" Caroline breathed, her frustration fading as she realized that she was about to hear the answer to a very old mystery.

"The night I lost my human life," Robin said with a nod. "You see; I had loved Corisande very much. One of Handel's favorite sopranos, she had been my mistress before we married."

"So that's why there is no record of it," Caroline interjected, moving closer to him so she would not miss a single word of his soft voice.

"An unsuitable match for Lord Merritt. Fortunate for me, many would have said, that she died so shortly thereafter. I buried her in a miserable little churchyard in London. As befits her rank as lawful wife of Lord Merritt, Corisande ought to be here, of course, in the family crypt. I remember the thought of it tugging at me all afternoon as I was made ready for my new betrothed."

"The guilt."

Robin turned his head to look at her keenly. "Yes, that's exactly right."

Caroline reached out and laid a gentle hand on his forearm. "All the historical information we have indicated that your match with Elizabeth Gwayr was a joyous love match."

"Oh, I had no qualms about wedding Elizabeth. She suited me and my situation very well. I found her very beautiful. I desired her."

Caroline felt another jab of jealousy and chewed her lip. She reckoned he must be almost three hundred years old so, of course, he would have had wives, lovers. Even if it made sense, she didn't like it.

Robin covered her hand with his and intertwined his long fingers with hers. "I just did not love her in the way I loved my wife — or you."

She reached up to kiss his cheek.

"I will tell you what I can remember of what happened to me," he said. "It will be the first time I have ever spoken of it and even I don't understand much of what occurred."

YORKSHIRE, 1750

"I do not wish a black patch," said Robin irritably.

"But, my lord," protested Sudeley, his favorite dresser, "the patch finishes a gentleman's countenance. One on your lordship's cheekbone will…"

"'Tis enough to be covered in hair powder." Robin waved him away while staring at his gilded reflection in the full-length mirror.

He thought Elizabeth might really prefer the Lord Merritt with windblown hair and muddy riding clothes to the artificial perfection he saw in the looking glass. He gleamed from head to foot, a sort of ice king: white hair pulled back with a black ribbon, flawless white linen and rich black frock coat, even the polished silver buckles on his shoes shone in the candlelight.

"All of you go," he commanded to his little army of dressers. "I would take some time alone."

They glanced at each other warily.

"But, my lord," Sudeley volunteered cautiously, "Your gracious mother has requested your presence. Would you have us fail…"

"I would take some time alone," he repeated. "Harcourt, pray inform Her Ladyship, the Countess, I will be attending her shortly. Jenkins, a glass of claret and be gone — all of you."

They made the usual sniveling noises and fled. Robin wondered idly as he watched the heavy door close behind them if they would retreat to the servant quarters with tales of how Lord Merritt was in a fine temper before his own betrothal ball.

Robin emerged from his dressing closet. He picked up the glass of claret Jenkins had dutifully set out and took a sip. The warm taste was fortifying.

He looked about his main room and marveled that Elizabeth Gwayr who was always happier out in the fresh air with horses and dogs than at needlework, would also one day call it her own.

She would be in the Great Hall now. Beautifully gowned and branded with her mother's best jewels, waiting for her future husband to appear. Elizabeth was performing her duty, what she had been brought up to accomplish for her family. She was making a powerful alliance.

Fortunately for Elizabeth such an alliance was not an unpleasant outcome of her girlish years. She actually loved him and he was very fond of her. They would be kind to each other and it would an enviable match.

Robin almost sighed. Yet it was his duty to keep her pinned like a specimen butterfly by filling her with as many children as her small frame could endure producing.

He thought it had not occurred to Elizabeth what she was really exchanging for the right to be Lady Merritt — or perhaps it had, and in that peculiar way women had of coping, she offered up her youth to him simply content in the knowledge he was not a coarse boor.

"I pledge, Elizabeth Gwayr," Robin said out loud, lifting the glass of claret in salute, "you shall have your fair share of horses and the moor."

A voice sang in the distance, light and airy: "When he returns, no more will she want, no more will she grieve."

Startled, Robin broke the paper-thin crystal in his hand. The wine spilled over his fingers as the glass shards crumbled.

"Corisande?" his voice had gone hoarse.

But no, it could not be. Corisande was dead. It had to be one of the singers Oliver had hired for the ball's entertainment but that particular aria from Galatea was Corisande's signature piece. Oliver would never allow it to be sung again in his presence.

It came again. Clear high white notes. "No more will she grieve."

Robin backed up in horror. Why was Oliver allowing anyone to sing from Galatea? It was like a knife to the heart, a terrible reproach.

Then he heard a scratching sound like a bird was beating against one of his windows. He swerved to look but nothing was there.

The soprano voice caught his attention again. It seemed closer now — in the very hallway outside his rooms.

He strode to the door and flung it open.

"How dare anyone sing that…" Robin began furiously, until his mind absorbed the fact that the hallway was deserted. Even the usual footmen were missing, as everyone was needed down below.

The soprano voice floated down the empty corridor. "When he returns, no more will she want."

The shimmering notes sounded so much as if they belonged to Corisande. She had possessed a true 'white voice' — a rarity among opera singers. Was there another young singer in all of England who could produce such clear uncolored phrases?

He heard quiet footfalls on one of the rear staircases and then the rustle of a lady's gown.

"Please!" Robin called as he followed in pursuit. "I must speak to you!"

But the voice and the footsteps always just eluded him. They took him down to the ground floor where the beautiful white voice seemed doused by the rumble of activity swirling through the castle's most important rooms.

Robin followed what now seemed to be only a relentless instinct. He moved around brilliantly liveried footmen and other servants as they handled serving carts and trays. He forced away the lovely crisp notes that the musicians were playing and the cheerful roar of his parents' guests in the distant Great Hall.

He followed this instinct out of a side entrance and into the cool night air of the formal gardens. Here he could again perceive the gentle rustle of a gown or a footstep on the pathway.

Further and further he went into the terraced lawns of Lavec's design. Further and further away were the sounds of Hawkesmoor's betrothal ball until it was simply a pleasant murmur underscoring the calls of a night bird and sudden breezes through flowerbeds. He was running now — hoping for just one glimpse in the moonlight of the mysterious singer with Corisande's voice.

God's teeth, Robin swore as he finally came to a stop. He took off the peerless black frock coat and tossed it onto one of Lavec's neoclassical benches. What in blazes was he doing? What would a hired singer be doing this far away from the other musicians?

He pulled at the neck cloth and threw that after the coat, taking in a few deep breaths of the earthy grass-scented air.

"Robin?"

He looked up. Around the edge of a rose briar stepped a slender form he had not expected to see again in his lifetime.

"Corisande," he managed to force from his throat, sinking to his knees on the damp grass.

She was as he had first seen her — the acknowledged beauty of the opera stage. All the cruel ravages of the consumption gone: the alabaster skin was flawless, the famous red hair fell in heavy curls to her waist and, perhaps, most wondrous of all, there was no more pain in her luminous blue eyes. She even seemed to glow faintly in the moonlight, as if her exquisite white gown was dappled with fairy dust.

"Will you not greet me, husband?" Corisande said, holding up her arms towards him. "Do I not please you?"

"Corisande," Robin's voice broke, "how can it be you?"

"Let us not trouble ourselves with what cannot be understood." She came towards him with outstretched hands. "Can we not rejoice?"

"But you are dead," he replied miserably.

Corisande stepped close enough to reach behind his neck to untie the black ribbon from his hair. She slipped her cool fingers into the long powdered locks and pulled them free about his shoulders.

"What a shame, "she murmured, "to cool such amber flames."

Robin wrapped his arms about her slender hips, resting his head against the white silk velvet at her waist. He could feel Corisande's solid physical form in his arms. He could feel her body rise and fall as she breathed. Somehow, incredibly, she was with him.

"I've missed you, Corisande," he said brokenly. "You must never leave me again. Never."

"Dearest, Robin," Corisande whispered. "You must not cry."

Robin pulled himself up off the grass, laughing as she wiped at his streaming eyes with the edge of her sleeve. He kissed her forehead, then found her mouth and kissed her with more passion than he had allowed himself to demonstrate during the final stages of her terrible illness. She returned his feelings with a sensual ferocity he could not ever remember her expressing towards him in the past.

"Corisande," he breathed, pulling away for a moment, "let us go back. You are my rightful wife."

"No," she whispered before she kissed him again. "Do you bind yourself to me?"

"You are my wife." Robin felt almost faint from the power she was exuding. He had never known Corisande as such a sexual creature. She had always done her best to please him but her long illness had made her rather fragile. It had always been like handling a rare piece of glass.

"Are you mine forever?" Corisande persisted, her arms sliding up around his back.

Robin could not find the strength to utter a word as he gave in to her desire to kiss him deeply.

"Are you mine forever?" she repeated once she had released him from the hungry embrace.

"Yes."

He felt like a man unable to swim, caught without a life line, in deep water, gasping for air.

Corisande let out a triumphant cry. He felt the lithe figure in his arms begin to alter shape. Her glowing white form guttered out, replaced by something ancient, dark and awful, crafted of misshapen sinew and bone.

Robin felt then that he was lifted up. High into the realms of the night sky where owls hunted their prey, as if the creature had simply taken to wing. The cold air pulled cruelly at his hair as they left Hawkesmoor behind. He knew what it was to be the stunned sparrow in the talons of the hawk.

The thing dropped down in a little grove of trees Robin recognized, despite the frozen horror that had paralyzed his senses. It was the Roman copse. The place the farmers spun stories about, insisting that something evil haunted the old trees.

He was carelessly thrown to the ground. Before he could recover from the force of it, he felt himself being yanked to his feet and his arms stretched apart as if he were about to be drawn and quartered. Lifting his head, he saw that he was strung by the wrists between two of the copse's trees.

Dazed, he searched the darkness for his attacker.

"You are wondering why you have been selected," said a cultivated voice to his left.

Robin moved his head to find the speaker. The thing was altering form again. An elegant figure wrapped in the patrician robes of a Roman took shape before him.

"I come here now and again," said the creature, indicating the copse with an arm cuffed in heavy beaten gold. "It is one of my touchstones. You came here yourself not long ago with a maiden, did you not?"

Robin stared at him and nodded, remembering the afternoon he had spent with Elizabeth.

"Both of you... So beautiful... so young,"

It came closer. Robin took in the aquiline face with its chiseled Octavian features. The new shape was that of a very handsome older man, perhaps fifty years of age from the thick silver hair and gentle creases about the clear gray eyes.

This shape moved with great ease, as if it were a mask the creature worn often and was very comfortable with.

"But, of the two, you were the prize." The gray eyes looked him over with real pleasure, expressing the same pride of ownership a gentleman might have for a particularly fine horse.

"You will bear my mark well." The Roman shape reached out and tore open Robin's linen shirt. "I prefer such pale skin." It stood back a moment to admire Robin's heaving chest. "Why I often choose one from these isles."

"My oldest pronounceable human name is Morvidus." He traced a long finger along one of Robin's ribs and circled around his heart. "It's beating so fast — just like a little bird."

Robin could only stare back at him, unable even to push away from the entity's cold touch. He had never known such pure fear. He had never been completely subjugated before anyone or anything.

"The revenants call me 'The Old One,'" the Roman shape continued. "Once you walk among them, Robin, I shall finally be able to see the Corpse Road fall."

Robin tried to find his voice. When he finally managed to speak, it left his throat low and ravaged.

"My father will avenge my death."

The Roman laughed with real amusement. "What a gallant idea."

He crossed his arms and pondered Robin's face for a long moment.

"Shall I tell you what I am going to do to you? You should know that the mark of Morvidus is considered a royal line among the revenants—highly desirable not only for its symbolic value but as a mark of having endured incredible pain."

Robin felt his knees give way. He sank as far as the bindings at his wrists would allow. There would be no quick execution, no momentary flash of pain followed by blessed darkness and peace. The entity was going to make him suffer. He wondered dully if at the end of all the pain, he would finally find release—and the mysterious God the family priest promised existed somewhere draped in glory and divine forgiveness.

"Rather surprisingly it appears my children possess a much less invasive way to hunt, kill or multiply." Morvidus cocked his head to the side in thought. "Some sort of evolutionary improvement, I expect. But that concept has no meaning for you as yet, does it?

"I am," Morvidus said, taking his cool fingers to Robin's skin again, his voice gentle and almost calming, "going to rip you open from here to here."

He traced an icy line from the bottom of Robin's throat to the top of his left hip.

Robin knew he was going to be sick. He dropped his head, gagging on saliva and the claret Jenkins had poured out for him.

"I am going to take out your heart while it is still beating," Morvidus lifted Robin's chin off his chest so he could continue, "and drain you of blood."

Robin was trembling so badly that Caroline put an arm about his waist.

"Please," she said, "you don't have to say anymore."

He let out a shaky breath. "I'm afraid there isn't much more to tell."

"That horrible scar on your chest… is that the Morvidus mark?"

Robin nodded and moved back a little so he could open her father's old leather jacket to reveal the black wound vibrant against his pale skin.

"Morvidus was right," he said roughly. "The pain was unendurable and yet, I did endure."

Robin's elegant jaw tightened and he reached for the bottle.

"It's amazing you didn't go mad," Caroline said softly.

"I can remember begging God to die but I couldn't even faint. I now know that Morvidus' body fluids must have acted like some kind amphetamine and I had ingested his saliva when he had projected himself as Corisande." Robin finished off the whiskey. "I remember seeing my own heart out in front of my eyes, glistening blue black in the moonlight.

Yorkshire, 1750

"Drink, my bride," said Morvidus, as he opened a gash on his own chest. "Drink and the pain will lessen."

He pulled Robin's head to the wound. Robin felt cold thick blood ooze across his parched mouth. It was a sick-making sensation and yet he did as he was bidden. He was thoroughly broken. He would have given his own mother to Morvidus if such an act would stop the pain.

"You will see me again," Morvidus murmured, cradling Robin as he drank from the gushing wound, "when the gate is open and all of mankind hides in the dark."

"That's the last I remember of Morvidus." Robin shivered despite the bright English sun. "I woke days later in France to discover I was now owned by another vampire named Anthony Fortesque."

"Owned?" She frowned at the word.

"He was my master. It's a common thing in vampire society. A newly created vampire does service for an established one." He shrugged loosely. "It was not a pleasant time. He treated me badly but I was finally able to leave and after a few other minor adventures, I ended up teaching history at NYU."

Caroline, wordlessly, wrapped her arms about him, wondering if she would ever be able to find anything soothing or reassuring to say in reply to such a tale.

It was there, with her head resting against his chest, that a ghastly thought came unbidden into her head.

"Robin?"

"Yes, love?" His voice sounded far away as if he was still in the past, remembering the ribbon of horrors that had tied up his life.

"Your heart — he showed you your own heart."

Caroline felt his body stiffen. Hearing the story coming back at him in her voice had the power to rattle him. She wished she didn't have to ask but the idea was invasive, it demanded an answer.

"Did he put it back?" she whispered.

To her surprise, Robin relaxed and laughed. He kissed the top of her head affectionately.

"Oh love, I am sorry," he said still laughing. "What lady would wish to marry a heartless man?"

Robin stepped back from her and touched the old black scar with his hand.

"Yes. Morvidus put it back, which I must say was almost as awful as losing it." He held out his other hand to her. "Come here, darling."

Caroline accepted his hand and allowed him to gently guide her head to the scarred section of his chest.

"Hear it beating?" he asked, pressing her against him.

"Yes," she replied almost breathlessly, when the steady dull thudding in his chest cavity became clear. "Yes — I can hear it!"

Robin seemed to find that funny as well and began laughing again. It wasn't until Caroline stood up to share in his remarkable good humor that she realized he wasn't laughing at all.

"Oh," she said, putting her arms about his shaking frame.

Suddenly she had a very clear sense of why they were both standing there on Hawkesmoor's lonely Great Walk. Robin needed someone to mourn for who he had once been.

"You've never allowed yourself to feel sorrow for that Lord Merritt, have you? Never a drop of pity for that frightened young man in 1750 — only guilt for the life the vampire has lived."

It wasn't until the long shadows that summoned late afternoon fell across the Great Walk that they finally came down, ready to face the night.

43

"You are a veritable vision, Lord Merritt, sir," said Hugh, as he entered the small room just off the Norman chapel where Robin was waiting for the ceremony to begin.

Robin, dressed in white tie he had possessed since the 1930s, offered Hugh a tired smile.

"I might be careful about whom you call Lord Merritt around here," he said. "I relinquished my claim to that title a very long time ago."

"Mr. Dashwood," Hugh grinned and made a slight bow, "I can tell you that nearly 100 percent of the country gentry from hereabouts have gathered out there. I don't think I've ever overheard so much excited curiosity about a groom. Usually that sort of stuff is reserved for the bride's dress."

"God," said Robin quietly.

"But the good news is Winnifred, Gabriel and I haven't spotted a single errant ghost or mysterious shadow entity — nor has a vampire friendly or otherwise, crossed our paths yet."

"Do you think all is ready?"

"The new Lord Merritt's finally arrived with Caroline's little sister who was not best pleased about being herded into her hunt ball dress from last year." Hugh patted him on the shoulder. "So, shall I inform the good father that you will emerge?"

Robin let out a short breath and nodded.

"Right then!" Candlethorne gave him another encouraging smile. "Be back in a little minute."

The hired musicians out in the chapel shifted into another Bach adagio and Robin smiled, thinking how the harpsichordist must be going slightly mad trying to keep his instrument tuned in the ancient room's inconsistent temperature.

He ran a comb through his hair one last time and checked the status of his occasionally capricious cuff links. Vaguely, he was aware of how much he wanted a drink. A glass of sherry would do.

Christ, he was freezing. Since his system's biological change he found he was always rather cold — as if the vampire's naturally lower temperature was now being perceived as such by his resurrected human faculties.

Hugh came in through the door. "Time, Robin."

"Do you think," said Robin, "we could have a quick sherry — for courage?"

Caroline nervously pressed her hands against the heavy satin of Elizabeth's magnificent dress. She was about to marry the mysterious Lord Merritt of the unsigned portrait. The Lord Merritt who had become a vampire. Maybe it really was all just a particularly detailed dream. She'd wake up to discover everything was the result of too much Shepherd's Pie at dinner and the Americans had arrived with earth moving equipment to start their car maintenance facilities.

"Thank the lord," came the crisp tones of Miss Shaw, "there you are!"

Caroline turned to focus on the officious caterer as she came into the Great Hall. No, it was not a dream. She was going to marry a vampire.

Miss Shaw had brought the Earl and Hannah in tow. The Earl looked suitably dignified in his white tie, while Hannah looked lovely but uncomfortable in her hunt ball gown. The teenager glowered at them all.

"I hate this stupid thing," she complained. "I hate dressing up."

"My dear," said her father, ignoring his younger daughter completely. He offered his arm to Caroline. "Shall we? I imagine the whole pack of them are slavering to get at the dinner tent."

"Thank god!" called out Peter's cheerful voice from the main staircase. "I'm not late after all! Hang on, everybody!"

Miss Shaw let out a startled gasp as Lord Merritt, clad in his immaculate evening clothes, sat on the edge of the long winding banister and slid all the way to the bottom.

Robin tried not to appear anxious as he walked to the required spot near the village priest. He felt every eye in the crowded room upon him. The intrigued murmurings of the assembled neighbors and friends was intense enough to be mildly embarrassing. He felt a little like he was once again up on the table in Madame St. Cere's salon being sold to the highest bidder.

He held his head up and scanned the guests jammed into the small chapel, with what he trusted passed as a serene gaze. Most had the 'just brushed the dog hair off my evening clothes' look of the country set. He spotted Mark Halsey glowering in a rear seat. More worrisome was the sight of Gabriel and Winnifred standing by the heavy arched wood doors, having what seemed to be a rather agitated and urgent whispered conversation. They both glanced at him in concern and then exited as if fleeing a sinking ship.

Robin turned abruptly around to face the beatific Father Hazelton, who offered him an expression of warm sympathy.

"I did always think the practice of having the groom wait in front of the assembled masses was rather a biblical torture," he said kindly, "like being thrown to the lions."

Robin stared at him, unable to frame a reply. Why were Winnifred and Gabriel rushing away and was Caroline in any danger?

"Spot on, padre," interjected Hugh who was acting as Robin's best man. "Why can't the groom hide out?"

Then the arched doors opened with an ancient thud and the assembled musicians began a work-a-day transcription of Handel's aria "Every Valley Shall Be Exalted" from The Messiah. Robin spun on his heel, feeling, suddenly, that some sort of trap was being set.

Peter slipped in first and moved to the left to find a place in the audience. Utterly baffled and dismayed, Robin watched him join up with what were presumably old family friends since they were middle-aged fox hunting types and seemed overjoyed to see him.

"What's up?" asked Hugh breaking polite form by whispering in Robin's ear.

"Winnifred and Gabriel — something's not right."

Robin heard a sharp intake of breath from Hugh but before the doctor could reply there was more movement in the doorway indicating another member of the bridal party was about to enter the chapel.

It was Hannah, all awkward teenager in her white dress, trying to walk in a smooth cadence but obviously longing to lope along in a comfortable pair of paddock boots.

And then there was Caroline with her father. The chapel audience let out an absolutely delighted gasp at the first sight of her. The bride was not wearing white as had become traditional since Queen Victoria's wedding to Prince Albert. She was in a sumptuous celadon green dress with the opulent peach trimmings in a perfect mid-18th century style. The heavy satin gown glowed in the soft lighting as Caroline began the walk down the aisle. She was breathtaking, a creature who might have stepped down from one of the castle portraits. Her strawberry blonde hair was swept up into an exquisite arrangement of peach roses and pearls. This was a graceful reverence to Robin's past. A sweet and meaningful gesture done just for him.

But for an awful instant Robin confused Caroline with Corisande. He felt light-headed and nauseated as the beautiful vision floated down the aisle towards him.

The last time such a fairytale creature had approached him he had lost everything dear to him and all he had known was mind-bending pain. It must be part of a trap — the reason Winnifred and Gabriel had fled the chapel. Something had gone terribly wrong.

He must have weaved a little on his feet for he felt a steadying hand on his shoulder and heard Hugh's quiet voice asking him if he was quite himself.

With effort, Robin pushed away the Georgian vision and its unnerving associations. It had to be Lady Caroline DeBarry coming towards him. Caroline — courageous enough to give herself to him despite all she had learned about his past. Caroline — who loved him enough to take his hand despite what she knew might confront them in the future. Caroline — the woman he loved above all others.

The Earl offered him Caroline's hand as they finally reached the altar. Robin accepted it with a gratitude and respectfully bowed his head to the current the Earl of Hawkesmoor.

Then he pivoted gracefully and offered Caroline the formal bow he would have offered to a noble lady of his times. The assembled guests murmured their surprise and appreciation at the arcane act of reverence.

Robin kissed her hand. "Madam, you are beyond beautiful."

Caroline beamed at him. Then they turned to Father Hazelton.

44

Anxiously, Robin scanned the enormous reception tent for either Winnifred or Gabriel. It was filled with people milling about enjoying drinks before being seated for dinner. Cheerful wedding guests had spun out into many chattering collectives, seeking out old friends and recounting what they thought of the event so far.

Miss Shaw had done an admirable job on short notice. The tent glowed with tables and fixtures done in the same pale green and peach color as his new wife's spectacular wedding dress. White and peach roses abounded as well, hanging from gilded baskets and on every available surface. Strings and strings of fairy lights brought a romantic glint to the tent's cavernous corners.

The musicians had their own small elevated stage to the rear where they were currently engaged in trying to tune the harpsichord again. Crisply uniformed staff members moved quickly through the undulating crowd and saw that everyone had a full glass. If it all more closely resembled a summer champagne concession in the long gone public pleasure park Vauxhall Gardens, so be it. He'd have to be the only one who could draw the comparison.

He noted vaguely as he searched the room that it was all very pretty but a bit anonymous. It was a shame the Earl's guests would not be allowed to sit down to a meal served on Hawkesmoor's own notable possessions.

On occasion, his mother used to have a table laid with plates made of sterling silver and priceless Venetian glass. He wondered if the silver dining service or the glass still existed after generations of different servants had handled them. There was that magnificent bone china service too, with gold worked throughout.

Richard Robin Francis DuPlessis, Lord Merritt. It was a whisper in his left ear as if someone had crept up behind him. He swerved around and saw nothing beyond standard issue wedding guests as they clustered about waiters brandishing appetizer trays.

Well, if it isn't you.

He turned again sharply, nearing knocking into a sturdy matron in radioactive green. She cheerfully forgave him — as he was the anxious new husband — and dove at a tray of caviar and toast as if she hadn't seen food since the Thatcher years.

At last.

Robin pushed past the amiable matron. He was positive that he had almost seen someone this time. Someone or something that had slipped away through the crowd like a Halloween will-o'-the-wisp.

Robin snatched champagne from a passing waiter and knocked back half a glass, craving the warm sensation it dropped delicately over his nervous system. He was shaking. One of the few things that really frightened him was the thought that Petherbridge, Lord Scyon, would learn of Caroline's pregnancy and somehow get a hold of her.

"You look awfully glum — considering," said Caroline as she joined him.

He took a quick swig of the champagne. "Oh, I was just hoping that no errant castle ghosts would turn up to scatter your guests into the night."

"I'll settle for no more vampires. Not that I don't like your friends — I do," Caroline murmured, taking the glass from his hand so she could have a sip as well; then remembering her current state, she gave it back with a disappointed sigh.

Robin sipped some champagne for her. "So far so good."

"You know," Caroline slipped an arm under his, "we don't have to stay for whole thing. Once the dancing starts, we could slip away."

"My god," Robin said in dismay.

He felt Caroline's body stiffen beside him.

"What is it?" she asked, looking up at him with a pale worried face.

"It's that Miss Shaw descending upon guests like a starving kestrel," he replied. "I think she wants everyone to sit for dinner."

"Oh, you!" Caroline gave him a light punch on the upper arm. "Don't do that! I was expecting — well, never mind."

Kate Ashby tossed her head nervously and looked around at Hawkesmoor's Great Hall and the other vampires who occupied it. She was the very image of young Hollywood — long and impossibly lithe sheathed in a red Prada silk minidress that seemed the antithesis of not dressing to upstage the bride.

"You'd better take me to see Robin right *now!*" She seemed on the verge of actually stamping her foot. "He'll be very upset that you've treated me this way!"

Hugh looked puzzled. "Robin really took this one as a bride? Really?"

They were circling the frightened young American vampire who turned about anxiously, unsure which one was the most dangerous.

"I told you he did!" Kate cried, her American accent harsh and shrill. "Robin loves me. Just ask him. Ask him now."

"Who sent you? Lord Scyon?" asked Winnifred.

"He can be hard to refuse," added Gabriel with a sympathetic smile. "Imagine Petherbridge sending a neophyte like this to face three old vampires like us."

Kate teetered around in six inch Chanel pumps. "I keep telling you, nobody sent me here! I just want to see Robin. He made me and I'm his. Why don't you just ask him?"

"I want a blood sample," said Hugh as they moved closer to the increasingly frantic American.

Kate's eyes grew wide at his request. "Blood sample? What do you want with a—"

Winnifred stepped deliberately and aggressively into Kate Ashby's space. The panicked girl jumped back directly into Gabriel's arms. He broke her neck with a quick and brutal snap.

"Petherbridge had to know we would destroy her," Gabriel said, tossing the American vampire aside without a backward glance. "Bastard."

"Either way, he'd establish that Robin was back in England." Winnifred was unsheathing a dagger. She dropped down next to Kate's body and nicked open a vein in the girl's throat so Hugh could collect his sample.

Hugh looked grim. "He knows about Robin. This creature was just a simple warning."

"Or misdirection." Winnifred plunged the dagger into Kate's temple, destroying the brain and any possibilities of reanimation, and then expertly re-sheathed the blade.

They all instinctively looked in the direction of the wedding tent. Lord Scyon could be there now, sitting next to Caroline and lifting a glass of untouched wine to her good health.

"I'll go," sighed Hugh. "You two can get rid of the body."

"Don't tell him," Winnifred said quietly. "It's his wedding night."

Dinner gave way to coffee, wedding cake and Edwardian dancing music. The well-fed and satisfied guests took to Miss Shaw's portable wood floor in droves to perform sloppy variants of their ancestors' dance patterns.

Robin watched the dancing, enjoying the sight of Caroline going round and round with her father. He sipped his champagne and wondered why he couldn't shake the sensation that someone or something predatory was tracking him. Every time it seemed possible that the hunter might reveal itself from behind a tent pole or an attentive waiter, Robin saw nothing but celebrating humans and busy catering staff.

He had another sip as Peter cheerfully pulled a reluctant Hannah onto the dance floor. Maybe his vampire enhancements and instincts were simply going haywire as his body shifted towards a hybrid state.

"There you are, Robin," said Hugh sliding into the chair beside him. "Good. I need a word."

Robin turned to look at his friend. "Did you find them?"

Hugh's handsome jaw tightened. "Winnifred's up on the Great Walk. We've got a Black Monk wandering about and what appears to be someone's former deer hound galloping around driving the living dogs mad."

"Dear," sighed Robin. "This is the most haunted of castles."

"Can you get Caroline out of here?" Hugh moved a bit closer. "Back to your rooms in the west wing?"

Robin frowned. "Yes, certainly. I think she's quite tired, actually."

"Would you mind if I had a look at her?"

"Of course not," Robin replied, his frown deepening. "Can you tell me why?"

Hugh shook his head. "Not here. Go get Caroline."

Robin immediately made his way to the dance floor. He nimbly wove through the moving pairs, spotting the Earl and Caroline just as the music came to a bright finish.

He saw Caroline wipe her brow as everyone else applauded the efforts of the hired musicians. She had the gray feverish pallor to her skin that he'd noted before when she was having spells of not feeling well.

"Caro," Robin heard the Earl say as he drew up to them, "you ought to sit down now. You look tired."

"Robin," she breathed gratefully upon seeing him.

"Just the man!" The Earl patted him on the shoulder. "Caroline's a little winded."

"Oh, I'm all right." Caroline made a weak dismissive gesture with her hand. She looked exhausted.

"Come on, darling." Robin slipped a supporting arm around her waist.

"Go to ground," advised the Earl with a wary glance around the tent, "or that confounded Miss Shaw will lead the kill. She's already given us two bulletins about throwing some kind of floral arrangement."

"Traditional bouquet toss, Dad," Caroline said wearily. She brushed a bead of sweat away from the bridge of her nose.

"Any suggestions, sir?" asked Robin.

The Earl thought for a moment and jerked his head to the side. "Side vent for the musicians. Go! I'll hold off the slavering hounds!"

Robin was pouring himself a steadying whiskey when Hugh at last came in to see him.

"God, how I wish I could have one of those." Hugh gazed enviously at Robin's full glass. "That golden bite as it makes its way through the system."

"How is she?"

"Fever's down a bit," said the doctor. "I expect she's wanting to spend the rest of the evening with her new husband."

"I worry, you know," Robin paused to take a long sip of the whiskey, "that this baby is killing her."

"These half-caste pregnancies are a new thing for me," Hugh sighed and plopped down into one of Robin's vaguely Japanese chairs. "Can you tell me — have you noticed any paranormal events when Caroline's having one of her fevers?"

The question set Robin back on his heels. He looked up from his whiskey, eyes narrowed in thought.

"I had not considered the idea before," Robin thought some more, "but yes — it's possible."

"Fascinating." Hugh shook his head slightly at the complexity of the situation. "I've done a sort of routine obstetric examination. I think these fevers and bouts of light-headed exhaustion are connected to a metabolic condition."

"Is it dangerous?"

"I'm not really sure," Hugh admitted slowly. "From Caroline's own recollections, the bouts are less extreme than they were, which would seem to indicate that things are progressing as a half-caste pregnancy should."

"A metabolic condition." Robin took a chair near Hugh's. "That sounds as if the baby isn't some sort of vampire feeding off its own mother."

"No, your child is not that." Hugh smiled at Robin's palpable relief. "But I think it is a powerful being. If I'm right, it's capable of producing enough psychic energy to make Hawkesmoor's paranormals jump around."

Robin stared at him. "You must be joking."

"Oh, I don't think it's a conscious decision on the baby's part or anything. It simply is powerful." Hugh leaned forward to make his point. "Look you — in your human time you possessed the greatest faerie attributes of your bloodline. Indeed, so great was your connection to your Tylwyth Teg ancestors that even after being made vampire by Morvidus, your faerie blood eventually reasserted itself — hence your evolution into a sort of hybrid.

Not difficult to imagine biological offspring of such a hybrid might be immensely gifted."

Robin sipped his drink, thoughtfully. "When Winnifred stabbed me, the voices sang to me in old Welsh. They said my daughter would take my place one day."

"And she's wasting no time, either," the doctor added with another envious glance at the glass. "The metabolic condition I mentioned?"

Robin frowned. "Right. Go on."

"Caroline's gestational clock is speeding way ahead of schedule. Her human body is working at a furious pace, trying to keep up with the rapid growth of your daughter. That's why she has periods of seeming to burn up with the effort," Hugh explained. "It must have something to do with our revenant healing process. Somehow it's applied itself to the baby's gestation."

The long hand that held the whiskey glass shook, spilling some of the amber liquid.

"My god," said Robin hollowly. "How soon?"

"Soon."

Robin's face was ashen. "You won't," his soft voice had a catch in it, "you won't let this destroy Caroline, will you?"

45

"Seems a logical conclusion," said Gabriel as he and Hugh took their turn on the Great Walk after the wedding guests had departed, "that Morvidus didn't just stumble upon the beautiful Lord Merritt by accident."

Hugh nodded. "I think he knew the DuPlessis carried faerie blood and the idea threatened him somehow."

"Still," Gabriel mused as they strolled the medieval stonework, "when a revenant decides to create another, there is usually some kind of prior relationship. We don't just turn up on doorsteps and grab the first person who answers the bell."

"I doubt Morvidus did anything in the fashion to which we are accustomed," Hugh said. "From what I was told once by a revenant who actually saw him, he was every inch a patrician Roman, much taken with the idea of Gods swooping unexpectedly out of the sky to deal out destiny to pathetic humankind."

"Point granted," Gabriel bowed slightly. "Still, getting Lord Merritt out of his castle on the night of his official wedding announcement — that took some tactical foresight."

"Point taken," Hugh returned the bow. "But I don't think that question is half as interesting or as pertinent to our current situation as why the DuPlessis faerie bloodline intimidated Morvidus so much that he had to destroy the last carrier."

"But Morvidus disappeared. Lord Merritt was the last of his brides."

"Interesting." Hugh paused to think. "I wonder," he looked up suddenly, "if Miss Ashby or what's left of her might hold part of the puzzle."

Robin skillfully removed another hairpin and lifted out the last of the peach-colored roses as Caroline sat at her dressing table. He remembered the many times he had done much the same for an exhausted Corisande.

"Thank you," breathed Caroline gratefully, as her strawberry blonde hair fell down about her shoulders. "You're very good at that."

He tossed the roses on her dressing table.

"A vampire my age has had practice at many things."

She ran her fingers through the loose locks and gazed at her pale reflection in the mirror a little despondently. Robin slipped his long fingers into her hair and bent down to kiss her neck.

"Let me help you out of this great puff pastry of a dress," he murmured in her ear. "I want to go to bed."

"Puff pastry?" Caroline laughed and reached up to tap his cheek playfully. "Thanks a lot!"

He caught her hand and kissed the top of it.

"Don't even try." She pulled her hand away. "Your fancy 18th century manners have no effect on me."

"Oh," Robin raised an amused eyebrow, "Really? And why do you imagine you're in this fix?"

Robin lifted his head from Caroline's shoulder. He had made love to her twice and she was drifting off in his arms. However, he was alert and aware — now that his attentions were not entirely focused on his new wife — that the dark room seemed to hide the same predatory presence he had sensed earlier. It was the damnedest thing. His vampire sensitivities should have been able to detect a human, revenant or ghost in the room even without light.

He peered through the night-shrouded air and tried to perceive *anything* producing a signature, either hot or cold. Nothing. The bedroom was completely clear. Maybe, Robin thought for the second time, restoration of his human aspects was responsible for creating false alarms in his system.

Robin quietly extricated himself from Caroline and pulled on his dressing gown. There was a decanter of sherry in the sitting room. He slipped away and poured a drink. Appreciating again the lovely warm glide of the stuff across his chilly system, Robin wandered over to Caroline's bookcase, hoping to find a lurid detective novel. As he did so, something unique sitting on one of the lower shelves caught his eye. Something he had not seen since 1750.

Robin retrieved the ornate Chinese puzzle box he had been so pleased and amused by in his human years. One of his 16th birthday presents from his mother.

He ran his long hands over the delicate wood and enamel surface, marveling at how well the intricate surface with its pearl inlay had survived the centuries.

"I wonder," Robin said out loud, "if the secret catches still work."

Sliding onto a chair, Robin placed the box on his knees and began the first of the three maneuvers that would cause the box to reveal its interior. He pressed into the pearl inlay on the lower right side until he heard the little joint click in, and then he was free to push a thin panel back on the rear side where he could slip a finger inside to depress another tiny jointed mark. Once that was accomplished, he was able to lift and rotate the handsome lid to the left.

It was open. He used to keep intimate letters from Corisande safely hidden within its silk lined recesses. Robin looked into the space, wondering if any of them had survived.

Odd, he thought as he reached inside, his letters were gone but there were several small leather books tied together with a black ribbon. He supposed it was possible someone had cracked the puzzle and had used it for their own purposes — perhaps even Caroline.

Robin lifted the collection out and gazed at the well-worn cover at the top. They were old pieces with bindings not uncommon to his time. Definitely not secured items of Caroline's.

He untied the black ribbon and cracked open the leather cover of the first book and almost dropped it in dismay.

His own mother's diaries, beginning in the year 1750.

Of course it made a sense. It had been her birthday present to him and she had been the only other person to know the box's secret catches.

Robin sat back in the chair, dazed. It was a very long time before he opened the diary and read the first line in his mother's fine hand:

All of England is now of one mind: my only son is dead.

<h1 style="text-align:center">46</h1>

Winnifred took her turn about the Great Walks, enjoying the night air and allowing it to push away any mild regrets she had about destroying the American vampire.

All was quiet now. There was no sign of anything more eerie than the call of an owl tracking prey in the fields.

A state, she reflected, that was not going to last forever. Petherbridge knew where Robin was and he obviously had a desire to square up some old dispute between them. A plan that would be deadly enough without the vampire king discovering Robin's mutation and how it had succeeded in creating a bloodline which might, if Hugh's surmises were correct, prove more powerful in the revenant universe than even the mark of Morvidus.

Perceptions of power would shift. Ancient leaders could be toppled and new alliances forged. Any vampire king's nightmare.

Winnifred paused, catching sight of a figure up ahead on the castle walk. Robin, she noted from the glint of amber hair in discreetly placed security lights. He was standing alone, hands in the pockets of his trousers, staring out over the silvery moor.

"Odd spot to spend a wedding night," she volunteered when she came within earshot.

Robin did not look away from the shrouded moor. "I just needed a breath of air."

"You seem rather subdued, if you don't mind me saying so." Winnifred leaned against the castle wall next to him. "I haven't seen you quite like this since you discovered that little seamstress had gone to the guillotine."

"Poor little thing." His voice was hollow. "All she had done was to earn her way hemming Madame St. Cere's vulgar gowns."

"'Tis in so many ways a cruel world," Winnifred said, turning to follow his gaze out over the moor. "But such a beautiful one as well."

"No trite philosophies tonight," Robin said in a harder tone. "I beg you."

"My apologies," she replied without rancor, "for being trivial. What has happened, Robin?"

He pulled a small leather-bound book from his trouser pocket and laid it on the gray stone in front of him.

"My mother's last diary of life here at Hawkesmoor. This was before my cousin Ambrose Westmacott, in his position as the seventh Earl of Hawkesmoor, withdrew his favor and she was forced to seek a roof with her brother like a charity case." Robin rested one of his spidery hands protectively on the little volume.

"And this diary has upset you?"

"It is, actually, one of three. The earliest dates from the very week I disappeared in 1750. She left them in a secret place where only I could find them." His voice thinned. "You see, she always believed I was alive somewhere and would come back. She thought I would want to know what had happened here."

"I'm sorry," said Winnifred. "I know Elizabeth met a tragic end at the hands of your cousin."

"If only it were that simple." Robin sighed deeply. "My father had a massive stroke shortly after I disappeared. Perhaps, because of his Tylwyth Teg blood, he held on to life for twelve years — blind, unable to speak or to move more than his right arm. My father was such a dignified man. Can you even imagine his despair?"

He picked up the diary and returned it to his pocket.

"My father finally did die, thus allowing my cousin Ambrose to begin ransacking the family money. He could, at last, mark paid to huge debts he had incurred in London by flaunting the title of Lord Merritt in gaming circles and at all the fashionable tailors."

They walked together along the castle battlements as Robin continued his story.

"Before I was attacked by Morvidus, I fought an early morning duel with Ambrose over some remarks he made about Elizabeth. It was a silly business: Ambrose had the first shot and missed. I couldn't kill him after he started blubbering so I just shot up in the air and walked away. Most men might have been grateful for such an escape but not Ambrose. He hated me and he hated my second — my friend and music teacher, Oliver Tupin."

Winnifred slipped her arm under his as they walked along the ancient stone path. She said nothing, allowing him to collect his thoughts and memories.

"My mother writes of an incident shortly after my disappearance in which Oliver was robbed by footpads who were," Robin paused to steady his voice, "who were careful to break his hands in ways that left them useless. Oliver left my parents employ over my mother's protests and apparently managed to hang himself some while later in a London poorhouse."

"My god, Robin. Horrid."

"Oh, 'tis only the beginning." Robin began to walk again. "Elizabeth Gwayr, the charming girl I was to have married, found herself yoked to a monster who proceeded to break her spirit and her body with the same alacrity he later demonstrated in draining Hawkesmoor's accounts. For a lady of the 1740s, my mother is very picturesque in her descriptions of the bruises and savage wounds Elizabeth tried to hide under her clothes."

Robin paused again, his chest rising and falling rapidly with agitation. He pulled away from her and turned around pointlessly a couple of times. Pacing two steps forward, he stopped to look back at Winnifred.

"From my mother," Robin's voice seemed to stop in his throat. He tightened his elegant jaw and tried again. "From my mother's attempts to interpret what servants told her of how he tormented Elizabeth, I could see these were the sort of specialized practices he had learned in only the most accommodating of London's brothels."

"Dear Christ in Heaven," Winnifred breathed, "and they allowed the poor child to wed this foul man?"

"I'll tell you why." A tear spilled from his left eye and coursed down over his cheekbone. "Two months after I vanished, it was discovered Elizabeth was carrying my child. My mother and Elizabeth's family thought that if the baby proved to be a boy it would ensure my son's birthright."

"That poor girl," Winnifred said, genuinely moved.

"Almost seven months later Elizabeth did give birth to a son. My son, Simon Richard Oliver Westmacott." Robin spoke Ambrose's surname through clenched teeth. "What they failed to understand, in their attempts to do the right thing for Elizabeth and my child — and what my mother came to learn to her eternal regret — Ambrose did not agree to marry the compromised Elizabeth out of a sense of duty to Hawkesmoor or out of pity for her and my family. He married her because he hated me. Because he could do all the things to Elizabeth he would have liked to have done to me."

"But even Ambrose could not deny your son the Earldom eventually." Winnifred thought for a moment. "I remember reading a court circular years ago about the eighth Earl — son of Ambrose. He wrote a manual on fly-casting or something."

"The eighth Earl was the result of a union between Ambrose and his mistress, whom he promptly wed after Elizabeth was killed," Robin replied.

He seemed to weave on his feet, as if struck by an invisible blow to the body. Then he sat down in the middle of the Great Walk, his arms flailing loosely with defeat and lapsed into a dazed silence. Winnifred dropped to the cool stone floor next to him.

Robin stared ahead at some fixed point only he could see. Another tear dropped from his eye.

"My mother received a cursory note from Ambrose's secretary once she had left Hawkesmoor. It informed her that a recent outbreak of smallpox in the village had taken the lives of many, including that of my son."

Winnifred reached out to lay a hand on his. "Your mother did not believe that, did she?"

"Of course not." He wiped the tear from his cheekbone. "She made discreet inquiries and sent a family retainer to the village to ferret out what the locals were saying. It didn't take long. People were eager to gossip as none liked the Earl or his new coarse countess."

Robin dropped into pensive silence again.

"And what was your mother's man able to tell her?"

"Not long after my mother left Hawkesmoor my son disappeared. The tutor and the boy's valet had been dismissed and sent away from the village with unseemly haste. The official story held that the boy died of smallpox and to protect the household, his body was committed to the grave with extreme unction."

He swallowed roughly before continuing. "Rumor among the locals was that Ambrose had my son murdered by a couple of his London thugs, who got rid of the body somewhere in Merlin's Tower." Robin closed his eyes. "My mother learned that the servants thought the job had been botched and my son — my son had been walled up alive."

"That mustn't be the truth." Winnifred moved closer so she could stretch an arm around him. "You remember how servants used to embellish gossip."

"Because it's very odd, you know," said Robin in a crystal thin voice, "to find oneself praying that one's son had his skull successfully caved in or that the garroting wire held true."

"Oh, Robin," she said, grieving with him.

"My mother's writing stopped after that. There weren't any more entries until much later, when she returned to Hawkesmoor one last time to see Ambrose buried in the family crypt. He had died of overindulgence: fat and gouty."

"A remarkable woman, indeed." Winnifred tightened her embrace. "Small wonder that you are the creature you are."

Robin ignored her comment altogether. He pulled away and stood up, walking unsteadily several paces as if following some unseen vision. Then he stopped abruptly and pivoted to focus his green eyes on her.

"I am the Lord of Time," Robin said, an imposing figure with his red hair billowing in the night wind and his green eyes flashing. "I don't care if the physics of it destroys the gate and hell opens up. I'm going back for my son!"

47

"He's bloody going to do *what*?" asked Gabriel as he came into Winnifred's sitting room.

She yawned. "I'm not going to explain the whole thing again simply because you overslept."

"And you, a monk," said Hugh.

Gabriel threw him a withering glance. "Nobody can bloody time travel! Not even the most powerful revenant."

"Apparently it is an attribute of Faerie." Winnifred raised an eyebrow pointedly. "Especially for Robin DuPlessis, Lord Pwyll."

Hugh explained. "Lord Pwyll is the Druid god of time."

"The Druid god of time?" The former monk made a face when the other two vampires nodded in response.

"He probably can't manage it anyway." Gabriel dropped into a chair and eyed his friends seriously. "Have either of you noticed how much Robin has taken to drinking?"

Hugh nodded, his jaw tightening for a moment. "Aye, I have."

"If you knew his story as I do," Winnifred rose immediately to Robin's defense, "you might understand why."

"Damn it, Winnifred." Gabriel looked disappointed. "Can you actually be asking us to tie our fortunes to a vampire hybrid who may be an alcoholic?"

"He's not an alcoholic!" she shot back.

"Not yet," Gabriel countered quickly.

Hugh held up his hand for calm. "Please — this really isn't helping us at all."

"Who will help us," the former monk demanded, "when Petherbridge turns up?"

"Highly likely that Robin's revenant system repairs any damage from drink," Hugh replied as if the subject was of little interest. "Moot point. Let him enjoy a stiff drink. God knows he's earned it."

There was a long awkward silence. Gabriel rubbed his jaw and looked as though he was attempting to cool a rising temper.

"Well, said Gabriel at last. He eyed the wine glasses full of blood from Hugh's bottled supply and said in a deliberately light voice, "can we plan a brief excursion to a metrop? Blood bank fare is all very well but I'm beginning to dream of humans wandering like deer in docile herds."

Hugh had a drink from his glass. "You know; I can't tell the difference anymore."

"Neither of you hunt anymore," Gabriel pointed out as he took a glass from the table. "I'm not a voracious hunter — I just prefer small, polite drinks from the original source."

Robin had forgotten how much he loved a good country gallop. Hannah's big Irish bred mare, Firefly, was as eager as he was. Her long legs swallowed up ground as they galloped along the far edges of Hawkesmoor's northern border.

Robin squeezed the reins, asking Firefly to ease back to a walk. She did so quietly and without any of the skittish nonsense Hannah had been complaining about. He patted her neck and dropped the rein to the buckle, giving Firefly her head as they walked along.

It was calming to get a little distance from the castle. As much as he loved the place, almost everywhere he glanced conjured up a memory.

But most of all he dreaded the possibility of seeing the castle's most mysterious ghost: the boy who usually walked near Merlin's Tower. The boy whose face his mother had drawn in the pages of her last diary—his son Simon.

Caroline finished tying her hair up in a ponytail and gave herself a critical once over in the mirror. She now possessed the decidedly pregnant silhouette of a lady much further along in the process.

Thanks to Elizabeth's big pastry of a dress she had been able to look pleasantly round, as if knocking off rigorous riding competitions had allowed her to put on a few pounds.

But after the last bout with metabolic fever, as Hugh had decided to call it, the baby had another growth spurt. She wasn't going to be able to hide from notice and awkward questions any longer.

Caroline pulled at the hem of one of her father's old shirts, which she had swiped to wear over a skirt with a very forgiving elastic waistband. There was no doubt. She turned sideways to the mirror again. She had a Hitchcockian profile.

Just how was she to explain to her father that she was carrying the physically precocious child of a man who was a vampire?

A quiet knock interrupted her thought. Thinking it might be Robin; Caroline hurried across from her dressing room and happily flung open the door.

"Darling! Where have you…?"

The vampire Winnifred stood out in the hall. She gave Caroline an apologetic smile. "How are you feeling?"

"Pretty well, thank you. No fever." Caroline stepped back to allow her to enter. "Please come in."

"Most kind," murmured Winnifred.

Caroline instantly envied the vampire's slender elegance as Winnifred came in from the hallway. It made her feel all the more like a large hard-boiled egg on legs.

She also had a moment to feel a huge pang of self-pity; it was really hard to imagine herself as the proverbial 'lovely new bride' when a revenant goddess like Winnifred floated about. Especially one who had been Robin's lover. She could easily imagine that this glamorous creature was skillful and passionate in bed.

"I know this sounds really pathetic coming from a new bride," said Caroline, "but have you seen my husband?"

Winnifred looked sympathetic. "He's out hacking."

"On a horse? Without me?"

The vampire nodded, still radiating concern and sympathy. "There is still a little of the 18th century Whig left in Robin, I fear."

Caroline let out a short laugh just to be polite. It was the morning after her wedding and she was getting well-meaning advice from her husband's former lover — a flawless creature that had known him far longer and better than she did. She felt like dissolving into tears, something she seemed to do a lot of late and loathed.

"Speaking of Georgian times," Winnifred held out a small collection of leather-bound books, "are you at ease reading an 18th century hand?"

Caroline took a moment to put her emotions in check, not wanting to turn into a soppy puddle in front of Winnifred. She accepted the books. "I've had to read quite a lot of antique inventories and documents."

"Read these — lost diaries of Robin's mother," Winnifred said with genuine kindness. "You'll come to know your husband's past better. Hopefully understand why he must attempt something rather extraordinary."

"So," said Gabriel, once he was sure the immediate area was clear of humans, "you were up all night with your doctor's bag. Find anything unusual?"

Hugh pushed away his cold, uneaten plate of eggs and toast. "And *how*," he replied.

"Carry on, carry on." Gabriel waved his hands in mild frustration. "What were you looking for and what did you find?"

"You know that I find it intriguing that Morvidus vanished after he made Robin," Hugh said, as he leaned back on his chair. "I wanted to run some tests on Kate Ashby's blood because we suspect she is the only revenant Robin ever created."

"The connection still eludes me." Gabriel made a sour face. "Me, a mere monk."

"Blood tests confirmed to me that Kate Ashby was a dying vampire. She had about six months, maybe a year, before the cell destruction in her revenant system completely crashed her three-dimensional form."

"What? A terminal vampire? Impossible!"

"I found dead blood cells, dying blood cells, weirdly deformed and mutating blood cells. Her whole revenant chemistry was imploding." Hugh shrugged. "You remember how weak she was. She hardly put up a fight."

"Well, yes… but Robin was a weak vampire too, according to Winnifred." Gabriel shifted uncomfortably in his chair, as if the whole idea of sick vampires made him distinctly queasy. "Can it be surprising that his own brides would be weak, too?"

"In a way, it's all connected," Hugh said and leaned forward. "Robin is now powerful because his intrinsic faerie bloodline has reasserted itself and has strengthened his revenant abilities. I think his unborn child is powerful because his faerie kind, the Tylwyth Teg, have successfully interbred with humans in the distant past. I just don't think it quite works that way in the vampire exchange."

"You mean Robin's faerie blood is toxic to us?" Puzzlement crossed Gabriel's handsome aquiline features. "But, if that's true, why didn't Robin die centuries ago?"

"He's of the faerie bloodline. It's not alien to him. Besides, he wasn't exhibiting powerful aspects of his faerie background in 1750. He was essentially human. I do think, however, that Robin was a one in a millennium genetic throwback, and he would have evolved into faerie on his own if the vampire intrusion hadn't slowed the process down a few centuries."

"'Strewth!" Gabriel rubbed his right temple. "So you're postulating that Robin's blood destroyed," his voice dropped to a whisper, "Morvidus?"

Hugh looked uneasy. "Maybe… I don't know. I do, however, have a theory about the vampire race."

"Go on." The former monk sighed. "I think I can handle more information."

"Well, not to bore you, but I've long been searching for some kind of proof or clue to our genetic background."

"Sorry," Gabriel shook his head, "it's all Greek to me — except, of course, I'm fluent in ancient Greek."

"It's pretty simple if you really mull it over." Hugh sat back in his kitchen chair again and made an expansive gesture that indicated a far distance from where they sat. "If the Tylwyth Teg once came through to this plane and took human mates, our ancestors must have also done something like it as well. All vampires must be descended from another ancient bloodline — from *another* race of inter-dimensional visitors."

Firefly suddenly shied to the right, leaping up and landing stiffly on all fours like a startled cat. Robin rode out the awkward maneuver with the sure instincts of a man who had spent many lifetimes on a countless variety of horses.

He looked up at the gathering of trees situated on one of the highest rises in the local geography. The little copse where soldiers of Imperial Rome had once established a look-out point and had, according to legend, tortured locals for information and amusement. Even earlier, the Druids were said to have found the copse a place of special power, visiting it when they were traveling in the north to deal their gold work.

"Let's take a look, shall we?" Robin murmured to the mare as he gathered his reins.

Gabriel sat back in his chair and regarded the vampire doctor with an astonished expression. "Another inter-dimensional bloodline."

Hugh nodded. "It could explain Robin's reference to a dark army."

"My earliest documentation of vampire courts all seem to fall around the time of the Third Punic War — the Roman and Egyptian vampire courts emerged in 147 and 54 B.C., respectively." Gabriel thought for a moment. "Rinthon Annaeus was the first recorded vampire king."

"Nothing before 147 B.C.?" Hugh asked in some surprise.

"Well, yes. All sorts of human references to horrible supernatural dark things that rend the flesh and drink the blood: the Utukka of the Assyrians, Babylonia's Ekimmu, the Rabbinic Lilith, the Ch'ing Shih of China, the Penanggalan of Malaysia, the Greek Menads." The former monk shrugged. "But these are all ancient mythic beings, not truly vampire as we understand the term. These are things that go bump in the night. The first revenant originated writings occur in 147 B.C."

"Or are they just mythic beings created by human fear of death and darkness?" Hugh leaned forward to make his point. "Could these creatures be the very species we vampires are derived from? Insatiable, greedy hunters from another dimension preying on humans for food. While the faeries enchanted humans and loved them, these creatures ate them."

"And then, somehow, they can't make the jump here anymore," Gabriel added, his voice rising a little in his excitement.

Hugh nodded again. "Yes, but go the extra step — imagine that one of them stayed behind. It was trapped, maybe hiding in some kind of human form in order to hunt with anonymity. Somewhere along the way, this thing-that-goes-bump-in-the-night discovered that it could create creatures not completely unlike itself."

"Morvidus!" Gabriel exclaimed.

Hugh raised both eyebrows. "*The Oldest One.*"

Firefly hesitantly stepped forward to begin the climb to the copse of trees. She was edgy now, dancing a little to the left and right in her mistrust of the way forward.

From the moment Robin felt the moor breeze and heard it shiver through the leaves, he also heard the songs. The old Welsh language of the Tylwyth Teg rose with the wind — many, many voices singing, rising and falling harmonically with capricious air currents.

He urged Firefly on until they reached the center of the copse. Halting the mare, he allowed the voices to swirl around him. It was almost like returning to Cader Idris or the storm above Britain. The songs were so clear here, so intrinsic to his system that they seemed to flow in and out of his body as if he were some sort of musical tuning device.

Much of what he heard was ancient — songs he recognized from Cader Idris and even earlier, from his human dreams. These were lyrical tales of the Tylwyth Teg's past on the human plane — a kind of vocal history: song stories of love, courage and adventure in a time when faeries walked with mankind. There were songs of dark days in which the doorway was closed, and tales of legendary humans whose existences were forever intertwined with the faeries: Merlin, Gwydion — and songs of simpler humans who carried the faerie bloodline.

There were new songs too. Voices that were trying to speak to him of the doorway, of his daughter Arianrhod, and warning of dangerous forces that sought re-entry into the human plane. Black forces that fed on more than just human flesh and blood. The voices gave him devastating glimpses — *bloody massacre of Huguenots at Vassay 1562, the nationalized insanity of the Tulip Mania of 1637, the Reign of Terror in France 1793, the charnel house rise of the Spanish Inquisition 1478, Hitler's hellish Final Solution for Jews and Gypsies 1942, the bestial 1969 Manson Family murders, mass slaughter in Rwanda 1994 and September 11h, 2001* — when the gate weakened and shadow slipped through the bars

He cried out in panic and grief, pressing his hands against his ears to stop the sound. The cruelest songs had the power to overwhelm and immobilize. He had to learn how to filter through the vast harmonics to isolate particular voices with things to tell him. Surely this was the special ability of humans like Merlin and others with powerful faerie gifts — they had disciplined themselves into learning how to separate the musical strands so they didn't go mad.

Yet, whenever he had contact with the Tylwyth Teg, he always came away knowing more than he did before, as if the musical currents entered his being and left a residue of information.

The wind was beginning to die down and the voices faded as well, leaving Robin shivering and alone.

He was suddenly aware of how cold he was despite the spring sunshine.

Gathering his reins, Robin remembered it was also the place where he'd lost his human life. He remembered being strung up between these trees — whose leaves and branches now carried the voices of the Tylwyth Teg to him — and being torn apart by Morvidus.

Hadn't Morvidus told him that night that the copse was a touchstone for him? His place of torture and death. Morvidus had also been attracted by the power the place possessed.

A breeze gusted through the treetop and the voices rose with it — one reminding him that he had once made love to Elizabeth Gwayr here. Arthur Pendragon was conceived in such a place; a fading voice sang to him as the wind left the trees again.

Firefly was anxious to flee the trees and Robin had to hold her back from breaking into a canter — for fear she might clatter into some of the exposed roots and injure herself. She gave a low whinny as they came out of the trees, and to Robin's considerable surprise, another horse whinnied in return.

Robin turned his head sharply. A big handsome bay horse stood just off the traveled path. Sitting aboard it was Garnet Petherbridge, Lord Scyon.

"Well, if it isn't *you*," said the vampire king.

"Lord Scyon," said Robin as he wheeled Firefly around to face the vampire king. "It has been a long time."

"Yes," Petherbridge replied—always the master of studied indifference. "You've been in the colonies, I hear—an academic, no less. "

"It passed the time," Robin allowed, his voice quiet and wary—a tone he always tended to adopt around vampire kings, as if they were strange dogs dripping suspicious foam.

Petherbridge idly dropped the second rein of the pelham onto his horse's neck. "I was so dismayed not to have received a proper invitation to your second wedding. A simple oversight, I'm sure."

Suddenly panicked, Firefly sidestepped awkwardly and tried to wheel about in the direction of the castle. Robin lost the chance to frame a reply as he expertly sat into the green mare, squaring her up again.

"Tell me, is she another creature possessed by both divine gift and a tragic flaw?" the vampire king was saying as Robin swung Firefly back around.

"Let me make myself completely clear," Robin said calmly. "I will destroy you if you go anywhere near my wife."

"And now, since the velvet gloves are off: allow me to issue you an edict." Petherbridge straightened in the saddle. "If you intend to live in this country, you owe me complete and utter allegiance. I was foolish once to allow you to exist outside my influence. Never again, Lord Merritt."

"I owe you nothing," Robin spat back as Firefly danced sideways in fear.

"Defy me at your peril, Lord Merritt." Petherbridge swung his leg over the saddle and dismounted. "Would you do me the kindness of returning this bay gelding to its rightful owner?"

The vampire king tossed the reins to Robin who managed to catch them despite Firefly's increasing anxiety.

"Explain," said Robin, drawing the gelding up next to his jigging mare.

Petherbridge smiled pleasantly back at him, the very picture of English geniality at its aristocratic zenith.

"I just happened upon the modern Lord Merritt preparing for his morning ride."

Robin felt a wave of dread so dark and so deep wash over his senses that he thought he might actually drown in the effect.

"You remember the old Marquess of Southbrook, don't you?" Lord Scyon's eyes lit up at the memory. "He took days to burn."

"No," Robin tried to clear his swimming head, "No, not Peter."

"Humans just do not possess the same staying power. Rather a letdown really."

Robin spun Firefly on her hocks, jerking the bay after.

"This is not over," he promised over his shoulder as he drove the willing Firefly forward into a hard gallop.

Petherbridge gave a small wave. "We will meet again."

"Caroline!" Hannah was hysterical. "Caroline! Do something!"

The vampires were quickly moving the black, rigid body from the box stall where Hannah had discovered it to the stable aisle where light was better. Peter was barely recognizable as human. His flesh had been burned black and where the fire had not been as direct, raw muscle had shriveled away from tortured bone.

"I… *can't*," Caroline heard herself saying. She had only the power to watch as Hugh ran his expert hands over Peter's seared flesh.

"Petherbridge?" Gabriel was asking as Caroline forced herself to move closer to her brother's shuddering frame. "It's certainly his style."

"No doubt," Hugh murmured as he rapidly filled a hypodermic needle. "This may stabilize him a little but he'll go into cardiac arrest at any minute. It's a miracle he's still alive."

Petherbridge took in a deep breath of the earthy odor and found a seat on a fallen limb well inside the circle of the trees. He pulled an 18th century snuffbox out of his jacket pocket and ran his beautifully manicured thumbnail over its elegant gold hinges.

The destruction of the witless little Hollywood vampire bothered him more than he might care to admit. Gabriel, Hugh and Winnifred had been fixtures in English vampire society for centuries and had never given him a moment's pause since his violent *coup d'etat* and rise to unquestioned power in the British Isles.

As his emissary, Kate Ashby should have been given room to perform her mission—a simple information gathering assignment. Why had these old vampires decided to risk his considerable ire in this way?

And what was it about Robin DuPlessis that always seemed so different and more dangerous than any other revenant he had ever known?

Petherbridge corrected himself . It went back much longer than Robin's vampire existence. He had been a peculiar human as well, with his inexplicable passion for his sister's descendant, the opera whore.

The vampire king opened the snuff box and enjoyed once again the anguished screams of the disembodied Marquess of Southbrook as he begged for release from endless torment.

He ran a hand through his gleaming blond hair, connecting in a physical way with the shadowy being he had harbored in his revenant system since 1750.

"One day," Lord Scyon said out loud, "you will explain to me why you had to have Lord Merritt of Hawkesmoor Castle, an unimportant northern rustic?"

But it did not reply—never did on any conscious level Petherbridge was ever aware of.

It used him: but there had been rich reward for such service. A kingdom and the unquestioned power to hold it.

Petherbridge made a sour face. How tedious that he owed even the honor of serving such an ancient and incalculably powerful being to Richard Robin Francis DuPlessis.

Oh, but he would pay Robin DuPlessis back—in full.

"I can't save him," said Hugh as Winnifred knelt down, murmuring prayers for the dying. "I'm sorry."

Hannah let out a howl and buried her face in Caroline's shoulder, sobbing until the stable was filled the wrenching sound of the teenager grieving for her brother.

There came a thunder of hooves across the stable yard gravel. It was Robin at a hard gallop. Firefly careened into the stable aisle, lathered with sweat and snorting with exertion. He pulled up the mare and leaped to the ground.

"Is he alive?" Robin asked as he ran towards them.

"Just barely," Hugh said, pulling the needle away from Peter's trembling arm.

"Out of my way," Robin commanded tersely. "All of you!"

"I beg your pardon." The doctor looked baffled.

Robin shoved the astonished Hugh to the side and fell onto his knees next to Peter's destroyed body. He reached out and delicately laid his long fingers on raw wounds at Peter's temples.

"Robin, for pity's sake!" Hugh protested as Peter groaned in agony at the touch.

Robin let out a small cry, half-choked and took in a ragged breath. He shook his head as if dazed and seemed to refocus his thoughts on Peter, who was arching his back in response to Robin's attentions.

"Oh, my god!" Hannah choked out through her tears.

Robin jerked away from Peter as if propelled by a powerful unseen force. He fell back against a stall door with a sob and curled up into a fetal position. Robin's frame began to convulse. Peter's blackened flesh, in turn, began to retreat and take on a healthier color.

There was a collective gasp from human and vampire alike. Peter was healing at an incredible rate. His flayed muscles began to seal together and rebind, the ghastly exposed bones disappearing into the rapid repairs. He was literally reconstituting his form in front of them.

But as Peter was restored, Robin disintegrated into a rigid mass of burned flesh and oozing tissues.

Caroline felt the ground beneath her feet shift and her vision blurred. She wondered desperately, in the brief instant before she fell, if the baby would be all right.

49

"It's a bit like the Battle of Sterling Bridge all over again," said Hugh a bit wistfully as he applied a cold compress to Caroline's forehead. "Darting from one fallen soldier to the next."

"What did you think of William Wallace?" asked Gabriel in genuine interest. He leaned against the lower left post of Caroline's handsome Regency bed, watching as Candlethorne looked after his patient.

"Very nice fellow." Hugh shrugged and lifted Caroline's limp wrist so he could find her pulse. "Mad about oat cakes. Always had 'em squirreled away in his sporran."

"How is she?" asked Winnifred, appearing out of thin air.

"Feverish," Hugh replied, not glancing up from reading the second hand on his wristwatch. "I have no real experience with vampire-faerie-human pregnancies, but my guess is Lady Caroline is in the early stages of labor."

"Christ in heaven." She made an instinctual sign of the Cross.

Hugh replaced Caroline's arm gently on her bed. He shook his head with another sigh. "Her pulse is racing. She's burning up and non-reactive. I don't know if it's safe to give her anything for fear of hurting the child. It could all be perfectly normal. I just don't know."

A knock came at the door and Robin slipped inside. He was dressed again, in jeans and a black sweater — looking completely well, and not at all like the destroyed creature they had carried into the castle.

"How is my wife?" he asked softly but with urgency.

"Holding her own, I think." Hugh stepped back from Caroline's bedside. "In labor."

"How long have you known you possessed empathic ability?" Gabriel asked Robin.

Robin bent over Caroline and kissed her forehead with a devotion that made Winnifred's ancient heart ache at what she might have possessed. "I can't do it for vampires. Only humans.

"Hence it must be a faerie trait," Hugh interjected. "Fascinating."

"Take care of her for me, Hugh. I have something I must do."

"You're not going to engage Petherbridge?" Gabriel asked sharply. "He's too much for you alone."

"No, not Petherbridge." Robin pushed away from the bed. "Something I should have been around to do a long time ago."

"Well, that makes perfect sense," Hugh said angrily. "Look here, Lord Merritt, sir — your lady may well be in labor. You could be a father before morning. You're needed here."

Robin's elegant jaw tightened. "Petherbridge will return. I may not get the chance again."

Gabriel shook his head in disbelief. "Hugh's saying Caroline could die, Robin. Your child could die."

"I know what Hugh is saying," Robin's voice was strained, "but still I must go."

Regret pulled at the corners of Robin's eyes. He turned slowly to gaze back at Caroline as if memorizing her face. He broke off his stare abruptly and headed for the door.

Robin shed his gear upon entering the burial crypt. The spade and pick-axe clattered to the flagstone flooring with a crash that seemed to rattle through the entire tower.

"Where are you?" Robin asked, his voice echoing slightly in the shadowy space. "Where did those bastards put you?"

"Can you sense any trace of him?" Winnifred found a seat on the edge of one of the older freestanding sarcophaguses.

He shook his head in frustration. "I was never a talented vampire, Winnifred. I never could track people by impressions."

"Hmm," she raised an eyebrow. "Pity."

"But I know he's here somewhere. I can feel it in my bones — I know my mother was right about Ambrose hiding my son's body in here. It makes a certain sense."

Winnifred crossed her long legs and thought for a moment.

"If you make sense of it intellectually — then why not try to find him the same way?" she mused finally. "Where would have been the easiest, safest place to put the poor boy's body?"

Robin's green eyes widened in appreciation. "Some place where the signs of burial wouldn't be too obvious — in case my mother's family came looking."

"Perhaps not in the crypt at all?" Winnifred suggested. "How about the old stores?"

Robin backed up two paces — his face suddenly drawn as if he might be physically ill at any moment.

"Elizabeth." He wrapped his arms about his chest. "Is it possible that Ambrose put the boy in with his mother?"

"Robin," Caroline said trying to sit up. A powerful cramping sensation seized her midsection. "Is he all right?"

"He's perfectly well," Dr. Candlethorne assured her with a professional smile. "His revenant attributes saved him again. Peter is fine, too. It's you I'm more concerned about at the moment. You're feeling some contractions?"

She nodded with a wince as another bore down on her.

Hugh reached for his blood pressure cuff on the night table and began to wrap it around her upper arm with quick practiced movements.

"I think you're going to have your baby in the next 24 hours," he said, pumping up the sleeve. "You do understand why your husband feels it would be a mistake for you to go to an ordinary hospital?"

"Yes," Caroline replied, watching intently as he put the stethoscope to the inside of her elbow, "of course — too many awkward questions."

Robin slammed the pick-axe into the gray stone with all his vampire strength. A goodly section obligingly splintered and crumbled to the floor.

He lowered the tool, moving in to check his progress. The wall had given way sufficiently to reveal the black interior of a small man-made cavern.

Robin was suddenly struck by the idea that the girl he had expected to marry had been lying behind the cold stonework for centuries.

"Well, you've done it," Winnifred announced, breaking into his thoughts. She peered at the dark opening he had created. "One more blow ought to prove whether you could earn your keep as an historical detective."

When he failed to answer, she laid a hand on his shoulder. "This must be terribly hard for you."

He wiped at some dust on his forehead.

"Yes, 'tis rather," he allowed quietly.

Winnifred gave his shoulder a comforting squeeze.

Robin forced his hands to grip around the tool's handle and he lifted the pick-axe up again. "No time like the present, is there?"

"Oh — I've been saying that for hundreds of years." Winnifred grinned and stepped back to allow him room to swing.

He gritted his teeth and swung the axe into the crypt wall. A large section shattered with a really deep cracking and fell away, providing a gaping hole that offered easy access to the man-made tomb.

Robin dropped the pick-axe and reached behind him for the flashlight he had given Winnifred to hang on to. She handed it to him silently.

He reluctantly brought the flashlight around so its yellowish beam could shine directly into the black hole. It revealed a simple wooden coffin shrouded in centuries of dust.

Robin shuddered involuntarily and lost his hold on the flashlight. It clattered to the floor, returning Elizabeth's coffin to the blackness.

"Hell!" he sputtered, feeling like an idiot. He was a vampire, for Christ's sake — death, decay, coffins, the smell of a burial site: it was all part of his twilight world.

"It's all right, dear," said Winnifred, retrieving the light. "No one could blame you for feeling a little overwhelmed."

He had a sudden flash of memory — Corisande being lowered into the muddy ground of St. Giles. She had been so terribly ill that death had seemed almost a kindness. It was a different thing altogether to imagine the young vibrant Elizabeth, who had been at her happiest riding out on a windy moor — now trapped behind a stone wall, rotting away like some discarded bit of broken furniture.

"If you want to find your son, we have to look," Winnifred said, as she held the flashlight up so that the beam once again illuminated the interior of Elizabeth's grave.

Robin forced his frozen muscles to obey him. He walked forward until he could grasp the edge of her coffin lid. He felt sick. The wood under his fingertips was like powder — splintered and dissolving from centuries of damp English weather.

Biting his lower lip, he shifted the old lid, which made a moaning sound as the soft decaying wood moved for the first time in almost three hundred years. He would have preferred a good sharp crack to the mewing sound, which was strangely repelling, as if the coffin had a life of its own and was losing it to some horrible cancer of the wood.

Yards of tattered velvet, black with age and water stains, seemed to dominate the interior of the coffin. When he focused more intently it seemed possible that the fabric had once been green in color.

The putrid velvet belonged to a once-handsome day dress that now possessed more shape and presence than the sad little collection of bones that lay inside it.

Robin's throat constricted painfully. There she was — all that was left of Elizabeth Gwayr. The fragile bones protruding from the heavy dress were not a tidy white like the ones observed in Halloween decorations and science classrooms. Elizabeth's body had endured the same devastating element as her coffin and clothes — her skeleton was a mottled brown with blackened joints where sinew had turned to rubbery gelatin.

Most terrible however was the condition of her skull. It simply lay in several dirty pieces on her *pont de lac* lace collar, attesting to the severity of the mortal blow that had killed her. The impact to her head had been so powerful that the skull had been unable to hold its shape after death.

Robin covered his mouth with his hand as bile rose up in his throat. He choked on it, unable to tear his eyes away from the sight of Elizabeth's broken head lying on its rotting bed of hanks of hair and lace.

Ambrose had buried her with nothing. Even the gown was bare of decoration. She lacked even a simple brass cross. There was nothing to indicate this had been a highly born lady deserving a certain degree of respect.

How like Ambrose Westmacott. He had probably taken all of her things, even the Gwayr family jewels, and made a present of them to his mistress.

"Forgive me," Robin begged, reaching out to touch one of her skeletal hands. "I never meant to leave you. I am so sorry."

"Robin," said Winnifred putting a hand on his back. "The boy is not here. Let us replace the coffin lid and allow the Countess peace."

50

Caroline wished Hugh would come back. The vampire doctor had excused himself in order to talk to her father who had been pacing the hallway outside.

She wondered what her father would say when he discovered she was having the baby now instead of following a normal human cycle.

Perhaps it really was all just a long complicated dream she was having. She'd wake to discover she was still in New York for the opening of the exhibit.

A powerful contraction made her wince and reevaluate her last thought.

"No," she concluded with a gasp. "We're stuck with it."

Caroline opened her eyes as the painful grip of the contraction began to ebb away.

The blond boy stood at the bottom of the bed, staring at her with his large unhappy eyes. He was as clear and solid as any breathing person at Hawkesmoor.

"You!" she breathed, wishing he had chosen another time to visit the living.

He seemed about to speak — then glanced sharply to the side as if he had heard something alarming that she had not — and vanished.

"He could be anywhere," Robin said sitting on the edge of one of his older ancestors' freestanding tombs. "I don't know where to begin to look."

"It's a puzzlement," Winnifred admitted. "I suggest we try the stores."

"Ambrose could have had his body thrown in a moor bog for all we know."

"I owe you my life," came Peter's voice from behind them. "How can I be of help?"

"Oh," Robin sighed softly so only Winnifred could hear. "Brilliant."

They turned around to find the modern Lord Merritt walking towards them. He blanched a little at the sight of Elizabeth's opened grave but did not otherwise comment upon it.

"Hugh had a go at explaining," Peter said, his gaze going from Robin to Winnifred and back again. "All of you. You're not actually real, are you?"

Robin cleared his throat. "We're not real humans if that's what you mean."

"Not real humans anymore," corrected Winnifred firmly. "We were once, you know."

Peter's eyes widened. "Vampires," he said in awe. "Vampires exist?"

"Revenant," she gave a small nod, "is the more elegant term."

He let out a shaky breath. "And I thought the corporate Americans were a foreign concept. Dad's a bit shaken up — seems he hadn't counted on his favorite daughter marrying a vampire but I expect he'll survive."

Peter's voice trailed off as he gazed at Robin.

"You're Richard DuPlessis," he said finally in utter wonderment.

"I was always Robin."

"You are the rightful Earl of Hawkesmoor," Peter continued, still staring at Robin's face. "I should have seen it in the portrait — of course it's you."

"No," said Robin as he stood up. "Your father is the Earl of Hawkesmoor just as you will be, one day."

"I know it's sounds silly but I'm," Peter's voice almost cracked with emotion. "I'm awfully glad you didn't die some horrible death in 1750. You see, as children we all used to rather worry about you."

"Thank you." Robin held out his hand and Caroline's brother shook it warmly.

Caroline opened her eyes after a particularly nasty contraction. Again, the phantom boy stood at the end of the bed with his long beautiful hands resting lightly on the Regency woodwork.

"They would have me protect you," he said in a hollow sort of tone as if he were talking through a Victorian clerks' speaking-tube.

"They?" Caroline forced her dry throat to produce the word.

"The singers at the end of time," the boy replied unhelpfully. "One of the strands from the song of songs."

She gritted her teeth as pain began to rise up in her system again. "I'm sorry but I'm not very clear-headed today."

"Time and song are threads reaching through," he said as if he were rapidly translating a foreign stanza of verse, "doorways. Doorways and circles. A silver wheel."

"A silver wheel?" Caroline asked in frustration before another contraction started to reach its peak and all she could do was stare helplessly at him over the bed linen.

"I will stay as long as I am able," he said, losing the singsong quality. "He is looking for me."

Peter's face was melancholy as Robin finished the tale of Ambrose Westmacott and his blood-soaked journey to the Earldom.

"What a wretched bastard," he spat. "I wish the Westmacotts had not been our cousins."

"Well, he was my cousin, too," Robin pointed out and they both nodded in resignation.

Winnifred picked up a chipping of stone from Elizabeth's tomb and tossed it aside fretfully. "So, do you have any brilliant ideas about where Westmacott would have had Robin's son hidden?"

"Then you really haven't seen it?" Peter looked mildly surprised.

Robin cocked his head to the side. "Seen what, exactly?"

"You're sitting on it."

"*Sitting on it?*" Robin repeated, perplexed. "You don't mean old Auguste DuPlessis here?"

"Oh, move for heaven's sake, dear." Winnifred strode over to the freestanding sarcophagus Robin was leaning against.

He obediently stepped aside to allow the other revenant access to the old stone. "I can't see how my great-grandfather is useful."

Winnifred knelt and wiped dust from the plaque near the base of the tomb.

"Richard Robin Francis DuPlessis: born 1718, died 1750," she read aloud. "Why, that's you."

"Not possible!" Robin said before dropping down next to her. He ran his long fingers over the chiseled letters. "I don't believe it — this was my great-grandfather's grave."

"Ambrose Westmacott wanted to ensure everyone understood you to be dead and buried," Peter explained. "He had your great-granddad moved into a wall crypt. That way he could put your name on one of the really big important gravesites. He then proceeded to invite a large cross-section of people to a memorial service so they could see first-hand that you were most certainly considered dead by the family. There would be no further question of his right to the coronet."

"He certainly was industrious," Winnifred commented dryly.

Robin's elegant jaw tightened and he looked away from the plaque as if the sight of it made him ill.

"If it's any consolation, your mother fought him tooth and nail over it but naturally she lost." The new Lord Merritt shrugged sadly. "Ambrose was the acting Earl after your father's stroke — he had all the real power at Hawkesmoor."

"Well, it would be the ideal spot to put the boy," Winnifred pointed out as she rose to her full height. "It was standing empty just waiting for an occupant."

"Let's shift the lid and find out!" Peter's voice grew bright with excitement. "All through our childhoods, Caro and I longed to stumble across missing skeletons."

Caroline braced for an oncoming contraction. They were getting very intense.

"A dark army gathers, lady," the phantom boy said. "You must be ready."

"You know," Caroline paused to ride out the peak of the contraction and then continued in some real annoyance, "these eerie riddles and dire warnings are not especially helpful to a woman in labor. I don't want to explore any metaphors — I just want the pain to go away!"

The boy backed off suddenly — his large eyes conveying both fear and worry.

"I must go," he said anxiously. "I fear you will not see me again."

Caroline sucked in a gasp of air as a really powerful contraction roared over her senses, overwhelming her like a rogue wave at sea.

"Hugh!" she cried hoarsely. "I think the baby is coming."

"Jesus Christ," said Peter, recoiling from the first glance. He turned away from the open grave looking as if he might well be physically ill.

Winnifred laid a hand on Robin's shoulder. "I am sorry, my dear. Terribly sorry."

Robin said nothing. He simply stared down into the stone coffin, transfixed by the sight before them.

His son was no mere blackened skeleton like the pathetic remains of Elizabeth Gwayr. His son's body, due to some inexplicable environmental conditions in the ancient stone sarcophagus, had been mummified into a ghastly parody of youth. The brown leathery skin encased in its final costume of a simple white nightshirt, now grayish-green with age, told a very clear tale of the boy's final hours.

A knotted rope was wrapped around his throat, embedded in the dried flesh. The boy had been brutally strangled by a crude sort of garroting device long favored by Whitechapel footpads.

But the murder had only been partially successful — even more distressing was the boy's expression of pain and horror clearly etched in the hard skin. His hands were clawed, fingertips worn away and nearly destroyed — frozen forever in a frenzy of fear. He had been alive when committed to the grave.

Strangled into unconsciousness by Ambrose's inept London street thugs, the boy had revived to the stale blackness of his own coffin and had known only the sheer madness of the prematurely buried until he slowly suffocated.

Robin could almost hear his son's faint tortured sobs echoing throughout the ancient tower crypt:

Mother, where are you? Please, I am so frightened. Help me. Help me.

He put his hands over his ears to block out the sound.

"I'm going back, Winnifred." His voice rose sharply to be heard over his son's cries of pain. "I must go now!"

<h1 style="text-align:center">51</h1>

"You are doing beautifully, Lady Caroline," Hugh said as he took her blood pressure again. "I know you're tired but stay with me."

"I don't know if I can go on," she whispered.

Hugh didn't look up from his study of the pressure gauge. "You can and you must."

Robin rested his hand on the boy's withered chest, his fingertips feeling the rough surface of the ruined nightshirt. He focused on the voices threading through the air, calling upon the Tylwyth Teg for direction and aid.

A shiver of energy coursed through his nervous system. His physical frame seemed to flicker like a guttering candle and he felt his entire structure lose mass and density. He was dismantling but instead of drifting in common air molecules like an invisible glider, he was hurtling through space with the force of a stealth bomber.

"Her blood pressure is sky rocketing," Hugh told Gabriel quietly at the door to Caroline's bedroom. "She's been stuck at seven centimeters for an age, dehydrated from the metabolic fever and she's losing strength."

"Oh, dear," replied Gabriel with a wary glance over his shoulder at the Earl who was pacing the hallway and trying to come to terms with the new reality thrust upon him.

"I'm going to lose her, Gabriel." The doctor lowered his voice another notch. "I've been running a line of fluids into her bloodstream with a little portable unit I carry in case of emergency but it's not designed for anything but a short ride to hospital. It's woefully inadequate for what I'm asking it to do."

"You're going to have to tell her father," the other vampire said. "He should know."

"I'd rather tell her husband!" Hugh's face grew angry. "Robin ought to be here."

Sound and vision restarted with a whir and click not very different from an old film projector jolting into action.

He found himself staring at the double keyboards of a harpsichord. His long fingers flew across the keys, enmeshed in a complicated phrase from Bach's D-Major Concerto.

Glancing up, he saw Oliver Tupin running his bow over the strings of his violin in support of Bach's relentless score.

And just to the music tutor's right was his father playing the cello section with meticulous care. The Earl lifted his head as if he'd heard Robin call out to him. He managed to smile fondly at his son despite the demands of Bach.

Robin smiled back at him, almost hypnotized by happiness at seeing his father again. His hands faltered on the keys, destroying the finely wrought pattern of musical spirals.

Oliver pulled the violin out from under his chin.

"We shall never be ready!" he announced in annoyance. "Lord Merritt, sir, you really must apply yourself with more vigor."

"Forgive me," Robin murmured, content to continue staring at his father's aquiline countenance. "I found concentration lacking."

"I doubt such an insight will carry any meaning to Mr. Handel." Oliver tapped Robin's shoulder with the end of his bow. "If we attack the figurations of the right hand as we have just done, I suspect the Master will find the call of the supper room simply too great to endure."

"Odd's fish, Tupin. 'Tis only a small gathering of friends," interrupted the Earl as he sat back in his chair. "Do not fret so. I am told 'tis bad for the digestion."

The music tutor immediately lost the taut outline that betrayed his anger and turned to give the Earl the polite bow known to all those who served their betters.

"My pardon, your lordship," replied Oliver. "We lose the light in any event."

No, thought Robin suddenly, this was not right. It was far too early — Corisande was still alive, singing on the stage in London. He had to move forward in time or risk being trapped.

But it was so lovely — the chilly gold of the late autumnal light as it streamed through the music room's windows. He could have a sherry with his father by the library fire and they would laugh together over some small incident garnered from daily life at Hawkesmoor Castle.

Robin shook his head to clear it. A voice whispered old Welsh into his ear.

Take heed, Lord Pwyll. You can so easily lose your way. Wandering through time is not unlike an ice storm — the enticing warmth as one begins to freeze to death.

"Bobbity," came his father's voice.

Bobbity. He had not heard that in two centuries. Only his parents continued to make use of his nursery name.

"Bobbity, the room grows cold," his father continued, handing off his cello to an attentive footman. "Thank you,

Cottington. Come, young Tupin: let us gather round a fire and discuss the forthcoming event."

Tupin gave a smaller secondary bow. "Your servant, sir."

"God's teeth, I think our Robin is distracted by thoughts of his mother's present." The Earl looked bemused. "Have you seen the bay? Zounds, she outbid all the young bloods at Tattersall's — took old Bellows by surprise, I can tell you. He is unused to ladies making their own bids but my dear wife when she decides upon a thing — one might as well try to stop the sun rising in the East."

A picture rose in Robin's mind of a gleaming seal bay with four white socks and a blaze. What a generous, stouthearted beast he had been.

An anguished cry shattered the vision. A cry of such power that it seemed to tear a rent from one veil of time through to another.

"Caroline!" He stood up from behind the keyboards.

Both Oliver and the Earl turned towards him in surprise at his outburst.

"Bobbity," frowned his father, "are you quite yourself?"

Robin watched his father and his friend fade like old sepia-inked pages.

It was the Hawkesmoor that belonged to ghosts who walked its byways. He was not time traveling now. He was simply stuck in some half world — a sort of inter-dimensional crawl space.

A gray twilight world where shadowy outlines of ancient dress moved slowly as if through heavy water. Everything seemed to be submerged in a spectral glue that held together many times and spaces.

Robin walked with no such hindrances. He ignored the gray forms that lumbered towards him, seemingly attracted by his vitality. He had come across the molecular leavings of the dead many times before in his long existence. They had never interested him particularly.

A door opened in grey hallway. Robin saw the castle entities pause in their pathetic shamblings and turn towards the cold white light that emanated from the open door.

He saw Hugh emerge from the room and lean against the wall with a long disappointed sigh. The vampire doctor pulled the stethoscope from around his neck with a short tired jerk.

"It's no use," he heard the doctor say in defeated tones. "She has no strength left."

"Hugh," said Robin, his throat tightening with grief, "you must try."

The doctor could not hear him. He rubbed his eyes wearily and went back into Caroline's room.

"She will live," came a musical voice behind Robin. "I will heal her.

The voice had spoken in old Welsh.

Robin turned away from Caroline's doorway. A pale enchantress of a girl, dressed in a crimson gown of ancient design, stood in the hallway. She gazed at him with large, intense gold eyes.

She was no ghost — but not exactly human, either. The beautiful angular face had an elfin cast with up-swept eyebrows and delicate slightly pointed ears.

He realized that he knew this shimmering creature. He had always known her. She had sung to him — songs of courage, protection and hope.

"Ceridwen."

She came towards him with arms outstretched.

"You have my promise," the girl said in the singsong of Welsh

Robin took one of her elegant hands and bowed over it. "I can sense your strengths, Ceridwen. You are far more powerful than I."

"No, I am Ceridwen but I am also Aeron, Gwydion, Beli — and I am you." She pulled away to smile up at him. "You will not need to hold the gate alone."

"Tylwyth Teg," he said in wonderment.

"You must go now." Ceridwen reached up to lay a cool hand on his cheek. "Your son carries the Teg bloodline, too — almost as strongly as you do. In death, he returned here as a guardian."

Robin watched, too moved to speak, as Ceridwen indicated Caroline's doorway. A moment later he heard the crying of a healthy baby and knew his daughter existed on the human plane.

"She will have the name Arianrhod," said Ceridwen. "I will see to that as well. Go now, Lord Pwyll."

He turned away from Caroline's door and refocused on the past, willing himself to bind with the essence that had been his son until he dissolved.

"Well done, Caroline," said Hugh gazing down in awe at the serene face of the sleeping newborn. "She's absolutely perfect."

Caroline smiled, grey with exhaustion. "Thank you for everything, Hugh. I wonder what my father will make of her."

"She's gorgeous," replied Hugh protectively. "He'll adore her. Her name is Arianrhod."

"Those lovely ears," she smiled again and closed her eyes to rest. "Not exactly human."

52

R obin felt his surroundings click into real time. He was on one of Lavec's laboriously pleached paths facing Hawkesmoor's Tudor era dower house.

A summer's night. The sky was black as ink and the air warm, scented with Lavec's meticulously arranged flowerbeds. The breeze caught at leaves here and there. An owl called as it tracked prey over the fields. The genuine quiet of the world was profound — the ever-present electrical hum of the 21st century gone.

The low-level rumble he had grown so accustomed to had completely vanished. He hadn't realized how glorious such peace had been. If his visit wasn't so urgent, he would make his way up to the castle battlements as he had so often in his human life and find a solitary spot in which to count the stars.

The thought made him return his gaze to the dower house. A gilded glow of candlelight guttered in one or two of the rooms. The place was occupied. In his day, it had been used as a kind of basic surgery and nursing home for ailing, aged or injured servants and their families.

How like Ambrose Westmacott to deprive the common people of their small comforts and install an obsolete Countess there when were many well-appointed apartments went begging in the castle proper.

He walked towards the brown and white timbered house but when someone approached on the gravel footing, he ducked behind a large hedge. It was not his intent to frighten anyone with a sudden reappearance and he did not wish to alter Hawkesmoor's history in any way. He only wished to whisk away one long, long-forgotten boy.

Gabriel blinked in confusion and tried again. He asked his revenant system to dematerialize — a simple command for a talented old vampire like himself — but not a single molecule answered his call.

"What the actual hell?" He stared down at his solid exterior in mystification. "This has never happened before."

Hugh nodded balefully as he paced, rocking the sleeping baby in his arms. "I can't manage the simplest things either. It's as if our power has been drained off."

"Wonderful," said Gabriel. "So when Petherbridge decides to make an appearance, he'll just slaughter us all."

"At least if we were at full power, he would have to break a sweat," Hugh concurred. "I wonder just what being burned at stake will feel like."

"Oh, deeply uncomfortable," the other vampire promised gloomily.

"He's foul that Ambrose Westmacott," said one of two underfootmen who were outside sneaking a gulp or two from a flask.

"Aye," agreed his companion with a nervous twitter in his voice. "I miss the old Earl. He and his were very fair to the likes of us."

"To the old Earl," said the first footman lifting the flask with an arm banded in black. "God's speed, my lord."

"Things would be different if the proper Lord Merritt had lived," he continued as he handed off the flask to his mate. "Bit of a bluestocking, but he would have done. Bred for the job — not like that swine in there."

The other had a long sip from the metal bottle. "Now all the true masters of this keep are dead."

"The DuPlessis are no more," he gestured at the dower house, "except for her."

They gazed at the quiet house for a long reverent moment, had a last pull at the flask and reluctantly returned to the castle. Robin slowly rose from his crouch by the hedge. It was not hard to deduce that his father had just died and his mother, with unseemly haste, had already been exiled to the dower house.

He glanced about for any more truant household staff and seeing none, continued on his way.

All the lamps in the Earl's study began to flicker ominously before winking out completely, plunging the room into twilight. Indeed, all various electrical hums and rattles associated with modern life had seemed to cease.

The two vampires exchanged worried glances and went to the large leaded windows to look out — all manufactured light was gone as far as their eyesight could stretch. The castle's outdoor security lighting was down and even the distant twinkling from outlying farms and Beckdale had disappeared.

In the distance a storm was gathering. The heavy clouds were illuminated by streaks of lightning so powerful it seemed to suggest the missing electricity had been stolen to give it life.

"So much for refrigerated blood," Gabriel pointed out airily. "I hope you like the life fluid of sheep."

Winnifred stared out at the massive storm. She winced at a particularly loud crash of thunder overhead. "And thus, the whirligig of time brings in its revenges," she murmured.

"Oh, my lady, he fire will soon do its work," said a voice plaintively as if the speaker were praying the recipient of the homespun *bon mot* would be cheered by such modest news.

Robin had slipped in through a servant entry in the rear of the dower house, stealthily making his way through shuttered and barren rooms towards the soft glow of a functioning fireplace.

He marveled at the gall of a man like Ambrose Westmacott who could send a new widow out to an ill-prepared icebox of a house without a shred of self-reproach.

The dower house might as well have been the castle cold rooms for all the amenities it provided. There was little furniture as most of its original decor had been removed to provide sick rooms for the local people. Even the serviceable furnishings of the infirmary had been stripped from the house. No servants prowled its chilly hallways save the one who had spoken.

His mother had been reduced to a state of penury. Little wonder she had been forced to return to the Dashwood family seat in Sussex.

The operating fireplace was located in what once had been the dower house's small library. He stood in the hallway, peering through the archway which seemed to lack the rather handsome rounded top door that had once hung there. He had vague memories that some of the dower house's fine sixteenth century interior doors had been removed to make passage in the infirmary a simpler matter.

"It does not matter, Dora," came his mother's weary voice.

Robin felt his throat tighten at the familiar contralto.

She sighed. "It does not matter one jot."

"Oh, ma'am!" His mother's long time lady's maid and chief dresser sounded stricken. "The room shall soon warm and I will away to fetch a hot drink."

"Dear Dora," replied his mother with affection in her tired tones, "do not fret so. I am well enough for one who has but lo, this very day, buried her husband."

"That devil Ambrose Westmacott!" Dora cried hotly. "One day he will answer for what he had done."

"It is of little service to rage against that which we can neither influence nor change. What is done cannot be undone."

"But, your ladyship," Dora began.

"The hot drink, Dora—I pray you," Augusta interrupted gently. "It would do much to restore my spirits."

"Oh ma'am," the ladies' maid sounded almost giddy with relief at having been given something useful to do, "I will attend to it immediately but it shall take some little time as I fear I must go back to castle to fetch it."

"Yes, yes—go," his mother said.

Robin backed away into a dark corner as the maid hurried from the former library—her busy footsteps echoing through the empty shell of a house.

He emerged and stepped with revenant quietness into the room.

Dressed in a severe black gown that threatened to drown her small frame, his mother was sitting in one of the Jacobean wing chairs from his rooms. Her feet rested on a small needle worked ottoman and she stared pensively into the glowing fireplace, the fingers on her left hand tapping a repetitive pattern on the upholstered chair arm.

Softly and deliberately, Robin cleared his throat.

His mother did not look away from the fire. "How good of you, Dora. Put the tray nearby and get you to bed. I shall attend to myself this night."

"Begging your forgiveness, madam," said Robin quietly, "seems woefully inadequate."

Augusta's fingers abruptly ceased tapping. She very slowly turned her head and when her astonished gaze finally drank him in, she half-rose from the chair, radiant with joy. Then fell back against the yellow damask with a strangled sob.

"I go mad!" She buried her face in her hands. "My son is dead."

"No," Robin said, moving forward to kneel at her side. He gently pulled her trembling hands down from her face. "I am not dead."

She stared at him with wide wild eyes. "Then you are the very devil sent to torment me!"

"No," he repeated. "I am only your son."

The fear began to fade in her eyes, replaced by wonder. Augusta lifted her hands and gingerly put her fingertips against his face, tracing the familiar bone structure with a delicate touch.

She reached out and laid a hand on his head as if testing the weight and quality of his amber hair against what she remembered of her lost son.

Tears spilled from her large green eyes. She made no attempt to wipe them away as if she feared losing the physical connection with Robin would cause him to disappear.

"Are you a ghost?" Augusta asked in a hoarse whisper.

He gazed up at her considering various options as to what he could tell his mother.

"In a way," Robin admitted, "I am."

Augusta ran her hand over his cheekbone, caressing his skin as she had when he was a little boy.

"How strange." She searched his face thoughtfully. I always felt you existed. That you were trying to return to Hawkesmoor."

"The Lord Merritt you remember was murdered that night in 1750," he said and swore softly at himself when she bent over in the pain inflicted by his words.

"Madam, that was well tactless of me," Robin apologized, searching about her little side table for a linen square. He found one and quickly handed it to her. "Forgive me. I did not intend to upset. I only wished to explain."

"No," his mother shook her head as she dabbed at her eyes with the linen, "you must forgive me, Bobbity. I am the one who lacks the strength to hear your words."

"Mother, my time here is short." Robin's voice was full with regret. "There is little to be done to right the many injustices my disappearance has wrought. But there is one thing I can do that may put your mind at ease."

Augusta sat back in the yellow damask wing chair with an expression of comprehension dawning over her patrician features.

"I know now that you are a dream," she said. "A wonderful illusion come to comfort me."

"No, Mother. I am no illusion."

"Your father always said the faerie folk spun wondrous dreams for those at Hawkesmoor." Augusta gave him a kind smile. "Many nights he sat up on the battlements because he said they sang their songs to him there."

Robin's eyes widened at her revelation. "Father heard faerie song?"

"He said he never understood what they sang but the beautiful sound always sent him to bed with dreams." She sighed. "I believe they sang to him in his great infirmity until the moment he died. That, you must understand, Bobbity, is part of my dream."

Robin nodded, unable to express how moved he was by her recollection. Then he gathered a way he could fashion a useful conversation with his mother.

"Mother," he said taking her hands in his and kissing the backs of each one. "You are wise to understand that I am a creature composed of cobweb and faerie lights."

"You are a beautiful dream," she agreed and her green eyes were once again luminous with tears.

"My time here is short," Robin repeated. "I have come to both comfort and aid."

"Aid?" Augusta regarded him with puzzlement.

"You possess, deep within you, an as yet unspoken terror that the boy — my son — lives in mortal danger."

She inhaled sharply, panic rising in her face.

Before his mother could frame a reply to his revelation, Robin continued in the most soothing voice as he could muster.

"Your fears are well grounded. Ambrose Westmacott will murder Elizabeth and once he has forced you home to Sussex, he intends the same for my son."

Tears overflowed their barricade and coursed down her pale cheeks. A soundless sob shook her small person.

"That poor sad little boy," she wept. "He has been so brave and Elizabeth — the cruelties she has endured are beyond my powers to describe or fully comprehend."

"I know." His voice hardened as he remembered her diary entries concerning Elizabeth's treatment at the hands of his cousin. "For your sake, do not dwell upon it."

"We were wrong," his mother went on. "We knew he was a preening, tedious fop but we thought to protect the child's birthright and Elizabeth, in her condition, was hardly suitable for another marriage arrangement. It was a terrible mistake."

"Madam, I am here to claim my son." Robin squeezed her hands. "Tell me where he sleeps this very night and I shall go to him."

"Oh, Robin! You would take Simon with you?" For the first time hope entered her large expressive eyes.

"When you receive the news that the boy is no more — do not mourn despite what tales my cousin will spin. The boy will be with me."

"When I was afforded the luxury, I kept him near me." Augusta's voice rose in excitement. "You will find him in a small room in what was once my own."

"I will away," Robin rose to his feet and bowed formally over her hand. "Madam, you are a great lady."

She found a smile for him. "Are these strange garments the raiment of faerie folk?"

Robin glanced down and realized he was still in Peter's old blue jeans and the black sweater he'd worn to dig up his son's grave.

"I cannot say I care overmuch for the fashion." Augusta turned her head quickly towards the library door as the sound of footsteps approached. "That will be Dora. You had best be off, Bobbity."

"Ever your servant, madam," he said and moved to shroud himself in the shadows.

He hid near the door until Dora appeared with a tray heaped with food and drink, exiting silently behind her as she passed through the arch.

"Why, my lady, you are looking much refreshed!" He heard Dora say over the tinkling of silver and china.

"A dream can restore the soul," came his mother's reply. "God speed, Bobbity."

"Well," said Gabriel as Peter and two security guards pulled open the massive doors to the Great Hall, "this is another interesting development."

Framed in the doorway were three figures. They stood shoulder to shoulder at the threshold. Dressed anonymously in hooded capes that concealed their faces and standing against a backdrop of jagged lightning strikes, they were an intimidating trio. Behind them was a small army fanning out over Hawkesmoor's wet lawn.

Hugh, Winnifred and Gabriel immediately stepped forward as they would still be viable defenders even without their special attributes.

"Peter, the guns," said the Earl tensely. "Hannah, upstairs with the dogs. Go now."

All three figures reached up and pushed back their hoods with a smooth, almost choreographed movement.

"Perhaps we can explain," said one of them in a calm voice.

"Sita!" breathed Gabriel in real surprise. "Good heavens, is that really you?"

The elegant Princess of ancient Ceylon stepped forward as she divested herself of the wet cape.

"How very nice to see you again, Gabriel Addington," she said pleasantly as if they were all arriving at some conference's welcoming cocktail party.

"Revenants?" asked Peter pointlessly. Hannah, her young face anxious, slipped her arm under his. He patted her hand in reassurance.

"Yes. All of us," replied a soft drawl. A tall, lanky man with clear blue eyes and chiseled American features was shrugging off his rain slicker. "Eli Walker. Formerly Major Elijah James Walker, U.S. Cavalry, Arizona territory."

"Kwang Tse," the third said as he too removed his dripping cape. "Former aid to Sun Yat-sen and the Chinese Democratic Republic."

"Brilliant!" Peter exclaimed. "I wrote a paper on Sun Yat-sen! He was *light years* ahead of his time for turn-of-the-century Asian politics. He's *still* light years ahead for Asian politics…"

Kwang Tse blinked through his small round glasses and offered Peter a polite bow. "I thank you, young sir."

"None of us can access our usual strengths," Hugh said, ignoring the introductions. "You?"

"Our power seemed to wane once we came within range of the castle," Sita replied, extending a hand to an uneasy Earl who took it briefly. "Very odd."

"Why are you here?" ventured Hannah in a small voice from her place clinging to Peter's arm.

"We have brought local people to Hawkesmoor," the elegant Indian vampire explained and then directed her words to the castle vampires. "I fear that Lord Scyon is summoning his forces and intends to destroy Robin DuPlessis as well as anyone or anything who gets in his way."

"We came to help you out." The American nodded with a grim expression. "I do not like bullies. This Lord Scyon y'all so worried about, is just one hell of a bully."

"You can say that again," Gabriel said dryly.

'We did not want Lord Scyon to be able to use your friends and neighbors as cannon fodder." Kwang Tse gave another polite bow to the Earl.

"Or as a convenient feeding source," Eli interjected.

Sita leaned forward to kiss Gabriel's cheek lightly.

"We agreed they would be safer here behind the castle walls," she said. "At least for a while."

"At least," Hugh agreed, "until Petherbridge gets here."

53

Caroline kissed the crown of her sleeping baby's head and wondered how it was possible to love something so much so instantly.

Arianrhod. Caroline rested her head back against the pillows with a tired sigh. Apparently the beautiful infant had arrived with it, fully equipped. Hugh had insisted that the ancient Celtic name was for her daughter. Nothing else would do. So much, she reflected, for quietly refined names like Pamela or Alice.

More name me, yes? A child's voice in her head asked her with such concerned sweetness that it riveted her attention.

Caroline half sat up and looked over at her baby. Arianrhod's large eyes had opened. The infant's drowsy face gazed up at her with absolute adoration.

"Did you just talk?" Caroline shook her head. It just wasn't logical. Babies simply didn't construct sentences, telepathically or otherwise.

Arianrhod yawned and closed her eyes again.

Me am sleep.

A vampire council met in the Earl's study while villagers and farmers ate a reviving meal downstairs. The only humans allowed to be present were Peter and the Earl. They sat, gobsmacked, as

Hugh explained his theories about Morvidus, dimensional gates and powerful Celtic deities.

"It has long been known to me as an old vampire," said Sita, crossing her long thin arms in thought, "that Morvidus was very powerful and very strange. The courts used to whisper of it until the great Roman vampire king, Rinchon Annaeus, disappeared forever under mysterious circumstances. Revenants were too frightened to talk about Morvidus after that."

"And when did Rinchon Annaeus disappear?" asked Kwang Tse in interest.

Sita shrugged loosely. "I'm not sure anymore but about the time the Alrava tesh vara Temple was built in Darasuram."

The Chinese vampire stared at her blankly.

"1073," answered Gabriel. "The same year Gregory VII became Pope. William the Conqueror was on the English throne."

Hugh cleared his voice. "Let us assume for the moment that Morvidus destroyed Rinchon Annaeus because he wished to muddy his true origins and his first-born knew too much."

"Actually," interrupted Sita, "all the early Kings and Queens are gone."

"Some of those can be accounted for." Gabriel stood up and stretched. "Accident, intentional suicide, human intervention — we took a terrible beating in Eastern Europe in the 14th century."

"Well, we deserved to." Winnifred made a sour face. "That Wittelbach idiot creating new vampires everywhere he went — using the spread of the Black Death as a magic carpet. Small wonder humans finally got irritated."

"Some of us got fairly greedy in all the confusion," Gabriel said, by way of explanation to Peter and his father. "So many were dying anyway, you know — who'd notice a few more?"

"Brilliant," said Peter in awe. His face lit up with an historian's bliss at discovering he was in the presence of collaborative witnesses to some of the most dynamic events in the human time line.

"It does introduce another issue." The Earl sighed deeply, signaling his fatigue with the new vampire. "Now that the power is out, I'm assuming your portable blood supply is no longer viable. I don't think any of the locals will appreciate being fed upon."

"I packed the lot in ice," said Winnifred, to the tangible relief of the other revenants present. "It won't last forever but it will hold us for now — hopefully until things get sorted out."

"If Petherbridge hasn't been affected by this power drain, it'll be a moot point, I assure you," Hugh added.

"So he's that powerful?" Eli asked, his blue eyes brightening at the thought.

Peter shuddered. "He's a monster."

"He is legion," Gabriel said flatly. "When Petherbridge needs it, he possesses the strength of many vampires."

"But he is not a particularly old vampire, is he?" Kwang Tse asked with a frown.

"The old Marquess of Southbrook took him as a bride in 1643," said Gabriel. "I believe young human Petherbridge was then editor of *Mercurius Aulicus* at Oxford."

The historian in Peter gasped audibly. "The Cavalier newsletter? Why, I've handled their very pages in Bodley's Library!"

"By all means," said his father without humor, "before he sets you on fire next time, try to pry some reference notes out of him."

"Besides," continued Winnifred, "Robin is now incredibly powerful. He became one of us in 1750."

"But Robin's different. He's this odd hybrid," Gabriel countered swiftly. "Let me assure you: no one's ever claimed that Petherbridge is half faerie!"

Kwang Tse raised an eyebrow at that. "But if you have one hybrid, why not two?"

Robin slipped into the castle through the door that he hoped would lead him to the common rooms. If his memory was accurate, it would be the most effective place to launch himself into the Hawkesmoor Castle of the 1760s. After all, servants had to be able to fetch and carry at their employer's whim, in a sense. All roads in a great country house led to the servant quarter.

He was gratified to note that a line of hooks in the antechamber wall held up a collection of well-worn aprons and smocks. These did not belong to the well born in the household — he had indeed remembered the castle's general layout.

But he didn't recall it as a dour and depressed place. He could feel melancholy like a physical force in the air, pulling at him with black strings as he covertly made his way through an exceptionally quiet common area.

The lack of servants was odd, Robin thought as he stepped around a corner to allow two exhausted scullery maids with soot blackening their uniforms to pass unhindered.

It was late. Many might have retired to their small rooms but there ought to be a skeleton crew ready to serve their betters at a moment's notice. His mother had liked a cheerful environment throughout the castle. She had always encouraged her staff to socialize among themselves and to make Hawkesmoor their home. Because of her enlightened attitude, the servant quarters had always been warm from well-tended fires built to be every bit as large as ones in more rarefied parts of the castle. Even in the slow hours, friendly conversations could be heard from comfortably appointed rooms in which servants were well fed and kindly managed.

Not like this cold prison.

Granted, their much-loved master had just been placed in the family crypt but the joyless atmosphere seemed entrenched as if Ambrose Westmacott had managed to pollute and poison the entire castle.

A resounding crash made him spin towards the direction of the hideous clatter. With apprehension tightening his chest, he pressed into shadowy corner as a footman ran towards the servant quarter.

"Jesus, Mary and Joseph!" cried the footman. "I'll none of this!"

Elizabeth! Robin's thoughts flew to his betrothed. Had Ambrose just pushed her down the staircase? He emerged from his hiding place and broke into a run, heading to the Great Hall.

Gabriel snorted. "A hybrid of what? A hyena? No — a famous jackal like Anubis!"

"No, no," Hugh said shaking his head in disapproval. "Don't be so quick to dismiss Kwang Tse's thought. What if Morvidus and his kind inhabited other bodies, other forms as a way of hunting humans on this dimensional plane?"

"Like Invasion of the Body Snatchers?" Gabriel rolled his eyes.

Hugh threw him a withering look. "We can guess that Morvidus took various human forms to stay in hiding after the door to this dimension closed."

"But how does Petherbridge fit in?" Gabriel lifted up his arms in a wide gesture of bewilderment. "He was off tormenting and drinking up hapless slum whores in Robin's day."

"Ah, but he wasn't always slitting the throats of the poor and unlamented," Hugh replied triumphantly. "There is a connection between Petherbridge and Hawkesmoor Castle. Petherbridge told me he had developed a fascination for Robin, then Lord Merritt, and his love affair with the opera singer Corisande Belfield."

Peter let out a short whistle at his words. He and his father exchanged stunned glances at learning previously unknown tales in their castle's history.

"Yes," Winnifred said as she walked closer to the fireplace. "Robin married Corisande just before she died. She was the great love of his life, I believe." She threw the Earl a guilty look. "Until he met Lady Caroline, of course."

"Lord Merritt married before his own betrothal ball to Elizabeth Gwayr?" Peter's voice was breathless. "Love matches among the landowners were only beginning to gain credence in the last gasps of the 18th century! He went against all social convention — fascinating!"

"Well," said Winnifred dryly, "in all fairness — and you know I adore Robin but she was on the verge of a terrible death from consumption. I don't expect he ever imagined he would have to present her to his family as Lady Merritt. I think he just wanted to make her last hours happy."

"Then!" announced Hugh, taking back the floor pointedly, "Petherbridge decides to hotfoot it up to Hawkesmoor — relieve his boredom with some refined acts of cruelty and ploughs right into the disembodied consciousness of Morvidus whose ability to manifest in three dimensional form has been destroyed by Robin's faerie blood."

Sita gasped. "Morvidus *is* Garnet Petherbridge?"

54

Robin found the Great Hall empty. The terrible sound of random destruction had begun anew, so he followed its direction. He was careful to stay out of the sight and it was with silent stealthy steps that he approached the vortex of all the violence — his former rooms.

His throat ached at the sound of Elizabeth's frightened voice rising above the din.

"You must not do this. 'Tis very cruel," she begged. "It will kill your poor Aunt."

Something made of glass shattered before Ambrose's studied drawl deigned to reply.

"This night has been long anticipated," he said. "I would have you to see all that is left of my cousin destroyed. Tell me — is it just a little like watching Robin being chopped for firewood?"

"You," Elizabeth said with revulsion, "will rot in hell one day."

"And you are nothing more than one of Robin DuPlessis' whores — and believe me, he had a weakness for doxies." Ambrose was enjoying himself. "I've been told he possessed quite a keen appetite for bedding his mistress but alas, you, my little flower, seemed to inspire much less interest."

There was a horrifying pause before Elizabeth spoke and when she did, her voice trembled with emotion.

"Ambrose Westmacott, you can take apart his possessions, scatter his books, break the spirit of those he loved," she said, her courage growing stronger with her conviction," but you shall never be the true Lord Merritt of this keep. Just as you will never be a real Earl of Hawkesmoor. Despite how you would muddy his memory, you will never destroy the connection I possess with him. Never!"

Robin felt a tear drop onto his cheek. He brushed it away, pressing into a darkened doorway as a servant girl with a candle stepped carefully out from another room down the long hallway. She paused uncertainly and held out her candle as if vaguely aware that someone else might be nearby in the shadows.

"Never?" came Ambrose's voice cold with fury. "I am lord here and madam, you shall learn it!"

The maid jumped at his voice and gathered up her skirts. She ran — headed to the safety of the servants' hall much as the footman had done earlier. Robin held his breath as she darted past, hoping the servant would not catch sight of him and alert the entire castle to his presence.

But the darkness continued to shield him from detection — one benefit from the time of candle power. He let out a relieved breath and had just the barest moment to ponder what he ought to do for Elizabeth.

If he rescued Elizabeth from her fate, the future as he knew it could be altered forever. Caroline might never be born. He would never see her again. A terrible cosmic riddle: choose Elizabeth and lose Caroline forever or choose Caroline and Elizabeth's terrible fate is sure.

A thudding sound came from his rooms. A ghastly sort of heavy wet thud followed by a second thud and then a third. Finally, there was an obscene cracking to break the sickening cadence.

A profound silence followed.

Robin moved out of the darkened corner. He clasped the handle of the door, turned and pushed it open.

Wild-eyed, Ambrose Westmacott was staring at blood that glistened as it dripped from his fat fingers.

Elizabeth was slumping to the floor from between Ambrose's heavy hands. She fell into a crumpled heap with yards and yards of a pale blue muslin underskirts pooling around her. It was staining rapidly with an expanding tide of her blood.

Her face fell to the side, exposing the damage. Her head had literally cracked open, revealing brain and bone. Elizabeth's left cheekbone had shattered causing her once delicate jaw to hang useless and one eye was obliterated completely.

From the relative positions of Ambrose and Elizabeth, it wasn't hard to deduce that his cousin had seized her in a violent rage and with incredible force repeatedly smashed her face into the heavy Jacobean bedpost.

So, it had not been the stairs at all. Ambrose would throw her body down the staircase in the Great Hall and bully the household into accepting his version of the facts.

Already Ambrose's remorseless mind had leapt to this course of action and he was bending down to pick up the small shattered body.

"You really have gone too far this time, cousin," said Robin in a quiet but deadly voice. "History will remember you as a murderer of this defenseless lady."

Ambrose's corpulent face had been radiating a kind of terrible excitement but now mutated to ashen panic. He looked up from his grisly task, staring at Robin with disbelief.

"You!" he breathed, backing away from Elizabeth. "But this cannot be. You are dead!"

"You are quite right. I am dead," Robin agreed as he advanced on the retreating Ambrose. His hated cousin was scrambling backwards, crablike, over the floor. "I am also a monster."

"It was an accident!" Ambrose cried, holding up one bloody hand in a futile gesture of protection. "She fell. Her little foot caught on the carpet and she fell."

Robin used his vampire strength to reach down and pick up Ambrose by the collar. He lifted his struggling cousin off the floor, content to let Ambrose gag for air. "I want you to heed my words, Ambrose Westmacott, and heed them closely." Robin shoved Ambrose's back against the wall, pinning him there with one hand at his cousin's throat. "Do you understand me, cousin?"

Westmacott was turning blue from the agonizing lock on his throat. He gagged but managed to execute a ragged nod of his head.

"When you bury Elizabeth, it will be with the full honors due her." Robin tightened his grip on Ambrose's windpipe. "You do agree?"

Ambrose coughed painfully and made another attempt at a nod.

"You will not bestow Elizabeth's family jewels on your mistress," he continued. "You will return them to Manwaring in the proper time. Agreed?"

Again, Ambrose nodded. His eyes were bulging now and his skin had taken on a nasty grey pallor.

"Then we have a contract." Robin let Ambrose drop to the floor.

Robin turned and located the handsome medieval dirk that had belonged to Sir Francis DuPlessis, sitting in its usual place on the chimney piece.

He strode over to the fire and took it off the mantel.

"And in the unfortunate event that you consider casting aside our contract." Robin unsheathed the ancient weapon and returned to Ambrose who was still balled up on the floor, moaning and gasping for breath. "Perhaps this will remind you of me."

He grabbed a handful of Ambrose's greasy hair, yanked his blubbering cousin's head up and plunged the dirk tip into Ambrose's left eye.

Westmacott convulsed with a hoarse attempt at a scream, muted to a raspy whine by Robin's bruising of his voice box.

"One last thing, cousin," said Robin, discarding the dirk and moving towards Elizabeth. He knelt to pick up her small broken body.

Despite the excruciating pain, Ambrose paused in his agonized rocking to listen. He stared at Robin with his good eye, a fat hand clamped desperately over the ruined one.

Robin lifted up Elizabeth and began to head for the door. Then he paused in answer to Ambrose's hoarse entreaty to know that one last thing.

He turned, looking down at the pathetic figure of Ambrose Westmacott clutching at his destroyed eye.

"Know this, Ambrose Westmacott," Robin said coldly. "Many years from now, when at last you die, I will be waiting for you in hell. Then I shall have all of eternity to make you suffer for what you have done to my family."

Any lingering regrets Robin felt at not being able to carry out his prophecy fled as he saw mind-bending horror that wash over what was left of his cousin's face. Ambrose Westmacott would spend every waking moment in a kind of gut-churning dread. It was enough.

Robin bent to lay Elizabeth's body down with exquisite gentleness at the top of the stairs. No one could possibly believe that she had fallen to her death but Ambrose was devious enough to find a way to make his lies stick.

He kissed the palm of each of her hands.

"I would have been proud to call you wife," he whispered. "God speed, dear Elizabeth. God speed to wherever it is human souls belong."

A break in the storm revealed a burnished glow emanating from behind a rise; a long thin line of flickering copper and gold that finally reached the summit of the rise and stopped there, seemingly content to dominate the moor.

"Is it a fire?" asked Winnifred, frowning as she leaned against the old stonework of the Great Walk. "Awfully organized for a wild fire."

"No," murmured Gabriel. A cool breeze ruffled his hair as he stared across the dark expanse to a ribbon of gilded light. "It reminds me of an earlier time. Long before electricity."

"Of course," she said, "torches. Many of them lined up."

"In intimidating battle formation," Gabriel finished for her.

Hugh swung back sharply to look out at the copper glow. "A medieval army in full shoulder-to-shoulder column."

"I'll go," said Gabriel. "I'll go tell them Petherbridge is here."

55

Robin reached his mother's former rooms just as a panicked hue and cry went up in the Great Hall behind him. A servant had discovered Elizabeth's battered body and the unnaturally silent castle was coming to terrified life.

He slipped inside the sitting room just as a random assortment of servants ran down the hallway to see why their limited world appeared to be coming to an end.

"Stay child, I pray you!" came the voice of a younger man. "I shall see what is afoot this night."

The boy's tutor, Robin guessed as he faded into shadows thrown by a massive Tudor wardrobe.

"I am *not* a child," returned the steady voice of his son as the sound of multiple shrieking voices reached the room. "It sounds terribly important, Mr. Forbes-Hamilton. Please do have a look."

"I certainly shall," his tutor replied. His voice became louder as he neared the small antechamber in which Robin was hiding. "But you, Mr. Westmacott — stay by your fire and continue to translate your paper into legible Greek."

"Yes, Mr. Forbes-Hamilton," the boy sighed glumly. "As you wish."

Robin watched from his dark corner as a rather handsome Mr. Forbes-Hamilton came into the room bearing a small lit candle. Without a glance in Robin's direction, he made his way quickly to the door and let himself out.

Westmacott indeed! Robin clenched his jaw. If Ambrose was styling himself as the new Earl of Hawkesmoor Castle, then by rights the boy should be Lord Merritt.

But it was a courtesy title and Ambrose had obviously failed to extend it to the boy. Robin thought longingly about returning to Ambrose amidst the rubble that had once been his lovely Jacobean furniture and putting his cousin's other eye out.

Ambrose hadn't lent Simon the right to be styled Lord Merritt because such declarations left trails and he wanted history to forget the boy ever existed.

"You are telling me," the Earl blinked and turned to survey the band of light in the distance, "that is an army of vampires?"

"I'm afraid so, your lordship," replied Gabriel apologetically. "My guess is he's rounded up all revenants under his control and imported others who owe him favors or who just fancy the job."

"Life used to be bloody simple around here until you people turned up. Oh yes, on occasion we had a farmer who enjoyed one too many trips to a concession tent at village fetes but never vampires in full battle mode." Caroline's father looked annoyed. "Why is he just waiting around then? Why not polish us off and be done with it?"

"I suspect they're experiencing the same power drop off," Gabriel said, "or believe me, Petherbridge would already be here polishing us off."

"You mean he and his friends can't just pop into the castle willy-nilly anymore?"

"Correct. If we stay powerless, he's reduced to attacking the old-fashioned way." The former monk's eyes scanned the long thread of glowing light. "He does have an awful lot of us with him, though."

The Earl raised his eyebrows and said sharply, "We will simply defend our castle the old-fashioned way too. Gabriel, call everyone together in the Great Hall. We don't have much time before dawn."

Simon was sitting at a little table before a crackling fire. His head bent intently over his lesson work as he struggled to scratch down a sentence.

Robin almost smiled. The boy's long handsome fingers were stained with black ink from the quill he was laboriously using to copy his Greek. He remembered his own fingers, black with ink from Mr. Pitt's lessons.

"Simon," he said, "how I see your mother in you."

The boy's head jerked up. He looked startled at Robin's presence, his large green eyes widening in fear.

He had his mother's heavy tawny blond hair but the highly planed, angular face belonged to the DuPlessis bloodline. There could be no doubt as to who his real father had been. Every soul within a crow's flight from Hawkesmoor would know the boy had sprung from the DuPlessis family. He was no Westmacott.

"Who are you, sir?" he breathed, his chair squeaking a little as he edged backwards nervously. "I must warn you — my tutor will soon return."

Robin stepped clear of the shadows and watched as Simon's intelligent eyes scanned his face.

"Do not fear me, Simon," he said in a quiet voice. "I have little time to explain and you have no reason to trust me — but you must."

"God's teeth!" Simon gasped, recognition taking fire in his eyes. "You are the man in the portrait. The one Aunt Augusta keeps on her bedroom wall!"

"I am Richard Robin Francis DuPlessis." Robin nodded and held out a hand. "Come with me, boy. We must away, you and I. Time grows short."

"But you," the boy tried to make sense of what was happening, "disappeared. Father said you well-nigh abandoned Hawkesmoor!" Simon looked embarrassed. "Mother says I should not always heed his words."

Robin extended his hand again. "Come with me, Simon."

"But are you not dead?" Simon tilted his head to the side in such a quizzical fashion that Robin could, with a painful mixture of sadness and elation, recognize the gesture as something he did himself.

Robin shook his head. " 'Tis deuced difficult to explain. To some I am dead but to others, my heart beats. I draw breath."

Simon's beautiful face shadowed with regret. "I wish I could come with you." His voice dropped to nearly a whisper. "I would not miss my life here."

But then he straightened his spine and lifted his chin with impressive courage for one so young. "But I have a duty to this keep. One day it will be mine."

Robin glanced over his shoulder as heavy footsteps of more servants clumped past in the hallway.

"Simon, I mean you no alarm but you must listen to me and listen with care," Robin said, his gaze returning to his son's face. "Do you understand me when I say that by birthright, you are the true Earl of Hawkesmoor and yet you will never be master of this keep?"

A variety of emotions flickered across Simon's angular features from thoughtful to momentary panic. He settled, at last, on resignation.

He glanced away from Robin, swallowing hard. He slowly picked up the quill and replaced it with care in a specially made silver stand.

"The stable boys tease me," Simon told him as he threw a pinch of sand from the stand over the wet ink on his page of writing, "when they know they will not be caught. I was puzzled by what they said for quite a long time."

He looked up from his books and papers. "But the stable boys know more than I, do they not?"

Robin let out a short breath. "I am your father. You are Simon DuPlessis."

"Then *I* am a bastard," Simon pointed out with a raised eyebrow.

"You are my son," Robin replied strongly. "You are the rightful heir to this keep."

"I am the rightful heir to *nothing*!" Simon's voice was bitter. "You saw to that, did you not? Deserting my mother after she..." He could not bring himself to utter the thought.

"We tarry here too long," Robin tightened his jaw and wished he could return to inflict more damage on his vile cousin, "or would you rather Ambrose's footpads jerk a garroting wire 'round your young neck?"

"You are able to see into the future?" Simon's tone was dismissive.

"Actually yes," he replied. "In this case I can. If you refuse my help, you will die in a way I would not wish upon a cur dog."

Simon paused and reevaluated Robin. He looked at Robin's face intently for a moment and then slowly, his head began to nod.

"I admit, the prospect of denying my *father* the pleasure of seeing me dead intrigues me," he said with remarkable calm. "What must we do?"

Hawkesmoor hummed with life in a way it had not in many generations. Vampire and humans worked together to fortify the old structure against the expected onslaught of Petherbridge's army. Instead of succumbing to a hideous wait and imploding, everyone was given job. Skillful builders aided Kwang Tse in the construction of a device designed to pour hot embers and oil upon the invaders. Others helped to organize and prepare what weaponry could be found in the castle. Some crafted bows and arrows as Winnifred and Gabriel instructed them. Hannah and other horse savvy teenagers saw to the animals, erecting makeshift stabling and bringing them within the castle walls.

"I wonder if Peter has gotten the antique weapons up and operational," The Earl said to his stableman, Evan, as they watched a group of farmers sharpening long sticks for lances. "By God, this is almost fun — and everyone's taking it awfully well. They've taken to the notion of blood-sucking immortals with a stiff upper lip."

"Yes, your lordship," Evan concurred, "but then, we're British, aren't we?"

"Is this *quite* where you meant for us to travel?" asked Simon in wonder.

Robin blinked. They were still in the boy's rooms but the castle seemed different somehow. The lighting seemed wrong — unbalanced and too far over into the blue-green tint on the spectrum. It was also seemingly deserted.

No comforting and familiar sounds of people going about their business. Instead, there was an almost electric energy to the place as if the inhabitants had just been sucked away into oblivion and the zing in the air was a residual whoosh.

"I," Robin began hesitantly, "fail to understand this. I do not know where we are."

"Oh, Lord Merritt! Come out, come out!" sang a voice from the hallway outside. "Lord Merritt, you can't hide from me!"

Simon flashed Robin a questioning look and frowned as his father motioned urgently for him to find a hiding place. He obeyed despite his qualms, slipping into one of the large wardrobes and pulling its door shut.

Robin turned to face the door squarely as Sir Anthony Fortesque strolled in. He looked much the same as he had in the late Georgian — still a dandy in black leather trousers and a silk shirt, his hair pulled back into a ponytail.

"How really nice to see you again," he drawled, walking towards Robin. "I've often thought of you over the years, Mr. DuPlessis."

"And I, you," replied Robin, watching his former owner warily.

"You look very well, I must say." Sir Anthony laid a beautifully manicured hand on Robin's left shoulder and ran it over the soft black cashmere of the sweater. "Three hundred-odd years hasn't blunted your appeal."

Robin brushed Fortesque's hand away. "Don't."

Sir Anthony looked delighted. "How really wonderful! Misbegotten dignity. It's so old-fashioned."

"Surely you must have more pressing matters."

"Actually, I don't. Petherbridge sent me to track you down and by the way, the boy? He was most particular about the boy."

Robin almost wove on his feet with surprise. *How had Petherbridge come to learn about his son?*

"I don't know," he stammered, struggling to find a response. "We were separated, trying to link back to the present."

"How I hoped you would say that!" Sir Anthony stepped forward and slammed an elbow into Robin's ribs. He fell with a choking cough to the floor.

Caroline, can't bear the pain! You must help me!

Startled, Lady Caroline pushed up to her elbows. In the flickering candlelight, she could see her new daughter sleeping nearby in a small crib that had served DeBarry infants since the Regency. But no one else. The room was peaceful and pleasant.

"Robin?" she said tentatively, positive that she had heard his voice. He sounded panicked, even traumatized.

Her inquiry brought no response. Caroline rubbed her eyes. Perhaps she ought to go and find her father — find out what the state of things were in the castle.

I need your help! Just say yes so we can link together.

Robin's voice was ragged and desperate. It drove Caroline to her feet. She stumbled from her bed and took a few unsteady steps across the carpet, looking everywhere for some sign of her husband. The room remained still, untouched by any hint of strife.

But Robin was some sort of trouble. He needed her.

"Yes," she said out loud, without knowing exactly why. It just seemed the only thing to do.

56

"Rush lights," explained Gabriel, as he carefully placed a clipped stalk into a makeshift tin holder. "It was one of my duties centuries ago at the monastery. This will last for an age once I light it and saves the wax candles for more important tasks."

"Excellent!" replied the Earl, pleased. Then he turned his attention to his rapidly approaching son. "Peter — good. Any indication that this Petherbridge has moved his forces?"

"None." He shook his head, long blonde hair falling about his face haphazardly. "All is currently quiet."

"Oh, Gabriel," came Hugh's voice.

"Yes?" He glanced up from his rush lamp.

The vampire doctor peeked around the kitchen doorway and smiled rather too broadly at everyone who stood at the old refectory table in the heart of the 'new' castle kitchen.

"Could I borrow you for a little minute?"

"Can it wait a bit?" Gabriel asked as he placed another shoot in a tin box. "I've got many rush lights to do."

"No, it just *couldn't*," Hugh replied too lightly.

Before Gabriel could reply, the Earl stepped away from the kitchen table.

"Hugh," he said forcefully, "you've got some troubling news. Tell us what it is."

"Well," the doctor reluctantly came into the kitchen, "it's Lady Caroline." He lowered his voice to near whisper. "She's gone missing."

Caroline looked around. She seemed to be in one of Hawkesmoor's smaller rooms but she didn't recognize it at all. What was it she was supposed to accomplish for Robin here?

"Who's there?" Caroline said, as a shifting sound caught her attention. "Robin… is that you?"

Please say yes. Please say it's me — Robin. I'm going to stay by your side until we are both safe at home in our Hawkesmoor, she thought anxiously, and then gasped, spinning as a hinge squeaked in protest behind her.

A large wardrobe door was slowly opening. Caroline backed up apprehensively: wanting to know who was inside the heavy piece of furniture and just as happy never to know at all.

In her nervousness, she knocked into a little table, sending it flying. She turned awkwardly in horror to see what she had done and promptly sent a standing vase spiraling to the floor.

"God's teeth, madam! You shall have the wretched hound down upon us," said an annoyed voice, echoing slightly in the confined acoustics of the wardrobe.

Robin wondered how long he would last under Sir Anthony's interrogation. He had already taken a beating and with his vampire repair process compromised by the re-emergence of the faerie cell structure, there would not be much to work with once Fortesque really started to enjoy his favorite hobby.

But, Robin thought, there were two important issues he must not allow Sir Anthony to own. One was the presence of Simon DuPlessis in this dimension because to do so was to place his son in the hands of Garnet Petherbridge and the other was his physical evolution away from the vampire. That information could endanger the lives of everyone he cared about.

"Once again, Mr. DuPlessis," Fortesque's deadly drawl broke into his thoughts, "where is the boy?"

Robin threw his former owner a disinterested glance as if the vampire was just some vaguely annoying person in a train compartment.

Sir Anthony approached him. "I will break you."

"Oh, not you again!" Caroline groaned as Hawkesmoor's boy ghost climbed out of the wardrobe. "Have you no spot in the hereafter to call your own?"

"Madam, you speak in riddles," the boy said, brushing a cobweb off his shoulder. "Kindly inform me as to where we are and to whom I am speaking."

She stared at him. "You don't know?"

"What 'tis the meaning of your word 'don't'?" he asked with a frown crossing his patrician face. "You speak most strangely and affect a peculiar mode of dress. You are of this place?"

Caroline glanced down and realized she was still wearing a large shapeless nightgown.

"Bloody hell," she said in surprise. "I must look ghastly."

The boy cocked his head to the side, quizzically. "No. Merely *odd*."

"Thank you." Caroline made a face.

Winnifred was showing some of the locals how to properly line up an archery shot when Hugh found her. She pulled back on the bow with an elegance built from centuries of skill and let the arrow fly.

It whistled across the courtyard and impaled itself into the center of the target with a dead-on thud. The collection of local men and women gathered about her applauded with genuine zeal.

"Anyone can do it," she said, once the clapping had died down. "Steady and consistent. Remember to aim for the head. It's the only really vulnerable place for a revenant. You can slow them down with injuries elsewhere but a head shot destroys the brain — and the vampire."

There was a lot of impressed chatter as Winnifred left the knot of would-be vampire slayers to join Hugh who was adjusting a makeshift baby sling around his shoulder.

"You look silly but weirdly noble," she said upon reaching him. "You're taking Arianrhod to safety — outside these walls?"

Hugh nodded as he made sure the sleeping Arianrhod was safely secure. "Robin's gone." He looked down at the newborn. "Her mother is missing. I don't think she's safe in the castle."

Winnifred only smiled sadly at him. "I'd never question your instinct."

"True. 'M a very old vampire."

"Hugh," Winnifred asked with sudden urgency, "is this a *real* sort of good-bye?"

The vampire doctor swallowed roughly. "Yes, I'm afraid it might be. Yes."

"Don't come back if it's bad, Hugh," she said, laying a soft hand on his forearm. "Just stay wherever you are and survive."

"I don't want you to face Petherbridge without knowing," Hugh struggled to find the right words, "without knowing how I feel. You have always held that vampires like us don't love. We only confuse desire with love because we miss our human components but I submit that you are wrong. I love you, Winnifred. I always have, you know."

"Hugh Candlethorne," Winnifred replied in mild frustration. "I haven't given that old theory of mine any credence since the French Revolution."

She stepped forward, slipping her arms gently about him and the baby. Hugh moved a little closer so he could kiss her properly.

Hugh pulled away and awkwardly shifted his weight to check on the sleeping Arianrhod. He looked up at the sky. It was just beginning to show signs of a lighter hue.

"Mind how you go, Winnifred Turchil."

57

Caroline stared at the boy in real puzzlement. "Is this Hawkesmoor Castle or not?" she persisted. "Let's make this even simpler. Have you seen a tall man with long reddish hair? I need to find him and quickly."

"Richard Robin Francis DuPlessis?" he asked. "Once Lord Merritt of this keep?"

"Yes! Where is he? Can you take me to him?"

The boy seemed to crumble at her questions. He gazed at the floor, fighting back tears. His jaw clenched and unclenched.

Suddenly Caroline understood the boy's place in all of it. She wondered if Arianrhod's faerie abilities had lent her occasional flashes of extraordinary mental clarity as well as a miraculous recovery from the tedious after-effects of childbirth.

Of course, it was all laid out in the diaries Winnifred had suggested she read.

Caroline squeezed the boy's shoulder, afraid his 18th century upbringing would recoil at a more familiar gesture. "Robin is your father," she said softly, "and he came back to find you, did he not?"

The boy she knew as Hawkesmoor's most poignant ghost lifted his head to her and nodded.

"Madam, how do you know of such things?" he breathed, tears finally escaping his green eyes and rolling down his cheeks. He wiped them away roughly with his shirt sleeve.

"Simon, as odd as I appear to you," Caroline indicated her comfortable old nightgown, "I am rightly your stepmother."

Simon gasped. "Stepmother?"

"Call me Caro. My family and friends do," she said as cheerfully as she could manage. "Let's get on to helping your father. It appears to be his turn for a rescue."

"All you have to do is tell me where the boy is," Fortesque said sympathetically, "and this can end."

Robin, weakened by Peter's empathetic healing, was no match for the powerful Fortesque. His former owner hauled him toward a restraining table used in medieval times when the castle had a fully functioning dungeon in which to house political enemies and local miscreants.

"God," murmured Robin in dazed reaction to the pain. Sir Anthony threw him hard against the darkly stained wood and locked his throbbing wrists down under metal bars.

"You say that as if you think such a being, if he exists, would actually help *you*, Robin DuPlessis. You — a vampire. You — bride of Morvidus, the old one."

"Listen," said Robin, with a pronounced wheeze, "leave the boy alone. He's nothing to Petherbridge. Garnet only wants to revenge himself upon me."

Fortesque sat on the edge of the torture rack as if it were a hospital bed and he was casually dropping by to visit an old friend. He idly traced a line slowly down the front of Robin's black sweater with the point of a knife.

"Hear me out," Robin wheezed, trying to lift his head from the wood panel. "If you let him go, I'll come with you. I will be your slave. Anything. Just let him alone."

Fortesque's eyes brightened. "You're offering yourself to me?"

He used the knife to rip a long shred in the black cashmere. Pushing aside the ruined sweater, Fortesque gazed down at the black mark of Morvidus that Robin bore over his heart, and reached out to run his fingertips over the rough scar.

"Yes," Robin said, watching Sir Anthony with revulsion, "I am."

"Mr. DuPlessis," he dropped a kiss on Robin's forehead and stayed down to whisper in his ear, "I *will* have you."

Robin stared up at the vaulted ceiling of the dungeon counting the beams. Counting the cracks in the beams. Counting the cobwebs that shimmered in the cracks — anything to will his mind elsewhere. A survival technique he had learned long ago as Fortesque's indentured property.

Sir Anthony dropped down, hungrily kissing the side of his face and then his mouth. Robin inhaled a long breath once Fortesque had pulled his mouth from his and exhaled slowly as his former owner stared down at him in fascination.

He shifted his focus and gazed back dispassionately at Sir Anthony.

"You own me. I hope it brings you nothing but pain."

Sir Anthony's hand left his chest, making a lazy arc down and across his abdomen. His icy fingers sought out the broken rib with exquisite accuracy. Robin flinched, his body automatically trying to move away from its tormentor.

The protective response elicited a growl of pleasure from Sir Anthony who bent down to kiss him with a suffocating passion.

"That's right, Lord Merritt," he whispered hoarsely, as Robin tried to pull his head away, "Remember that room in Paris where I brought you to your knees?"

Robin had a blinding flash of a small sweltering room on a Paris summer night. The weather had been unseasonably hot and Fortesque's dressing room had become almost unbearably airless. The claustrophobic room had been swimming in red-flocked velvet and an overpowering stench from the streets seeped in through its one open window.

He had been so hungry. Starving. He was sick. His stomach was twisting with dry heaves. He didn't know how to hunt. He depended on Sir Anthony to bring him food but now Sir Anthony was refusing. Sir Anthony was offering a sort of arrangement. He had a new demand — alien desires. No, he couldn't meet such a price. He had been Lord Merritt, after all. But the hunger was so intense. He had to feed. He was starving. He didn't know how to hunt and he depended on Sir Anthony for so many things. Perhaps it would not be so bad. Maybe he could do it just once. That was what Sir Anthony was promising. Just once.

Caroline and Simon carefully made their way through to the Great Hall. Hawkesmoor seemed entirely deserted, like an eerie stage set.

"Do you hear something?" she asked referring to a clattering and a crash in the distance.

Simon nodded, listening intently for another bang. "In the old stores, I fear."

"We should try it," said Caroline, "but with extreme care."

"Our servants have their own staircase," Simon interjected, before she could suggest the possibility of using a back staircase. "I have never transversed it but I know such a thing exists. I am told on good authority that it is actually far quicker than our own means of descent."

"Simon," Caroline threw him an amused glance, "you're really going to like the 21st century."

Robin caught his breath as Fortesque shifted over him and compressed the damaged rib. His master murmured a guttural appreciation of his pain and kissed him again with increasing violence.

58

"Petherbridge will destroy you," said Sir Anthony, as he lifted his head to look at Robin. "Give him the boy and that will end it."

With a gentle hand, Robin brushed an escaped lock of Sir Anthony's hair out of the vampire's face. It was a small, intimate sort of gesture that seemed to promise the moon and stars without being especially specific as to what that might actually mean. It was a gesture not entirely lost on Sir Anthony.

"Our arrangement is contingent upon you having a care for that child," Robin reminded him quietly, sliding his arms slowly up and around Sir Anthony's neck. "You and I both know what must happen."

Fortesque's cruel face hardened. "He will put you on a pyre of wood and set it alight just as he did the old Marquess."

Robin tried not to shudder. "And so it must be."

"You'll burn for *days.*"

"Just tell Petherbridge you could not find the boy," he said. "That is all I want."

Robin pulled him down into an embrace—the first time he'd ever initiated such a thing with Sir Anthony Fortesque. He slipped his long fingers into Fortesque's hair, giving the kiss all the energy he could muster.

As a dodge away from Simon, it worked beautifully but success came with a completely unexpected peril of its own.

He felt Fortesque respond to him with a fierce hunger that would rapidly become overwhelming. Robin inhaled sharply, throwing his head back in agony. He felt crushed against the more powerful vampire as if Sir Anthony was purposely trying to snuff the life from his body as if he were a candle flame.

Oh, Caroline, he thought as shadow seemed to fold in around him relentlessly like gravedigger's dirt. *I should liked to have seen you one last time.*

Tim cried out from the castle battlements, "They're on the move!"

The vampires on the Great Walk scanned the distance. Petherbridge's revenant army was descending from the distant rise. The line was solid and organized. It moved with deadly purpose.

Winnifred turned towards Eli Walker whose clear blue eyes regarded her with the sort of high seriousness she remembered from earlier eras of battle and human bloodshed.

"Lock and load, Madam General?"

"Yes, Major Walker," Winnifred replied. "Remember, your guns are our most valuable asset. Hang back and treat what ammunition you have with respect. Let my archers take the first flight."

"Yes, ma'am." He gave her a brief nod and wheeled about to organize his line.

"Set your bucket brigade into place, Mr. Kwang," Winnifred said quietly. "I hope your science project works."

The Chinese vampire bowed quickly. "Ropes and pulleys have worked admirably for many centuries: I think they will see us through this as well."

Then Winnifred shouted an order. "Major Walker, you are on deck!"

Hugh, on horseback, wheeled around at the sound of Winnifred's commanding voice echoing over the moor. He saw Petherbridge's vampires begin their descent. Soon they would reach the castle walls and it would begin.

It was all he could do not to spur the bay and gallop back to Hawkesmoor. He wanted to stand with Winnifred and all the brave humans who hoped to hold back the revenant horde. They would need him too. They would need a doctor.

But he was charged to protect the child.

"Winnifred," Hugh said like a benediction. He turned the horse from the castle, heading away at a hard pace.

"Hold!" Winnifred warned her archers, as the moving line of Petherbridge's vampires dropped down the rise and began coming across the moor. "No one is to shoot until I give the order. Remember Petherbridge doesn't know we intend to defend Hawkesmoor."

Robin slowly opened his eyes. Sir Anthony Fortesque had vanished and along with him the crushing pain. Wincing with effort, he pulled himself up from the ancient torture table and scanned the deserted chamber. Inexplicably, the ghastly Sir Anthony was gone and he was alone. For a moment Robin felt a giddy hope wash over his damaged frame — he'd find Simon and take him to safety. He knew Caroline's generous and kind spirit. She would welcome Simon to her Hawkesmoor.

Again, Robin was struck by the eerie sensation that he being stalked by an unseen force. He froze on the wooden table, trying to make sense of the abandoned dungeon and seeking some evidence of his stalker. It wasn't a complicated space. Just a large room with stone walls lit with flaming braziers as they once did in bygone eras. No real place to go to ground. No obvious coverts.

But then, in the wavering reds and gold of the light, Robin began to see that shadows falling across the tower's old stonework had energy of their own. Shadows, blacker than night and more solid than ordinary darkness, twisted across the flickering walls — each an entity in its own right and yet deeply interconnected with the others.

A lance of bleak sorrow twisted through him as if the shadow entities had stabbed him with desolation and pain. Robin struggled to push away its numbing effect. He remembered the almost unbearable litany of human cruelty: *The bloody massacre of Huguenots at Vassay 1562, the nationalized insanity of the Tulip Mania of 1637, the charnel house rise of the Spanish Inquisition 1478, France's Reign of Terror 1793, Hitler's hellish Final Solution for Jews and Gypsies, the bestial 1969 Manson Family murders and mass slaughter in Rwanda in 1994.*

Robin watched as the shadows slithered across the room, intent on reaching him. The vile race from the faltering Corpse Road gate. Black forces that fed on more than simply human flesh and blood. They were here.

"Fire!" shouted Winnifred, releasing her arrow, aimed at a rather beautiful blond man as his line reached the castle wall.

She remembered him from somewhere and wondered if he wasn't that Swede Fortesque had taken a shine to some time back in the 1920s. He'd been rather a good sculptor in bronze. Her aim was true and slammed into the Swede's high forehead. A fountain of blood and gray brain matter obliterated his fine features.

"So much for art," she said, feeling an acute sense of dismay that she was killing and maiming in battle. It was something she had hoped never to do again.

The rest of her archers held together well. Their arrows finding marks that, if not as accurate as Winnifred's, succeeded admirably in forcing the vampires to fall back in surprise.

They clearly had expected very little if any resistance to their quest to take Hawkesmoor and they stumbled, a momentary confusion in the ranks. A vibration of shock rose from the roiling lines of vampires. Three of their comrades with destroyed heads fell onto the grass and badly wounded revenants were struggling to find a safe spot to await repair to their systems.

A ragged cheer went up from the human contingent, dazzled and relieved at their modest success.

"Odd," Winnifred said to Gabriel in the brief lull. "They lack direction."

The former monk nodded. "Reasonably big group but I don't see Petherbridge, do you?"

"Encamped on the rise, watching." Winnifred was pulling a fresh arrow from her quiver and placing it against the bowstring. "Most of the vampires down there are just court followers and indentured servants."

Gabriel also yanked an arrow into place. "I don't think Petherbridge reckoned on the complete power loss. He expected his revenants to nip in and seize the castle without much of an altercation. Lacking their vampire traits, his army is just as ragtag as ours."

"Position!" shouted Winnifred as Petherbridge's assortment of allied vampire kings regrouped their forces and urged them forward.

Her archers again took up their places, their unease every bit as taut as the bowstrings they leaned into.

For humans who tended to equate beauty with goodness, the vampires presented a primordial sort of aesthetic construct. They were beautiful, these creatures on the grass below. They were mesmerizing, angelic, full of grace.

How could such creatures be capable of hurting anyone? How could they be legendary monsters? Surely maiming or killing one was tantamount to pulling wings off a dragonfly?

"Fire!" Winnifred urged as a rebuilt line of Petherbridge's vampires tried another direct assault using rope and grappling hooks.

A flight of arrows sang their shrill song through the crisp morning air as they flew fiercely towards their targets.

Winnifred and Gabriel's arrows found their marks, destroying the heads of two vampires who were in the process of throwing their grappling hooks. They sank in bloody heaps as their climbing hooks tumbled uselessly to the wet grass. The other arrows took out less this time as the attention of the archers began to fragment under the pressure.

"Archers, drop back," Winnifred cried, realizing the moment was gone and they needed respite before going on. "Major Walker, you're up!"

"Thank you, Madam General!" he called back, as his rifles dropped into the spots being hurriedly vacated by her archers. "Lock and load!"

A second line of vampires roared at the castle walls, using their superior strength and agility to climb the ancient stone like elegant bats. Enraged by the destruction of their kind, they realized taking Hawkesmoor wasn't going to be the cakewalk promised by confident kings under Petherbridge's sway. They might be drained of their most unusual powers but a handful of humans couldn't stand against them.

"Wait for it," warned Walker to his rifles as the humans, unnerved by the sight of the rapidly ascending vampires, shifted in their positions eager to shoot. "Wait for it."

In another moment, Petherbridge's second line reached the battlement, preparing to swoop on the humans for blood and vengeance. They were so close that the farmers and villagers could read the anger in the revenant faces. They fought fear and sudden mistrust. *Why wasn't there an order to fire? Maybe all the vampires were in this together?*

"Now!" shouted Walker as he found the instant when the attacking revenants were most vulnerable. Close enough to be hit often and fatally by inexperienced killers, far enough away from their own kind to seriously slow support efforts.

Relief was palpable as the rifle contingent fired an opening volley. Several of the beautiful creatures fell immediately. Some from direct shots to their heads and others sustaining massive wounds elsewhere that would take time to regenerate.

The Earl calmly took out a tattooed woman clad in black leather with a blast from his prized Purdey shotgun. The vampire's intricate face tattoo vanished in a crude implosion of blood and brain matter.

Peter missed a snarling Slavic-faced vampire, hitting only its shoulder. The wound seemed to be of little hindrance to the agile monster. He leapt with incredible speed at Peter who froze, unable to sort out a response.

Eli Walker pivoted with even superior speed and fired. The Slav's head flew apart, drenching Peter in gore. With a primal cry, Peter shoved the destroyed vampire backwards and the body tumbled through a machicolation, dislodging another climbing revenant in the process. Both fell hard to the moor ground below.

In the heavy barrage, more vampires fell with satisfying results to the moor. As yet, no human suffered more than gut churning dread and panic. A third line attempted to achieve the same success in scaling Hawkesmoor's grey stones but this time Walker didn't allow them the opportunity. Volley after volley of gunfire convinced Petherbridge's undisciplined army to fall back and regroup.

"They're mad as hell now," said Eli Walker as the vampire army retreated with their dead and wounded.

"They'll be back — with better ideas and more weaponry," Winnifred said as she waved encouragement at the jubilant humans who were cheering and congratulating each other. The Earl of Hawkesmoor, shotgun cracked over his elbow as if he were in a genial shooting party, tipped his hat to her and Major Walker.

Kwang Tse approached and gave them both a small bow of respect.

"Winnifred," he said, "Eli, that was most well done."

"When they return, we will need your dragon's fire to turn them away," she said. "Now they understand we can hurt them with arrows and bullets. Your oil bath will be the last thing they'll expect."

The encroaching shadows spun upwards in an arc, spiraling into one cantilevered cyclone. It made a high pitched sound like a medical saw or a symphony of unified screams. Robin had the whimsical notion that he now understood the phrase: black as sin. These shadow entities were unrelenting black matter — seeming to exist by sucking all the energy from any unlucky environment near enough to strike. He slid back on the table, wondering if his brutalized frame would allow one last burst of energy. Just enough to get him to the stairs.

59

As Winnifred predicted, Petherbridge's makeshift army was far better organized after it had retreated to the rise and regrouped. After determining that they weren't going to saunter into the castle for a monumental feast of villagers cheerfully lit by burning pyres of vampire traitors, they had taken a serious look at the tactical problems. Winnifred Turchil and Eli Walker weren't the only old vampires with considerable battle experience. When Petherbridge's vampires reappeared on the crest of the rise, they had weapons and a visible sense of order. They were on the run across the moor — fierce and focused.

"This is a whole different war," said Major Walker to the assembled force inside the castle walls. "They now recognize that we are fighters; but if we can't make our three lines of defense work with split-second timing, they will take the castle this time."

"And I don't know about you lot," said Peter, stepping away from his position against the battlement, "but I don't want to end up as a convenient food source for this Petherbridge and his friends!"

"Aye!" shouted a farmer from Sita's pike group. "We'll not become cattle for the likes of them!"

Winnifred lifted her bow and slipped an arrow into place. "Two minutes, I reckon," she said. "It's been an honor to fight with you."

Two minutes later to the second, Petherbridge's revenants attacked with renewed vigor. It was like a tidal wave striking the castle walls. They threw hand built ladders against the walls. They scaled the stone under their own power. And this time, humans did not go unscathed. Three villagers were pulled, shrieking in terror, to their deaths below. Vampires on the ground drained their blood as if it were some sort of battle narcotic.

"Oh, for the simple ability to pop in and out again," breathed Gabriel, as he released an arrow into the vampire horde. Petherbridge's army successfully placed yet another hand built ladder against the castle wall and began scaling it with revenant strength and speed.

"It's not going particularly well, is it?" Peter asked as he flipped around, his back to the castle wall, to reload his shotgun.

"We don't possess the ammunition for a long siege," Gabriel conceded, dropping back to find a fresh arrow from his quiver.

The castle barbican was being assaulted by old-fashioned battering ram. It's powerful blows ringing even above the chaotic combat.

"If they can succeed over there," Gabriel indicated the embattled barbican, "it's all over."

Kwang Tse's vats of linseed oil and burning embers unleashed their boiling rain through the castle ancient oil gutters. The thunderous blows to the castle gates ceased, replaced by terrible shrieks of those bathed in the scalding fluid. In the momentary confusion, the battle turned in favor of Hawkesmoor Castle.

In the flickering light of a single torch on the wall, Caroline took a long look around the central core of the castle's old prison. It certainly possessed more nasty artifacts than her Hawkesmoor. Most of the instruments of torture belonging to her castle had been used for firewood or melted down for horseshoes probably in early Georgian times.

There was a metallic clatter behind her. Caroline spun, biting her bottom lip to prevent a frightened cry from escaping and giving away their exact location in the shadow-shrouded room.

"God's teeth!" came a soft swear.

A figure in the near blackness emerged from behind a collection of old wooden crates and livestock wire, very much the kind of wonderfully familiar farm detritus found in her Hawkesmoor.

Simon came into the quivering torchlight. He was brushing cobwebs from his shoulders. "Sadly, I lost my foothold upon the…"

"You have to be more careful!"

"Thank you, madam," Simon replied as he readjusted his now sooty shirt, "I really am very *nearly* recovered from my fall."

"Yes, yes. You're young and resilient." Caroline made a dismissive gesture. "Do we go on this way?"

Simon sighed. "It occurs to me 'tis possible we are being led in this direction as if we were blackbirds on a trail of bread crusts."

Caroline turned to look at him with panic pulling at her face. "What do you mean?"

"As with the blackbirds and bread crusts, we are feeding on light," he explained softly. "We are forced to seek the next lit torch in order to continue our quest."

60

"I do not understand Lord Scyon's vendetta against Robin DuPlessis. I never have," Said Remy Baptiste, a muscular black man with the lilting tones of the Caribbean. "I only came because of an old treaty with Lord Scyon."

"Aye," agreed a Scottish voice as a massive red-bearded revenant pushed forward. "I be Ewan McLeod. I think some o' ye may know me and had I known Winnifred Turchil would be against Petherbridge, I dinna think I'd hae come."

There were sympathetic mutterings in what was left of Petherbridge's vampire army. They jostled around for the best vantage spot to listen to their leaders.

"In fact," continued Baptiste, "had I realized who would be here to support Robin DuPlessis, I might have brought my forces in on his side. Winnifred Turchil, Gabriel Addington, Kwang Tse, Eli Walker, and Sita: these five comprise some of the most significant revenant history known to us."

"And tha' bluidy Garnet Petherbridge, *Lord Scyon!*" spat out the Scottish vampire in disgust. "What is he to us but a mean-spirited git we're all afeared to cross 'cause we remember the burnings?"

"I say we parley. Listen to what these revenants have to tell us," said an English voice, as another vampire stepped up to join Baptiste. "They can tell us why they are here to protect Robin

DuPlessis and why a quiet writer of history books is such a threat to the all and powerful Lord Scyon."

Hugh Candlethorne looked around the ancient trees. Something about it had suggested that it might be the right place to give the child a bit of a rest. Funny, it did have a certain aura as if the trees had been waiting for them.

He dismounted, careful to avoid bumping Arianrhod against the saddle. A few minutes to rest and regroup. Then he'd put hell to leather getting them to a real town with modern transportation.

"We're here, poppet." He looked down at the infant's small face. She gazed back at him, almost seeming to smile. "What next, I wonder?"

Arianrhod's green eyes glittered at his words.

Winnifred, Major Walker, Gabriel Addington, Sita and Kwang Tse were standing in almost ceremonial order on the Great Walk as their attackers streamed into the courtyard, holding up a white flag of parley. The Hawkesmoor vampires resembled not so much wearied figures of battle but five royal standards of revenant history and accordingly Petherbridge's invasion force seemed confused and uneasy at the sight.

"Where is Petherbridge?" asked Gabriel. "Surely he's not resting in his battle tent waiting for you to put the conquering standard on the castle turrets?"

Remy Baptiste raised an eyebrow. "We were issued demands to make our courts available for his use. He disappeared during the battle."

"Petherbridge is a master of misdirection," Kwang Tse said.

The comment made a distinct impression on revenants gathered in the castle courtyard. The ranks tightened around their leaders as they moved in closer to listen with rapt attention.

"Aye," McLeod bellowed. "We be too busy fightin' ourselves to fight *him*!"

"I think we need to hear what you revenants at Hawkesmoor have to say," announced Remy Baptiste over the murmuring of the courts. "We would like to understand."

61

The swirling column of shadow spun out revealing a nightmare at its center. Stepping free of the sentient onyx ribbons, the aquiline Roman walked towards Robin wearing a rictus smile. The shadows dropped back, retreating as if to wait and watch.

"Morvidus," said Robin in a dry voice.

The oldest revenant gave him a small bow. "Lord Merritt," he said.

Robin backed off the torture table, glad to have the massive piece between them. "So it's been you all the time."

The Roman morphed into gilded Garnet Petherbridge. "In a way, yes. I fused with this one. He was *very* useful."

"Sir Anthony was never here?"

Morvidus reconfigured briefly as the vicious Fortesque and then returned to Petherbridge's more elegant persona. "I've been watching you since your return to Hawkesmoor imperceptible to even your hyper-senses."

Robin edged slowly to his left, still hoping to find a way to survive the encounter. "You move freely here," he noted. "Not imprisoned in Petherbridge."

Morvidus smiled and ignored his observation. "You're a flawed, sentimental race hopelessly in love with your prey."

"I am no longer vampire," Robin said with disdain. "You have no claim over me."

"Imagine you can bar the gate against my kind, do you? *Tylwyth Teg!*" he spat. "You are unworthy."

Then Robin understood. Some of the song strands he had heard humming in the electricity of the storm cell and in the skies above Cader Idris made a terrible sense to him now. *Hawkesmoor was the doorway. It had always been the doorway.* Here in the ethers, he would become both bridge and barrier. He would hold back the black horde and all its horrors for humankind. He could not fail. To fail was to lose Caroline and his children to shadow. They would drown in blood.

Robin took a breath to steady his nerve and moved to confront Morvidus. Black channels, turgid and thick like bloody viscera, began to pool on the floor. They undulated towards Morvidus until winding about him — the mantle of an emperor.

"I am the Lord of Time,' Robin said quietly. "You shall not pass this way."

They gazed at each other. Light and shadow. Ancient foes.

Then the shadows draped about Morvidus spiraled up –an onyx viper. It splintered into shards that became black scorpions with slashing claws. Robin choked and staggered to his knees, impaled. The shadows attacked, winding about him like mummy wrappings. They wove in and out of his consciousness like voracious maggots draining away everything save desolation and despair.

YORKSHIRE, 1750

"Go to hell," he said after Oliver wished him a son and heir on his wedding bed.

Oliver grinned and patted his shoulder. "No more drink, Robin. You'll not possess the …"

"Stomach for the task?" Robin asked, leaning somewhat unsteadily against a sideboard in the west wing hall.

"I was going to suggest a certain sort of vitality," Oliver threw him a look of sympathy. "Well, good night, sir. May angels sing you to your rest."

"You bastard." Robin pushed off the mahogany table and resignedly turned to his rooms.

He went inside, rubbing his right temple already throbbing with headache from all the wine imbibed since the wedding breakfast.

His presence caused a bit of a stir in his antechambers. A collection of household servants was laboring at arranging left over wedding flowers around the sitting room. They froze at the sight of him and his glowering expression.

"Thank you," he said waving a dismissive hand at them. "That will be all."

They stared at him, petrified like animals in the poacher's lamp light.

"That will be all," he repeated more strongly. "Thank you."

His man, Sudeley, sprung to life and clapped his hands with the brisk authority of the highly favored servant.

"His lordship no longer requires you," he said priggishly. "Off you go."

The servants broke from their domestic tableau like sparrows taking to wing. They rushed past him, one or two of the maids trying to suppress giggles as they went. The heavy door thudded shut as the last footman pulled it after him.

Robin held out his arms for Sudeley to remove his flawless frock coat.

"Is she here?" he asked as Sudeley bustled forward to divest him of the coat.

"Indeed yes, your lordship," the servant replied, slipping the frock coat off his shoulders. "We have attempted to make her ladyship most comfortable in her new apartments."

Something in his valet's tone made Robin swing around to look at him more closely.

He frowned and rubbed his aching temple again. "Lady Merritt has found some fault with her care?"

Sudeley looked positively pained. "Her ladyship has most exacting requirements, sir. We have attempted to satisfy them to her standard."

"I see." Robin found himself grinding his teeth.

Sudeley moved to begin the process of untying Robin's elaborate cravat but stopped when Robin held up a restraining hand.

"Off to bed with you, man. I can manage on my own."

Sudeley blinked in some surprise. "Yes, your lordship. Thank you, your lordship."

Robin groaned, heading for the room that held his bed and his new wife.

Pross Gwayr was kneeling by her priest, Father Blacknell, receiving some kind of blessing when Robin came through the doorway.

He noticed with annoyance that his favorite chair had been shifted from its usual spot to make room for a religious sanctuary complete with a prayer kneeler. He hated the sentimental embroidery on its cushioned top, but not nearly so much as he loathed Father Blacknell.

The religious figure looked up in disapproval as Robin wandered into the bedroom. Blacknell patted the top of Pross' bowed head in some kind of spiritual encouragement.

"Your lordship, will you not join us," he asked in his curdling syrup of a voice, "in prayer?"

"Are you planning on staying for the entire event, Father Blacknell?" Robin countered, as he poured another drink from the small decanter of sherry that Sudeley left for him on the night table.

Pross gasped and opened her eyes.

"Lord Merritt!" she breathed, mortified. "You are addressing a man of God."

"Madam," Robin saluted her with the sherry glass before knocking back a good half in one swallow and turning to Father Blacknell.

"Get out," he said in a dangerous timbre.

Blacknell blanched at the implied threat and sputtered out something about the moral responsibilities of those who ministered to men's souls. He gathered his black skirts and left the room with undignified urgency.

"You would deny me my very prayers?" Pross asked, still kneeling by his Jacobean four-poster.

"You may pray anywhere you like save my rooms, Lady Merritt," Robin replied, sipping his sherry. "If I find Blacknell here again, he will be on a coach back to the hole he climbed out of."

"Very civilized." She stared up at him, her face severely arranged into an expression of disapproval.

God, he thought in something close to despair. She was the very image of a crow. The elaborate silk and satin dressing gown did little to distract from her thin black hair and failed utterly to conceal the sharp dreadful edges of her skeletal frame

His wife until one of them had the good fortune to stop breathing. His duty as Lord Merritt of Hawkesmoor Castle.

He walked across the room and extended a hand so she could get to her feet.

Pross registered fear by sucking in a quick breath and gazing at him with panic in her small dark eyes.

"Madam," he said, withdrawing his offer of aid and untying his cravat instead. "I am going to my bed. You can join me or you can sleep on the floor. I do not much care which."

He threw his neck cloth over the foot board and unbuttoned his waistcoat, noting that Pross had weighed his words and was slowly rising to her satin slippers.

Robin shrugged off the waistcoat and tossed it without care after the neck cloth. He stiffened his spine, surprised to feel Pross behind him touching the black ribbon that held his hair.

She pulled the knot loose and slipped the ribbon away.

"Madam," he said quietly, "what would you have me do?"

"I have long yearned to see your hair without benefit of the ribbon," Pross replied. "It is most handsome, my lord."

Robin turned around, suddenly conscious that Pross Gwayr might be a colorless little creature without much in the manner of an intellect, but she was a woman and he had always known how to please women.

He could do this. He could trade his hopes for a happy domestic arrangement for one that resembled the sort most of his married friends possessed. His parents' marriage was really quite exceptional. He could do this for Hawkesmoor. He could shoulder the responsibility of his keep — not fail. Not fail again.

Pross stepped back as he turned around. Her eyes widened in apprehension as if she imagined he was going to chastise her for remarking on his personal appearance. Many gentlemen would take offense as it was certainly not a lady's place to do so.

Robin moved towards her, closing the gap. He reached out, laid a heavy hand on her shoulder and considered how best to proceed. He could feel her trembling. She was afraid of him. And why not? Pross Gwayr had been a spinster of thirty on their wedding day. She knew nothing of men save what her priest chose to tell her.

"Wife," said Robin, running a hand slowly from her quaking shoulder to the side of her face, "'tis your duty to please me."

Pross instinctively backed away from him again.

"My duty is to please God." She failed to force her features into an expression of pious certainty.

"But, doubtless, it pleases God when women faithfully serve their husbands."

Pross swallowed roughly and tried to think.

Robin found that the pleasure of confusing and unnerving the supercilious Pross had ignited genuine desire. He would press his advantage and see the narrow-minded wretch at his feet.

He pulled her roughly towards him, ignoring her thin cry of protest. Cruelty had lent him a brutal passion and he kissed her harshly.

Ah, he thought, as Pross struggled against him, so this is hell.

There was an absolute silence in the castle courtyard when Gabriel finally completed his synopsis as to the origin of vampires, the bleeding inter-dimensional gate and how Robin DuPlessis had to hold it fast against Morvidus' dark army.

"My God," offered a stunned Remy Baptiste at last.

"So, if Garnet Petherbridge and Morvidus be one and tae same — where is he?" asked Ewan with a shake of his shaggy head. "Dinna he care we took the castle?"

"I admit that makes no sense." Winnifred shrugged. "Why go to all the bother to fight for a castle if he doesn't need it?"

"Begging your pardon," said Kwang Tse politely, "but perhaps Morvidus and his kind cannot exist for long periods on this plane. Perhaps they require hosts for extended visitations."

"They'd need a helluva lot of hosts for a dark army," Eli Walker pointed out with a raised eyebrow.

Kwang Tse bowed in appreciation of Walker's point and then held up an arm silently to indicate the gathering of vampire courts.

There was a collective intake of breath throughout the courtyard.

Remy Baptiste's face twisted in disgust. "Slavery."

Gabriel's voice was awed. "It didn't matter who won or lost. It just mattered that we'd all be present here at Hawkesmoor."

"I'll not be a nag for some parasite to ride!" Ewan snapped definitively.

Hugh turned around slowly. The Roman Copse had drained of color. It was a strange blue like a world inside a ship's bottle.

"He is very nearly lost," said a sad voice behind him. "He has made his own hell and will not be easily turned from it."

A dark haired girl in medieval crimson stood in the center of the copse. She was slight and lovely but her face shone with sorrow. She was Tylwyth Teg. Hugh saw an otherworldliness glimmer off her like phosphorous in a night sea. He quietly tightened his hold on Arianrhod who let out a small sleepy cry of protest.

"His hell is a construct of guilt and regret — he attempts to correct the past by choosing another path," she explained. "But he cannot undo the past and the effort simply drains what is left of his energy."

Hugh took a cautious step towards the big bay horse. He had no intention of allowing this creature anywhere near Arianrhod until he knew the truth of her. She might well be some chimera devised by Petherbridge.

"I am Ceridwen," the girl said, raising a graceful arm towards them. "I will show you my truth."

Yorkshire, 1750

"No," said Oliver Tupin tapping his bow sharply against Robin's music stand. "You lost the phrasing in your left hand."

Robin pulled his hands from the harpsichord keyboard and nodded regretfully. "Forgive me. I find I am not quite myself today."

"Well, enough then." Tupin lifted his bow so he could swat Robin's upper arm with it in an affectionate manner. "By the by, the servants are circulating tales that you are failing to sleep most nights."

Robin let out a small groan and rubbed his cheekbone wearily.

"Who would have guessed Pross Gwayr harbored such passions?" Oliver raised both eyebrows as he considered the idea. "Marriage has set the caged bird free."

Robin bent forward and dropped his elbows against the lid of the harpsichord. He rested his chin on his hands.

"I wish I could despise her completely," he said dully, "but I must confess, I cannot. She is narrow-minded and certainly no one could accuse her of thought. Yet those same qualities which I loathe also seem to make her quite a useful Lady Merritt. She manages a large household very well—every spoon accounted for in the silver closet, every candle put away to dry properly, every ounce of flour noted in the ledgers. She is forever doing her Christian duty for the poor and her high moral standards impress the farmers."

"It seems she will make an excellent Countess," Tupin observed dryly, "if you live."

"I think it is quite simple, really," said Sita, her gold cuffs clinking together as she pointed to Hawkesmoor's Barbican. "You must gather your courts and leave Hawkesmoor immediately."

"Slow 'em down some," added Eli in his American drawl. "Even if DuPlessis fails."

Remy Baptiste registered his agreement by signaling his court to prepare for an exit. "Then it is agreed. We return to our kingdoms and await word."

"Aye and it'll be a long journey without our usual methods." Ewan waved at his small band of tough Scotsmen. "We might as well be getting a leg up."

YORKSHIRE, 1750

"Thank you, Lady Merritt," murmured Robin as she brought him tea, laying the delicate cup and saucer on the table by his wing chair. "Most kind of you."

He turned the page in his book and tried to return to the words but reading Latin seemed rather more tiresome than usual.

"And how has your morning passed, madam? Tolerable, I hope," he inquired, setting the book to one side as she began her extensive recitation of the tenant families with sick children, to whom she had taken generous baskets of restorative broths, blackberry jam and freshly baked bread.

He rested his head against the chair, listening to her prattle, and wondered if all gentlemen knew his sensation of suffocating exhaustion — understood it was merely a sign of age — simply something that all men with estates to care for and a tedious wife came to in the end.

"I do believe it shall be a most charming affair," Pross was saying with that radiant enthusiasm she seemed to produce endlessly now.

He had the odd thought that it almost seemed as if his wife was siphoning off his strength and adding it to her own.

But perhaps any man lashed to a tiresome wife, regardless of his station, came to learn such things.

"Forgive me. You have arranged something — an evening's entertainment?" Robin asked, forcing himself to focus on his wife.

Pross looked mildly concerned. "Even you cannot have forgotten the ball we are giving this very evening in honor of your cousin Ambrose Westmacott's birthday. Why some of the carriages will be arriving in a matter of hours."

The room seemed to swim before his eyes.

"I have agreed to no such thing," he sputtered in disbelief. "A ball for my cousin?"

She looked at him in pity and moved to kneel by his side. "My poor husband. I know you have not been well. Can it be that you have truly forgotten such a thing?"

Robin shook his head, trying to clear his thoughts. "I do not know."

Pross took his hands softly in hers and laid her cheek against the backs of his long fingers.

"My poor husband," she repeated.

Almost beyond his control, Robin found himself pulling one of his hands from her grasp, and with the lightest touch, stroked her black hair.

He thought of her morning spent delivering strengthening food to Hawkesmoor's ill and elderly — a task he would find stupefying but was perfectly suited to her tastes and reflected very well on him by association. He thought how he was indebted to this creature who had so securely anchored Hawkesmoor for him with her tireless acts of Christian duty.

Robin leaned forward and kissed the top of her head.

"I shall try to be polite to my cousin," he murmured next to her ear, "in honor of you, madam."

She picked up her head and gazed at him in something like wonder. Beyond the conventions of social civility, it was the first truly kind thing he had ever said to her.

"Why, thank you," Pross breathed, a kind of avian beauty slipping into her aspect with his words.

It was strange how she managed it, Robin thought, running his eyes over her small body. Like the old tale of Sir Gawain and his Green Lady, there were times late at night when the candles had guttered out; he had found her almost beautiful.

"I should," Pross glanced away from his intense gaze, "I should have my ladies organize my clothes for this evening."

If he had thought her intelligent enough to deploy astute strategy, he'd be positive Pross used modesty and shyness as weapons to entrap his interest.

Robin brushed her cheek with the back of his hand.

"Have you some arcane knowledge of poison, wife?"

She looked at him blankly. "Poison?"

"Nothing, m'dear." He half-smiled at the nonsense of it and sat back in the chair, feeling rather drained by his encounter with his wife.

"Are you unwell?" Pross asked in concern. "You have gone quite pale. Shall I fetch Sudeley?"

"Perhaps, madam," Robin said closing his eyes as the room seemed to tilt and spin, "you ought to fetch your priest."

He felt the darkness pull him down and swallow him whole.

The Hawkesmoor vampires stood up on the castle battlements and watched as the revenant courts crossed over the moor country.

"Quite impressive and medieval, isn't it?" Gabriel held up an arm as several of the departing vampires turned to wave farewell.

"A sight I never thought to see again," said Winnifred a bit wistfully.

"Frankly, I'm glad to be seeing anything at all." Gabriel slowly lowered his arm and let the cool moor breeze wash over him. "I thought my eyes would have exploded in the hellish flames of a lit pyre by now."

Winnifred shivered. "Must you be so graphic?"

Eli Walker shambled towards them, a smile breaking across his clear American features.

"Y'all think it might be nice to let the humans know they can come up out of the dungeons?"

Hugh had to admit it was fascinating.

Ceridwen had shown him the delicate drop of water balancing on a leaf. Within it, manifestation of a private hell. Resembling an intricate revolving stage of Hawkesmoor Castle, an area only existed in fully complex order when Robin was in that location. The other elements dissolved when he no longer focused on or needed them. A servant brought him champagne on a silver tray and then faded away to nothing once beyond Robin's presence.

Hawkesmoor's ballroom was the most detailed in the castle. It was ablaze with candlelight. The floor filled with sumptuously dressed people following a minuet while a vast array of household servants saw to every want.

Robin stood off to the side, watching the complex minuet. Even at a distance, Hugh didn't think he looked well. Ceridwen was right when she said what was left of Robin was weakening under the strain of projecting his nightmare.

YORKSHIRE, 1750

Robin watched his wife as she maneuvered through the crossing pattern and changed partners. She did not move like water as some of the other more skillful dancers did.

Pross had come to enjoy many frivolous endeavors since her marriage had freed her to do so and dancing was one of her favorites. Although she did not perform the complicated steps brilliantly, she laughed with genuine pleasure as she made mistakes and then caught up with the other more experienced dancers.

Her Father Blacknell did not approve of the social dance. He glumly put up with it since his meager salary was provided by a husband who disagreed with his narrow view. He was frankly unhappy that his pupil had been encouraged to discover joy in such things. Even now, Blacknell was pouting in the corner, studiously trying to appear as if he wasn't glowering at the licentious minuet.

A pity he did not feel quite himself, Robin thought, eyeing the gloomy priest. It might have been amusing to needle Father Blacknell, see if the pompous lout could bleed.

He raised his glass and took a sip of his champagne. It was wonderfully cold and did a little to ease the burning sensation in his lungs.

It was not usual of him to fall victim to chills but one had certainly entered his lungs with a vengeance. His chest hurt when he breathed and the night air had encouraged a wheeze.

God's teeth, he thought, watching as Pross came around her new partner and dipped a small curtsy, she looked quite acceptable. Pretty even, in one of her new gowns from Paris.

He felt his chest tighten painfully and decided to step outside on the fashionable new terrace where he would not disturb their guests with his cough. Robin pulled the handkerchief away from his mouth and stared down at the white linen, now heavily spotted with blood.

"God," he said quietly and wondered what would happen to Hawkesmoor if he died without an heir.

"Lord Merritt?" asked his wife behind him. "Is the evening not to your liking?"

He crumpled the linen in his hand and slipped it into his coat pocket before turning around.

"'Tis a lovely ball, madam." He was careful not to take in a deep breath of the rose-scented air lest it start the cough.

"You have done very well." He tried to hide his wheeze by pretending to clear his throat.

"Thank you." Pross almost blushed.

"Pale pink suits you," Robin said, referring to the heavy satin gown she wore. "'Tis a color you should wear often."

She did blush this time. "I know I am no beauty, sir. Champagne has dulled your senses."

"It is rude to contradict one's husband." He held out an elbow for her to take. "Come, walk with me. I would away for a time."

Pross dutifully accepted his arm. He led her into the formal gardens where they strolled on one of the pathways, saying very little but drinking in the fine summer night.

Robin paused to catch his breath, his chest burning with the effort.

"Pross," he said, "would you mind terribly if we sat for a moment on this admirable neoclassical bench?"

"Please, you are not well." She looked at him in real concern. "Will you faint again; do you think?"

"No, no." Robin gave her an encouraging smile as he slipped onto the bench. "I am quite well."

He pulled her down next to him.

"I simply wanted to get you a safe distance from the mob."

Pross' face took on a panicked expression. "But, sir, we are… in the gardens."

"You must learn to call me Robin," he murmured, bending to kiss her bare shoulder and then her neck.

"Someone will miss us," she protested as he made his way up her throat. "Father Blacknell might come looking!"

"Father Blacknell is interested in the prospects of more Christians to bully, is he not?" Robin kissed her and reached around to undo the top row of her bodice hooks.

"Robin," Pross pulled her mouth away from his, gasping as her gown slipped further down her shoulders, "please! I could not bear to be discovered."

He kissed her again and felt her body press against his, unable to deny his hunger. If she would only get with his child. Hawkesmoor would need another DuPlessis heir all too soon.

"Lady Merritt! This can only be the devil's work!"

Predictably, perhaps, Father Blacknell had chosen to follow them.

Robin tightened his hold about Pross' thin and quaking frame, preventing her from bolting. She hid her face in his chest, a sob muffled against his waistcoat.

"You, priest, are finished at Hawkesmoor," Robin said in disgust. "Go and collect your belongings."

"I shall go to her father," Blacknell threatened. "He will have this marriage annulled. Only a dissolute rake such as yourself would submit his wife to such indecency."

"Your duty is shepherding men's souls," Robin replied coldly. "Mine is begetting sons."

Pross lifted her head from his chest, her dark eyes wet and luminous with tears.

"Pross." Robin reached for one of her hands but she recoiled and backed away as if he were a diseased dog.

They watched as the woman in the pink gown ran from the garden and then, once out of Robin's range of focus, dissolved like a snowflake in a warm winter wind.

Hugh winced as Robin struck the priest in some kind of rage.

"Now we can enter his world," Ceridwen said, taking Hugh's hand in hers. "He is angry. He has unconsciously created a situation that rebuilds the negative energy sustaining his dream."

"But if Robin is your mystical Lord of Time, why doesn't he just zap himself out of this mess and save the day?"

"Because he is all too human." Ceridwen squeezed his hand tighter.

"But what does that *mean*?"

"He has not yet evolved to the elemental—a sentience that binds all that is light," came her enigmatic response as she reduced their three-dimensional bodies to nothing. "We must help him. Your world is in the balance"

Yorkshire, 1750

"Do not dare to threaten me of annulment, priest," Robin spat as Father Blacknell picked himself up from the flower bed. "Do not dare to threaten me at all."

"You would strike a man of God?" Father Blacknell wiped at the blood dripping copiously from his nose.

"I will horsewhip a man of God," Robin promised, "if he does not get out of my sight with alacrity."

"You have turned her from religious instruction," the priest offered in a kind of high-pitched whine. "Her family will demand an annulment."

"Our families require an heir!" Robin shot back with more desperation than he ever intended to reveal to anyone, least of all Father Blacknell. "Hazard a guess as to what they and your church will consider a more valuable use of time."

He threw up his hands in despair and turned away from the stunned priest. His chest was wheezing with effort. He was in agony.

"Nice," said Hugh, taking in the rich appointments. He reordered the sling on his shoulder and looked down at Arianrhod's delicate face as she slept. "It's been awhile."

She ignored him, scanning the crowded ballroom for Robin.

The room had a rather eerie quality; there was much music and graceful dance patterns, yet it all seemed oddly quiet and devoid of any real human animation, as if what they were seeing was some sort of beautifully designed image on pause in an elaborate video game.

"We must convince him to leave this construction," she said, as they edged around the elegant groupings of guests scattered around the dance floor. "If he fails, the Gate falls."

Hugh sighed, exchanging a polite bow with one of Robin's guests, a flawlessly dressed gentleman who seemed, as did all of the people in the ballroom, surreally robotic. He wondered if when Robin entered the room, they all regained their personalities in full.

An answer came in the next moment. As if a mysterious player somewhere had chosen his next move in a game, the people in the ballroom came to dazzling natural life. Vibrant human laughter and bright conversation filled the air. The faces of Robin's guests took on the lines and shadows of real people.

"There he is!" whispered Ceridwen. "Coming in from the garden. We must stay with him."

Robin stood; scanning the guests with the same intensity as Ceridwen, then broke off his scrutiny with a small shake of his head. He refused champagne offered by an attentive servant and moved forward with purposeful steps.

"I bet he's looking for the woman in pink," Hugh said as they skirted the crowd to pursue him.

"We must stay with him," she replied, nipping around a servant carrying a tray of sweetbreads. "If he leaves this room, it may disappear with us still in it."

<h1 style="text-align:center">62</h1>

Robin paused to cough. Hugh and Ceridwen slipped in close enough to hear him speak to a darkly handsome man in a simple brown velvet frock coat and waistcoat that lacked the intricate decoration of other gentlemen present.

"Oliver," Robin said, clearing his throat slightly after the coughing had ceased, "perchance, have you seen my lady wife?"

His friend shook his head and squeezed Robin's shoulder affectionately. "Is she not dancing or at the supper tables?"

"We had a scene in the garden." Robin's jaw tightened. "I hit Father Blacknell."

Oliver looked impressed. "I suppose Saint Peter has just placed a large black mark next to your name."

Robin bent forward and coughed again. "Blasted chill," he wheezed.

"Best away to the library fire," Oliver advised, slinging an arm around his friend's shoulders.

"Perhaps," Robin stopped for a moment to catch his breath, "perhaps that would be a good idea."

"You are not well, sir," Oliver said with a frown. "If you do not mind me saying so."

"'Tis just a chill," he replied, pressing a hand against his chest, "though I confess, I wish my lungs would cease this dreadful ache."

"Shall I fetch Tibbitts the surgeon?"

"No, no, I will be quite all right." Robin gave him a weak smile. "A glass of port by the fire?"

"My lord," Oliver murmured, as they moved off in the direction of the library.

"Oh," said Robin, stumbling, "'tis just a chill."

He fell then.

The ballroom inhabitants began cries of dismay but they were cut off abruptly. The lights flickered dangerously and the ground rocked violently.

"Bloody hell," said Hugh as everything went black.

YORKSHIRE, 1750

"My lord," his father's personal secretary, Everett, bowed deeply, "if you will but sign this final document you can rest contented in the knowledge that her ladyship will have no fears as to her well-being."

Robin coughed weakly and made his hand grasp the quill one last time to scrawl his name across the heavy vellum.

"Thank you, Everett," he wheezed as he scratched down his title. "You will see to it that the bequests to Oliver and Sudeley are made immediately? Sudeley is too old to start again with a new master."

Everett moved to take the quill from Robin's shaking fingers.

"You have been most generous, my lord," he murmured, deftly removing the little writing table from Robin's lap. "Please rest without further care on their behalf."

Robin allowed his head to settle back on the massive Jacobean headboard. The hot pain that gripped his chest would soon overwhelm him like the sea rolling over a tide pool. He knew he was dying. A rare poisoning of the blood. The surgeon had bled him several times and found dismal results.

"Thank you," he said again.

"My lord," Everett executed another of his exquisite formal bows, "it has always been an honor to be of service."

"Thank you," Robin said one last time and turned his head to offer his wife a smile as she came in, carrying a small basin.

"Do not cry, Pross," Robin said with as much vim as he could summon. "I am not quite dead yet."

Everett made a smaller bow to Pross as he left with the documents.

She sat on the edge of his bed, a tear running down her face and took a cool cloth from the basin to apply to his forehead.

"Do not make light of such things." Pross shook her head. "It mocks God."

Robin wheezed deeply before he could marshal enough energy to reply.

"Your God is such a bully," he whispered, as she wiped the perspiration from his clammy face.

A now alert Arianrhod cried in panic. Hugh clung to the shuddering staircase with one arm entwined in the elaborate spindles, while the other held with unbearable pressure to Ceridwen's wrist.

She was dangling over an abyss, a kind of endless night sky, a yawning void where once a lavish ballroom had stood.

Robin's last energy drain had sent his Hawkesmoor into collapse. The ballroom had flown apart as if a bomb had struck the castle.

Hugh threw all his vampire strength into one last effort. Ceridwen was pulled upward as far as he could maneuver. She cried in pain as her ribcage crashed against the edge of the sheared stair that hung in midair. Arianrhod continued to wail, instinctively terrified by all the tumult.

"Sorry!" he called out to both of them and tried to catch his breath.

Hugh made another attempt and this time managed to drag her up and over the ledge. They both fell from the force of Ceridwen's rescue and rolled backwards against the ruined staircase with considerable violence. Hugh shielded the agitated child, taking the brunt of the fall with his right side. He made sure Arianrhod was in one piece despite her distress.

Seconds later the bottom step vanished. Another instant and the next dissolved into the black void.

"Come on!" Hugh shouldered the baby sling and pulled her to her feet.

They scrambled up the long set of stairs, too frightened of losing their footing to notice or care where they were going. A low growl in the air intensified as the abyss swallowed more and more of Robin's dream. The last stair disintegrated. Ceridwen gave a small cry of alarm, throwing her arms about Hugh's neck.

"I have forgotten what it is to feel sensation," she gasped in his ear.

He threw himself at a door and twisted the handle, hoping it would actually open. It did, far more easily than he might have wished. They both fell through with a crash. Ceridwen gave Hugh a bemused look as she attempted to right herself.

"I shan't forget you, Hugh Candlethorne," she said. "We may meet again if the elements are right."

He nodded politely, unsure of whether the idea appealed to him or not. Vampires were complicated enough. After checking to be sure very unhappy Arianrhod was all right in her baby sling, Hugh helped Ceridwen pick herself off the floor.

"Are you are agents of death come to claim me?" Robin gazed at them through dull, glassy eyes. "Somehow I had reckoned on a more frightening vision."

They were glad to see that he was alone. Always a doctor first, Hugh rushed across the room to where Robin lay in his bed and picked up one of Robin's limp arms, staring at it in dismay.

"You've been bled!" Hugh winced, "Idiots!"

Ceridwen sat on the other side of the bed and took Robin's free hand in hers.

"You are a pretty little creature," whispered Robin, gazing at her in vague interest. "Pity about the ears though. What is that ghastly sound?"

Hugh released Robin's arm and turned his attention to Arianrhod, soothing her quiet again. He stood, rocking Arianrhod, as Ceridwen smiled reassuringly at Robin and squeezed his hand.

"Lord Pwyll, you must seek the light and no longer walk in darkness."

A tear dropped from Robin's eye.

"Hugh," said Ceridwen without looking away from Robin, "either way his construction will be destroyed."

Then she bent over, whispering urgently into Robin's ear.

63

Caroline and Simon crept around the last bend in the stairs, finding themselves in another dungeon room. While the others had been stores for exhausted castle hardware, this one still seemed fitted for cruel purpose. Even the atmosphere radiated a dark, unquiet energy. It was tomb-like and ominously lit from iron braziers that cast broad, flickering shadows against massive walls.

Simon froze in the archway. "'Tis is a horrible place. We must away from here."

She was about to agree when the sound of clanking metal riveted their attention. The darkness seemed to draw back like theatre curtains, revealing a massive wooden table. Now illuminated by one of the glowing braziers, a man was chained to its surface.

Caroline recognized the red-gold hair instantly. She crossed the hellish room at a run. "You've been hurt!"

Robin was chained by the wrists to a nasty restraining board, splattered with his own coagulating blood. He had been pretty badly beaten; a battery of bruises mottled his alabaster skin, dried older blood had dripped from his forehead and mouth, cruel ligature marks about his wrists testified to the prison's ability to perform its original mandate.

"Darling," Robin said hoarsely, "release me."

Caroline reached immediately for the ancient pins that held the metal cuffs in place. Free at last, Robin reached up and laid a bruised hand against her cheek. "I thought never to see you again," he whispered.

Tears rose to Caroline's eyes. Suddenly she felt cold despite the glowing prison braziers. Cold, exhausted and distraught — she wondered why she even cared about going home to Hawkesmoor.

"That is *not*," Simon's voice was behind her, "my father."

Thunder of extraordinary depth hammered the sky above Hawkesmoor. An electrical storm of myth-making potential swept over the moor. It created a fierce rain that drove at the castle's old stone as if it were an army of nail guns and seared the sky with lightning, sending sudden shafts of disorienting light through the huge Elizabethan leaded windows.

Humans and vampires alike hunkered down in the Great Hall, gathered tensely around collections of battery operated lanterns and flickering candles. Everyone hoping that once the massive storm had passed, they could go home and return to normalcy after a profound supernatural experience. Everyone was exhausted and severely rattled by the vampire siege.

"Now there's something you don't really expect to see," said Gabriel lightly to Winnifred, who, with her usual calm, was leaning against a window ledge watching the storm.

Winnifred spun away from the window ledge and from her silent prayers of thanksgiving. Gabriel was right. From all directions, ghosts were streaming into the Great Hall: men, women, children from every era, pale and colorless yet present and intact down to the smallest detail of costume.

"Good God," said the Earl pushing off the stair he had been sitting on. "Frances DuPlessis, August DuPlessis, Lady Jane DuPlessis."

There was nothing particularly frightening about the Hawkesmoor ghosts. The human contingent seemed fascinated by them as they made their pale stately way to the hall's center.

"Of course!" Gabriel gasped as the idea occurred to him. "This represents the DuPlessis bloodline. These are no ordinary ghosts: they carry the faerie genetics, too."

Hugh felt his knees hit the stone floor of the Great Hall with stinging pain. "Bloody hell!" he muttered from the floor, while making sure that the sling with Arianrhod was in place and that she was safe.

Then he became aware that oddly silver gray feet shod in medieval velvet slippers of the same strange shade, were right under his nose. He followed the silver gray legs up to an aristocratic figure in a perfectly lovely late 13th century costume. The gentleman peered down at him curiously.

"Hugh!" Winnifred cried.

She darted past the medieval ancestor and dropped down next to the vampire doctor, throwing her arms uncharacteristically around his neck.

"You actually made it back!" She kissed him several times. "You perfect idiot."

"Why, Winnifred," Hugh looked at her with dazed delight, "that's the nicest thing you've ever said to me. What's the story with Prince Valiant?"

"He's a DuPlessis ghost — one of many that have suddenly shown up." Winnifred stood and offered him a hand up. "Gabriel thinks that their faerie bloodline has given them more clarity than the run-of-the-mill ghost."

"I admit," Gabriel ran up to thump Hugh's shoulder affectionately, "the Maypole thing has got me confounded!"

Hugh widened his focus and saw that the ghosts had made a large circle in the Great Hall as if they intended to dance some kind of reel, except they stood, backs to the center, without moving. More silent sentinels than social dancers.

But shadows in the room were slowly lengthening and taking on their own individual shapes in a distinctly menacing manner. It was fascinating — like watching a room of shadowy anacondas uncoiling, on the hunt for prey and ready to strike with supreme speed when the moment was right.

Silver wheel, he heard Robin's voice as if the former revenant had spoken into his ear.

Hugh turned words over and around in his head. Silver wheel… round… wheel… circle…

"It's them!" he shouted urgently, noting as he did, the coiling shadows seemed to hear him as well, rearing back like a hydra. "Everyone must be inside the circle!"

The Great Hall at Hawkesmoor could have been the center of a massive tornado or a freight train roaring out of control. Everything seemed to be spinning as the vampires led the panicked human contingent through the grey ghosts to the center of the Silver Wheel.

The shadows that had seemed to seep so slowly from the very walls now ribboned about the circle with speed and volition. They whirled around the gray DuPlessis ghosts like vicious spectral weasels searching for a way into a barred hen house. The DuPlessis bloodline was resolute.

"Stay in the circle!" shouted Gabriel against the high-pitched shrieks of anger and frustration emitted by the incessantly moving shadows. "Don't move! No matter what happens here!"

Hugh held both Arianrhod and Winnifred close. "It's the Silver Wheel."

"*That* is my father," said Simon, choked with emotion.

Fighting back a sob of despair, Caroline pulled away from Robin's touch and looked. Simon in a flood of tears, pointed up to a corner of the ceiling high above them. Hanging on a crossbeam by ribbons of slithering black was her husband, Robin

DuPlessis. He stared at them, his dead green eyes glittering like glass. The shadow entities wove in and out of him like voracious graveyard maggots.

"Robin!" she cried, horrified. The shadows were devouring him.

"Lord Merritt can't help you," said a cultured voice. "He's in hell."

She and Simon turned again — the other Robin morphed seamlessly into imperially handsome blonde with cut glass features and a flawless black suit. They both instinctively shrunk back from his powerful presence.

"Thank you for bringing the boy," he said pleasantly. "I knew you would agree to come."

Caroline frowned. "I never agreed to come anywhere."

"*Please help me. I need you, Caroline!*" He beamed as a terrible comprehension crossed over Caroline's face.

"I was hoping for the baby but he'll do. They all carry the wretched bloodline."

"He'll do for what?" Caroline pulled the shivering Simon back against her protectively.

The exquisite Englishman shrugged eloquently. "In his way, Simon is also a doorway. He can carry me into *their* realm."

He reached up then and with a series of short savage jerks, pulled his face from his skeletal frame. The patrician features ripped, exposing bone and muscle. His lovely cornflower blue eyes exploded and something began to bore through the bloody sockets. Something that wanted to be free of its old body.

Like a cobra shedding its skin, something black and glistening with blood oozed from the blond's ruined head. Then the thing stopped almost as if it were an animal pausing to sniff the wind for danger.

He called upon his ancestors and all of his kind — his voice made hoarse by desperation and despair. Without hesitation they answered. Voices began to weave through and around him. The nightmare Hawkesmoor fell away like discarded paper and he fused with the silver thread that bound all things of light. He was a prism. He was alone. He was joined with all elementals — a single sentience that permeated every aspect of the universe. He was the Lord of Time.

Robin suddenly threw his head back as if surfacing from too long under water. He gasped for air and forced words from his straining throat. "The beginning and the end. All shadow banished from this place."

Then he was free of the shadow bindings. The hydra of entities reared back and retracted as if violently shocked by an electric current. He dropped to the stone floor, as everything seemed to tilt and spin, fade in and out of focus — a ship capsizing in a storm.

The parasitic creature began to rise up and reformulate into a human shape

"Caroline," shouted Robin above the roar, "Simon — you must go!"

"We can't leave you!" she cried, clinging to Simon in the fierce wind.

Robin looked at her with longing — it seemed possible to Caroline that time actually stopped. Eyes locked, without words, they exchanged an entire lifetime of depth and devotion. Then — jarringly — real time kicked in and Robin refocused his attention on a powerful, evolving black entity. He raised his arm, his fingers outstretched. Caroline felt an electrical vibration wrap around them like a warm cloak.

"Father!" Simon started forward.

But Caroline knew it was too late. She flung her arms around Simon as the mysterious otherworld Hawkesmoor flew apart. The entire construction collapsed like an ingenious picture in a children's pop-up book, closed by a capricious child or a sudden gust of wind.

The Silver Wheel remained unbroken. Human and vampire huddled together as the shadows spun about the silver-gray circle of resolute DuPlessis ghosts, unable to enter but increasingly desperate to find forms to inhabit. Faster and faster the onyx ribbons threaded the circle, searching for one tiny crack, one tiny flaw in the wheel.

An electrical growl crackled above them. Something huge, black and foul dropped to the stone floor near the circle. It hurled itself against the Silver Wheel and for the first time, the DuPlessis ghosts shuddered under the impact. The phantoms wavered ominously like sputtering lights in the Titanic as it sank.

"Stay in the circle!" shouted Gabriel as some of the villagers began to panic.

The massive black entity—a tornado of jagged teeth and claws — attacked again, brutishly slamming the circle. Great Hall itself seemed to tilt sideways with supernatural force. DuPlessis ghosts staggered –their internal lights dimming.

Hugh pulled Winnifred and Arianrhod tightly to him. This was it. Another attack and the shadows would devour them.

Then a new sort of sound rose against the hungry growls of predatory shadows. It began like a breeze; a soft dusting of a song drifting through the hall, growing in strength and direction.

"The Alpha and the Omega, the beginning and the end. All shadow banished from this place."

"Robin," breathed Winnifred in wonder.

A flare strobed though the darkness as if the atmosphere itself had ruptured. The shadows shrieked with a pitch so high and harsh that everyone within the ghost circle clamped hands to ears in hopes of blocking out the jagged sound. The shaft of light widened and steadied, revealing Robin within its glimmering motes. He walked with grim purpose across the Great Hall, trailing in his wake — echoing images of Tylwyth Teg as if they were part of a wondrous golden cloak.

"All shadow banished from this place." Robin raised his arms and the glittering beings spun out, spiraling about the Silver Wheel and joining with the DuPlessis.

"Not this time," sneered the entity. "Not when I am about to inhabit your daughter."

Robin broke into a run, headed for direct confrontation. The entity, an obsidian whirlwind, moved forward to engage. It snaked out, piercing Robin directly in the heart as if it were made of steel. Clearly the blow struck deep — Robin staggered and nearly fell.

"Can't we do something?" Gabriel demanded over the roar of the shadow entities. "They're killing him."

Hugh shook his head, unable to formulate any rational response to what he was seeing. Hunched against him, helping to shield Arianrhod, Winnifred was reciting quiet prayers.

Hungry shadows encircled Robin. Unsteady, he tried to right himself as they wove about him and began to burrow into his frame like voracious eels. He shuddered under the onslaught and disappeared under the undulating black swarm — lost to them all. Some of the humans harbored within the circle cried out at the sight. Others stared dully, all hope lost.

The Silver Wheel began to falter again. The freight train roar of ravenous shadows rose to unbearable levels. Hugh sent out a last thought that he wished he'd done better to protect the innocent child in his arms.

Then a higher, more plaintive note cut across the insatiable growl. A pinprick of white-hot energy appeared within the relentless whirlwind. Shadows flung back as if scorched, shriveling in distress. Robin emerged from the swarm — wherever shadows had driven into him, shafts of light now sprung from the wounds. He lifted his arms out and it was as if he had become a prism, refracting power. Lines of energy soared out from Robin fusing with the others who had gone to hold the circle.

Suddenly a wheel of violent sentient power surrounded humans and vampires. It pulsated and expanded — shadows caught within its spokes were ripped apart, disintegrating with shrieks of agony. Then with one collective scream born of sheer rage, the surviving shadow entities recoiled into the ethers and vanished.

The brilliant lines of energy began to withdraw, returning to Robin who stood quietly with his arms outreached. His wounds healed as the light returned as if it cauterized them. Tylwyth Teg drifted apart from their phantom descendants, glimmering back into Robin's golden shadow.

Robin let out a breath. He nodded as one of the Teg shimmered at his shoulder. Hugh couldn't be sure but he thought it was Ceridwen in the fragmented light. Robin turned to go.

"Wait!" Hugh pushed clear of the circle. "Robin — your daughter." He lifted Arianrhod from her sling and held her up so her father could see her. As if the infant understood, Arianrhod was glowing. She gazed out at him with peace and contentment.

Robin smiled. A wistful smile — more than a little sad. Hugh found himself glad Caroline wasn't there to see it. Then the Teg surrounded Robin, a scattering of stars. It seemed a gesture of comfort and support. Then they were gone. The man who had once been Richard Robin Francis DuPlessis, Lord Merritt of Hawkesmoor Castle was gone as well.

The storm outside ceased and a pale, almost tentative morning light filtered in through the windows. Tranquility and blissfully ordinary peace wafted in from the moor country.

The DuPlessis phantoms turned in unison and bowed with great formality to the current Earl of Hawkesmoor. It was as if they were paying long overdue tribute to the ranking member of the DeBarry line for having taken such care of their keep. Then they too vanished.

The lights flickered and hummed as they came back online. A tired round of applause greeted the return of modern conveniences.

"Good Lord," the Earl let out a long tired breath, as farmers and villagers began to sort themselves out. "I dearly hope that is the last we will see of unwanted tourists at this Castle."

"Oh, Dad," said Hannah with a relieved grin. Exhausted, she threw her arms about him in a tight embrace.

"This ever gets out," grumbled a shell-shocked farmer as he blew out his candle, "we'll become a magnet for all the nuts in England."

"Stars and garters!" gasped a woman's voice. "It's Lady Caroline!"

Peter turned at her words and saw his sister and a boy in 18th century clothing descending the steps two at a time. He darted forward in relief. Hannah and the Earl at his heels.

"Caro!" he called. "Caro!"

He ran through the collection of tired, slightly staggering locals to the base of the sweeping staircase. Caroline flew at her brother, hugging him fiercely while the boy lagged back as if terminally shy.

"You managed to come home!" he cried, squeezing her tightly. "Clever, clever Caroline."

"Where's Robin?" She asked, looking about expectantly. "He must be here. You should have seen him! He was incredible! He..."

Peter shook his head. "He's gone. Robin saved us — Hawkesmoor, England — everything."

Caroline straightened her spine even as she fought back tears. She lifted her chin — she was a DeBarry of Hawkesmoor Castle. She would be worthy of the sacrifice he had made.

"Oh, Caro," murmured her brother in utter dismay, "I am so sorry. So sorry."

"Here's someone," came her father's voice, "needing you."

Caroline looked over Peter's shoulder and saw that her father was holding Arianrhod wrapped in his arms. She felt the mother's instinct tug at her like an invisible wire and she pulled away from Peter, going to her new daughter.

"Hello," said Peter, extending a hand to the handsome blond boy who waited shyly on the staircase. "I'm Peter."

"Oh," interjected Caroline with a sniffle to clear her throat, "I completely forgot! Peter, Dad, Hannah, this is Robin's son, Simon DuPlessis. He will be living here with us now."

Simon wiped at his tear-stained face and slowly came down the remaining stairs.

"If such an idea would suit," he said quietly.

The Earl cleared his throat. "This is your home as much as it is ours, boy."

"My God. *Another* Lord Merritt," Peter breathed in fascination as he shook Simon's hand warmly. "Welcome back."

The start of a smile lit up Simon's wan features and then he looked away, overwhelmed.

"He's *so* gorgeous," whispered Hannah into Caroline's ear.

Caroline raised her eyebrows and turned to take in her sister's moonstruck expression. It suddenly hit her that the DuPlessis bloodline might well go on at Hawkesmoor for quite a long, long time.

Richard Robin Francis DuPlessis, Lord Merritt of Hawkesmoor Castle who had given his life so that his children might live in peace and safety, would have been so very pleased.

Arianrhod opened her green eyes and gazed at her mother with newborn adoration. Caroline bent to kiss her small forehead, knowing she would be grateful forever that he had left her with such a tangible way to remember him.

"Caro?" said Peter.

She looked up to find Peter smiling at her, an arm already slung affectionately around Simon's thin shoulders.

"Have we got stories to swap!" he announced. "How about we fry up whatever is left in the kitchen for breakfast and tell all we know!"

Caroline stepped into the warm circle of her family. There would be time later to grieve. *Forever and ever and ever.*

Epilogue

Arianrhod laughed, tittering unsteadily on her one-year-old legs as she tried to follow the striped ball her grandfather had rolled across the grass.

Caroline breathed in the rose-scented air of a perfect English twilight and thought what an ideal summer's night it would be for the faerie folk of her old children's books — the tiny fictional characters who wore costumes made of flower petals and took delicate fairy baths in morning dew and not the powerful Celtic variety.

Nearby, Simon, Hannah, Peter and the Earl's beloved Harold played a game of football without any rules save stealing the ball and kicking it away from all comers as brutally as possible.

Caroline sipped her lemonade and tried to return to the spy thriller on her lap, but the light was just at the turning point when reading became difficult, so she simply rested her head on the chair, content to absorb the wild beauty of the summer moor.

Life had returned to something approaching the normal in a year that had seemed to pass so quickly. Simon had taken to life in the modern world with a fascinated verve, and had so thoroughly ruined his speech patterns it was getting really difficult to tell he was not just another British teenager with hobnail boots and Assassin's Creed posters on his bedroom walls.

Caroline grinned and glanced over at her father, who was playing with Arianrhod in the long cool summer grass.

A pity Simon had such a flare for playing the electric guitar. It was driving her poor father around the bend except when unexpected foreign tourists turned up to see the castle and he secretly encouraged Simon to jam at full blast on the floor just above the State rooms.

Winnifred and Hugh bought a nearby squire house. They visited often, as did Gabriel. The former monk came up from London when he needed a break from a massive updating of the vampire library and wished to confer with Winnifred, who had been asked by the British vampires to replace Garnet Petherbridge as their sovereign.

She believed that vampires had new purposes to follow in the human world — those of watcher and guardian — and felt strongly that until a great deal more was understood about gateways and the ribbon of time, Morvidus or other dimensional beings would continue to be a major threat. Winnifred was passionate about establishing a kind of vampire knighthood that would serve to protect the human plane — and while many revenants shared her enthusiasm, the more vicious among them emphatically did not. It was proving a dangerous, volatile time for all vampires, regardless of whose standard they followed.

Caroline tried never to allow her thoughts to travel to such frightening places. She left all that to braver souls like Winnifred Turchil and Hugh Candlethorne. She preferred just to be the mother of Arianrhod and Simon, working quietly on the restoration of Hawkesmoor.

Her father was worried about her. He felt she ought to consider the possibility of accepting some of the dinner invitations that had begun to come her way from some of the perfectly acceptable men in their social orbit.

"I am not suggesting that you should marry Mark," he had said only that morning over breakfast. "I just think you might let him take you over to Middleborough for dinner once in a while. Do you good — get you out of this place for a change of air."

Caroline smiled, waving at Arianrhod, who was chortling with delight as she managed to levitate the striped ball so it spun in the air like a top.

Arianrhod was really getting the hang of the telekinetic thing and Hugh, her vampire godfather, was incredibly proud of her. Her thoughts returned to Mark — how to explain to her own father that Robin DuPlessis had ruined her for anyone else?

She looked away from her father as Firefly let out a loud whinny and began galloping around her paddock. *Silly old mare,* she thought, *Evan must be upping her grain allotment again.*

"Someone coming across the moor!" called Tim from the castle battlements where he patrolled in the evenings. "Shall I go warn 'em off?"

The Earl was annoyed. "I'll bet it's that wretched French gardener again, coming to lecture me about restoring Lavec's formal designs. I'd like to force feed him his pretentious beret."

"I'll go," Caroline said, setting aside her book. "I'd like the chance to stretch my legs anyway."

"Well, if he tries to show you his blasted portfolio, give me a signal," replied her father in obvious relief, "and I'll have Tim shoot him."

"Dad," she said, "you can't just go round having Tim blow away annoying Frenchmen."

He made a sour face. "And they say we're progressing in this country!"

Caroline shook her head in mock despair and turned to walk down the gravel pathway. She scanned the distant moor looking for the figure Tim had spotted on Hawkesmoor land. Probably just a rambler who had wandered off the public paths.

To the southeast she caught a glimpse of movement in the twilight blues and grays. Focusing, she squinted to make out whether the person was wearing a rambler's club jersey or even the telltale beret of the contentious little French gardening expert.

No… Caroline's throat went dry and started to ache. Tim's walker was tall and pale, and even in the gathering twilight, she could make out long strands of amber-colored hair blowing in the light breeze as he came across the moor.

It just couldn't be. She stumbled forward, breaking into a run.

But Caroline was sure by the time she had sprinted the first hundred yards. It was him. She'd know that graceful stride anywhere.

"Robin!" she cried in a voice raw with emotion.

She saw him look up and catch sight of her, too. He paused, seemingly frozen with the realization of who had just called out his name.

Robin stood, dressed in the same black cashmere sweater and trousers she'd seen in the dungeon, and looking quite as if he had never left Hawkesmoor at all.

She slowed her run about a foot from her husband.

"Robin! How can this be you?"

He seemed unsteady on his pins as he tilted his beautiful head to the side; his green eyes seemed dazed and were straining to focus on her. She wondered if he had sustained some damage to his sight.

"Caroline," he said hoarsely, as if he had not used his voice in a very long time and had to force such sounds from his throat.

Caroline took a step nearer and raised a trembling hand to touch his face. His skin felt cool and real next to her fingertips. She gasped at the wonder of it.

"You came back," she pointed out uselessly, running her hand down to his shoulder, savoring the reality of his being there.

Robin tried to speak but then stopped for a frustrating moment, seeming to need to concentrate in order to produce vocal sound. "How can I…?"

His voice failed.

"So they let you come back?"

She stared at him, afraid of the answer. Afraid to learn the Teg had permitted him only a mere few minutes to balance his old world before drawing him back to faerie.

"Quite a long time from now," he said in his uncertain voice, "I shall die in a car accident not far from where we stand. Then I will truly and finally belong to the elements."

"Oh, Robin!" She threw her arms about his neck.

"How can I balance universes with my heart here with you, Caroline?"

He slid his arms around her stiffly, as if his physical form was also something he had not used in a long while. Awkward at first, he kissed her cheek and tried to move the kiss to her mouth but paused instead, letting out a long shaky breath.

"It is too much … sensation," he admitted, resting his chin on the top of her head. "You will have to have patience with me, love."

"Forever and ever and ever," she said very softly, for herself and for the life it promised her.

"I beg your pardon?" Robin pulled back slightly. "I fear I did not hear you. My senses are returning but rather slowly, I'm afraid."

Caroline smiled at him. "Would you like to see your children?"

His face slowly lit up, as if at a thought glimpsed many miles away. "Please. I would be so grateful."

"Well," she slipped an arm around his elbow, "off we go then."

"Hawkesmoor," he said, as they turned to begin the short walk back to the castle.

"It is beautiful, is it not?" Caroline murmured, gazing too at its curves and battlements — a silver ring fashioned by faeries set down in the wilds of the moor country.

"Yes, but not as beautiful as you." Robin cocked his head as various noises drifted across the moor from the castle. The bell-like laughter of Arianrhod could just be heard over the cheerful dynamics of a very human game of football. "Not nearly as beautiful as that sound."

Caroline turned to gaze at his elegant, angular face — one that had been part of her life since she was tall enough to see paintings on the Hawkesmoor walls, and rose to the balls of her feet, kissing his cheek.

"You won't miss your faerie realm?"

For one unguarded moment, Caroline caught a certain yearning in his large green eyes. She saw that he had been one with horrors and splendor far beyond human comprehension, and that despite his resemblance to the imperial Lord Merritt of the painting, he was now quite a different being. He had come because he could not bear her loneliness and her grief.

She also saw that at times, the urge to return to the Teg would become almost unbearable but that he would honor his promise and stay with her until the day he died.

Robin glanced away from her and she lost the connection.

"I have a life to finish on this plane," he said simply.

"To give up so much — are you really sure you want to?" Caroline asked quietly.

He returned his green-eyed gaze to her. All the tantalizing dreams she had seen in his eyes had been masked — only genuine affection remained.

Robin nodded and stumbled forward, unbalanced, as she pulled him rather abruptly after her.

"Just wait until you hear what everyone has been up to! Arianrhod's learning to walk and Simon is playing the electric guitar," she told him brightly, thoroughly enjoying his horrified expression. "He's really very good, you know."

"Well," said Robin, "thank god I came back."

Anne Merino

Photo: Erin Judd

Anne Merino grew up in Arizona and Wales, devoted to horses, hounds and books. The daughter of an American classical philosopher and a Welsh mother who loved to tell her eerie tales of ghosts, elemental beings and mortals who built bonfires to Ceres, it is, perhaps, unsurprising that story and theatre became her passion. Anne went on to become a professional ballerina and choreographer for notable companies in the US and abroad. Now happily retired from the stage, she writes novels and plays. Married to a filmmaker, she also has two fascinating sons and a retired working dog named Hector.